Book 1: Simple Machines

Charlotte E. Bennardo

What are the animals in your backyard doing?

Char

EVOLUTION REVOLUTION

Book 1: Simple Machines

By Charlotte E. Bennardo

Also by Charlotte E. Bennardo

Sirenz

Sirenz: Back in Fashion

Blonde Ops

Beware the Little White Rabbit

Dedication

To my mother, Jeanne. She believed in this story from the very beginning and refused to let me give up seeing it born. And to my son Alec, the inspiration for this story when he brought home his third grade science homework; my son Thomas, who played in the sandbox with his trucks which gave the me idea for the wheel; and Collin, who loves all animals. You continue to be my muses. Thank you for your humor, skepticism, and unique way of looking at things.

Contents

One: Eat or Be Eaten

Two: Rolling, Rolling, Rolling

Three: Sisters!

Four: The Sound of War

Five: A Time to Gather

Six: Rock'N Rolling

Seven: The Great Plan

Eight: If Everyone Works Together

Nine: Not Another One!

Ten: Crispy Whiskers

Eleven: It's in the News

Twelve: The Plan, Part Two

Thirteen: The War Goes On

Fourteen: Stare Down

Fifteen: Fluffed and Stuffed

Chapter 1

<u>Eat or Be Eaten</u>

If he didn't run faster, he would be eaten. His legs pumped harder, every breath painful, but he pushed for more speed. A hot breath tickled his back. He ran even faster, afraid of the snapping jaws moving closer.

He leapt. His claws gripped the bark and never had he climbed so quickly. Only when he was high in the tree, the branches so slim they bent under him, did he stop.

"I will get you, Squirrel," came the hiss from below.

With his fur shining in the light, his tongue lolling out of a slack mouth, the fox trotted off, heading back into the deep woods.

The squirrel waited; he knew Fox's tricks. He might be hiding behind a fallen log, just waiting for him to climb down from safety in the tree. Then Fox would pounce. No, he would wait.

When a chipmunk scrounged for nuts below him, he knew it was safe. Clambering down, he leapt the last bit and took off, away from the woods and towards the humans. It would be even more dangerous there, but he'd find food.

From under a leafy bush, his sharp eyes followed every move the humans made.

He sniffed rapidly. Fresh seed. No nuts, only seed. That was fine; he had a whole store of nuts ready for when the cold came.

Unlike Fox, the humans moved slowly and clumsily. Filling bird feeders with seed, they plodded around, making too much noise. No gentle whucks to other humans, no soft chitters to each other. Silently, he moved as close as he dared without being seen, and listened carefully.

"Stan!" shrieked the very round human. The other one, long and straight like a tree, turned around.

The name for the skinny human was *Stan*.

"Bring me the chair."

"Eh?"

"Bring me the chair." The round human pointed at the thing humans sat on.

"What, Gracie?"

"Bring me the CHAIR, Stan!"

"Huh?"

"Chair, chair, CHAIR!" screeched the round human, pointing wildly. And Stan brought over the sitting thing.

Chair. Slowly he was learning more human names and sounds and what they meant. Humans used so many; he would learn as many as he could.

He watched as the round human, female from her scent, put another obstacle on the bird feeder—an owl, but not real. One thing he knew; humans put out seed to attract the pretty birds, not hungry, hoarding squirrels. This human constantly tried to devise new ways to keep him out. She used wires, bells, and sticky stuff on the poles and feeders. It never worked. What she and other humans didn't know was that he watched her put on the traps, and learned their sounds while he waited, hidden. He knew *wire, bell, pole, bird feeder, road*, and others. Then they'd leave, going back into their human den, and he would work through the traps and pilfer the seed. He had patience, cunning, and sharp claws that could grip anything except glass. He even figured out how to get around the wire with the sharp metal thorns. New puzzles excited him. He learned quickly.

Holding a can, the female plodded over to the next group of feeders. Under the bush, he was only a short distance from her, but human eyes and noses and ears were weak, and she didn't see him or smell him or hear him. She put down the bag on the grass. Standing on the chair, she filled the last feeder. The delicious smell of seed tickled his nose and stomach. He was hungry.

He could have run right over to the bag, stuffed some in his mouth and filled his paws, but she would scream. That awful sound froze him in his tracks. And then she'd grab something to hit him with or throw at him. He knew her tricks. No, he'd wait till she was gone.

Now she was opening another can. A strange smell wafted through the air. His nose wrinkled in distaste—whatever it was, it was made from meat. Fox or Owl had a smell like that on their breath after they hunted.

She rubbed the mud-like stink stuff on every pole, and even on the feeders. The birds would not be happy, but they would eat anyway. Birds weren't choosy about their food. Some would eat dead animals, stinking and drying on the road.

Now she even put some of the stink mud on the grass under the feeders. The rats would really like that. The female would screech when she saw them. Almost all humans did.

The horrible smell wouldn't keep him away. One fall of water and most of it would be gone.

"Do you think that's enough lard, Stan?" she asked.

"Eh?"

"LARD!" she shouted gratingly, pointing to the can.

Another name. *Lard*. Meat mud.

"Do you want some more?" Stan asked.

"Never mind!" she yelled back, shaking her head so that the fur on it, which looked remarkably like a twisted and frazzled gray squirrel tail to him, swung back and forth. Stan rubbed his head. He looked like an owl, with only little tufts sticking out around his ears. It was the saddest thing the squirrel had ever seen. Bad enough no tail, but no fur? He shivered at the thought.

"Gracie!" yelled Stan. Nothing happened. He yelled louder. "Gracie!" This time, the female turned around to look at Stan. Gracie was Stan's mate. *Gracie and Stan*, the bird feeders, squirrel chasers. He'd remember that.

Stan sat on one chair while she dragged over the

one she'd been standing on to fill the feeders. He felt the ground shake when she plopped down heavily next to Stan. It would be a long while before they left. It was warm and bright, with a cooling soft wind that ruffled both leaves and fur. There would be no seed for him until they were gone, if the birds didn't eat it all.

He left. Scampering under a gray metal fence with lots of holes, he ran to the next human den. In front of a tall and red wood fence, he stopped to listen. Many sounds filled his ears; distance softened the harshness of Gracie and Stan's sounds to a hum. Even farther were the sounds of machines that moved with deadly swiftness on the roads. Mixed in were echoes of so many animals: Robin calling, Gopher digging, and Chipmunk scurrying. And then there were those gentle clinks, almost like the hanging metal strips humans put in trees to make noise in the wind. How they could stand the constant banging was a puzzle to him. Slow, noisy, and they couldn't see or hear well. Poor humans.

But what was that clinking sound? Curious, he had to find out. Nimbly, he climbed the wood fence and perched on top to investigate. A human, smaller than Stan, sat in a shiny chair, pawing through shiny strange things strewn across the table. They had no names that he knew; there were no squirrel sounds for these things.

He sniffed. Nuts. The human had some—his favorite, too—the kind that humans smashed until thick like river mud. It was smeared all over a sweet fruit. He rubbed his paws hungrily. Maybe he could get some if a bit fell from the table into the grass. He didn't get any seed from the feeders and he was so very hungry and hunger always won over fear.

"Whuck! Whuck!" he called in hopeful greeting. Rat called these small humans boys or girls. The boy's head snapped up. His mouth curved up at the ends. A friendly sign.

"Whuck! Whuck!" he called again.

"Hello, little friend!" answered the boy. "I'm glad you came to visit."

What was he saying? The squirrel understood when someone spoke kindly to him. There was no trickery in the boy's voice, not like when a human would hold out a tasty nut and call to him trying to lure him close enough to be caught. He learned this lesson the hard way. A human did that to him once, and he bit the man. Running away as fast as his legs could move, he never went near that den again, knowing angry humans would be looking to trap squirrels. He warned Sister to stay away, too. When humans set out traps for biting squirrels, sometimes friends, or mothers, didn't come home.

This boy, with his skin dark brown, the color of wet wood, was different. He never left his funny looking chair, not even when he went into his home; chair and boy always went together. He'd watched the boy many times, but from a safe distance. Each time he visited, though, his curiosity forced him a little closer. He knew the boy saw him. Unlike Gracie, the boy never chased him with the long stick she used to brush out the dirt from her nest, or threw smelly things taken off feet.

"Want a banana?" The boy held up the sweet fruit, covered with the chunky nut mud. *The boy was offering food*. Slowly, cautiously, he crept down the wood fence, crossed the thick grass, climbed up onto the table, walked around the strange things, and snatched the fruit. Hurriedly, he backed up out of reach—just to be safe. But the boy sat quietly and didn't try to catch him, chase him, or get any nearer. He liked that in a human. He ate and watched.

While he chewed the nut-mud covered fruit happily, he and the boy stared at each other in silence, until the boy broke it with his soft voice, so unlike Gracie's screeching.

"You need a name, squirrel. I see you almost every day, and now that you feel safe enough to sit on my table, we're friends. And friends have names. I'm Collin, but I guess you can't say that. You can call me "whuck," whatever that means. Since I can't speak squirrel, I'm going to call you Jack," he said, smiling at him, "after my favorite pirate. He was a wily guy, too."

"Collin, Collin," he said, patting himself.

"Jack, Jack," he said, pointing to him.

The boy was *Collin* and he was *Jack*. He understood. He liked his human name. He would let the boy call him Jack. In agreement, he trilled and flicked his tail.

"Well, Jack, have a seat while I work on my remote control car. I'm building it from this kit, and you can watch."

While Collin put pieces together, Jack devoured the last of his banana. Suddenly, loud voices and terrible noises cascaded over the fence, and he froze. Clanging, banging metal and splintering trees stung his sensitive ears. He smelled something burning; not wood, but something thick and black. Something from machines. The scent of fresh sap mingled with it in his nose. He twitched his tail and gripped his paws in distress.

"Ta-cherr! Ta-cherr!" he chattered.

"What's the matter, Jack?" asked Collin. A machine snarled as it destroyed more trees.

"Ta-cherr!"

"I know, the noise bothers me too," said Collin nodding, as he returned to pushing things around in the box. "They're building another house. Maybe even some across the street. Too bad. I liked to watch the cardinals that lived in the nest in the huge maple tree." He stared at Jack. "I hope *you* don't live there, Jack."

Chapter 2

<u>Rolling, Rolling, Rolling</u>

Jack stood on his hind legs, listening to the machines as they continued their clamorous destruction. Many big machines. When machines came, animals fled and trees fell. Food got scarce. And then humans came to stay.

Jack turned toward Collin. He looked in the boy's eyes, and saw calm softness. With no fur and big eyes, it took no effort to see what humans felt. It wasn't like that with animals. Fox wore the same face whether he was just sitting or he was eating your brother.

"You can live here," continued Collin. "Our yard has lots of trees."

Jack merely stared at Collin, understanding no more than 'trees.'

Collin's trees? His tree? Dead trees?

He would have to learn more names from this boy.

Collin grabbed something, but dropped it on the table. It rolled across until Collin caught it as it fell off the edge. To Jack, it looked like a nut when it dropped from the tree and tumbled on the ground.

"This is a *wheel*," said Collin, holding it in one hand and pointing with the other. "It's *round*." His finger circled its edge. "And it *rolls*." Collin put the wheel on the table and gently pushed. It rolled until Collin caught it and held it out to him.

Frozen with fear at first, Jack didn't move, but Collin's slow calmness eased his fear. He took the wheel. Another name.

He examined it, turning it over and over in his paws. He put the wheel, like Collin had, on the table and pushed. Slowly it wobbled across the table. Collin caught it.

"Unbelievable, Jack," he said with a crooked smile. "You're one smart little guy." Again, he gave Jack the wheel to roll. They did this rolling a few more times.

"Now you know one of the simple machines," said Collin, a smile lighting his face as he dumped the wheel into the box.

Jack stuffed the last chunk of banana into his mouth, and finished by licking his paws clean.

"I wonder what else you know." Collin said, pushing the box of things carefully forward.

Jack hopped toward the box and inspected the contents, pushing aside wire, more wheels, and tiny metal things the length of a rose thorn with deep grooves winding up the side. Human things. Sitting up on his hind legs, he looked at Collin.

Abruptly, he hunkered down. He stole a wheel, and then scampered across the table.

"Jack! Bring that back!" shouted Collin. By the tight lines in the boy's face and the downturn of his mouth, he knew Collin was not happy with him for stealing the wheel. Collin's tone of voice was not nice; it was harsh. Jack understood. Collin was mad. He would be mad if Collin snatched his stash of nuts. But he wasn't going to keep or eat the wheel. He was only going to roll it.

Leaping down from the table, he landed on the middle of the hard pathway where humans walked. Collin turned his chair around and started to roll toward him. Jack twittered, holding up the wheel and Collin stopped, staring at him. The two stripes of fur over Collin's eyes rose up.

Jack put the wheel on the path and rolled it.

Collin laughed. When the wheel rolled close to the chair, Collin snatched it up.

"Okay, wise guy. You're brilliant. But I need this wheel for my car." He flipped the wheel back into the box with the other things.

Climbing back onto the table, Jack watched Collin push the big wheels on his chair. Collin's chair rolled.

He spied something next to the box.

"Whuck! Whuck!"

Collin looked up. "You called, Sir Jack? What do you want?"

Leaning forward, Jack sniffed part of a banana forgotten by Collin.

"More banana? Here, you can have mine, you furry little pig." He held out the chunk, which Jack quickly snatched.

Plain. No nut mud, but still tasty. He took it and rammed a chunk into his mouth, which forced his cheeks to puff out. It had the slight bitter taste of human mouth water, but he ate it anyway. It wasn't as bad as that stuff humans put out for cats to eat.

The ground shuddered and a low rumble rolled over the green grass. Jack leapt off the table and skittered up the fence. While he watched, a man holding a screaming machine felled trees; young saplings and full-grown trees alike shuddered, their trunks falling onto bush and grass.

"Ta-cherr! Ta-cherr!" he scolded, swishing his tail as towering oak and red maple were cut, then crushed by yet another machine. Its gaping mouth with metal teeth chewed the trunks until they were nothing more than chips of bark. He watched helplessly at the destruction. Sorrowfully, he ran for home.

Chapter 3

Sisters!

Through patches of light slipping down between branches, over a ground soft with fallen leaves and pine needles, he ran, a rippling wave of silver fur. Branches bent under his weight as he leapt from tree to tree, till he came to his own. Deep in the woodland, the oak was tall and strong. And safe. No machines.

"Where have *you* been?" scolded his sister, peeking out from their nest. "You've been gone so long, it will soon be dark." She perched on a high branch staring at him with hard, glittering eyes. She was mad. Sister was grouchy these days. Time for her to build or steal her own nest.

"I've been visiting that young human."

He scampered up the tree to sit beside her. They touched noses in greeting.

"Nuts! Where did you get those nuts? Did you bring some for me?" Her eyes shone bright with hope. She rubbed her front paws together.

"I didn't get any seed from the feeders. The boy gave me a fruit that had nuts all smashed on it. I was very hungry and ate it all."

Her eyes dimmed. "Oh." They sat quietly for a while, scanning the woods for visitors, predators, or friends. They found none.

"Do you want to know what I learned?" he asked.

She fluffed an already perfectly fluffed tail, ignoring him.

"You're mad because of the nuts, aren't you? There was only a little," he lied. "And the nuts were smashed like mud."

"Mud? Like from Beaver's river?" She sounded as though she didn't believe him.

"Yes. It was stuck on the fruit. Then it stuck to my fur. It was hard to lick off."

She snorted softly and turned away.

"Maybe if you come with me, you could get..."

"Are *you* nuts? Go visit a *human? I* don't visit humans." She proceeded to search for fleas.

"This boy is different. He sits in a chair, quiet, no grabbing. And the fruit is very good."

She leaned forward to sniff his breath. "What kind of fruit? Apple? Cherry?"

"No, he calls it banana. It's delicious."

"It smells delicious. But no humans for me. Just bring a small piece home for me next time. With the nut mud."

He wanted her to come with him and meet Collin, but arguing with Sister was useless. He'd rather fight other squirrels to protect his territory than have to argue with her. At least with other squirrels there was a chance he'd win.

"He calls me Jack. He is Collin. We're friends."

"Nice."

She was in a snit. When she was like that, there was nothing to do but get his tail out of there—fast.

"I'm going to collect more nuts." She made no reply, so he scrambled down and hopped a distance away. He hoped it was far enough. He stopped to pick up a nut.

"No, not that nut, this one!" she said, pointing in the opposite direction. Sister had decided to help. By ordering him around. It was all a squirrel could do not to pull out his fur.

I hate being second born.

"This one's bigger, it will give us more food," he argued.

She shook her head. "That nut is too heavy for either of us to move. Bury it in the dirt right there. Just remember where it is when we're hungry."

"With all the nuts that are too heavy and have to be buried where they fall," he muttered, "I'll never have time to dig up half of them. I wish we could find an easier way to move the big ones closer." He clawed the soft damp dirt and created a hole barely big enough to bury the nut. Rubbing his paws on the nut to give it his scent, he then pushed it into the hole. As he was about to cover it with dirt, he paused. Would he remember this exact spot, next to this small white rock and so far from the nest? Rocks and other clues would be lost under a layer of cold white. Suppose the machines came and he and Sister couldn't sniff out and move the nuts in time? They might go hungry, unless they stole from other squirrels. That always started trouble. And if the machines came they would lose their nest. They'd have to build or steal another. If the leaves were all gone and covered with white, it would be even harder to make the nest warm.

Jack stared at the nut. Too big to hold in his mouth. Too heavy to carry. He looked around at all the burial spots. They were scattered far apart. Each hole was just where the nut rolled after falling.

Rolled.

Like Collin's wheel.

"Sister!" he screeched excitedly. "Come here! Hurry!" With lightning quickness, he started to dig up all the nuts. He called her again, more insistently.

"Okay, okay," she snapped, "keep your fur on." Gracefully and unhurriedly Sister came scampering down a nearby tree. Her fur was flat on one side. She had been dozing while he worked.

"What are you doing?!" she twittered angrily. Swishing her tail rapidly, she stopped right in front of him. "Why are you digging up all our nuts?"

"To put them together in a bigger hole."

"In a bigger hole? Some nuts are too heavy to

carry, Brother."

"Call me Jack. And don't carry, *roll*."

She tittered in amusement. "'Jack' is such a funny name. And what is rolling?"

"*I* like the name. Now watch." He pushed the nut out of the hole. It rolled a short distance and stopped.

"You want me to push nuts from one hole to another? Why? I don't want to."

"If you don't want to roll, you can dig up the rest of the nuts or dig the bigger hole."

"But if they're all together in one pile, then chipmunks or..."

"Or stealing meadow squirrels?" he asked suspiciously. She looked away. He knew she was sneaking off to see one. Great. Her young would grow up to be lazy stealers too. Sometimes family was a pain in the tail, but she was all he had left. And now he was going to lose her when she mated and left their nest.

"We're not going to put *all* the nuts in one hole. We'll make holes here, here, and here." He ran around, stopping at the places he wanted the holes dug. They'll be closer to the tree. Every nut won't be in its own hole, scattered all over the place."

She sighed. "Too much work. It will take a long time. I can't help you."

He stopped digging to look at her. "Why not?"

"You buried them, you know where they are better than me."

"You know my scent! If I *move* all the nuts, then I *eat* all the nuts! Get busy."

Still she hesitated. "I want to visit... Rabbit. Yes, visit Rabbit."

Jack snorted. "Since when are you and Rabbit friends? You're slinking off like a fox to visit a meadow squirrel. I can smell him on your fur. Move nuts, then slink." He turned away and stared across the wood, darkness growing almost as he watched. He cocked his head to listen.

"When I was at Collin's den, I heard the machines," he chittered softly.

"We always hear machines. Stupid things are everywhere."

"No, Sister. Machines chewing up the trees next to the boy's den. I think they might come here."

She twittered. "*Here?* Into our woods?" She grunted. "They won't cross the road. This is our woods. You worry too much." She went back to work digging up nuts.

He didn't argue. It was useless. His fear wouldn't go away, though. All while he rolled nuts and reburied them, the fear was there and growing. He'd keep an eye on the machines to see if they crossed the road. If they did, all the woodland animals and trees were in danger.

Chapter 4

<u>The Sound of War</u>

Light shining into the nest woke him. That and those noisy birds, chirping and tweeting. Stretching, Jack sniffed. It would be just right outside his tree; not too warm, not too cool. Perfect for a run through the woods and Collin to sit outside. After he ate some dried mushrooms and drank dew pooling in a curled dry leaf, Jack headed for Collin's home. Halfway there, he stopped to enjoy his woods. There was the damp little cave where he'd hidden from loud boys and found a secret stash of mushrooms that he hadn't shared with Sister. Here was the gnarled oak, black, and burned smelling from a light strike. A shush of wind rushed across the ground, stirring dead leaves. Standing up, he sniffed machine smoke and dying flowers. He got a whiff of human scents, too. None were in the woods now; the wind carried their odor over the distance from the dens that bordered the woods. But they were getting closer. His stomach twisted, and not from hunger.

With slow steps, Jack felt the wetness of decaying leaves and black soil under his feet. His fur, tickled by a flea hiking down his back, rippled. He shook vigorously, trying to throw the flea free. The pest hung on, so Jack had no choice but to eat it. Fat from feeding off him, it snapped crisply in his mouth. Not bad tasting, but he'd rather have a mushroom or his treat from Collin.

The light was almost at its brightest but getting shorter and colder. Away he dashed, leaving cool woods behind, and crossed the black road, nicely warm from the light, in front of Collin's den. The machines were quiet this light rise. A very large bare spot replaced grass, thicket, and tree. Alert for danger, he sniffed, listened, and searched. No humans, but plenty of stink. He did not trust the humans or the machines to stay on Collin's side of the road. Small gray squirrels got killed by both.

He sailed off a branch, over the fence, onto Collin's grass. Sitting in his chair, Collin slowly glanced at Jack. Once Jack sat on the table in front of Collin, he offered Jack a treat of apple pieces and nut mud in silence. No greeting.

"Whuck! Whuck!" Jack called softly. Collin barely smiled.

"Whuck whuck to you too."

Something was wrong. Collin was not wearing a happy face. Every once in a while, Collin sorted through his strange shiny things in the box. Jack didn't see any brightness in his eyes, any quickness in his movements.

What was wrong? When Sister was unhappy, Jack would leap from branch to branch, pretending to fall, but suddenly catching on at the last moment. Scaring her like that always made her chitter, but she was more amused than frightened. She loved tricks.

Humans loved animal tricks, too. Dogs, grown silly living with humans, did stupid things, earning a treat when the humans laughed. Swiftly he scaled the nearest tree. *I'll do tricks.*

"Whuck! Whuck!" he called. When Collin looked, Jack leapt gracefully through the branches, as though flying like Robin. He stopped on one thick branch to see if Collin watched. He did, but there was no liveliness in his face. His eyes were still dull. He continued to sit there, unmoving.

Jack ran down the tree, then over to the birdfeeder. Birdfeeder tricks always amused humans, right before they chased squirrels that stopped to eat with long sticks. Skillfully, he climbed the pole up to the feeder. Like the one at Gracie's home, when Jack stepped onto the edge, the seed holes closed up. Jack dug in his claws, sharp from climbing, and hung upside down from the top, opening the holes. He reached in and pilfered the seed.

"Whuck! Whuck!"

The boy's smile lasted for a moment.

"Sorry, Jack, I'm not feeling well today. It

happens sometimes. Tomorrow will be better."

Unsure, Jack hung there, swaying slightly. He didn't know what else to do. He let go, flipped in mid-air, and landed softly in the lush green grass next to the pole. He skittered over, and up onto the table. Sitting there, he smoothed his whiskers and stared at Collin who laid his open hand on the table. Cautiously, Jack sniffed it. No more treats. On the road, machines smaller than those that chewed up the trees moved but soon passed beyond Jack's hearing.

Except one loud one. It stopped on the other side of the fence.

Jack leapt off the table, climbed up the fence and perched on a fat pole. The yellow machine, with a great yawning jaw, bit a huge hole into the ground. It swung its mouth and long neck around to the other machine. The jaw opened, dropping dirt, rocks and roots into another machine. When that machine was full, it rolled slowly onto the road, spitting out gusts of black, burning air, which made Jack sneeze and cough. His eyes watered and his fur smelled awful.

He stretched up on his hind legs, ears listening, eyes searching, tail twitching, chest pounding. Voices grated in his ears. Humans calling, humans walking around the hole as it grew larger and larger. He smelled the fresh dirt, almost wet.

It was beginning.

"Ta-cherr! Ta-cherr!" Jack called angrily, wishing the machines away. His tail trembled with rage while his paws quivered with fright.

"Whoa, Jack, easy little guy," soothed Collin.

"What's the matter?"

Jack shivered. He spit at the humans.

"Do the machines scare you, Jack?" asked Collin as he wheeled over. Collin, in his chair below, couldn't look over the fence. He waited.

Jack peered down at Collin, then turning toward the machines, he screeched, "Ta-cherr! Ta-cherr!" once more.

"I guess to you they are bad machines, cutting down the trees."

Jack watched in horror as one machine rolled away—to push through brush and small trees on the far side of the road, which led to his woods. He flew off the fence, scuttled under the gate, and ignoring Collin's shouts, scurried into the trees. There was going to be a fight over territory. Humans and machines against the animals.

Chapter 5

A Time to Gather

"Sister! Sister!" he chittered before he was even close to his tree. He continued to run and call. He crouched, panting, at the bottom when he reached it. Sister poked her head out of the nest.

"This better be good if you're screeching like Owl and interrupting my meal."

"You're always eating lately," he managed to gasp, "This is bad. Very bad."

"What could be that bad? Unless you've had a treat and didn't bring any for me." Jack looked away guiltily. He'd forgotten about bringing something back for Sister.

"Like I can't smell nuts and apples from here," she twittered crossly.

"The machines have crossed the road! They're in our woods!" he huffed.

Sister stood still. She flicked her tail several times. "What are we going to do?"

"We have to call a Gathering. Tell every animal."

She snorted. "What good is that? With all the noise those things make, the others must know. Before the machines tear up our nest and food stores, we have to find a new tree far from here. We have to build a new nest. We have to dig up and move as many nuts as we can." She ran up and down the branch in agitation.

"I'm not running away!" Jack screeched. "We have to think how to stop the machines."

Sister stopped, looked at him and mumbled, "Fur must be growing inside your head if you think we can do anything against machines!"

"We have to try. I'm going to Owl's. She can spread the word. When the light is dying, we should all meet at Speaking Rock." With that, he ran off as fast as his legs could carry him.

When darkness started to surround the woods, Jack waited patiently for the rest of the animals to show. Balanced on a fragrant pine branch, he took a deep whiff of the freshening breeze that soon would bring rain. He struggled to put bits of thoughts together.

As the animals arrived, he listened. No one looked up, which surprised him. Animals were not that careless. They checked all around for danger. They were afraid, but now they had a reason to be even more careful.

"Do you know what this Gathering is about?" asked a woodchuck.

"No," replied Rabbit. "Owl only said that Squirrel wanted all of us together. It must be important," she said, nodding toward a dark corner of the hollow. "Even Fox is here." She glanced nervously at Fox and the other meat eaters crouching together in back.

Jack wasn't worried about the meat eaters; they always behaved themselves at a Gathering. Afterwards was a different story. Fox wasn't called sly for nothing. Looking at Rabbit, Jack watched her nervously darting eyes always keeping Fox in sight.

The animals moved about restlessly, impatient for the Gathering to begin, but Jack waited for Sister. He didn't want to start without her, pest that she was. The squawking, chirping, growling, and other animal sounds grew louder with each passing moment. Finally, Jack skittered down the tree into the clearing. Sister should arrive very soon.

He climbed onto the largest boulder, called the Speaking Rock. The final shreds of light were disappearing below the mountains in the distance. The animals of the dark were jumpy. It was feeding time and they were impatient to eat. For the animals of the light like Jack, Bird, and Rabbit, it was time to curl up and sleep. He was ready for his nest, but not until they all heard what he had to say.

Seeing him, they quieted.

"What's this Gathering about?" asked an impatient young possum.

"Have you seen them?" Jack asked.

"Seen what?" said Rabbit.

"Probably a stash of nuts he's lost," joked one of the thieving meadow squirrels. Jack recognized him. This squirrel kept discovering where Jack secreted a good portion of his nuts. Jack saw him stealing them.

Lazy squirrel! Jack swished his tail and twitched his whiskers. His paws clenched and unclenched. Woodland squirrels did not like meadow squirrels that saved themselves from hard work by taking what they needed from Sister and him. They were too many and Jack couldn't watch all of them. Or stop them.

He eyed the thief. "It's something more important than you stealing our stash of food." There were a few titters from the chipmunks. The meadow squirrel slunk down into the long sweet grass. He belonged to the meadow. So why was he here anyway?

"If you don't listen, none of us are going to have *any* food. I was visiting a human..." he began. Upon hearing *human*, half the animals started muttering suspiciously, and some began to leave.

"No! Wait!" he tried to chitter above the din. They ignored him and wandered back into the woods. Jack's bushy tail drooped. He only wanted to warn them. He knew they distrusted humans, he did too, except for Collin. But the animals should trust *him.*

An ear-piercing scream filled the hollow and echoed off the trees. The animals froze.

"Good of you to stay," said Owl softly. "Now that you're all silent and still, please listen to what my friend Squirrel has to say. It's important, or I wouldn't have wasted my sleep time spreading the call to come here. And, you must obey the law of the woodland; every animal has a say on the Speaking Rock. He wasn't finished."

There were no arguments against the old mother of the woods.

She stared at each animal in turn, making him or her shiver. When again they settled down, because no one dared disobey Owl without fearing for their feather or fur, Jack stood up. Nervous, he smoothed an errant clump of tail fur, and began.

"The machines are coming. We must do something."

Screams, chirps, growls, and caws filled the night air. Rabbit cowered. Buck snorted angrily, stomping hooves. Birds, in chaotic formations, circled overhead.

"My young!"

"The machines are coming here?!"

"We have to run!"

"HOOOOOOOT!" Owl screeched again, but it did

no good. The animals were frightened, agitated, and running wild. Jack trembled, afraid to get trampled, bumped, or bitten. Until the animals worked off their panic, nothing could be said. During the upset, Owl's head swiveled toward the darkness.

No doubt listening for her meal, thought Jack as he nervously fluffed his tail from safety from on top of Speaking Rock. Sister snuck in sometime during the arguments. He knew she was searching for that meadow squirrel. Jack's tail flicked angrily.

Meadow squirrel! Whuck! She should have better sense than to run with those squirrels. A scraggly-tailed city squirrel would be better. At least they lived in trees, not ground holes.

The noise was dying down, the animals were tiring. Owl leaned forward.

"Squirrel, finish what you have to say. There are young to be taken care of."

Jack stood once more.

"The machines are on our side of the road."

"But they haven't come far," interrupted a gopher, "they're just on the edge. Only a little. Maybe they won't come in farther."

"They *always* come in farther," snarled Fox. "We must leave. Now." The panic started again.

"But I can't move the young yet! They're too small!" whined Beaver.

"See you," said the Jay. And she left with a snap of wings.

"We should do something!" twittered Jack as loudly as he could.

Only a few actually heard him. He could tell because they looked at him with blank eyes. It was a blankness caused by great fear. The only time he'd seen eyes look like that was when an animal was mesmerized by road machine lights—right before they got smashed under wheels. They were too afraid to move.

Then the whispers started. As more animals spread Jack's last words, more blank, then terrified eyes looked back at him.

"Uh oh," muttered Sister. "This is *not* good. Maybe you should run to the human's den until they don't look like that anymore," she whispered into his ear.

Jack's tail bristled. "No. I'm not running from my nest, not with cold coming."

"Did he say we should *do something?*" questioned Skunk, sitting by herself on a rock closest to the woods. And downwind.

"He meant we should do something like get ready to leave. Right?" asked Beaver, shaking.

"No! I meant we should fight, protect *our* territory," said Jack.

Fox sneered. "I don't know whether to laugh at you or eat you, Squirrel. Do something? Do *WHAT?*"

So many eyes, and all on Jack. He twittered nervously.

"I don't know. Yet. But the human boy I visit shows me things and I learn. Maybe I could learn something to stop the machines."

"What could we learn from humans?" spat Rat, who had a nasty temper. "They catch us, ruin our dens, and destroy our food. Humans are good for nothing, except to steal from and bite."

There were soft murmurs of agreement; most animals hated the humans. All feared them. Each had stories of cruelty at the hands of humans; traps set and family never returning, guns which maimed or killed, and those smashed by the shiny machines that sped by on roads.

"Squirrel is friend," chirped Cardinal. "Listen."

"Oh, sure, we knew you'd say something like that," said Rat nastily. "You're the humans' favorite. 'Pretty bird!' they say, and then throw out delicious seeds for you. They even put up all those water holders for you to drink and bathe. What do they do for rats? Set out traps and foods that kill."

"Yes," agreed Cardinal, flying down from her perch in a scraggly cedar to the Speaking Rock where Jack sat quietly grooming his back fur.

She continued. "Rat picks scraps from large cans on road. Squirrel takes seed from bird feeders. Rabbit eats from gardens. Whine about cats and dogs that lick human hands. Forget they are animal. Good things and bad things from humans. My nest is here. I stay." There were grudging murmurs of agreement. Cardinal spoke the truth.

"What plan do you have?" asked Owl.

Jack looked at her in surprise. "None, yet."

Owl twisted her head, cocking it slightly. Something rustled just beyond the large tree. Jack heard it. And felt sorry for it. Owl was hungry.

"If you have a plan to stop the machines before

they clear the trees up to the stream, I will call another Gathering. Once the machines pass there, it is time for all to leave." With that said, she spread her large wings out and almost silently lifted up into the darkness. Moments later, the small rustling stopped.

The animals began to leave. Some mumbled and grumbled, others said nothing. Soon, nothing was left but trampled grass and two squirrels.

"Let's go to our nest, Jack," said Sister. He perked up at the use of his new name. Good thing he hadn't mentioned *that*. They really would have gone wild.

He climbed down off Speaking Rock. "Yes. While we have a nest."

Darkness swallowed them up.

Chapter 6

<u>Rock 'N Rolling</u>

The machines made no move the next light rise or the one after that. Whispers around the woodland hinted the machines would not come any closer. The trees and animals were safe. Jack knew better. It was only a matter of light rises before they started up again. Just like the machines next to Collin's home, these wouldn't stop until the trees were gone and humans lived there.

After a stuffing of food and a fluffing of tail, Jack was ready. As he was about to leap to the ground, Sister popped out of the nest, fur still matted down from sleep.

"Where are you going?" she chittered gently.

"To watch Collin."

"Don't, Jack, it's dangerous. You could..." But the rest of Sister's nag was lost in the rustling of dead leaves on trees as he ran.

Jack flew from limb to limb, leapt across the thick wires that hummed, and scampered down a tall pole onto Collin's grass, shaded with trees. Collin sat at his table, with box and treat. Jack sniffed appreciatively. Nut mud. He licked a whisker.

Hopping up on the table, Jack sat next to Collin's arm.

"Jack! Hey buddy. Hungry?" Collin reached into a box and brought out apple pieces with nut mud. Jack wished he could have food like this all the time. Gently, he took a piece. Then he grabbed another piece and put it beside him. He'd bring Sister a treat this time so she wouldn't look at him with mad eyes.

"Saving one for later? Here you go." Collin put down a piece of white paper with more treats. Jack could stuff himself till he couldn't move and still have some for Sister. *Not all humans are bad. Just most.* He started gobbling.

Collin was fitting shiny metal pieces together again. It looked like a little road machine. This one wouldn't smash Jack, but he was still leery of it.

Bzzzzzz! Bzzzzz! The little machine hummed to life. Jack jumped with a squeak and took off for the wood.

"Jack! Jack!" Collin called. "Whuck whuck whuck!"

Jack stopped. It almost sounded like Collin was trying to call him—in squirrel! He turned around.

"Whuck, whuck," said Collin once more.

Collin was holding out the treats. The little

machine was silent.

Should I go back? Collin hasn't hurt me. The machine didn't move, only made noise, and it was little. Jack was simply startled. And if he went back to the nest without a treat for Sister again, she might be more fearsome than Collin's machine. He went back.

This time, he didn't get quite so close. He sat on the other side of the box, away from the machine.

"Relax, guy. It's okay. I won't turn it on when you're here." Collin held out his hand, and Jack sniffed. Smelled like apples, nut mud, and metal. He sat back.

"Just keep me company, okay? I'm mostly here by myself. I like having you around. You should move into one of my trees so I could see you all the time. I'd probably make you fat, though, with all this peanut butter you're eating."

Pieces clinked against each other as Collin searched for something. Jack, curious, moved closer. *Wheel.* He stole it.

"Jack! Bring that back! Come back here!" Jack ignored the words as he scampered off the table. On the walkway, he set down the wheel and pushed. Collin turned his wheeled chair around just in time to see Jack rolling the wheel. Collin started to move toward him. Jack held up the wheel. Collin stopped. Jack again put the wheel down and rolled it. Collin hooted like Owl.

He was laughing! Jack didn't roll the wheel to make Collin laugh and give him more treats, like the dogs did for their humans. He hadn't finished what he had. He rolled the wheel once more, toward Collin, who caught it and picked it up.

"Okay, Jack, you remembered. You're one smart little guy, I know! But you have to leave my stuff alone. Can't build my car if I'm missing parts. Makes me wonder though, what else you can do."

Now Jack couldn't roll because Collin had the wheel. No nuts lay on the ground that he could roll. His keen eyes picked out a rock, smooth and kind of round, lying on the side of the walk. He picked it up and rolled it. Wobbling, it went a good distance on the white road that Collin wheeled his chair on before it came to a stop underneath the wheel on his chair.

"You've got this rolling thing down good. Now you don't need my wheels!"

Collin leaned down to retrieve the rock, but he couldn't reach it. When he tried to roll his chair forward, the rock lodged tightly under the wheels. The chair wouldn't budge.

Jack paused, looking at the rock, the chair, and the wheels on the chair. *When the rock is under the wheel, the wheel won't move.* His head was starting to hurt from the thoughts buzzing around in his head.

"I have to teach you more simple machines, Dude. You're just so quick to learn." Collin backed up the wheeled chair. Jack startled. Collin's chair had wheels; just like the machines coming into the woodland. *If this rock stopped Collin's wheels... lots of rocks could stop the machines.*

He ran home.

Chapter 7

The Great Plan

Jack couldn't race back to his tree fast enough. In his eagerness, he dashed right past the machine, silent in its menace, instead of taking the longer, safer way around, as he had been doing.

"Gathering at dark! Gathering at dark!" he called all the way through the woodland. "Gathering at dark!" Heads popped up, chirps silenced, and wings ceased as he spread the word.

"Sissssterrrr!"He trilled once he got close to the nest. "I have a plan!" He zipped up the trunk into the nest, but she was not there. The nest was cold. And a mess. A slight whiff of that meadow squirrel tickled his nose. It was mingled with Sister's scent.

Sister had gone with the meadow squirrel. Worse, she'd let him into their nest and let him eat their food. One light rise, Jack would wake up and there would be no food left.

He crouched there, sadly panting, flicking his tail.

I hope the meadow squirrels hear the news about the Gathering and share it with Sister.

Once rested, he scampered back down the tree to find Owl.

It was still bright; Owl would be sleeping. When awakened, Owl would be grumpy. Without a good reason for waking her up, Jack could be eaten. *Danger! Machines!* was all Jack could think about. *I have to wake Owl.* Standing back from the opening of her nest hole, Jack chittered softly.

"Owl! Wake up, Owl!"

She didn't stir. Owl was a deep sleeper.

He called once more, louder. "Owl!"

No movement.

How do I wake her?

The light would not last long, and Owl needed time to fly around spreading the call for the Gathering before the animals of the light curled up in their nests and dens to sleep.

He scrambled down the tree, and finding an empty nutshell, picked it up in his mouth, and scrambled back up. Standing in front of the hole, he tossed the shell in. There was no sound.

"Squirrel, if you don't have something good to tell me, say goodbye to your Sister, because I'm going to

eat you." In the dark of the tree hole, one glowing yellow eye opened.

"I know what to do!" twittered Jack, "we must call a Gathering!"

"Hmm hooot! You mean you want *me* to call a Gathering," she answered without moving.

"Yes!" said Jack excitedly. He waited. Finally, he heard a rustling movement. Owl was coming out. He backed up out of respect, and fear.

She filled up the entire opening of the hole, and twisting her head around, peered into Jack's eyes.

"Don't. Throw. Nutshells. Into. My. Nest."

"I, I, I couldn't wake you," he twittered nervously.

"Don't."

"No, Owl." Jack backed farther up the branch, unable to stare long into those unblinking eyes.

"I will tell the animals to Gather. You be ready to tell them what you want to do."

She leapt out of the hole, and with a bare whoosh of her wings, took off. She circled lazily once, gliding effortlessly. Before heading off toward the river, she hooted softly, "Good work, Squirrel."

With the dark came a deepening chill. Jack sniffed from his perch in an old nest, long abandoned by the squirrel that used to live there. Its scent had long since weathered away. In the air, he smelled not only wood but also fire; humans had no fear of fire. Sometimes they could control it, and had it burning in their dens. Sometimes it burned their dens. Poor humans. If they had fur, they wouldn't need the dangerous fire to keep warm.

His own fur was thickening rapidly. The thin undercoat for when it was warm had mostly fallen out, replaced by the longer and thicker one needed for cold. This cold time would be very long, and extremely hard. Lots of whiteness.

The animals gathered around the Speaking Rock. He could hear their excitement and fear. Fox, slinking by on almost noiseless pads, paused under Jack's branch. He sniffed, looked up, and seeing Jack, narrowed his eyes and laid back his ears.

Hunting behavior.

He then sat on his haunches, unblinkingly staring at Jack with his yellow teeth and flat eyes.

Jack was safe, if he stuck to trees for the rest of his life. That would be a problem because most of his nuts were all buried in the dirt. There weren't enough in his tree to survive for long.

"Well, Squirrel. Another Gathering. What is it this time? Why don't you come down and we'll talk about it?" He grinned, tongue lolling out, mouth water dripping down in sticky gobs.

"No. I'll wait right here," tittered Jack. Around the woodland there was a whisper that Fox ate Jack's brother last warm time. Fox didn't talk about it. There was nothing Jack could do about it. It was the law of the woods; be alert if you don't want to be eaten. His brother had been more interested in a delicious mushroom growing on a log than his safety. All Jack and Sister found was his tail, tumbling along the ground in the breeze. Some bird then carted it off to line her nest.

Turning away, Jack made a quick inspection of his tail. If he needed to run quickly or leap a good distance, a fluffed tail gave better balance.

"I suppose I could run up the tree to you," Fox snarled softly.

"I'd be halfway across the woods before you got here," replied Jack. Foxes, even with a running start, were slow climbers. And even without his tail, Jack could out climb, out run Fox. But he wasn't going to tell Fox that. Fox would remember, and that wouldn't be good if he ever cornered Jack.

"I could get you before you even got to the tree," replied Owl, staring at Fox as she landed softly next to Jack. Jack squirmed a bit. Owl was a meat eater, after all. "Gathering is starting. Fox, go. Squirrel, speak."

Fox looked at Jack once more, licked his lips slowly and thoroughly, and with drool still hanging from his snout, slunk off.

"He is not to be trusted, Squirrel. Remember that."

Jack chittered, agreeing.

"And warn your sister. You know the rumors." She stretched out her wings, forcing Jack to descend the tree. He leapt upon the Speaking Rock and the animals quieted.

Owl swiveled her head looking at Jack to begin.

Squatting on his hind legs, he said, "I visited Collin, my boy. Many times he does things I don't understand, but something happened that I need to share with you. He sits in a chair. He never gets out of it, so I don't think his legs work. This chair has wheels. Things that roll to make the chair move."

"What is rolling?" asked Rabbit.

Jack thought a moment. "A nut falls from the tree, and goes over and over, moving away from the tree," he said.

"Like rocks falling down the river bank into the water?" asked Beaver.

"Yes!" Jack.

"Like radishes falling off Farmer's machine and moving in the dirt?" asked Rabbit.

"Yes!" tittered Jack excitedly.

"Like my eggs moving in the nest as my chicks try to get out?" asked Cardinal.

"Yes!" He was so happy he ran in circles. They understood! When he calmed, he started again.

"Collin makes the chair roll to get from one place to another. When I was showing him how I can roll a rock, it got stuck under the wheels of the chair and the chair couldn't move."

The animals, expectant, looked around in confusion.

"The machines have wheels," explained Jack.

They still looked confused. Jack sighed.

"We stuff rocks under the wheels of the machines," he added as Sister dropped down from a nearby birch tree. Jack looked at her and happily clapped his paws together. She had come. And without a meadow squirrel or a bad mood, that was good for Jack. He turned back to the anxious group.

"With rocks stuck under wheels, machines can't move."

The animals stared at each other for a few moments, then they gasped. And then they went berserk.

Chapter 8

If Everyone Works Together

Chaos broke out. Screeches and howls, tweets and squeaks echoed around the hollow.

"Stop the machines?! Is he crazy?!"

"We can't stop them!"

"Did he fall out of his tree again?"

"I'd rather run!"

"HOOOT!" screeched Owl stridently, stilling most of the panicked animals instantly with her impressive size and power.

Jack shivered a bit, despite his fur coat.

It's never wise to ignore an owl, he thought grimly. *Especially a hungry one.*

He, Owl, Sister, and Cardinal sat still and waited quietly for the few still running about in a frenzy. Nothing could be done until they worked off their panic. Jack scratched his belly. Owl cocked her head, listening to sounds in the dark. Cardinal flitted about nervously. And Sister was smirking at that meadow squirrel.

Meadow squirrel! When had HE snuck in? Whuck! But Jack had other problems to worry about right now.

The noise was dying down. The animals were tiring. Owl leaned forward.

"Squirrel, please tell us how we can stop the wheels on the machine."

"Watch." He climbed down the rock and pushed a large green walnut into the midst of the clearing. Then he swiftly ran back and rolled a small pebble, lodging it snugly under the walnut.

"Sister, would you try to push the walnut?" he asked.

Sister hopped over and pushed. The walnut wouldn't budge. She pushed again. No movement.

"So??" asked Fox, clearly not impressed. "This doesn't prove anything. The machine is strong. It can rip out trees and chew big holes in the ground. A small rock isn't going to stop them."

"What a hare-brained idea!" said a young possum rudely.

"Hey! Watch your tongue! I'm related to the hares," hissed Rabbit. "Listen and leave out the insults."

The possum curled under its mother, leaving only two terrified black eyes peeking out from under white fur.

Jack groomed his whiskers thoughtfully. "Collin is big, but he couldn't roll over the small rock."

Rat grunted. He strutted forward, tail sticking straight in the air and ears pointed stiffly. "Watch *me.*" Walking up to the walnut, he pushed—in the opposite direction, and easily rolled the walnut away.

"Nuts," muttered Sister. Fox smirked and next to him, Rat snickered.

Jack, not minding any of them, circled the walnut, thoughtfully gazing it. Then the rock. And back to the walnut. He went over to the bottom of Speaking Rock, and loading his mouth full of more small pebbles, carried them over to the walnut. One by one, he pushed the pebbles under the edge of the walnut, till it was completely encircled.

"Now try it," he instructed. Rat sauntered over and pushed. Nothing. He pushed harder. Still nothing. Frustrated, Rat gritted his teeth, wiggled his whiskers, and shoved the walnut with all his weight and strength. And it went nowhere.

"It didn't move!" squeaked Sister, running over to give Jack a soft nuzzle.

"You want us to move a bunch of rocks because you *think* it's going to stop the machines?" jeered Fox. He shoved his way to the front of the group. "This whole Gathering is ridiculous! We shouldn't be listening to this! The machine will rip up the woods and you want to fight it? What will the next light rise bring? More machines, more humans, more dead animals, that's what!" he spat. Several grumblers agreed with Fox.

"Quiet!" ordered Owl. "Some of us want to hear

the rest of what Squirrel has to say, and he's on the Rock. Obey the law."

"Save our burrows!" yipped a skunk from the back.

"Let the squirrel speak!" growled a coyote.

Jack stood as tall as his small body would allow. "You saw how the walnut couldn't roll, with only small rocks. We can ram lots of rocks tightly under the wheels. And Beaver can chew down trees that we could roll, too. I think we could stop the machines."

"Or at least slow it down so we can flee," observed Owl dryly.

"Every animal has a say," interrupted Rabbit. "Yes or no. Each family will decide if they want to leave the wood or fight."

"I think it will work, but I can't do it alone," said Jack. "I need you to help me. *You,*" and he looked at all of them, but skimmed quickly over Rat and Fox, "live here. We all have to fight or flee."

"You're batty!" squeaked Rat, "if you think we can win against a machine by rolling a few rocks and logs. I think one too many nuts have dropped on your head, Squirrel."

"The boy calls me Jack, so use that name."

"Oh, so now we have a *human* name," said Fox snidely. "What's next? A human den too?" Fox bared his teeth and laid his ears back, seething.

Jack sighed softly. He knew this wasn't going to go over well with these animals; almost all were unfriendly to humans. "When you call me Jack, then I know you're talking to me, not Sister or one of the meadow squirrels. It gets very confusing when you say 'Squirrel' and so many of us answer." He tensed and his fur twitched. Fox and Rat were teaming up against him, riling the other animals to give up, before even trying to save their holes and dens and hutches. They wanted to make Jack look like a human pet because they didn't like him. He knew they were afraid of being killed before they could flee but they didn't have to act so mean to him.

Jack knew this could work, but it would work only if they all helped.

"Are you going to give *me* a name, *Jack*?" snapped Fox. A low rumbling gurgled in his throat.

"ENOUGH!!!" screeched Owl piercingly, flapping her strong wings. Clouds of dust erupted and leaves scattered in the whoosh of air. The animals cringed.

"We'll still be here arguing about dumb things like names when the machines wreck our wood! Fox, quiet! Jack, finish explaining. I want to know the rest of it before I die of oldness." Pulling her wings back, she preened some feathers, which had become quite ruffled during her screeching outburst. When the grumbles stilled, she nodded to Jack.

"Okay Jack, I think we're ready to listen. Again. Without interruptions," she glanced meaningfully at Fox and Rat. Then she nestled down on the low hanging branch.

Jack jumped to obey. "If we roll as many rocks and logs as we can all around the machine wheels, we'll stop the machine, like Beaver's dam stops the water. With everyone's help, the machines won't be able to go forward or go around, like Rat did with the walnut. If we do this in the dark, then the humans won't see us or stop us."

"Or catch us," interjected Sister, now standing beside him. Out of the corner of his eye, Jack noticed the slinking meadow squirrel trying to move closer to her. Jack's eyes could pick him out of the shadows halfway across the wood. Did that scruffy tailed squirrel really think Jack wouldn't see him? No squirrel could be that stupid, could they? He swished his tail. Saving the woods was more important than his Sister's choice of a mate, bad choice though it was.

"And what do we do," asked Owl, looking at Jack with those unblinking glowing eyes again, "if a machine pushes right past our rock and wood dam? Like Rat said, those machines are very strong." Rat nodded and Fox growled, both vigorously in agreement.

Jack scratched his ear, thinking hard. "We must build our dam high and strong. Make them back up, like Collin had to back up his wheeled chair. If they back up, no place to go but back onto the road or someplace else."

It was silent while the group considered everything. It was true; human dens surrounded the wood on all sides except for where the road ended abruptly. Machines would not cut down or crush human dens to get to the woods by another way.

"Humans do not give up so easily," warned Rat.

"I know," Jack agreed, "but we're fighting to save *our* dens. We will not give up easily, either."

"When start? What do we do? Call me Red," said

Cardinal.

Jack tittered happily. That bird was a true friend.

It took until well past complete dark for the animals to understand what each was to do. Smaller animals would hunt for and find rocks and logs; larger animals would roll or push them in front of the machines. Animals like Beaver would stack and build the dams. Jack was finally satisfied that each animal knew exactly what to do. They almost seemed eager to get started. Everyone except Rat and Fox.

Nothing but chasing away every single human would make those two happy, but we aren't able to do that.

"We need everyone's skills," urged Jack, hoping to enlist Rat's help. "Everyone has to work together, like one big herd, for this to work."

"Huh," snorted Rat. "What could one measly, nasty rat do that would possibly make a difference? I know what you think of me." He started to crawl away.

"A rat like that could provide me with food so I wouldn't have to stop working to hunt," replied Owl sleepily with one eye opening and focusing intently on Rat. Even though light time was far away, she rested her old wings.

"What do you want me to do?" sulked Rat, peering at Jack with half closed eyes and a dragging tail.

Jack had to think fast. *What can Rat do better than any other animal? I don't trust him, he's always sneaking off, hiding, and whispering, but we need every paw, every hoof.*

A thought flashed through his head. "You have

very sharp teeth, Rat," he said. "Chew their machines. If the machines don't work, it won't matter if the road isn't blocked."

"Sounds interesting," replied Rat, his tail, ears, and nose perking up. "I'm always ready for a little destruction. Rat against humans and the big machines. I like the sound of that. Something to tell the whole family."

"Since the machines are quiet when it's dark, while some animals roll rocks..."

"And logs! Don't forget my chewed trees!" piped Beaver.

"And logs," added Jack with an amused chitter, "others like you can chew through every wire on the machine. I've chewed a few myself, so I know you can do it easily."

"They're not going to zap me like those wires on tall poles that killed your other brother, are they, Jack?" asked Rat looking at him suspiciously.

"I don't think so," said Jack, pleased that Rat used his new name. "Machines go quiet. The wires up high are always humming. I told my brother not to chew the humming ones, but he didn't listen. If it doesn't hum, it doesn't work."

"Can I bring in some family to help?"

"Rat, bring as many as you want. You'll have to lead them because I'll be looking for rocks." Making Rat the leader of his family would keep him busy, happy, and away from Jack. A happy rat was a good rat.

"I'll bring my sewer family, they're tough," said Rat smirking enough so that all his jagged teeth showed, "we'll be done before the bats return to the cave."

"We'll meet at the big rotted tree near the machines when we're finished. We start next dark time. Remember," urged Jack sternly, "we have to finish before light rise. Hurry!"

Saying no more, Rat speedily darted off, his head and tail held high.

"What should I do?" piped up Skunk.

"Uh, um," hesitated Jack. He didn't want to send Skunk away, but Skunk hanging around would make it unbearable for them to work.

And it would make it unbearable for the humans too...

"As soon as the machines are blocked, and we're not downwind, you can add the uh, 'finishing' touch," he added brightly. Skunk nodded.

"I'll call you when it's time!" Skunk trotted off and Jack breathed in the fresh air gratefully.

"It's going to take a little more than some paw licking words to interest me," interrupted Fox, lazily chewing on some grass. He coughed up an irksome bone and spit it out next to Jack, who instantly jumped out of the way.

"Nice," muttered Jack.

"Fox," said Owl now fully awake from her nap, "this is a volunteer effort. If you don't want to help, that's your choice, but I will volunteer you for a midnight treat if you cause any trouble."

"I still choose not to help," he replied, tossing his head and tail airily.

Owl swiveled her head around to look at

everyone before turning back to Fox. Her eyes seemed to blaze even though it was totally dark.

"The machines are already past the end of the road. Your den, Fox, with your mate, is the first one they will squash. One might be on its way soon."

Fox dropped to a fighting stance, his ears pricked up in alarm.

"My den! What do I doooo?" he howled.

"Follow us and roll rocks," said Jack. "Your mate could help too," he added.

Fox snorted. "Think again. She'd rather visit her family before she lifts a paw."

Jack shrugged. It was worth a try.

"We're agreed," said Owl, "Now rest." She looked around at the group. "Everyone stay alert!" There were slow nods and agreeable mumbles. "I will watch the machines to see if any wake during the dark." Owl leaned her sharp, curved beak close to Jack, her yellow eyes staring keenly into Jack's.

"Remember to be careful around Fox," she warned softly as she blinked quickly, glancing at Fox sitting on his haunches, panting, and then back to Jack. "You, your sister, and even Cardinal must watch him very carefully. That one doesn't like you and is not to be trusted."

Jack nodded. Fox was whispering secretively to a weasel while stealing sly glances at Sister, him, and occasionally Cardinal. Jack shivered in his fur although it was a comfortable night.

"I need to eat." Owl flew off with a whisper of flapping wings, and was soon swallowed by the night.

Cardinal, Rabbit, Buck, and Beaver congratulated Jack. Sister added her soft chitter. Her meadow squirrel friend made no move or greeting whuck.

Rude squirrel. Jack turned away.

"I'm going to the nest, Sister. Be ready tomorrow at dark." He didn't wait for her; he knew she wasn't coming with him.

Chapter 9

Not Another One!

The next day, Beaver came chugging into Jack's territory, huffing and puffing. Jack scrambled down to meet him.

"What's wrong, Beaver?" he asked, "Why are you running so hard?" Jack had to wait until Beaver caught his breath.

"They're coming! What are we going to do? My dam! My lodge!" he wailed.

"Who's coming, Beaver? Humans?" Jack could hardly understand Beaver's ranting.

"Another big machine! Now two across the road! Coming to cut down our trees!" he cried breathlessly.

"Calm down, Beaver! We can't do anything with you running around like a rabid raccoon!" Jack shouted, trying to reassure the hysterical animal.

"What do you mean 'calm down,'" Beaver grunted back. "What is there to be calm about?! There is another machine! We need to run, save our families, find a new place. Oh, my dam was almost finished!" he wailed once more. Beaver ran in circles, whacking his strong tail with a hard thump on the ground, making Jack jump with each smack.

Another machine. In the woods where Jack, Sister, Beaver, Owl, Rat, Fox, and all the other animals lived. They had to choose: fight or flight. There would be no den, food, or territory once the machines did their work and humans settled here. Only some birds, a few rabbits, and of course, rats, possibly a squirrel or two, could exist so closely with the humans.

"Oh, be quiet and be still!" twittered Jack more harshly than he wanted, but it was necessary to stop Beaver's crying and tail slapping. "Let's go look. Maybe one machine left, they don't always stay."

Beaver quieted, but gave Jack a worried look. While he tramped as fast as he could, Jack followed nimbly through the trees.

Another machine in our woods. I knew this would happen. They always come, and they always destroy. And animals always suffer.

In the distance, Jack caught a glimpse of them. Glistening in the hot sun with silent menace, the machines waited on the edge of the wood by road's end.

"The new one was just getting here, and I ran as

fast as I could to tell you. Like Owl said, 'Keep alert.' And I did," Beaver huffed.

Jack moved closer to the machines, but Beaver, terrified, hung back.

"Careful!" he warned with a thwap of his tail.

Crunch! Snap!

Jack stopped and looked back. Beaver was chewing sticks.

"Stop making so much noise!" Jack tittered angrily. Did Beaver want to announce their arrival in this wood and the next? If humans were nearby, they'd come over to gawk at the animals moving in so close. Jack and Beaver could get caught.

"But I'm nervous!" Beaver cried.

"Then chew your claws, or groom your fur, but be quiet!" Once again, Jack slowly approached the machines. Human scents wafted through the air to his sensitive nose. Then came other smells—the stinky black smoke the machines spewed, tender green grasses crushed by the passing of the machines, and fresh run sap from broken branches on the maple trees—all which clung to the

metal. Silence hung thickly. He knew the birds, the small land animals, and even the crickets in this area were gone. The yellow machines loomed starkly against the brilliant blue sky.

They gave off no smoke, noise, or destruction. Warily, Jack scooted closer to the first one. It had a huge wall of metal, slightly curved, and vicious looking wheels with metal thorn-like points. Jack had seen one like this push a huge pile of dirt, leaving a large hole. The next one was a machine like Jack saw moving on the road, only bigger. The back was open and usually carried trash, dirt, or silly housedogs with ears flapping and tongue slapping in the wind. Jack tittered, thinking about the sight. Dumb dogs. They were too humanized to know how stupid they looked.

Jack saw enough. Having no words of comfort for Beaver, they retreated silently for their nests.

His mind churned over and over what he saw—and what he knew was going to happen. The anger started to build. By the time they reached Beaver's lodge, he was not angry. He was furious.

"I'm not going to lose my tree, Beaver! And you're not losing your dam! We are going to stop *every* machine they bring!"

Beaver stopped short. "Did you eat one of the bad mushrooms, Jack? Do you know what you're saying? It's one thing to stop a walnut. It doesn't fight back. It doesn't *kill*. One big machine was bad. There's another. Too many, too big!" he gulped.

Jack's mind was made up. "The machines can rest here, but they will not build here."

For now, the machines were still. That would change.

Chapter 10

Crispy Whiskers

Whispers about another machine coming into the wood raced like brushfire pushed by a dry hot wind. Red, with the help of the other birds of the light, spread the call before dark that all the animals were needed to fight. They would need to start their plan sooner. Good for them, the shortening light time meant a longer dark time.

We can do it, thought Jack as he rested a bit on a high branch, safe from Fox if he happened to be around. Jack had been running through the woodland encouraging any animal not to flee, but to help. With another machine, more logs and rocks would need to be moved. He hadn't seen Fox, but the meat eater's scent was all through the woods making Jack cautious.

Sister came back well past the start of dark time, slinking in, but Jack heard her. She woke after he'd eaten, scattering his neat stack of nuts and mushrooms. She chose the most tender, then quickly rubbed her snout clean. She didn't even bother to groom herself. Jack, seeing her tail and fur in disarray, tittered disapprovingly.

"I'm going to visit Rabbit's family," she announced as she jumped down. A bush, heavy with berries, shook as she plucked the fattest one and stuffed them in her mouth. When Jack didn't think she could eat more, she leaned against a rock and closed her eyes. A stray bit of late berry dangled off a whisker. She licked it into her mouth.

Jack, his eyes narrowed, pointed to a seed stuck in between two teeth. Sister sucked it in.

"That will take you a very long time," he chittered. "Rabbit's family lives everywhere I've ever been."

She is away from our nest more and more. Sister will be looking to build her own nest and family, thought Jack sadly. *Soon she won't come back at all. I wish she wouldn't go with that meadow squirrel.* He snorted. He didn't want any of her young growing up to be stealers.

But she would be safer away from the wood.

"It won't be hot anymore, so it's perfect for running, climbing, and visiting," she said, standing up.

"Perfect for sneaking, you mean," said Jack faintly. She wouldn't look at him. Yep, she was going sneaking to the meadow.

"Don't be silly, little brother," she tittered nervously. She sniffed a few times, checking for danger, food, and visitors.

"It will be dark before you see all the rabbits."

She didn't answer.

"If I see the meadow squirrels stealing our nuts I'm going to bite a few tails," he warned. "Don't be late for Gathering! You have to be there!"

Did she hear him, or was she pretending she didn't hear him, as she scampered with light hops through leaf piles, long soars from branches, and smooth leaps over rocks.

The worst part was she was happy.

Jack nearly flew through the trees. He checked on the machines. They hadn't moved. He ran on. Next to Collin's den, the gaping hole now had tall wooden poles sticking up and across. The start of a human den.

He might as well visit Collin until Gathering time. He looked across the road back to his wood. Same machines, no more. Somehow the silence bothered Jack more. It was the silence of the birds, the stillness of animals gone. He missed the chirping of the crickets, but with the machines coming and the increasing coldness, they were long gone.

Down the road, Jack saw humans, smaller than Collin, getting into a long bright yellow machine with flashing red lights. Once the humans were inside, the lights turned off and the machine lurched noisily forward. Out of the corner of his eye, Jack spied a chipmunk. It darted across the road. In front of the machine.

"Go back!" he squeaked. But over the roar of the large machine, his warning was drowned. The machine rolled right over the chipmunk, leaving only a flat bit of fur and a red spot. The machine chugged down the road and disappeared. A nasty crow, spying from on top of a nearby stump, flew over to pick at the mess.

Disgusted and angry, Jack, after checking both ways carefully, skittered across the road. He didn't want to see any human, including Collin, just now. He turned back for home.

A soft breeze, warm but with an underlying chill, skipped through the trees, stirring the drying and dying leaves. It wasn't time yet for the little points of light that sparkled in the dark, looking like many little eyes, but Jack wouldn't feel like gazing at them anyway. Something was going to happen, the woods were choked with fear that animals could almost smell or taste.

As he zipped through the trees, eyes alert for danger, Jack wished there were birds or bees making their sweet soothing sounds, but most birds were gone to a warm place and the bees were long asleep waiting for the next warm time.

Without knowing why, he ran to the machines. When he arrived at the area, he was greeted by the towering, voiceless threat. Something was different. What had changed from when Jack had been there before? Standing tall on back legs, he sniffed. An assortment of odors, mostly human, filled his nostrils.

His eyes detected no humans, and his ears picked up only the moaning of the lazy breeze. *The trees.* They had papers stuck to them. Jack had seen these things before. Humans tacked the papers, with marks on it, to the poles he climbed and on trees at the edge of the wood. Jack often had to scoot around them when climbing down from the poles. It looked like a little human den was on the papers, along with other marks.

What do the papers mean? What are they telling the other humans?

Jack couldn't worry about the papers. More machines meant more wheels, and that meant more rocks and trees to move. He curled up on the rotted log until he had to leave for the Gathering. Some curious chipmunks, rabbits, and a family of raccoons walked over to him.

"Can we help now, while we wait for the others?" asked Raccoon. His kits, grown fat and big, were almost ready to leave on their own.

"Yes!" Jack swished his tail, excited. He tried patiently to show each animal what to do, but they were easily confused. Excited, unsure, and not listening to Jack's screeches, the animals barely moved a noticeable amount of rocks and only a few small branches. It was almost completely dark once they and Jack met up with the other animals at Speaking Rock. As soon as Jack stood atop the rock, the animals quieted. Jack didn't see all the animals. Some had not come. That saddened him.

We need them all.

Rat wouldn't come until the next dark because most of his large family preferred to live closer to big human dens with a lot of garbage. Rat called them cities.

The animals that did come would have to work harder. Jack was ready.

When the larger animals arrived, they began to push rocks and logs into piles around the machines. Smaller animals moved twigs and stones. They all worked and worked until they were exhausted. Some, like Rabbit, cowered every time a meat eater passed them, or one log crashed into another as Beaver built the dam. But not enough rocks or logs were in place when the light rose over the distant hills and broke the darkness under the trees.

They had failed. In the distance, they all heard the thrum of more machines moving closer.

"Hide! Hide!" Jack squeaked anxiously. In a panic, the animals still there scattered everywhere. Some, like Beaver, ran haplessly in circles they were so scared.

"Go to your dens, your nests!" Jack ordered. "Gather by Speaking Rock at dark time! I'll watch the humans. Hurry!" His urgings heeded, within moments, every animal was gone. Good for them humans were not clever at noticing signs of animal activity or trails in the wood. They would not see leaves ripped away, or grass trampled, or even the breaking of little branches down low as animals rushed to get away.

Horrendous roaring and grinding noises filled the air. Several more new machines appeared, stopping at the edge of the wood. Looking for a safe spot, Jack found a tree close by and scurried up into a cozy but abandoned hole. He watched the machines move in. For the entire light time, so many humans and still more machines crowded into the small open space before the trees thickened. Spitting out burning black smoke that dirtied the air, the humans, male and female, lined up the machines facing the wood. The rock and log dam would have to be built in the wood. It couldn't be helped.

Next to the machines, workers unloaded giant blue boxes that carried the stench of human droppings. Jack, hidden well in the black maple, wrinkled his nose in disgust. A long white box, like a smaller human den with glass holes to peek out of and wheels, was carried by a machine almost as tall as his tree. It was put down near the stink boxes. Humans carrying papers went in and out of the box den many times.

Jack nearly fell out of the tree when he saw a man put a chunk of wood in front and back of every wheel under the box den.

They know how to stop wheels from rolling too! He panted. *Were all humans so clever?* Jack couldn't help but admire them, even if he feared them.

Men dug many holes the size of Fox's den around the clearing next to the road. Others came along and poured the grayish muck that hardened like stone. A female stuck a long metal pole in the muck. Right before Jack could feel, rather than see, dark coming, men attached fencing to the poles, circling the big boxes.

There isn't a fence that can stop me, thought Jack proudly.

The humans started to leave. None of the animals went anywhere near the area while the humans worked. The humans hadn't seemed to notice their small piles, easily kicking or pushing them out of the way.

Again we'll have to work the entire darkness moving rocks and logs. We might not finish, thought, his tail drooping tiredly. So many wheels. A lone man stayed behind after everyone else left. They couldn't work on their machine dam until the man left.

Jack's nose whiffed the arrival of Beaver, the air carrying the scent of wet fur. Then he picked up the scent of garbage. *Rat.* Beaver plodded noisily through the woods, the tramping of a lot of rodent feet mixing in. Jack's fur ruffled in the air as Owl landed smoothly in the massive birch near his maple. On her, he smelled fresh blood. Since she had eaten, she would be there throughout the night. The man never noticed the animals quickly massing.

Word must have gotten around that few animals showed up the previous dark time. Now it looked like every animal was there, and even more when Rat brought all his family.

Either alone or in groups, the animals gathered noiselessly, without alerting the man. They waited without moving while the man rattled doors, kicked wheels, and walked around. Finishing his tasks in the dark with a small light stick he pulled from his clothing, Jack saw him chuck a paper coffee holder into the brush without a second glance. That irritated Jack. He heard a few annoyed growls behind him. Humans and garbage always went together.

At last, the man clicked off the light, jumped into a dirty green, dog-carrying machine, and rumbled away, leaving total darkness and a harsh trail of choking fumes.

The woods stilled.

As soon as the machine's lights turned out of sight, Jack sprang into action. Animals popped up from holes, from behind trees, and from under leaf piles.

"Come!" announced Jack. "This time we have to work harder and faster. We might not get another chance."

"The rats are ready!" called Rat, coming up to Jack. Behind him Jack saw a whole horde of his kin. He was relieved because even if the machine dams weren't finished, everything on the machines but the metal would be chewed.

Jack looked at Rat. "You know what to do, Rat. You and your family rip and tear apart everything you can. When you're finished, let me know. We might need your help."

"It won't take us long," grinned Rat, wickedly licking his mouth. He marched off, heading toward the machine closest to the road. The rustling of many feet followed him.

Jack turned around. "Beaver, show the deer where you and the other beavers chewed down logs so they can roll them in front of the machines." Beaver thwapped his tail in acknowledgement. "Don't forget to put some on the sides, too. Only leave room for the machines to back out."

"I think we should put logs and rocks in back too," mumbled Beaver. "If they can't move at all, we won't have to worry where they are. If we need more logs, I can pull some from my dam," he offered. He puffed up his chest and whacked his tail on the ground, nearly flattening Rabbit. She hopped back hastily out of range and glared at him.

"True," said Owl, "but we don't want these things *staying* in our woods. We want them to leave."

"I don't want you to take apart your dam, Beaver," said Jack. "There are plenty of fallen trees in the woods to use." Beaver lumbered off to supervise the placing of the logs. Friends, offspring, and even animals from up the river and down in the meadow, frightened by the arrival of the machines in this wood, offered to help. Jack hopped close behind Beaver to watch the building of the dam.

"Not there," grumbled Beaver to a possum, "here!" His nose pointed to a spot in the middle of the dam in front of the machine that bit huge holes into the ground. Jack thought that one was the most dangerous. Possum, with her keen night sight, pushed a rock into the small gap Beaver indicated.

"That's better. It fills a hole, rather than just lying there on the ground doing nothing." He guided the placement of every single stick, rock, and log, seeming to know immediately the best place for them.

"Great job, Beaver!" exclaimed Jack, running up and down the barrier. "It's so strong! You're really good at building."

Beaver looked at him in annoyance. "It's what I do," he said dryly. "Now get off the dam and let me finish."

Free to hunt for rocks, Jack scrambled back into the deeper woods. Sister, who barely managed to show up on time, helped. Using their sharp eyesight, when they found a suitable stick, rock, or log, they twittered, calling Hawk or another strong bird to either carry it or fetch a larger animal to move it.

"Here!" cried Sister. Hawk swooped down, grasped the rock in its talons, and although he struggled a bit with the weight, he soared up. Hawk dropped it precisely in front of Fox, who was trying to claw some rocks closer to the dam for the digging machine with his paws.

"Watch it!" he snarled, but Hawk, screaming playfully, was already halfway back to where Jack stood calling for him. Hawk dropped down out of the dark, grabbed the thick branch Jack found, and took off once more.

"The deer pushed enough logs and rocks to almost bury one machine," said Owl, circling overhead a little while later. "There are some nice rocks down by the river, Jack. Maybe Gopher can roll them. If he can't, the deer can do it."

Jack, tired from running about non-stop, paused to take several deep breaths. "If only we had a machine to help *us* carry all the rocks!" he tittered tiredly. His little paws, rough and sore from work, rubbed his burning eyes. He needed a soft, warm nest. He needed a long sleep. Not now. Later.

After the machines are gone, he promised.

Overhead, Owl glided lazily on currents stirring up with the approaching light rise. Boasting of having the keenest sight, and easily threatening any animal that disagreed with her, she flew around giving reports to Jack on how well others were doing, on where there were more rocks or logs, and generally encouraging everyone to work harder. She alone did not have to push, chew, carry, dig, roll, or drag. She was the old mother of the forest. She simply flew. And watched.

Jack dashed over to check on the deer. They were magnificent. Using their antlers and strong legs, they pushed the larger logs with a speed that stunned Jack. As darkness began to disappear, he ran back to the machines. The rock and log dams were quite impressive, almost completely burying the machines, standing so high that it was about impossible for a human to climb into them without a struggle. Not only did they rise in front of the machines, but all around, leaving only the barest opening to back out.

This might work! thought Jack. His excitement revitalized his draining energy. Then, from a short distance, he heard Rat. He was singing.

RAT WAS SINGING.

"It must be good news, if Rat is singing," trilled Jack to a yawning Owl balanced on the sturdy arm of a creaky red cedar. Jack inhaled the sharp fresh scent. It gave him another little bit of happiness. They were going to save this tree and all the others, he hoped.

"No doubt," she said, yawning yet again. She had flown everywhere, never slowing or resting. "He never smiles, let alone sings. He's grouchier than a wet cat. I must stay awake long enough to hear what made him so happy."

Into the clearing stumped Rat, jauntily swinging his tail back and forth, followed by his troop.

"We're so great, Jack," he boasted, puffing his

chest out. "All the wires, tubes, seats, ANYTHING we could chew, we did. And," he paused, fixing his beady eyes on Jack, "for your information, even though the machines were quiet and there was no humming in the wires, they can still burn."

It was then that Jack noticed Rat's burnt whiskers.

"What happened?!" cried Jack.

"When I crawled up into the machine, I learned you cannot stand on metal while chewing on certain wires connected to a black box in the machine. It burns your whiskers and slams you about." Rat delicately smoothed the crispy stumps that were once his prized long whiskers. They crumbled some more.

"I'm sorry, Rat," said Jack sorrowfully, "I didn't know!"

"I know. I'm fine now. Forget it. But you owe me a favor," said Rat, "which you will have to pay someday, and it won't be a stinking nut. And, after I tell you what else we did, you'll owe me two favors."

Jack was thrilled. He couldn't sit still. With all the excitement, and even though he was very tired, he had to run a few circles and swish his tail several times before he could settle down. Rat was really getting into the mood of the fight. He might end up being well liked after it was all done.

"Tell me, Rat, what did you do?" he asked anxiously.

Rat stood up, smoothed down his grimy fur and pricked up his ears, trying to look sleek and impressive. It didn't work. He was still a dirty rat who now had crumbling, crispy whiskers.

"Oh, get on with it already," grumped Owl. "Don't make me cranky enough to eat you before I hear the story."

Rat sniffed. "Like I've said, humans don't give up that easily."

Owl sighed. "We know, we heard, spit it out." She twisted her head to stare right at Rat. She clicked her beak in a chomping motion.

Rat hastened his explanation. "Not only will they have to fix wires, tubes and seats, but also their wheels. We chewed off little tubes on every wheel and they went sssshhhhhh! Not round anymore." He grinned with pride. A whisker fell off.

"Rat, you're the best!" squeaked Jack.

"Thank you very much." His mouth stretched into a grin. It was a little scary with his long, curved yellow teeth.

"Ah, excuse me," interrupted Sister, "it's nice to praise each other, but it's time to leave. Humans are coming." All scattered as silently and swiftly as they could into the depths of the lightening wood.

Except Jack. He ran back up into the thinning maple. He was going to watch the storm erupt when the humans saw their machines. And what the animals had done to them.

Chapter 11

It's In the News

The wood echoed with many angry shouts.

"Who did this?!" demanded a man dressed in dark blue with a hard bright yellow hat on his head.

Peeking out from the maple branches, Jack observed the commotion and listened. The man's voice told Jack he was very mad.

He's wondering who did the damage.

"Don't touch anything and call the police," the man ordered. "Maybe we'll get some fingerprints. It's probably one of those nature-loving, tree-hugging groups, trying to stop the development." He stalked off, got into his dog-carrying machine and sped away, sending dirt and gravel shooting in all directions. The other men, shaking their heads, left soon after.

Jack tittered. From the anger in the man's voice, and understanding the words tree and stop, he knew his plan was a success. So far. If the humans fixed the machines, the animals would need to do something else to stop them.

Would there be enough time before the men fixed the machines? And how will I know what I need to learn? He sat in the tree, puzzled and worried.

A strong gust of chill air whipped the tall grasses and rattled the baring branches. The light was hidden behind thick grayness. Soon there would be rolling blackness and crackling booms. Jack sniffed the air, guessing that he didn't have long before the water fell very hard. He wanted to visit Collin, but stayed here. Someone had to keep eyes on the humans. Studying the machines, there was so much to learn, Jack realized. He would learn as much as he could—if he wasn't sleeping out in the cold because his tree was gone. Or worse, sleeping in the meadow, sharing a nest with Sister and *him.*

Few leaves were left on the maple to hide him. When he remained perfectly still, the humans never saw or heard him. Jack climbed over and perched in the cedar to be safe. He watched male and female humans come and go, carrying things and peeking into the machines. He chittered softly, watching them try to heave logs and push away rocks as they struggled to take apart the dams. There was no better builder than Beaver because the humans couldn't.

At one point, Jack had to grip especially tight with his claws and wrap his tail around the branch because he almost lost his balance twittering in glee at the men shouting below, anger and disgust in their voices and on their faces. They pointed to the animal droppings they stepped in constantly. And then there was the skunk stink—everywhere! It was especially heavy on the machines. Jack tittered again when the humans tied coverings over their faces to keep out Skunk's odor.

That won't help. Nothing can stop skunk stink.

Suddenly a number of road machines, white with flashing red and blue lights, and many humans in dark clothes and hats filled the area. Soon, lots of humans were standing in the road, leaning against the fence. Staring at the machines. Their eyes were big. They reminded Jack of animals who stopped to look at road machine lights.

The humans inside the fence stamped about, talking, pointing, and scribbling on paper. Jack watched them keenly. Then the water fell from above. Humans rushed into the smaller machines and zoomed away, or they ran down the street out of his sight.

One man remained behind. In the long human box, he peered out from the glass holes into the deep darkness as light streaked through the dark and rumbles cracked loud enough to shake the ground after each crack. Water slapped everything like Beaver's tail on the pond.

Smaller trees bent, then snapped off. Leaves and branches, ripped off by the strong gusts, littered the area. Jack clung to the cedar until he was so wet and cold. He returned to the maple and snuggled in an abandoned bird roost that smelled suspiciously like Owl and bones, but he was safe from the water and soon he'd be dry. The flashing light and booming, he knew from sight and sound, were moving swiftly toward them. From his hole he had a clear view of the man. If he only had some mushrooms, he'd have been quite comfy. Owl stink and all. Wrapped tightly in his tail, he slept.

Light rise brought a brisk coolness, which Jack liked. His fur grew better the colder it got. He stretched, dug up some nuts at the base of the tree he sniffed out that another squirrel had buried but abandoned, and tried to fluff the owl odor from his fur.

Done with his grooming, he watched humans arrive, then scurry around the machines through mud that sucked their feet and legs in, and trample through dripping wet woods while still more humans lined up at the fence, a good distance away from the machines.

Only some humans went near the machines, while the others stayed back. Were some humans afraid of the machines too? Jack wondered.

The humans brought things like new wires and seats for the machines. They changed flat wheels for round ones.

"Keep a safe distance," Jack warned some nosy young rabbits and chipmunks that appeared at the destruction site, "and try to act unstrange."

"What's 'unstrange'?" asked Rabbit.

"Well, it's, it's…" Jack stammered for the right words.

"If all the animals sit here and stare at the

humans, watching every little thing they do, like Jack here," said Sister suddenly appearing and nodding her head at her brother, "and they don't run away, that will look strange. The humans will get curious and try to find out why the animals are so brave. They might even," she chittered softly, "try to *catch* us."

Small gasps of fear burst from several of the younger ones.

"If a cute a little bunny or a *flat-tailed squirrel*," and Jack glared at Sister when he said that, "runs by, everything looks like it's supposed to. That's not strange. And how'd you sneak up on me?" he demanded.

"You mean how'd I sneak up on you *again*?" she replied sweetly, flicking her tail in his face.

Tail drooping, Jack sighed and shook his head. What kind of a squirrel was he? He'd better be more careful; if his not-too-quiet sister could sneak up on him, so could other animals. Fox came to mind.

"Okay. So what do I do to look unstrange?" asked Rabbit.

"Hop around a bit, make sure they see you. Stop and chew on some clover. The moment one of them moves toward you, or makes a sudden sound, run," advised Sister.

Rabbit grinned. "Oh, I understand now. Act like we always do around humans. Scared furless." Jack and Sister nodded.

The humans didn't seem to notice any strangeness in the animals' behavior, which surprised Jack, because too many animals constantly tramped through this part of the woods checking on them.

The humans don't see that trails are stomped all over the place, both meat eater and leaf eater, together. They can't smell our many scents. He sat thoughtfully, scratching his belly where a lone tick meandered across his fur, tickling him. Jack ate it without thinking, waiting only for the humans to leave.

Darkness fell and all but one man left. He sat in a smaller white machine with bright red and blue lights, looking at a big paper and drinking coffee. Sitting up, Jack inhaled deeply. He enjoyed the appealing scent of coffee drifting over to him. He knew what coffee was; once a human had left a paper holder with some coffee in it on the ground. Sniffing the delicious scent, Jack tipped the container over and lapped some up. It made his nose wrinkle. It was cold and bitterer than an unripe nut. He ran all the way to the river to scrub the taste off his tongue.

Because it seemed nothing exciting was going to happen, Jack ran back to his tree for a good long sleep. Maybe it would be quiet till light rise. He crawled tiredly into his nest, snuggled with his tail tightly wrapped around his body, and went to sleep.

Jack woke to a weak light rise. He ate, licked some dew that had hardened with the cold off a curled leaf, and then stretched. He hopped out of the tree as fast as his tail would let him see what the humans were doing. Mud crusted everything. Humans stood there, talking, shaking their heads, pointing to the hardened red mud, glistening with a coating of cold stiff water turned white, then left. It was full light. The humans threw aside more paper holders and finally left. There would be no machines working this light rise.

Freed from having to watch the humans and machines, Jack wondered about going to Collin's den. It was brisk; it would not get much warmer. Maybe it was too cold for a boy to sit outside in his wheelchair. He'd run over and see if Collin came out. He slowed as he got to the new den. Now it had a top, sides, and holes for glass. Humans, like bugs, climbed all over it, carrying small sticks that they would bang against the wood, shouting loudly to each other, and walking in and out, carrying big flat pieces of wood, freshly cut because Jack could smell the sap. He watched from under a thick bush. They were too busy to notice him. He scampered across the cold road. Perching bravely on top of the fence, he followed their movements.

One human, rounder than Gracie the bird-feeder squirrel-chaser, sipped coffee and ate something that smelled suspiciously, deliciously, like honey. She spotted Jack.

"Here little squirrel!" she called, and held out a chunk of the enticing treat. Honey was better than mushrooms, and Jack rarely got any. It wasn't worth the bee stings on his nose and paws.

When Jack didn't move, the human threw a piece to him. When he still didn't move, the female slowly moved closer.

"Ta-cherr! Ta-cherr! Ta-cherr!" Jack screeched angrily. *Go away, human.* The woman stopped. Laughing, she threw the rest of the treat toward Jack and turned back to the den. Jack ignored the treat and disappeared over the fence onto Collin's grass.

I don't want treats with human mouth water. Whuck!

Collin sat at the table, tightly wrapped in lots of soft things; around his legs, around his body, and even on his head.

If they had tails and fur, they wouldn't need all that, Jack mused.

Something metal was opened on the table in front of Collin. Jack knew what Collin was doing; Collin was learning things from the squiggly marks on it, just like the marks on the papers stuck to trees. All animals left some signal to mark territory or let a relative or friend know they passed. When the meadow squirrels came to steal nuts, they left footprints in the dirt. The marks told Jack they had been there. Jack was smarter; he always walked on leaves or logs to hide his footprints.

Meadow squirrels are not only lazy, they are dumb, too. He shook his head in disgust.

Some left a mark simply annoy the owner. Like Rat. He loved to chew Jack's tree for no good reason. Time after time, Jack, curled snug in his tail and nest, heard scritch, scritch, crunch, as Rat crouched below in the dark, nibbling on the tree. At least he didn't leave his water waste, like many animals did. Jack didn't do that because it smelled horrendous when the light warmed it. And it always seemed like he was downwind. Either way, Rat was pretty brave to be out in the dark when Owl, Coyote, or Fox were looking for a warm meal. Rat took a risk simply for the opportunity to pester Jack.

And it worked. Jack seethed whenever he scooted out of his nest to find another chunk of bark ripped off, the life sap running down into the dirt. One day Rat would kill Jack's tree. Or, maybe Owl would eat him. That possibility really amused Jack.

Walking silently down the long wooden table, Jack sat next to Collin's arm and peered over at the machine. There were many marks on the little metal window.

"Hey, Jack! Good to see you!" said Collin. He had on his happy face.

Jack hunkered down.

"Too bad you can't see what's in the news. Somebody tore up those construction machines big time. Even though they shouldn't have done it, maybe the builders won't put up new homes in your woods. At least, not for a little while. I worry about you, little guy."

Collin smoothed the fur along Jack's back with one slim finger.

Enjoying the rubbing, Jack saw a picture of the machines, covered by the rocks and wood the animals rolled around them.

"Where are you going, Jack?" chuckled Collin softly. He tried to slide the paper slowly out from under the squirrel. Jack put a little paw on the picture and tapped the page.

"Whuck! Whuck, whuck!"

Collin raised an eye fur.

We did that, thought Jack proudly. He wanted Collin to know. Jack watched while Collin's eyes moved quickly over the paper. He read aloud: "Police are baffled by the damage to the site and the equipment. No note was found from, or claim made, by a responsible group. Logs and stones were wedged tightly under all the wheels, and piled against the machines, almost completely covering them. Wires, cables, hoses, and seats were torn. Tires were punctured. Also confusing investigators, said Captain Joseph Greenly, was that the damage was so extensive, it would require a large group, yet neighbors neither saw nor heard any disturbance. And, there were a large variety of animal teeth and claw marks on both the logs and the equipment. Large amounts of animal droppings littered the site. Apparently, chuckled the Captain, some skunks seemed to be upset with the machines, leaving their signature spray all over them."

Collin looked at Jack, then back to the picture. He pointed to the picture. He stamped his paws.

"Whuck whuck!" Seeing Collin look at the picture

of the machines, Jack was sure the boy was reading about their attack. He patted the picture again, but the boy simply sat there, glancing back and forth between Jack and the picture.

Can he understand? wondered Jack. The way he sat there without saying anything, Jack figured he was going to have to show Collin.

As Collin watched him, Jack climbed down off the table and rustled in the flower garden until he found a small round rock. He rolled, and then wedged it under Collin's chair wheel. He ran back to the garden and under a bush, he chomped on a stick with his sharp teeth. That, too, he pushed under the wheel, lodging it snugly. Jack then climbed back onto the table, and waited.

Collin gasped. Then held his breath.

Now he believes, thought Jack proudly. He twittered and chattered, and clapped his paws together.

"I can't believe it. If you're that smart... No one would believe me..." The screen door slammed and Jack stiffened in surprise.

"Collin! Be careful! That squirrel could have diseases! He might have rabies!" Jack froze at the sound of the female's shrill voice. It reminded him of the sound his nails made when he slid down smooth glass. Jack knew what glass was because he'd slammed into it when bird feeders were stuck to them. He hadn't realized the glass was there since it was clear like water in the creek. The glass did not have ripples so Jack didn't see it until Thunk! Sliding and screeching, his claws couldn't grasp the smooth hard surface. Jack fell from that high glass onto the sticker bush below. Last time he made THAT mistake. He shuddered again over the female's grating sound.

"Oh, Mom," said Collin, stroking Jack's back, "he's okay. He's been coming here for weeks." Collin fished in his pocket, pulling out a round thing. It smelled sickly sweet to Jack. "Watch this! Here you go, Jack, show her!"

Should I roll for the female to see? Jack looked over at the birdfeeder. *She likes the birds. She might be a squirrel chaser, like Gracie. I don't trust humans with birdfeeders.* Jack inspected her closely. She was the same dark brown of wet wood that Collin was. She carried no sticks, she was standing still, and she stopped screeching. He decided to show her. Taking the round thing from Collin, he rolled it across the table.

"Oh, you've trained him! Amazing! He must be a smart little fellow." She fondly brushed Collin's head.

"Mom, you won't believe the things he can do. I think the animals ruined those machines at the construction site in the woods. It said in the paper that there were chew marks on the wires and stuff. Look at the picture!"

She laughed. "Collin! Squirrels chewing up bulldozers?" She laughed some more. "I see that he's very bright, but figuring out how to destroy big equipment like that?" She chuckled. "It makes a great story. Maybe you should write it down for your tutor. He'd enjoy it."

Jack watched her nuzzle the top of Collin's head before she walked back inside the den. She had to be

Collin's mother. Was she looking for ticks like his mother used to?

Collin sat quietly while Jack searched his belly for any nesting fleas. He hadn't gotten his snack from Collin and he was hungry. He was not going to eat the honey treat thrown by the machine human. He didn't need food *that* bad. Let another squirrel snatch it. On his tail, Jack found two sluggish fleas. The cold would kill them, but he decided he wouldn't wait. He didn't want any offspring showing up in his nest. They snapped between his teeth.

Collin looked at Jack, who stared back.

"I didn't really think she'd believe me," he said softly to Jack. "It's hard enough for me to believe. The development would destroy your homes, so you all worked together. Incredible. I still can't believe it, but somehow I know it's true."

Jack walked over and laid his tiny paw on Collin's large one. Collin slowly turned it over, palm up. Jack stroked Collin's palm.

Collin grinned. "A handshake? Dude, I'm going to have to show you how to do a high five, buddy."

Chapter 12

The Plan, Part Two

By the time Jack left for his cozy nest, the light was almost gone. He'd stayed as long as Collin remained outside. Once a bone biting cold set in, Collin shivered. His mother came out and pushed him into the den. She hadn't said anything to Jack.

"Go home, Jack. See you tomorrow." Collin waved and disappeared into the den.

As he flipped through a group of birches, a roar suddenly ripped through the woods. Startled, Jack missed a branch and had to check his fall by catching the next branch down. Luckily there was another one, and not empty space straight down to the ground. A fall from that high would hurt. Really hurt.

Jack knew that sound. It was the machines. They were fixed and ready to destroy again. His heart pounded. Time for another Gathering.

Jack ran to Owl's. He chattered loudly until the sleepy bird popped open one annoyed eye to gaze sharply at him.

"What is it now, Jack?" she asked. "This must be really, really important to wake up a tired, grouchy owl. I don't even care if you taste good anymore. I'll eat you just so I can sleep in peace."

Unafraid, Jack chittered, "The machines are fixed and roaring! We need to have another Gathering. Everyone needs to be there to make another plan." He was out of breath from running, leaping, and chittering.

"Your plan last time worked, Jack. Why not do the same thing?" Slowly her lids closed again. Owl spent more and more time sleeping in her hole.

Jack circled around several times, agitated. He wrung his paws together over and over before finally sitting down.

"But if they keep fixing the machines, we'll never get them out of the woods!"

Owl blinked once, twice. "You know human things, Jack. You know wheels and how to stop them. You will learn what to do." She hopped out of her tree hole, and spreading her wings, dove into the air. "I will call the others. Think, Jack." And then she was gone in the dimming light.

The animals gathered once more. This time, they looked to Jack without arguing about leaving.

"What are we going to do?" asked Rat, clearly ready for another fight. He was even grinning. "They've finished fixing the machines. We heard them roar, but they didn't move. What's the plan, Jack?" All eyes turned to Jack, sitting silently on Speaking Rock.

When Jack hesitated, Red spoke up. "Must do something! Cut trees at light rise! Danger!"

Again Jack hesitated and Fox shoved forward. "What's next?" he demanded. Clearly worried, he panted as he paced in circles around the clearing with his tongue lolling out the side of his jaw. His nervousness made the rest of the animals jittery, especially the smaller, easier to eat ones around whom he circled a little too closely.

Fox should be worried; he's still the first one in the way of the machines. At least now I don't have to be afraid that he'll eat me, Jack thought with some satisfaction, *he's too scared what will happen if I don't save his scrawny, stinky hide.*

Looking at all the hopeful eyes and smelling their fear, Jack stood tall and twittered for their attention. "The machines are fixed. More humans guard the machines now. We need something new."

"I'm ready. What do we do?" Fox repeated, inching closer. His hot, rotten smelling breath forced Jack back ever so slightly. He didn't want to think what Fox had eaten to make his breath smell that bad. It smelled *meaty and furry.* Jack shuddered. He turned in a circle or two, retreating to get fresh air. Jack brought his mind back to the problem and sighed softly.

Suddenly, he stopped short. *Fox moved forward, I*

backed away. His mind raced.

"You're not going to like it," Jack warned. The animals looked at each other, then back to Jack.

"We didn't like the rolling thing, but we did it and it worked," said Possum. "Share."

Still Jack paused.

This is dangerous. Jack didn't know a lot about humans even though he was friends with Collin, but he did know that humans liked to win. Always. That whole thing with the birdfeeder. No matter how many times Jack proved he could outwit any traps or obstacles Gracie built, she kept putting up new ones. She had to prove she was smarter than Jack. An enemy that never stopped was very dangerous.

He coughed up a piece of the last flea he'd eaten. His throat felt dry.

"We have to attack. When the humans are there. In the light."

A chorus of protests and yelps and refusals shredded the peaceful air of the hollow. Jack sat on his haunches and shrugged at the outbursts. He waited.

"Sometimes an animal needs to have his say before you can get them to listen," said Owl from over his shoulder up in the cedar tree.

"Whuck!" he agreed, watching her fly down from her branch to perch next to him on the rock. He wasn't afraid anymore. Not much. He guessed she never really developed a taste for squirrel. She only liked to scare him and the other animals. It was easy because she could snatch most of them up and eat them before they knew what was happening.

Waiting for quiet, Jack busied himself by grooming his fur and smoothing his whiskers. When the animals settled down, Owl spoke.

"Explain why we have to attack, Jack."

He sat up once more. "When Fox moved too close, I backed up. Fox can eat me, so I am afraid and move back to be safe. If we scare the humans, they will back up to be safe."

"Are we going to eat the humans?" asked Owl.

"Ughh!" choked Rabbit. "Not me!"

"No eating humans," said Jack. "Scare them. Attack, they back up."

"Why should the humans be afraid of us?" asked Fox. "They're bigger. They have machines."

"Animals stay in their territories. Rabbits with rabbits, beavers with beavers, and rats with rats. Humans know it's always been our way to be separate." Jack paused, twitching his head around to look at each animal.

"There are many types of humans. Light. Dark. Some with fur on head, some without. Many sizes. *They* work together. Round man carries papers. Tall female makes machine rip out trees. Man with face fur kicks tires and drinks coffee. Short female makes machine pour gray stuff that becomes hard like rock. They work together."

"We worked together!" blurted Fox.

Jack bobbed his head, saying, "Yes. For this. Humans have never seen animals do this. If we attack together in the light, they see us as one herd. They need to see us do the damage."

It was quiet while the group thought this over.

"Humans think animals are afraid and dumb."

"*They* think *we're dumb*?" snorted Buck. "Yeah, like those orange hunter hats. I can see them coming from a woodland away," he snorted again. Several other deer snickered.

"Humans made machines," said Owl quietly. "Thinking they are dumb will lead you into a trap."

"Or dragged away with your insides scooped out," said Fox. "I've seen it happen to deer and bear. And rabbits, turkeys and sometimes squirrels," he added, looking around.

"But not foxes," grumbled Rat.

"We have to stop the machines," said Jack. "We must attack humans every time they put machines in our wood. They will be scared."

"How? When?!" chirped Red, plainly frightened. She dove and circled in the air above their heads. A feather, loosened by her flying tizzy, wafted slowly down. Rat slyly snatched it, stuffing it under his body. Jack turned away when Rat snuck a glance at him. Rat collected feathers, bones, and other strange things.

"Nest! Chicks and eggs! Save tree!"

"I don't know what else to do," said Jack, his tail drooping. He thought and thought and thought about the problem. Attacking was the only thing he could think of.

"Can your human teach you something else?" Buck pushed to the front of the group, his large body blocking Jack's sight of everything but him.

Jack's tail and ears flicked in frustration.

"The machines are fixed and when dark fell, Collin went into his nest. He is a light animal." Jack looked up at Buck. "I don't know what I need to learn. I can't *talk* to him and ask," he replied shortly. He took a long breath. "The machines will start cutting and digging again at light rise." A stillness descended on the animals as they waited for Jack to solve the problem.

"Let's do it," volunteered Fox.

"Oh, look who's first to help now," said Rabbit dryly. "Fox. The why-should-I- learn-anything-human animal." She cocked an ear and looked at Fox with her large brown eyes, usually so gentle, now hard and cold.

"I wasn't the *only* one who didn't want to help. In the beginning." His eyes narrowed at Rat.

Unruffled, Rat answered, "Since *my* part of Jack's plan was so successful, my family have named me *King* Rat. *They* were *most* impressed with my leadership and my wounded whiskers. All the animals should call me King Rat, if you don't mind." He lifted his nose in the air, but it didn't appear to Jack that Rat impressed any of the others. Rat now had a new attitude—gone was the nasty part. Now he acted like his droppings didn't stink like everyone else's. Jack snorted softly.

"Uh huh," said Rabbit. She didn't look kindly at either of them. "This has to be agreed upon by all. Some of us may not want to attack the humans. As the mother of a large number of kits, I must think about this. I can't slink away to the city sewers to hide or swiftly run to the meadow with all my offspring if this doesn't work, like you two can."

By the way Rat's whisker stumps twitched, and

Fox's mouth started to snarl, it was time for Jack to interrupt.

"All of us don't have to attack the humans. Some can ruin the machines again, right Rat? Others, like Rabbit, can do something else, like spread the call again. The more animals that come, the better. A large crowd of different animals will convince the humans we are working together to stop the machines from destroying our wood. If Fox works next to Rabbit," and he saw her shudder at *that* thought although Fox grinned happily, "it proves to the humans we are one herd."

"That would scare me!" joked Beaver. Nervous titters broke out.

There were low discussions among the different animals. Jack heard the birds chirping their fright. They wanted to fly away from trouble. All their chicks had flown from the nests by now, and it was easier to simply build another nest elsewhere. So, the fickle creatures really didn't want to get involved. Except Red.

"Nest here. Not build another in strange wood. Cold coming. Show Red how to fight."

"We'll spread the word to other animals far down the river and across the meadow, down to the cornfields. They might come help," offered Crow.

"I can talk to the bats," said Rat.

"Don't bother," said Owl. "They won't come out of their cave before dark fall for anything. It's too painful for their eyes."

"If we have most of the light and some of the dark animals, we should have enough to frighten the humans," added Jack.

"We'll help," boomed the biggest buck whose antlers boasted eight prongs. "We need space, and with all these human dens and roads, there is no room or food for deer."

One by one, the animals either joined or left. In the end, only some birds and the rabbits refused to do anything that made them get close to the humans. Jack realized Rabbit was afraid for her offspring, and really, the attack would not be a success just because a bunny stood up on its hind legs and bared its big teeth. Rabbits just weren't scary enough. They were too cute to the humans.

"I'll make sure all the animals in dens and hutches, where birds can't go, know about the plan," she offered. Jack tittered, thanking her.

The animals were tense, yet excited.

"This is another first," joked Gopher. "Meat and leaf eaters united. What will we think of next?" Nervous snorts and yips rippled through the group.

Jack, bitten by another pesky flea, promptly picked it off and popped it into his mouth. Where were they all coming from? That meadow squirrel could have brought them to the nest. He shook hard, hoping they were all thrown off, then looked at the animals.

"The plan is simple. We all go to the edge of the wood. Rat, you—"

"Ah, it's *King* Rat, if you please." Rat pretended to stroke whiskers that weren't there.

"Sorry," said Jack, "*King* Rat and his group will chew and tear again. If the humans try to stop them, deer will push them back, and the rest of us will screech, jump on their heads, anything we can think of to scare them away. Leave piles of droppings on their feet, spray them, I don't care, but *No Blood*!" he insisted. "Just scare them! No biting, scratching, or making them bleed. Act like Raccoon's sister did when she got sick, dripping lots of white gooey stuff from her mouth before she died. Make noise and scare them back."

"If it gets nasty, they will come back angrier the next time, with more men and cages. I've seen it," said Rabbit quietly.

"Cages are nothing," added Buck. "They will be back with guns."

Chapter 13

The War Goes On

With stealth, the animals headed toward the road where the machines stood. The smaller ones with flashing lights and humans in blue were gone. In their place were more dog-carrying machines. Men moved about sluggishly, drinking their bitter coffee with steam curling up into the brisk air of early light rise. Jack's nostrils flared. The cool time will be short. Flowers that adored light and warmth were long gone. Leaves were almost finished changing from bright yellows and oranges. Most were already dead brown, falling swiftly. Before long it would be branch-snapping cold with piercing winds.

Peeking out from under a bush, Jack watched the animals creep forward. The deer, so large and obvious, hung back a distance, blending into the brown of trees, thickets, and fallen leaves, so the surprise of the attack wouldn't be ruined. Red flew around. She would chirp the order to attack to those animals too far away to hear Jack.

Behind logs, under bushes, and in holes, hid rats, foxes, gophers, raccoons, possums, and other land animals. Owl, Red, and a few crows perched in the trees. They would have frightened Jack any other time. A gathering of birds was not good. The crows were there to help with the attack, but Jack knew that they would get distracted if they saw anything shiny that caught their quick eyes. They just couldn't stop themselves.

While Jack did a silent search of the woods, Sister popped up next to him.

"Did I scare you?" she asked, cheerfully trying not to sound smug.

"Like you could."

"I've snuck up on you a lot lately, Jack. You're just saying that. I think I saw you twitch." She flicked her tail in his face.

Jack made a motion to grab it, but Sister was faster. This time.

"When you travel with meadow squirrels, you might as well travel with a herd of beavers. They both make a lot of noise. You came from the river. The bunch of you."

That wiped the arrogant look out of her beady eyes, thought Jack with satisfaction.

"They are kind of noisy," she admitted.

"Beavers or meadow squirrels?"

"Both," she chittered sheepishly. She took a couple of quick breaths. "After the attack, I'm leaving Jack."

Jack stared at her. "Did you build a nest with that scruffy-tailed meadow squirrel?"

"His tail is not scruffy and his name is Jerk!" she replied angrily.

"Is too." Jack turned away, and Sister scaled down the tree to hide with their cousins the chipmunks, who were there only to see the fight. They'd get stepped on in all the confusion. They decided they'd stay out of the way.

Now she can drive that meadow squirrel crazy, eat the best of his stored nuts, if he collected any, thought Jack irritably. *And the name that squirrel chose-Jerk. What kind of a name is that?* Sister said he'd overhead the name when he was spying on the humans and chose it. *Probably stealing, not spying. Leave it to a meadow squirrel to choose an enemy name. Well, she'll be taking her mess to Jerk's nest. Along with half the nuts that I worked so hard to find, roll, and bury.*

"Probably took the best ones already," he mumbled to himself.

The animals crouched, perched, and squatted, waiting for Jack to give the call. He smelled the scent from each of them while they forced wing, tail, and paw to remain still. He heard them breathe- some rapidly with fear like the beavers, or slowly with patience like the deer. And he felt the nervousness in the air. It was all around him.

"What are you waiting for, Jack, the river to dry up?" chittered Sister from below.

"I'm waiting for just the right moment," he whucked fiercely. His tail and fur badly needed grooming; they were flat and filled with bits of leaves and dirt. He put off grooming to be ready right at light rise. Although he was simply sitting and waiting, he didn't have time or desire now for a proper grooming. Jack kept eyes, ears, and nose tuned for the humans' arrival. He would do a victory groom when this was all over. If he survived.

Movement caught Jack's quick eye. Humans were trudging and gathering along the fence. Some came after the first attack; this time there was a woodland full.

"Why are all those humans here?" asked Jerk, climbing up to Jack's lookout.

Oh nuts. Him. Jack didn't bother to look at Jerk. He didn't want to talk to him either, but Sister was nearby. Probably listening and ready to stick her black nose into everything.

"Because humans always like to look," Jack explained. "Ever see a machine smashed against a tree? Humans stop to look at the dead and dying. Go back and get ready, Jerk," he ordered. It took Jerk, a slow mover for a squirrel, a while to get into place. Jack sighed. *It takes him too long to scurry. He's going to get caught by a meat eater.*

Jack stiffened.

Is that Collin and the mother with the other humans? It is.

Jack had no time for a friendly whuck to Collin. Once Jerk was ready, Jack screeched the order.

"Attack! Attack now! No blood!"

Red echoed the order and like one large herd, the animals moved forward, rolling like a wave of wind over meadow grasses.

At first the humans didn't notice. They drank, laughed, checked machines, and read large papers. One man, his back to the largest machine and his front facing the woods, squinted. He took a step closer toward the advancing animals, squinted again, holding his paw over his eyes to shield them from the brightening light. Then he backed up slowly, tapped another man on the shoulder, who then turned. Mouths open and eye furs lifted in surprise, they continued to back up together until a machine blocked their retreat. Just like Jack did when Fox moved forward with meaty breath and Jack backed up. Like Jack hoped the humans would.

Take your machines with you, he thought with a satisfied tail flick.

Jack leapt from his spot in the tree, scrabbled through hard dirt, clumps of mud and grass, and climbed up the greasy yellow machine in the center of the clearing.

"Attack! Attack! Save your dens!" screeched Jack. "Save our wood! No blood!" Only once did he spare a glance toward the humans. There was Collin. The boy was leaning forward in his chair, hands gripping the metal fence, eyes big. The mother stood behind him, her face showing a look of surprise and fear.

Jack had work to do, a wood to save. He turned

away.

"Rats, come out! Deer, push forward! Birds, drop your loads!" he shrieked.

Humans scrambled to get away from the oncoming attack. Shocked and panicked, they tripped over logs and each other, and then slipped in the mud trying to run. When they reached the road, they dashed. Most stopped after running past several human dens, but some kept going.

Seeing the humans flee in fear, the crowd at the fence screamed and ran in panic too. Jack's eyes darted about for Collin, but returned to check the movement of

the animals. Deer, after chasing away the last humans who were standing and watching, meandered gracefully back.

"Rest!" ordered Jack. Rats, raccoons, meadow squirrels, gophers, and possums popped out of nooks and crannies in the machines. One or two brave chipmunks, too. Rat still had a wire in his mouth and Raccoon had some white fluffy stuff ripped from a seat stuck to her whiskers and a bunch clutched in one paw.

Jerk and Sister rested under a dog machine. By their side lay a pile of everything they chewed, ripped, or broke off.

"Good work, Sister!"

She glared at him.

"And you too, Jerk," he added grudgingly. He still didn't like that squirrel. Much. Jack scampered through the mass of panting, sweating, and tired animals.

"Great work! We did it! We saved our woods!" He flicked his tail rapidly in excitement and twitched his ears.

The beavers banged their tails, adding to the din. Joining in, crows squawked, deer bellowed, and Fox howled. In the middle of the celebration, Jack looked across the fence for Collin. Like the other humans, he and the mother fled.

"What do you think the humans are doing now?" asked Rat, siding up to Jack.

"Still running," he replied.

"Ha! Good one, Jack. But really, what do you think they're doing?"

Jack looked tiredly at Rat who was so bouncy

with glee it irritated him. "Aren't you afraid the humans will come back with the next light rise? If Buck is right, they may return with guns."

Rat rubbed his snout, now sprouting baby whisker stumps, thoughtfully. "Yes, they will come back. But it's really hard to shoot a rat. Many have tried, few have succeeded." He grinned.

Jack shook his head sadly. "Squirrels aren't so lucky. Some humans like to kill for no reason. At least Fox kills to eat."

"Hope that he never gets hungry suddenly when you're around," whispered Rat softly. He snapped his tail smartly back and forth. "When do you think the humans will come back?

"I don't know, Rat. We'll have to wait."

The two sat, watching the celebration of victory in many dark eyes. It could be a very short celebration. And the last one.

"There is one thing I know," said Jack breaking the silence between them. "The humans will think we're as crazy as sick raccoons. No human or machine is going to take this wood, with our nests and families, away from us. If they come back, we will go crazy. No matter *what* we have to do."

Rat nodded silently. As dark descended, each headed off to a place nearby to rest. It wasn't over yet.

Chapter 14

<u>Stare Down</u>

With light rise, the animals gathered once more at the site to chew, rip, or shred anything they missed. Humans were nowhere to be seen, heard, or sniffed either in the wood or nearby. Farther down the road, humans moved about, but stayed well away and did not linger.

"This should slow them down even longer," encouraged Jack, checking out the damage to the machines. Wires, bits of plastic, chunks of wheels, and fluffs from seats littered the ground. He turned to Red. "Make sure the animals in the meadow and beyond know that we chased the humans away this time."

Then he turned to Rabbit. "Go tell your family too." She nodded, sucked a last bit of clover into her mouth and hopped away into the fading light. Word would spread in all directions quickly. The rabbits, like the birds, were a chatty bunch. Within a short time, every animal would know about their success.

"We've done pretty well," gloated Rat, plucking a bit of itchy wire wrapping from the claw of his front paw.

"This is only the beginning," warned Buck. "Now it's going to get nasty."

"Guns?" whispered Raccoon. Even sporting a dense fur, she trembled. She covered her eyes with her paws, afraid.

"Probably," answered Buck. He didn't seem too bothered by that possibility. Where the others were jittery, he appeared calm.

"What should we do?" Raccoon asked him.

After biting a bothersome tick on his flank, he answered, "Nothing you can do. You can't argue with humans, machines, or guns." Slowly, majestically, he trotted into the deep woods toward his thicket. The others headed toward their caves and nests and dens.

Except Jack. He had to see Collin. He sniffed the air. It was dark. Most of the leaves had fluttered down everywhere he looked. Only a few still clung to the oak trees. Zipping through the woods, he scaled trees with urgency in his short but swift stride. Crunching leaves sounded his flight over the ground. The tiny lights that appeared when dark came were hidden behind grayness, but Jack didn't smell falling water. Not yet, anyway. The air, clean and sharp, filled his nose and chest. Still early dark time, the coldness made his fur bristle and snap, giving off tiny blue bits of light.

If Sister were here, he'd touch her nose and zap her, like Rat got zapped from the machine wires. It would sting like a bee for a moment, but she wouldn't lose any whiskers from it. He'd titter, and then she'd get even.

But she wasn't here, and he was alone now. The nest was too big for one squirrel.

Those thoughts tumbled in his head as he ran the distance to Collin's home. He stopped short at the edge of the wood. As dark fall came, he saw the light on in Collin's den. Passing by the window was the mother.

Where is Collin? Jack ran across the road, now cool, over cold wet grass, and scrabbled up to the top of the fence to squat. He saw Collin through the glass. Collin was in his human nest, asleep. Jack watched him until he shivered as the cold deepened. The only sound came from the hunting cry of Owl far off. Jack ran home to sleep in his nest. He'd see Collin later.

At light rise, Jack waited until the humans came back. Lots of humans in blue clothes, humans with paper, and humans holding black boxes that flashed short, very bright lights. Every now and then the box would flash in Jack's direction, making him see spots before his eyes for a while, till he learned to look away. A crowd gathered, mostly standing around, looking and talking. Jack, hidden from their poor sight, watched and waited for the animals to return. Soon, all were assembled in their places, ready for action without the rest of the humans seeing them. Jack stood and gave the order.

"Attack! Attack! Save your homes! Protect your young! No blood!" Once again the animals stomped and clambered forward. Snapping twigs and crackling leaves marked their surge as they moved together. Rat and other rodents broke away and marched toward the machines. Buck and his kin advanced toward the humans. Jack raced to take his perch on top of one of the machines so the animals could see and hear him.

Some humans actually ran to meet the animals, flashing their little black boxes, but when the deer lowered their antlers at the challenge, they backed up, turned, and ran.

Faster than I thought they could run. Behind the fence, some humans were furiously making their marks on paper. On the far side of the road Collin and the mother stood, also watching the fight. Soon, lots of machines with flashing lights screamed their arrival. Smaller animals, like Beaver and Gopher, flinched. Jack did too, but seeing the deer unafraid, he stayed in his spot.

"Attack! It's only lights and noise! Don't stop till they leave our wood! No blood!" Jack chittered as loudly as he could. Owl repeated his words, crying overhead.

The tide of animal bodies drove the humans back; most now cowered behind the fence. Jack could feel, see, and smell the fear.

"They looked like *they're* caged in," observed Sister coming up behind Jack.

"Flying fur!" he chattered, jumping straight up. "Stop sneaking up on me!"

"Scared you, did I?" she smirked.

"You wish. I'm busy trying to lead a fight and you distracted me with your silly game." Jack looked around. "Where's Jerk? Stealing from my nut store while we fight the humans?"

Sister looked hurt. "He helped last time," she answered defensively, eyes narrowed. "He's around here somewhere."

Not for long, thought Jack. *Male squirrels never stay long in one place. But I will. I won't leave my tree.*

"Just make sure he doesn't get too close to the humans, they're unpredictable. If he gets caught, it means you'll move back into my tree again with your mess." His onyx eyes sparkled.

"You fleabag, I knew you liked him!" she chittered happily.

That's what you want to think. "Are you ready to move closer, Sister?"

"Right next to you, Jack. Lead on."

"Push! Force them out of the wood! No blood!" he called as he leapt over to the next machine, and then the next, until he was on top of one with the flashing lights. Sister landed right next to him.

Flash! A bright light temporarily blinded him and Sister. A human in woodland colored clothes used one of the little black boxes to pop a small bright light at them. Jack's fur stood up, and he stood tall in front of Sister, ready to bite if the human tried to take her. He was rammed aside. Jerk now stood in front, claws ready to scratch, tail flicking rapidly. He crouched in attack stance.

"Ta-cherr! Ta-cherr!" he threatened the man.

"Easy, Jerk," tittered Jack softly. "Stand still. I'll bite. You and Sister run if he moves." The man remained still. He simply watched them. Unafraid, his intent eyes gazed at the three of them. Jack saw curiosity in that stare, not sneakiness. Maybe they would be safe, but he was taking no chances.

The man slowly backed off, then took out a thick wad of paper and made lots of marks. Every once in a while, he would look up at them, but he never came closer.

"Let's go," said Jerk, nudging Sister. "The humans are running. Let's eat and nap." Jerk and Sister smoothly leapt off the machine, heading back into the wood together.

Jack and the human continued to stare at each other.

That's enough for me. Jack retreated to the top of the machine closest to the wood, watching the humans leave. When they were gone, the animals lined up around the edge of the wood and lay down to rest, blocking the humans from coming back in. Jack skipped up the maple tree where Owl's old nest once was, curling in a tight ball, and slept.

Chapter 15

Fluffed and Stuffed

It was the same thing the next light rise. When the humans arrived, the animals were ready. The humans inched forward. The animals drove them back. The humans ran. The animals rested.

On the third light rise, no humans or machines came. The woods fell silent, and like Jack, the animals felt relieved. The damaged machines were abandoned for a while, until large machines with strong wire came and pulled them away, along with the long white box den and the blue human stink boxes. Some grasses crushed under foot and hoof slowly started to spring back. The mud, now totally dried, cracked and hardened.

Saplings bent by the attack straightened, reaching for the weakening light. The air now stung with cold, but it was clear. No more thick black smoke or harsh smells.

The humans weren't completely gone. Jack, Rat, Owl, and Rabbit sniffed their scent in funny looking hiding places, which almost blended into the colors of the woods. Almost, that is, if you were as blind as a human. And as stupid as one, Jack thought as he spied on one from behind a rotted log, ripe with mushrooms. And as hard of hearing. These humans simply watched the animals, used their little black boxes to flash them, made squiggly marks on papers, and then talked into smaller silver boxes.

The silver boxes talk back. Jack couldn't make any sense of it, so he didn't try. His mind was tired from all the learning and thinking and watching and fighting.

"Like we can't smell them across the wood," mused Rabbit as she hopped up to Jack. They watched together while Jack proceeded to demolish a large and very tasty mushroom that by some wonderful chance had been overlooked by every other squirrel. He'd take whatever he couldn't eat back to his nest and dry it in the crook of a tree branch before storing it. When all was white and hard with cold, it would be a tasty treat from dried nuts. He carefully hid the remaining chunk to bring to the nest later.

"Humans are stinky, aren't they?" she asked.

Jack flicked his tail several times before answering. "Very." The willow tree and a huge pile of crispy leaves gave both of them good cover from the humans. Not that they were worried about either being

seen or caught. These humans didn't set out any traps. They stayed away from the animals. Also, Jack and the others were swift. And they knew all the hiding places if the humans start acting like hunters.

Every once in a while, the humans moved their strange little hidey boxes too close to an active den or nest. Jack, Buck, Rat, Rabbit, Owl, and Beaver would sit right in front and stare. Moving closer a little bit at a time. From light rise to dark fall, dark fall to light rise. Until the humans backed off.

For now, the humans seemed fascinated with them and no longer tried to destroy the wood. If anything, they prevented other humans from entering, even the young ones who used to run through and play there. They put up a fence all around the wood, and stuck papers with marks on trees everywhere. Buck kept knocking one section of the fence down to keep a trail open for the animals that migrated. Eventually, the humans left that part of the fence down.

It seemed to have worked out.

But Jack wasn't fooled. Gracie taught him that. She'd stop putting obstacles on the birdfeeders for a short time. Then she'd come back with something worse.

Sneaky humans. Always have to win. If animals and humans want the same thing, animals suffer. Sometimes die. We won this fight, but it isn't over. There will always be another fight, until the humans win.

Rabbit hopped off to her thicket as a few stray leaves rained down in whispers, landing almost noiselessly on the woodland floor. Jack, unable to resist, rolled in a particularly large pile, scampering and darting in and out. It was more fun when Sister played with him, but he still enjoyed the game.

Remarkably, it was a warm day, and Jack's thick fur was heavy and sticking to him. He sat and plumped his coat; first the top layer so cooling air could reach the under layer. Next he checked for any stray fleas or ticks. There were none. Finally, Jack groomed his tail.

His stomach growled. Spying a few red berries missed by Red and other birds, Jack deftly plucked them and popped them into his mouth. He forced himself to eat every last one. He wouldn't get a treat like this till the warm came.

Fluffed and stuffed, he walked the distance to

Collin's home. The boy, wrapped up in many layers of soft coverings, smiled when he saw Jack.

"Jack! You are the coolest! I'm so amazed. You and the animals scared the heck out of everyone! No one will go into your woods again. Even I'm gonna think twice about it!"

Collin held up his paw. Jack stood there, looking at him. Jack held up his paw, palm out. Slowly, gently, Collin touched his palm to Jack's.

"High five, Dude!"

"Whuck!" Jack touched his palm to Collin's.

"Un-be-live-a-ble!" whispered Collin. He smiled. Really big, showing a lot of large white teeth, but Jack wasn't afraid. Then Collin pulled out his box of strange things. And a bit of apple, with nut mud.

"So, are you ready Jack?" he asked.

Jack stood attentively. "Whuck! Whuck!" He was ready for his snack, even if his belly was already stretching his fur.

"Since you know about wheels, I think I'll teach you about axles."

About the Author

Charlotte Bennardo is the co-author of *Sirenz* and *Sirenz: Back in Fashion* (Flux), hailed as, "funny and entertaining" by Booklist and *Blonde Ops* (Thomas Dunne Books) which Booklist reported as "[a] hypercharged thriller of fashion, high-tech sleuthing, and power....highly entertaining, escapist fun." She is one of thirteen authors of *Beware the Little White Rabbit* (Leap) helping celebrate the 150th anniversary of Lewis Carroll's *Alice in Wonderland*. She resides in New Jersey with her husband, and is currently hard at work fighting for chair space with her cat as she works on her next project.

'A truly impressive achievement'   *Observer*

'Mr Aldiss' novel is suffused with grief at the loss of children . . . he uses the genre novel to explore themes of importance to him'   P. D. James

Also by Brian Aldiss

NOVELS

The Brightfount Diaries (1955)
Non-Stop (1958)
Bow Down to Nul (1960)
The Primal Urge (1961)
The Male Response (1961)
Hothouse (1962)
The Dark Light Years (1964)
Greybeard (1964)
Earthworks (1965)
An Age (1967)
Report on Probability A (1968)
Barefoot in the Head: A European Fantasia (1969)
The Hand-Reared Boy (1970)
A Soldier Erect (1971)
Frankenstein Unbound (1973)
The Eighty Minute Hour: A Space Opera (1974)
The Malacia Tapestry (1976)
Brothers of the Head (1977)
A Rude Awakening (1978)
Enemies of the System: A Tale of Homo Unifomis (1978)
Moreau's Other Island (1980)
Life in the West (1980)
Helliconia Spring (1982)
Helliconia Summer (1983)
Helliconia Winter (1985)
The Year Before Yesterday (1987)
Ruins (1987)
Forgotten Life (1988)
Dracula Unbound (1991)
Remembrance Day (1993)
Somewhere East of Life (1994)
White Mars Or, The Mind Set Free (with Roger Penrose) (1999)
Super-State (2002)
The Cretan Teat (2002)
Affairs at Hampden Ferrers (2004)
Sanity and the Lady (2005)
Jocasta (2006)
HARM (2007)

SHORT STORY COLLECTIONS

Space, Time and Nathaniel (Presciences) (1957)

No Time Like Tomorrow (1959)
The Canopy of Time (1959)
Galaxies Like Grains of Sand (1960)
The Airs of Earth (1963)
Best Science Fiction Stories of Brian W. Aldiss (1965)
The Saliva Tree and Other Strange Growths (1966)
Intangible Inc. (1969)
The Moment of Eclipse (1970)
The Book of Brian Aldiss (1972)
Last Orders and Other Stories (1977)
New Arrivals, Old Encounters (1979)
Seasons in Flight (1984)
The Magic of the Past (1987)
Best SF Stories of Brian W. Aldiss (1988)
Science Fiction Blues (1988)
A Romance of the Equator: Best Fantasy Stories (1989)
A Tupelov Too Far (1994)
The Secret of This Book (1995)
Common Clay (1996)
Super-Toys Last All Summer Long and Other Stories of Future Time (2001)
Cultural Breaks (2005)

NON FICTION

The Shape of Further Things (1970)
Billion Year Spree (1973)
Science Fiction Art (1975)
Science Fiction Art (1976)
Science Fiction as Science Fiction (1978)
The World and Nearer Ones (1979)
The Pale Shadow of Science (1985)
. . . And the Lurid Glare of the Comet (1986)
Trillion Year Spree (1986)
Bury My Heart at W.H. Smith's: A Writing Life (1990)
The Detached Retina (1995)
The Twinkling of an Eye or My Life as an Englishman (1998)
When the Feast is Finished (with Margaret Aldiss) (1999)
Art after Apogee: The Relationships between an Idea, a Story, a Painting (with Rosemary Phipps) (2000)

SF MASTERWORKS

Greybeard

BRIAN ALDISS

The right of Brian Aldiss to be identified as the author
of this work has been asserted by him in accordance with
the Copyright, Designs and Patents Act 1988.

This edition published in Great Britain in 2011 by
Gollancz
An imprint of the Orion Publishing Group
Orion House, 5 Upper St Martin's Lane,
London WC2H 9EA
An Hachette UK Company

5 7 9 10 8 6 4

A CIP catalogue record for this book
is available from the British Library

ISBN 978 0 575 07113 1

Typeset at The Spartan Press Ltd,
Lymington, Hants

Printed in Great Britain by
Clays Ltd, St Ives plc

The Orion Publishing Group's policy is to use papers that
are natural, renewable and recyclable products and made
from wood grown in sustainable forests. The logging and
manufacturing processes are expected to conform to the
environmental regulations of the country of origin.

www.brianwaldiss.org
www.orionbooks.co.uk

Written with love for
CLIVE and WENDY
who now
understand the story behind the story

INTRODUCTION

Greybeard is a novel about growing old, and about being old. Its every page is pregnant with the truth of that condition – that ageing is a ceaseless, decaying passage towards the impossible asymptote of our own death. But the fact that he is writing science fiction enables Aldiss to focus this human universal (it is hard, in fact, to think of a *more* universal human theme) with extraordinary clarity. For in his imagined world a nuclear accident has rendered humanity sterile: the old get older, but there are no more births, and no new generation rises behind them to fill their place. It is a bleakly brilliant conceit, and Aldiss works through its implication with a superbly restrained, almost Hardyesque rigour. In part this has to do with some beautifully observed, and beautifully handled, nature writing, the continuing fecundity of some (though not all) the wildlife contrasting bittersweetly with the sterile decay of humanity:

They came to a wide sheet of water, patched with small islands and banks of rushes. The lake was a sanctuary for wildlife; dippers, moorhens, and an abundance of duck moved over or above its surface. In the clear waters beneath their centre-board, many shoals of fish were visible. They were in no mood to appreciate the natural attractions. The weather had turned blustery, they did not know in which direction they should sail. Rain, galloping over the face of the water, sent them scurrying for shelter under the spare sail. As the showers grew heavier and the breeze failed, Greybeard and Charley rowed them to one of the islands, and there they made camp.

It was dry under the sail, and the weather turned milder, but a sense of depression settled on them as they watched shawls of water and cloud embrace the landscape. Greybeard husbanded a small fire into life, which set them all coughing, for the smoke would not disperse.

Aldiss has never written better, or more evocatively lyrical, than this. It creates a sense of the world as rounded, finely observed, pregnant with myriad beauties.

Greybeard is a potent elegy for the human condition. Like a later masterpiece Cormac McCarthy's *The Road*, *Greybeard* understands that humans do not endure through the grimmest times alone. Greybeard depends upon his wife Martha to give him purpose, and reason for living; and he is himself aware that being a fairly unimaginative chap is an advantage, since it prevents him from a capsizing comprehension of the approaching and inevitable end. But unlike the powerful but rather bludgeoning bleakness of McCarthy's novel, Aldiss' is shot through at all points with a weird, plangent beauty.

It will also remind the reader of P.D. James' derivative *Children of Men*, a book that committed nothing short of larceny upon Aldiss' (much better) novel and then failed to make anything much of its swag. James' take gets bogged down in religious allegory and political hi-jinks, forcing an artificial climax with some daft gunplay. The film adapted from this book – a much better work with very little in common with its source text – likewise pulled its key punch. In both cases there was a sense that a world in which parturition had come to an end could only be made comprehensible through hope: a pregnant woman, a new child, the dawn coming round again.

Aldiss is clearer-eyed. He tropes his existential theme as *anti-climax*, a figure that shapes many of the novel's set-pieces. Greybeard himself works as a contemporary historian, recording events for a future in which there will be literally nobody to read. Martha is kidnapped by a sex-maniac, chloroformed and tied up in a bedroom; but she is not raped. The novel's characters travel in the hope of reaching the sea, but we never get there. Even the novel's grand premise – that there are no more children – is eventually revealed as off-the-point.

Not to be pretentious (and in fact this novel is one of the most grounded, least pretentious ever written) but the resonance of *Greybeard* derives from the mellow skill with which it explores a crucial existential dilemma. We will all die. Some of us console ourselves with the thought that we will live again after our death, in a heaven perhaps, or reborn as humans in this world. Such fantasies are widespread, and for good reason, but they lack the heft of reality – they are, in the strictest sense, escapist, as if death were only a prison from which the obedient or the wily might break through. In our bones we understand the blanker truth: there is no escape from death. So we turn instead to another consolation; we die, but our children will carry on, and our DNA will wriggle its threadworm way through other organisms. There *is* some relief in this thought, and from a *longue durée* perspective it's kind of the point of our being here – humans are only one of the many ingenious methods DNA has lighted upon to make more DNA. But it would be a strangely aloof human being who could take personal satisfaction in that fact.

This is the genius of Aldiss' treatment. The discovery that children *are* still being born in the world is treated not as a flame of hope or redemptive twist, but – with brilliantly pitched anti-climax – as something largely irrelevant to the passing generation, a sort of knight's move. Greybeard and his wife are still on the way to death. *Greybeard*, fundamentally, is about seeing the world unencumbered either by fantasies of individual or species survival. That such a view is not merely depressing says something about Aldiss' enormous skill as a writer, but also – perhaps – it suggests that an existence beyond hope might be beyond fear as well. The theme is not in escape, but only in the fortitude with which we encounter the inevitable. That is the strength given to mortals, after all.

Given that it comes to many of us, and that most of us strenuously *hope* to reach it, it's perhaps surprising how few great novels there are that actually confront the realities of old age. Most – like Cervantes' seminal *Don Quixote* – are in fact fantasies of escape *from* decrepitude. Others, like Muriel Sparks' *Memento Mori*, explore the consolations of mortality. But Aldiss' novel takes a difference approach to either of these works. *Greybeard* is varied, beautifully observed and written, involving and profound without ever falling for the twin, related mendacities of 'consolation' and 'escapism'. It has a good claim to being Aldiss' most fully realised novel.

Adam Roberts

1

The River: Sparcot

A rifle was slung over his left shoulder by a leather strap. He moved silently along a path cut between coppiced sycamores as tall as he was. On the path ahead, a snake lay sunning itself. The day was warm for the time of year. He saw by its markings it was a harmless grass snake. It disappeared into the bushes at his approach. He had seen it there before.

As he came to the fish pond, a water rat jumped into the water with a smart plop. It always happened like that.

Greybeard worked his way round the bank of the pond among knots of elder which overhung the water. Crushing twigs in his progress, he smelt again the musty-sweet scent of their pith, a scent he had known since childhood. He looked down into the pond. The fish were as abundant as ever.

Everything was as before. The years ran through their cycles, but nothing changed.

He could see into the shallows where a chub waited under the bank among weeds. Or he could watch the surface of the water. There was reflected blue sky, patched with cloud. He stood where he was for a while, before recollecting himself. Then he could not remember what his thoughts had been.

Well, he muttered, half-aloud, all would be unbearable if it weren't for *her* . . . Martha . . . And that thought was no new one.

He turned away, to where a crumbling brick wall stood, bearded with fern. Once the wall had marked the boundary of a private estate. Now there were no private estates, the wall indicated the limits of the village of Sparcot, and the limits of Greybeard's patrol.

I

Sliding the rifle from his shoulder, he looked across the wall. His sense of danger was dulled by repetition. Twice a week for many a year, rain or shine, he had patrolled this flimsy border, had discovered snowdrops under the shelter of the wall, had seen the hedges thick with shining blackberries, had found the whole scene bright and barren under snow . . . Somewhere in the direction he was observing lay Grafton Lock, ruled by the fierce Gipsy Joan; but her tribe posed little threat. Men of the village said of Joan that she wore no knickers. He smiled to himself at the thought. Even to an ageing population, sex remained of perennial interest.

Then there was the possibility of another invasion by stoats, foraging along the river bank, such as had happened three times of recent years. But nothing moved on this peaceful day. Of animal life, he saw only a feral cat, motionless on a dead tree stump.

He waited to see the cat pounce, but it remained unmoving. He turned back at last. A slight haze lay over Sparcot and its grazing land. To his nostrils came the sardonic stone age smell of wood smoke.

All was as it had been. And would be again.

He knew not what the day of the week was called. But one thing was certain: in two days' time, he would be on patrol again, treading the same paths, watching the same vistas. And waiting.

The days were closing in towards the time people still called Christmas.

Four stoats swam a brook. Climbing from the chill water, they worked their way through dead reed and up the bank. Their bodies were low to the ground, their necks outstretched, the young ones imitating their mother. Keeping to cover, they looked out hungrily at rabbits seeking food only a few feet beyond their noses.

Where the rabbits frisked was once wheatland, cropping regularly under a farmer's care. Neglect had set in. Early one year, tractors had not arrived. Taking advantage of their opportunity, weeds had risen up, choking the cereal crops. Later, fire spread across the deserted farmland, burning down thistles and bind-

2

weed. Rabbits, preferring low growth, moved in to nibble the green shoots which thrust through the ash.

The shoots that survived this natural thinning process found themselves with ample space in which to grow. Many were now full-sized trees. In consequence, the numbers of rabbits had declined. Rabbits prefer open land. So grass had a chance to return to an old habitat. Now the grass, in its turn, was growing sparse under a spread of beech branches. The few rabbits ekeing out existence there were thin of flank.

They were also wary. When one rabbit saw the stoat eyes watching, it turned up its tail and bolted for cover. The other rabbits followed. The stoats were immediately on the move, brown flashes rippling across open space. The rabbits shot into their burrows. The stoats followed unhesitatingly. They could go anywhere. This world was theirs. In no time, their muzzles were bloody and they were feasting.

A day or two later, an old man was making a routine patrol of the same ground. He wore a coarse canvas shirt of red, green, and orange stripes which rendered him clearly visible in the tawny winter landscape.

Near the banks of the river, the wilderness had been cleared by corporate effort to allow space for cattle to graze. In the wilderness beyond, a pattern was still discernable to an educated eye. Large trees – to some of whose branches a raddled leaf still clung – marked the lines of what were hedges long ago. The trees enclosed entanglements of vegetation which had once been arable land. Brambles lacerated their way into the centre of the fields, in competition with elders, thorns, thistle and other sturdy growths.

Along the edge of one line of trees, a stockade had been thrown up, protecting an area of several acres which had the river on its longer side. It was by this stockade that the old man patrolled, whistling to himself as he went. His shirt, which furnished the only spash of colour in the landscape, was made from the canvas of an old deckchair.

In the branches above his head, rooks perching there did not bother to fly off at his approach.

Since the village was close, the barrier of vegetation was

punctuated by narrow paths trodden into the undergrowth. These paths led to latrines, holes dug in the ground and sheltered from the weather by roofs of wood or plastic. Such were the sanitary arrangements of Sparcot.

The village itself lay on the river in the midst of its clearing. It had been built, or rather had accumulated in the course of centuries, in the shape of a capital H, the crossbar being formed by a stone bridge which spanned the river. Though the bridge still threw its humpbacked span sturdily across water, it led only to a ruinous street, still known as Oxford Road or Oxfroad, and a dense thicket where the villagers gathered firewood, or attempted the gymnastics of antique passion.

Of the two roads forming the legs of the H, the one nearest the river, known as the High Street, had been designed originally as a quiet community street fringed by humble dwellings and a public house. One leg of this thoroughfare led to an ancient watermill, where lived Big Jim Mole, the boss of Sparcot. The other road, on the other side of the river, subject to spring floods, had once been a main road, leading to towns and cities, the very names of which were forgotten. Even before the line of houses petered out, in came the vegetation, stern and invasive as an army. The last house of all had been devoured by the weight of a rampant ivy.

All the houses in Sparcot bore the stigmata of neglect. Many were ruined. Some ruins were still inhabited. One hundred and twelve people lived here. None had been born in the village.

Where roads joined on the higher bank of the river stood a stone building which had served originally as a post office. These days, no post survived, no mail was ever delivered, nobody wrote letters. The upper windows of this building commanded a view of the bridge and river in one direction and the cultivated land in the other. Here was the village guard room. Since all the earlier frivolities which Sparcot had once enjoyed – video, bingo, car boot sales, church fetes – had become part of history, this room functioned as the centre of village life. And, since Big Jim Mole insisted that a guard be continually kept, it was occupied now.

There were three people sitting or lying in the old barren room. A venerable woman, past her eightieth year, sat by a

4

wood stove, humming to herself and nodding her head. She held out thin hands to the stove, on which stew was warming in a tin platter.

Of the two men keeping her company in the room, one was extremely ancient, although his eye was bright. Towin Thomas lay on a paliasse on the floor, staring up at the ceiling as if trying to puzzle out the meaning of the cracks there. His face, sharp as a stoat's beneath its stubble, wore an irritable look. Old Betty's humming jarred his nerves.

Only the third occupant of the guard room was properly alert. He was cleaning the rifle with the leather strap, running a piece of rag on a string through the barrel and then squinting up it to see that the rifling was perfectly clean. Greybeard was a well-built man in his middle fifties, without a paunch but not so starveling as his companions. He sat in a creaking chair by the window, occasionally glancing alertly out through the panes.

'Sam's coming,' he said. He had sighted the patrol with the colourful shirt approaching the guard house.

At his christening, Greybeard had been given the name Algy Timberlane, but it had become rather lost, like much else, as years went by. The nickname had gathered strength and stuck, even in a world of greybeards. Timberlane sported a thick hirsute growth which reached almost to his navel, where it had been cut sharply across.

His high and almost bald head lent emphasis to the beard, and its texture, barred as it was with stripes of black hair sprouting from the jawline, made it particularly noticeable in a society which afforded few forms of personal adornment.

When Greybeard spoke, Betty ceased her humming without giving any other sign she had heard. Thomas sat up on his paliasse, putting one hand on the cudgel that lay by his side; it was his constant companion. He screwed up his eyes in order to read the time from his wristwatch. This souvenir of a vanished world was Towin Thomas's most cherished possession, although it had not worked in a decade. A windup clock on a shelf gave him more reliable information.

'Sam's early coming off guard, twenty minutes early,' he said.

5

'Old sciver. Worked up an appetite for lunch strolling around out there. You better watch that hash of yours, Betty – I'm the only one I'm wanting to get indigestion off that grub, girl.'

Betty shook her head. It was as much a nervous tic as a negation of anything that the man with the cudgel might have said. She kept her hands to the fire, not looking around.

Towin Thomas picked up his cudgel and rose stiffly to his feet, helping himself up against the table. He joined Greybeard at the window, peering through the dirty pane and rubbing it with his sleeve.

'That's Sam Bulstow all right. You can't mistake that shirt.'

Sam Bulstow walked down the littered street. Rubble, broken tiles and litter, lay on the pavements; dock and fennel – mortified by winter – sprouted from shattered gratings. Sam Bulstow walked in the middle of the road. There had been no traffic but pedestrians for several years now. He turned in when he reached the post office, and the watchers heard his footsteps on the boards of the room below them.

Without excitement, they listened to the whole performance of his getting upstairs: the groans of the bare treads, the squeak of a horny palm on the hand rail as it helped tug its owner upward, the rasp and heave of lungs challenged by every step.

Finally, Sam appeared in the guard room. The gaudy stripes of his shirt threw up some of their color onto the white stubble of his jaws. He stood for a while staring in at them, resting on the frame of the door to regain his breath.

'You're early if it's dinner you're after,' Betty said, without bothering to turn her head. Nobody paid her any attention, and she nodded her old rats' tails to herself in disapproval.

Sam just stood where he was, showing his yellow and brown teeth in a pant. 'The Scotsmen are getting near,' he said.

Betty turned her neck stiffly to look at Greybeard. Towin Thomas arranged his crafty old wolf's visage over the top of his cudgel and looked at Sam with his eyes screwed up.

'Maybe they're after your job, Sammy, man,' he said.

'Who gave you that bit of information, Sam?' Greybeard asked.

6

Sam came slowly into the room, sneaking a sharp look at the clock as he did so, and poured himself a drink of water from a battered can standing in a corner. He gulped the water and sank down onto a wooden stool, stretching his fibrous hands out to the fire and generally taking his time before replying.

'There was a packman skirting the northern barricade just now. Told me he was heading for Faringdon. Said the Scotsmen had reached Banbury.'

'Where is this packman?' Greybeard asked, hardly raising his voice, and appearing to look out of the window.

'He's gone on now, Greybeard. Said he was going to Faringdon.'

'Passed by Sparcot without calling here to sell us anything? Not very likely.'

'I'm only telling you what he said. I'm not responsible for him. I just reckon old Boss Mole ought to know the Scotsmen are coming, that's all.' Sam's voice relapsed into the irritable whine they all used at times.

Betty turned back to her stove. She said, 'Everyone who comes here brings rumors. If it isn't the Scots, it's herds of savage animals. Rumors, rumors . . . It's as bad as the last war, when they kept telling us there was going to be an invasion. I reckoned at the time they only done it to scare us, but I was scared just the same.'

Sam cut off her muttering. 'Rumors or not, I'm telling you what the man said. I thought I ought to come up here and report it. Did I do right or didn't I?'

'Where had this fellow come from?' Greybeard asked.

'He hadn't come from anywhere. He was going to Faringdon.' He smiled his sly-doggy smile at his joke, and picked up a reflected smile from Towin.

'Did he say where he had been?' Greybeard asked patiently.

'He said he had been coming from up river. Said there was a lot of stoats heading this way.'

'Eh, that's another rumor we've heard before,' Betty said to herself, nodding her head.

'You keep your trap shut, you old cow,' Sam said, without rancor.

Greybeard took hold of his rifle by the barrel and moved into the middle of the room until he stood looking down at Sam.

'Is that all you have to report, Sam?'

'Scotsmen, stoats – what more do you want from one patrol? I didn't see any elephants, if you were wondering.' He cracked his grin again, looking again for Towin Thomas's approval.

'You aren't bright enough to know an elephant if you saw it, Sam, you old flea pit,' Towin said.

Ignoring this exchange, Greybeard said, 'Okay, Sam, back you go on patrol. There's another twenty minutes before you are relieved.'

'What, go back out there just for another lousy twenty minutes? Not on your flaming nelly, Greybeard! I've had it for this afternoon and I'm sitting right here on this stool. Let it ride for twenty minutes. Nobody's going to run away with Sparcot, whatever Jim Mole may think.'

'You know the dangers as well as I do.'

'You know you'll never get any sense out of me, not while I've got this bad back. These blinking guard duties come around too often for my liking.'

Betty and Towin kept silent. The latter cast a glance at his broken wristwatch. Both he and Betty, like everyone else in the village, had had the necessity for continuous guard drummed into them often enough, but they kept their eyes tracing the seamed lines on the board floor, knowing the effort involved in thrusting old legs an extra time up and down stairs and an extra time around the perimeter.

The advantage lay with Sam, as he sensed. Facing Greybeard more boldly, he said, 'Why don't you take over for twenty minutes if you're so keen on defending the dump? You're a young man – it'll do you good to have a stretch.'

Greybeard tucked the leather sling of the rifle over his left shoulder and turned to Towin, who stopped gnawing the top of his cudgel to look up.

8

'Strike the alarm gong if you want me in a hurry, and not otherwise. Remind old Betty it's not a dinner gong.'

The woman cackled as he moved toward the door, buttoning his baggy jacket. 'Your grub's just on ready, Algy. Why not stay and eat it?' she asked.

Greybeard slammed the door without answering. They listened to his heavy tread descending the stairs.

'You don't reckon he took offense, do you? He wouldn't report me to old Mole, would he?' Sam asked anxiously. The others mumbled neutrally and hugged their lean ribs; they did not want to be involved in any trouble.

Greybeard walked slowly along the middle of the street, avoiding the puddles still left from a rainstorm two days ago. Most of Sparcot's drains and gutters were blocked, but the reluctance of the water to run away was due mainly to the marshiness of the land. Somewhere upstream debris was blocking the river, causing it to overflow its banks. He must speak to Mole; they must get up an expedition to look into the trouble. But Mole was growing increasingly cantankerous, and his policy of isolationism would be against any move out of the village.

Greybeard chose to walk by the river, to continue around the perimeter of the stockade afterward. He brushed through an encroaching elder's stark spikes, smelling as he did so a melancholy-sweet smell of the river and the things that moldered by it.

Several of the houses that backed onto the river had been devoured by fire before he and his fellows came to live here. Vegetation grew sturdily inside and out their shells. On a back gate lying crookedly in long grass, faded lettering proclaimed the name of the nearest shell: THAMESIDE.

Farther on the houses were undamaged by fire and inhabited. Greybeard's own house was here. He looked at the windows, but caught no sight of his wife, Martha; she would be sitting quietly by the fire with a blanket around her shoulders, staring into the grate and seeing – what? Suddenly an immense impatience pierced Greybeard. These houses were a poor old huddle of buildings, nestling together like a bunch of ravens with broken wings. Most

9

of them lacked chimneys or guttering; each year they hunched their shoulders higher as the rooftrees sagged. And in general the people fitted in well enough with this air of decay. He did not; nor did he want his Martha to do so.

Deliberately, he slowed his thoughts. Anger was useless. He made a virtue of not being angry. But he longed for a freedom beyond the flyblown safety of Sparcot.

Beyond the houses were Toby's trading post – a newer building that, and in better shape than most – and the barns, ungraceful structures that commemorated the lack of skill with which they had been built. Beyond the barns lay the fields, turned up in weals to greet the frosts of winter; shards of water glittered between furrows. Beyond the fields grew the thickets marking the eastern end of Sparcot. Beyond Sparcot lay the immense mysterious territory that was the Thames Valley.

Just beyond the province of the village an old brick bridge with a collapsed arch menaced the river, its remains suggesting the horns of a ram growing together in old age. Greybeard contemplated it and the fierce little weir just beyond it – for that way lay whatever went by the name of freedom these days – and then turned away to patrol the living stockade.

With the rifle comfortably under one crooked arm, he made his promenade. He could see across to the other side of the clearing; it was deserted, except for two men walking distantly among cattle, and a stooped figure in the cabbage patch. He had the world almost to himself – and year by year he would have it more to himself.

He snapped down the shutter of his mind on that thought, and began to concentrate on what Sam Bulstow had reported. It was probably an invention to gain him twenty minutes off patrol duty. The rumor about the Scots sounded unlikely, though no more so than other tales that travelers had brought them – that a Chinese army was marching on London, or that gnomes and elves and men with badger faces had been seen dancing in the woods. Scope for error and ignorance seemed to grow season by season. It would be good to know what was really happening . . .

Less unlikely than the legend of marching Scots was Sam's tale of a strange packman. Densely though the thickets grew, there were ways through them and men who traveled those ways, though the isolated village of Sparcot saw little but the traffic that moved painfully up and down the Thames. Well, they must maintain their watch. Even in these more peaceful days – 'the apathy that bringeth perfect peace,' thought Greybeard, wondering what he was quoting – villages that kept no guard could be raided and ruined for the sake of their food stocks, or just for madness. So they believed.

Now he walked among tethered cows, grazing individually around the ragged radius of their halters. They were the new strain, small, sturdy, plump, and full of peace. And young! Tender creatures, surveying Greybeard from moist eyes, creatures that belonged to man but had no share of his decrepitude, creatures that kept the grass short right up to the ragged bramblebushes.

He saw that one of the animals near the brambles was pulling at its tether. It tossed its head, rolled its eyes, and lowed. Greybeard quickened his pace.

There seemed to be nothing to disturb the cow except a dead rabbit lying by the brambles. As he drew nearer, Greybeard surveyed the rabbit. It was freshly killed. And though it was completely dead, he thought it had moved. He stood almost over it, alert for something wrong, a faint prickle of unease creeping up his backbone.

Certainly the rabbit was dead, killed neatly by the back of the neck. Its neck and anus were bloody, its purple eye glazed.

Yet it moved. Its side heaved.

Shock – an involuntary superstitious dread – coursed through Greybeard. He took a step backward, sliding the rifle down into his hands. At the same time, the rabbit heaved again and its killer exposed itself to view.

Backing swiftly out of the rabbit's carcass came a stoat, doubling up its body in its haste to be clear. Its brown coat was enriched with rabbit blood, the tiny savage muzzle it lifted to Greybeard smeared with crimson. He shot it dead before it could move.

The cows plunged and kicked. Like clockwork toys, the figures among the Brussels-sprout stumps straightened their backs. Birds wheeled up from the rooftops. The gong sounded from the guard room, as Greybeard had instructed it should. A knot of people congregated outside the barns, hobbling together as if they might pool their rheumy eye-sight.

'Blast their eyes, there's nothing to panic about,' Greybeard growled. But he knew the involuntary shot had been a mistake; he should have clubbed the stoat to death with the butt of his rifle. The sound of firing always woke alarm.

A party of active sixty-year-olds assembled and began to march toward him, swinging cudgels of various descriptions. Through his irritation he had to admit that it was a prompt stand-to. There was plenty of life about the place yet.

'It's all right!' he called, waving his arms above his head as he went to meet them. 'All right! I was attacked by a solitary stoat, that's all. You can go back.'

Charley Samuels was there, a big man with a sallow color; he had his tame fox, Isaac, with him on a leash. Charley lived next door to the Timberlanes, and had been increasingly dependent on them since his wife's death the previous spring.

He came in front of the other men and aligned himself with Greybeard.

'Next spring, we'll have a drive to collect more fox cubs and tame them,' he said. 'They'll help keep down any stoats that venture onto our land. We're getting more rats, too, sheltering in the old buildings. I reckon the stoats are driving 'em to seek shelter in human habitation. The foxes will take care of the rats too, won't they, Isaac, boy?'

Still angry with himself, Greybeard made off along the perimeter again. Charley fell in beside him, sympathetically saying nothing. The fox walked between them, dainty with its brush held low.

The rest of the party stood about indecisively in midfield. Some quieted the cattle or stared at the scattered pieces of stoat; some went back toward the houses, whence others came out to join them in gossip. Their dark figures with white polls stood out against the background of fractured brick.

'They're half disappointed there was not some sort of excitement brewing,' Charley said. A peak of his springy hair stood out over his forehead. Once it had been the color of wheat; it had achieved whiteness so many seasons ago that its owner had come to look on white as its proper and predestined hue, and the wheaty tint had passed into his skin.

Charley's hair never dangled into his eyes, although it looked as if it would after a vigorous shake of the head. Vigorous shaking was not Charley's habit; his quality was of stone rather than fire, and in his bearing was evidence of how the years had tested his endurance. It was precisely an air of having withstood many ordeals that these two sturdy elders – in superficial appearance so unlike – had in common.

'Though people don't like trouble, they enjoy a distraction,' Charley said. 'Funny – that shot you fired started my gums aching.'

'It deafened me,' Greybeard admitted. 'I wonder if it roused the old men of the mill?'

He noticed that Charley glanced toward the mill to see if Mole or his henchman, Major Trouter, was coming to investigate.

Catching Greybeard's glance, Charley grinned rather foolishly and said, by way of something to say, 'Here comes old Jeff Pitt to see what all the fuss is.'

They had reached a small stream that wound its way across the cleared land. On its banks stood the stumps of some beeches that the villagers had cut down. From among these, the shaggy old figure of Pitt came. Over one shoulder he carried a stick from which hung the body of an animal. Though several of the villagers ventured some distance afield, Pitt was the only one who roved the wilds on his own. Sparcot was no prison for him. He was a morose and solitary man; he had no friends; and even in the society of the slightly mad, his reputation was for being mad. Certainly his face, as full of whorls as willow bark, was no reassurance of sanity; and his little eyes moved restlessly about, like a pair of fish trapped inside his skull.

'Did someone get shot then?' he asked. When Greybeard told him what had happened, Pitt grunted, as if convinced the truth was being concealed from him.

'With you firing away, you'll have the gnomes and wild things paying us attention,' he said.

'I'll deal with them when they appear.'

'The gnomes are coming, aren't they?' Pitt muttered; Greybeard's words had scarcely registered on him. He turned to gaze at the cold and leafless woods. 'They'll be here before so long, to take the place of children, you mark my words.'

'There are no gnomes around here, Jeff, or they'd have caught you long ago,' Charley said. 'What have you got on your stick?'

Eyeing Charley to judge his reaction, Pitt lowered the stick from his shoulder and displayed a fine dog otter, its body two feet long.

'He's a beauty, isn't he? Seen a lot of 'em about just lately. You can spot 'em more easily in the winter. Or perhaps they are just growing more plentiful in these parts.'

'Everything that can still multiply is doing so,' Greybeard said harshly.

'I'll sell you the next one I catch, Greybeard. I haven't forgotten what happened before we came to Sparcot. You can have the next one I catch. I've got my snares set along under the bank.'

'You're a regular old poacher, Jeff,' Charley said. 'Unlike the rest of us, you've never had to change your job.'

'What do you mean? Me never had to change my job? You're daft, Charley Samuels! I spent most of my life in a stinking machine-tool factory before the revolution and all that. Not that I wasn't always keen on nature – but I never reckoned I'd get it at such close quarters, as you might say.'

'You're a real old man of the woods now, anyhow.'

'Think I don't know you're laughing at me? I'm no fool, Charley, whatever you may think to yourself. But I reckon it's terrible the way us town people have been turned into sort of half-baked country bumpkins, don't you? What's there left to life? All of us in rags and tatters, full of worms and the toothache! Where's it all going to end, eh, I'd like to know? Where's it all going to end?' He turned to scrutinize the woods again.

'We're doing okay,' Greybeard said. It was his invariable answer to the invariable question. Charley also had his invariable answer.

'It's the Lord's plan, Jeff, and you don't do any good by worrying over it. We cannot say what He has in mind for us.'

'After all He's done to us this last fifty years,' Jeff said, 'I'm surprised you're still on speaking terms with Him.'

'It will end according to His will,' Charley said.

Pitt gathered up all the wrinkles of his face, spat, and passed on with his dead otter.

Where could it all end, Greybeard asked himself, except in humiliation and despair? He did not ask the question aloud. Though he liked Charley's optimism, he had no more patience than old Pitt with the too-easy answers of the belief that nourished that optimism.

They walked on. Charley began to discuss the various accounts of people who claimed to have seen gnomes and little men, in the woods, or on rooftops, or licking the teats of the cows. Greybeard answered automatically; old Pitt's fruitless question remained with him. Where was it all going to end? The question, like a bit of gristle in the mouth, was difficult to get rid of; yet increasingly he found himself chewing on it.

When they had walked right around the perimeter, they came again to the Thames at the western boundary, where it entered their land. They stopped and stared at the water.

Tugging, fretting, it moved about a countless number of obstacles on its course – oh yes, which it took as it has ever done! – to the sea. Even the assuaging power of water could not silence Greybeard's mind.

'How old are you, Charley?' he asked.

'I've given up counting the years. Don't look so glum! What's suddenly worrying you? You're a cheerful man, Greybeard; don't start fretting about the future. Look at that water – it'll get where it wants to go, but it isn't worrying.'

'I don't find any comfort in your analogy.'

'Don't you, now? Well, then, you should do.'

Greybeard thought how tiresome and colorless Charley was, but he answered patiently. 'You're a sensible man, Charley. Surely we must think ahead? This is getting to be a pensioner's planet. You can see the danger signs as well as I can. There are no young men and women anymore. The number of us capable of maintaining even the present low standard of living is declining year by year. We—'

'We can't do anything about it. Get that firmly into your mind and you'll feel better about the whole situation. The idea that man can do anything useful about his fate is an old idea. What do I mean? Yes, a fossil. It's something from another period . . . We can't do anything. We just get carried along, like the water in this river.'

'You read a lot of things into the river,' Greybeard said, half laughing. He kicked a stone into the water. A scuttling and a plop followed as some small creature – possibly a water rat, for they were on the increase again – dived for safety.

They stood silent, Charley's shoulders a little bent. When he spoke again, it was to quote poetry.

> ' "The woods decay, the woods decay and fall
> The vapors weep their burthen to the ground,
> Man comes and tills the field and lies beneath . . ." '

Between the heavy prosaic man reciting Tennyson and the woods leaning across the river lay an incongruity. Laboriously, Greybeard said, 'For a cheerful man, you know some depressing poetry.'

'That was what my father brought me up on. I've told you about that moldy little shop of his . . .' One of the characteristics of age was that all avenues of talk led backward in time.

'I'll leave you to get on with your patrol,' Charley said, but Greybeard clutched his arm. He had caught a noise upstream distinct from the sound of the water.

He moved forward to the water's edge and looked. Something was coming downstream, though overhanging foliage obscured details. Breaking into a trot, Greybeard made for the stone bridge, with Charley following at a fast walk behind him.

From the crown of the bridge they had a clear view upstream. A cumbersome boat was dipping into view only some eighty yards away. By its curved bow, he guessed it had once been a powered craft. Now it was being rowed and poled along by a number of whiteheads, while a sail hung slackly from the mast. Greybeard pulled his elder whistle from an inner pocket and blew on it two long blasts. He nodded to Charley and hurried over to the water mill, where Big Jim Mole lived.

Mole was already opening the door as Greybeard arrived. The years had yet to drain off all his natural ferocity. He was a stocky man with a fierce piggy face and a tangle of grey hair protruding from his ears as well as his skull. He seemed to survey Greybeard with nostrils as well as eyes.

'What's the racket about, Greybeard?' he asked.

Greybeard told him. Mole came out smartly, buttoning his ancient army greatcoat. Behind him came Major Trouter, a small man who limped badly and helped himself along with a stick. As he emerged into the grey daylight, he began to shout orders in his high squeaking voice. People were still hanging about after the false alarm. They began to fall in promptly, if raggedly, women as well as men, into a prearranged pattern of defense.

The population of Sparcot was a many-coated beast. The individuals that comprised it had sewn themselves into a wide variety of clothes and of rags that passed for clothes. Coats of carpet and skirts of curtain material were to be seen. Some of the men wore waistcoats cobbled from fox skins, clumsily cured; some of the women wore torn army greatcoats. Despite this variety, the general effect was colorless, and nobody stood out particularly against the neutral landscape. A universal distribution of sunken cheeks and grey hairs added to the impression of a sad uniformity.

Many an old mouth coughed out the winter's air. Many a back was bent, many a leg dragged. Sparcot was a citadel for the ailments: arthritis, lumbago, rheumatism, cataract, pneumonia, influenza, sciatica, dizziness. Chests, livers, backs, heads, caused much complaint, and the talk in an evening was mostly of the weather and toothache. For all that, the villagers responded spryly to the sound of the whistle.

Greybeard observed this with approval, even while wondering how necessary it was; he had helped Trouter organize the defense system before an increasing estrangement with Mole and Trouter had caused him to take a less prominent part in affairs.

The two long whistle blasts signified a threat by water. Though most travelers nowadays were peaceable (and paid toll before they passed under Sparcot Bridge), few of the villagers had forgotten the day, five or six years ago, when they had been threatened by a solitary river pirate armed with a flame-thrower. Flame-throwers seemed to be growing scarcer. Like petrol, machine guns, and ammunition, they were the produce of another century, and the relics of a vanished world. But anything arriving by water was the subject for a general stand-to.

Accordingly, a strongly armed party of villagers – many of them carried homemade bows and arrows – was gathered along the riverside by the time the strange boat came up. They crouched behind a low and broken wall, ready to attack or defend, a little extra excitement shaking through their veins.

The approaching boat traveled sideways to the stream. It was manned by as unruly a set of landlubbers as ever cast anchor. The oarsmen seemed as much concerned with keeping the boat from capsizing as with making progress forward; as it was, they appeared to be having little luck in either endeavor.

This lack of skill was due not only to the difficulty inherent in rowing a fifty-year-old, thirty-foot-long cruiser with a rotten hull, or to the presence aboard of fully a dozen people with their possessions. In the cockpit of the cruiser, struggling under the grip of four men, was a rebellious pack reindeer.

Although the beast had been pollarded – as the custom was since one of the last authoritarian governments had introduced the animal into the country some twenty years ago – it was strong enough to cause considerable damage; and reindeer were more valuable than men. They could be used for milking and meat production when cattle were scarce, and they made good transport animals; whereas men could only grow older.

Despite this distraction, one of the navigators, acting as lookout and standing in the bow of the boat, sighted the massed forces of Sparcot and called out a warning. She was a tall, dark woman, lean and hard, her dyed black hair knotted down under a scarf. When she called to the rowers, the promptness with which they rested on their oars showed how glad they were to do so. Someone squatting behind one of the baggages of clothing piled on deck passed the dark woman a white flag. She thrust it aloft and called out to the waiting villagers over the water.

'What's she yelling about?' John Meller asked. He was an old soldier who had once been a sort of batman to Mole, until the latter threw him out in exasperation as useless. Nearly ninety, Meller was as thin as a staff and as deaf as a stone, though his one remaining eye was still sharp.

The woman's voice came again, confident though it asked a favor. 'Let us come by in peace. We have no wish to harm you and no need to stop. Let us by, villagers!'

Greybeard bawled her message into Meller's ear. The white-head shook his scruffy skull and grinned to show he had not heard. 'Kill the men and rape the women! I'll take the dark-haired hussy in the front.'

Mole and Trouter came forward, shouting orders. They had evidently decided they were under no serious threat from the boat.

'We must stop them and inspect them,' Mole said. 'Get the pole out. Move there, you men! Let's have a parley with this shower and see who they are and what they want. They must have something we need.'

During this activity, Towin Thomas had come up beside Greybeard and Charley Samuels. In his efforts to see the boat clearly, he knotted his face into a grimace. He dug Greybeard in the ribs with a patched elbow.

'Hey, Greybeard, that reindeer wouldn't come amiss for the heavy work, would it?' he said, sucking the end of his cudgel reflectively. 'We could use it behind the plow, couldn't we?'

'We've no right to take it from them.'

'You're not getting religious ideas about that reindeer, are you? You're letting old Charley's line of talk get you down.'

'I never listen to a thing either Charley or you say,' Greybeard said.

A long pole that had done duty carrying telephone wires in the days when a telephone system existed was slid out across the water until its tip rested between two stones on the farther bank. The river narrowed here toward the ruined bridge farther downstream. This spot had afforded the villagers a useful revenue for years; their levies on rivergoing craft supplemented their less enthusiastic attempts at husbandry. It was the one inspired idea of Big Jim Mole's otherwise dull and oppressive reign. To reinforce the threat of the pole, the Sparcot men now showed themselves in strength along the bank. Mole ran forward brandishing a sword, calling for the strangers to heave to.

The tall, dark woman on the boat waved her fists at them.

'Respect the white flag of peace, you mangy bastards!' she yelled. 'Let us come by without spoiling. We're homeless as it is. We've nothing to spare for the likes of you.'

Her crew had less spirit than she. They shipped their oars and punting sticks and let the boat drift under the stone bridge until it rested against the pole. Elated to find such a defenseless prize, the villagers dragged it against the near bank with grapnels. The reindeer lifted its heavy head and blared its defiance; the dark woman shrieked her disgust.

'Hey there, you with the butcher's snout,' she cried, pointing at Mole. 'You listen to me, we're your neighbors. We only come from Grafton Lock. Is this how you treat your neighbors, you fusty old pirate?'

A murmur ran through the crowd on the bank. Jeff Pitt was the first to recognize the woman. She was known as Gypsy Joan, and her name was something of a legend even among villagers who had never ventured into her territory.

Jim Mole and Trouter stepped forward and bawled at her to be silent, but again she shouted them down.

'Get your hooks out of our side! We've got wounded aboard.'

'Shut your gab, woman, and come ashore! Then you won't get

hurt,' Mole said, holding his sword at a more businesslike angle. With the major at his side, he stepped toward the boat.

Already some of the villagers had attempted to board without orders. Emboldened by the general lack of resistance and keen to get their share of the spoils, they dashed forward, led by two of the women. One of the oarsmen, a hoary old fellow with a sou'wester and a yellow beard, fell into a panic and brought his oar down onto the foremost boarder's head. The woman went sprawling. A scuffle broke out immediately, despite bellowings from both parties to desist.

The cruiser rocked. The men holding the reindeer moved to protect themselves. Taking advantage of this distraction, the animal broke free of its captors. It clattered across the cabin roof, paused for a moment, and leaped overboard into the Thames. Swimming strongly, it headed downstream. A howl of dismay rose from the boat.

Two of the men who had been looking after the animal jumped in too, crying to the beast to come back. Then they were forced to look after themselves; one of them struggled to the bank, where there were hands to help him out. Down by the horns of the broken bridge the reindeer climbed ashore, its water-smooth coat heavy against its flanks. It stood on the far shore snorting and shaking its head from side to side, as if troubled by water in its ears. Then it turned and disappeared into a clump of willows.

The second man who jumped in was less successful. He could not reach either bank. The current caught him, sweeping him through the bridge, across its submerged remains, over the weir. His thin cry rose. An arm was flung up amid spray; then there was only the roar of green and white water.

This incident dampened the struggles at the boat, so that Mole and Trouter were able to question the crew. The two of them, standing by the cruiser's rail, saw that Gypsy Joan had not been bluffing when she spoke of carrying wounded. Down in what was once the saloon were huddled nine men and women, some of them nonagenarians by their parched and sunken-eyed aspect. Their poor clothes were torn, their faces and hands bloody. One woman with half her face missing seemed on the point of death, while all maintained a stunned silence more terrible than screaming.

'What's happened to them?' Mole asked uneasily.

'Stoats,' said Gypsy Joan. She and her companions were keen enough to tell their tale. The facts were simple enough. Her group was a small one, but they lived fairly well on a supply of fish from a flooded area next to Grafton Lock. They never kept guard, and had almost no defenses. At sunset on the previous day they had been attacked by a pack – or, some said, several packs – of stoats. In their fright, the community had taken to their boats and come away as quickly as possible. They predicted that unless deflected by some chance, the stoats would soon sweep into Sparcot.

'Why should they do that?' Trouter asked.

'Because they're hungry, man, why else?' Gypsy Joan said. 'They're multiplying like rabbits and sweeping the country looking for food. Eat anything, them devils will, fish or flesh or carrion. You lot would do well to move out of here.'

Mole looked around uneasily and said, 'Don't start spreading rumors here, woman. We can look after ourselves. We're not a rabble, we're properly organized. Get a move on. We'll let you go through unharmed, seeing that you've got trouble on your hands. Get off our territory as fast as you can.'

Joan looked prepared to argue the toss, but two of her leaders, fearful, pulled at her arm and urged that they move at once.

'We've another boat coming on behind,' one of these men said. 'It's full of our older unwounded people. We'd be obliged if you'd let them through without holding them up.'

Mole and Trouter stepped back, waving their arms. The mention of stoats had turned them into anxious men.

'On your way!' they shouted, waving their arms, and to their own men. 'Pull back the pole and let them get on their way.'

The pole came back. Joan and her crew pushed off from the bank, their ancient cruiser wobbling dangerously. But the contagion of their news had already been caught by those ashore. The word 'stoats' passed rapidly from mouth to mouth, and people began to run back to their houses, or toward the village boathouse.

Unlike their enemies the rats, stoats had not declined in numbers. During the last decade they had greatly increased, both in numbers and daring. Earlier in the year, old Reggy Foster had been attacked by one in the pasture and had had his throat bitten out. The stoats had extended an old occasional habit of theirs and now often hunted in packs, as they did at Grafton. At such times they showed no fear of human beings.

Knowing this, the villagers began to trample about the bank, pushing each other and shouting incoherently.

Jim Mole drew a revolver and leveled it at one of the fleeing backs.

'You can't do that!' Greybeard exclaimed, stepping forward with raised hand.

Mole brought the revolver down and pointed it at Greybeard.

'You can't shoot your own people,' Greybeard said firmly.

'Can't I?' Mole asked. His eyes were like blisters on his antique skin. Trouter said something, and Mole lifted his revolver again and fired it into the air. The villagers looked around in startlement; then most of them began running again. Mole laughed.

'Let 'em go,' he said. 'They'll only kill 'emselves.'

'Use reason with them,' Greybeard said, coming closer. 'They're frightened. Firing on them's no use. Speak to them.'

'Reason! Get out of my way, Greybeard. They're mad! They'll die. We're all going to die.'

'Are you going to let them go, Jim?' Trouter asked.

'You know the trouble with stoats as well as I do,' Mole said. 'If they attack in force, we've not got enough ammunition to spare to shoot them. We haven't got good enough bowmen to stop them with arrows. So the sensible thing is to get across the river in our boat and stay there till the little vermin have gone.'

'They can swim, you know,' Trouter said.

'I know they can swim. But why should they? They're after food, not fighting. We'll be safe on the other side of the river.' He was shivering. 'Can you imagine what a stoat attack must be like? You saw those people in that boat. Do you want that to happen to you?'

23

He was pale now, and looking anxiously about him, as if fearing that the stoats might be arriving already.

'We can shut ourselves in the barns and houses if they come,' Greybeard said. 'We can defend ourselves without deserting the village. We're safer staying put.'

Mole turned at him savagely, baring his teeth in a gaping snarl. 'How many stoat-proof buildings have we got? You know they'll come after the cattle if they're really hungry, and then they'll be all over us at the same time. Who gives orders here anyhow? Not you, Greybeard! Come on, Trouter, what are you waiting for? Let's get our boat brought out!'

Trouter looked momentarily disposed to argue. Instead, he turned and began shouting orders in his high-pitched voice. He and Mole brushed past Greybeard and ran toward the boathouse, calling, 'Keep calm, you bloody cripples, and we'll ferry you all across.'

The place took on the aspect of a well-stirred anthill. Greybeard noticed that Charley had vanished. The cruiser with the fugitives from Grafton was well down the river now and had negotiated the little weir safely. As Greybeard stood by the bridge and watched the chaos, Martha came up to him.

She was a dignified woman, of medium height, though she stooped a little as she clutched a blanket about her shoulders. Her face was slightly puddingy and pale, and wrinkled as if age had bound her skull tightly round the edges; yet because of her fine bone structure, she still retained something of the good looks of her youth, while the dark lashes that fringed her eyes still made them compelling.

She saw his faraway look.

'You can dream just as well at home,' she said.

He took her arm.

'I was wondering what lay at the end of the river. I'd give anything to see what life was like on the coast. Look at us here – we're so undignified! We're just a rabble.'

'Aren't you afraid of the stoats, Algy?'

'Of course I'm afraid of the stoats.' Then he smiled back at her,

24

a little wearily. 'And I'm tired of being afraid. Cooped up in this village for eleven years, we've all caught Mole's sickness.'

They turned back toward their house. For once, Sparcot was alive. They saw men small in the meadowland, with anxious gestures hurrying their few cows in to shelter. It was against just such emergencies, or in case of flood, that the barns had been built on stilts; when the cattle were driven into them and the doors shut, ramps could be removed, leaving the cattle safe above ground.

As they passed Annie Hunter's house, the desiccated figure of Willy Tallridge slipped from the side door. He was still buttoning his jacket, and paid them no attention as he hurried toward the river as fast as his eighty-year-old legs would take him. Annie's bright face, heavy with its usual complement of rouge and powder, appeared at her upper window. She waved a casual greeting to them.

'There's a stoat warning out, Annie,' Greybeard called. 'They are getting ready to ferry people across the river.'

'Thanks for the warning, darling, but I'll lock myself in here.'

'You have to hand it to Annie, she's game,' Greybeard said.

'Gamy too, I hear,' Martha said dryly. 'Do you realize, Algy, that she's about twenty years older than I? Poor old Annie, what a fate – to be the oldest professional!'

He was searching the tousled meadow, looking despite himself for brown squibs of life riding through the grass, but he smiled at Martha's joke. Occasionally a remark of hers could bring back a whole world to him, the old world of brittle remarks made at parties where alcohol and nicotine had been ritualistically consumed. He loved her for the best of reasons, because she was herself.

'Funny thing,' he said. 'You're the only person left in Sparcot who still makes conversation for its own sake. Now go home like a good girl and pack a few essential belongings. Shut yourself in, and I'll be along in ten minutes. I ought to help the men with the cattle.'

'Algy, I'm nervous. Do we have to pack just to go across the river? What's happening?'

25

Suddenly his face was hard. 'Do what I ask you, Martha. We aren't going across the river; we're going down it. We're leaving Sparcot.'

Before she could say more, he walked away. She also turned, walking deliberately down the hollow-cheeked street, and in at her door, into the dark little house. She did it as a positive act. The trepidation that had filled her on hearing her husband's words did not last; now, as she looked about her at walls from which the paper had peeled and at ceilings showing their dirty bare ribs, she whispered a wish that he might mean what he had said.

But leave Sparcot? The world had dwindled until for her it was only Sparcot . . .

As Greybeard went toward the stilted barn, a fight broke out farther down the street. Two groups of people carting belongings down to the river's edge had collided; they had lapsed into the weak rages that were such a feature of life in the village. The result would be a broken bone, shock, confinement to bed, pneumonia, and another mound in the beggarly greedy graveyard under the fir trees, where the soil was sandy and yielded easily to the spade.

Greybeard had often acted as peacemaker in such disputes. Now he turned away, and made for the cattle. They were as valuable – it had to be faced – as the rabble. The cattle went protestingly up the ramp into the barn. George Swinton, a one-armed old heathen who had killed two men in the Westminster Marches of 2008, darted among them like a fury, hurting them all he could with voice and stick.

A noise like the falling of stricken timber stopped them. Two of the barn's wooden legs split to ground level. One of the knot of men present called a word of warning. Before it was through his lips, the barn began to settle. Splinters of wood showed like teeth as joists gave. The barn toppled. It slid sideways, rocked, and collapsed in a shower of ruptured planks. Cattle stampeded from the wreckage, or lay beneath it.

'To hell with this! Let's get ourselves in the boats,' George Swinton said, pushing past Greybeard. And none of the others cared more than he. Flinging aside their sticks, they jostled after him. Greybeard stood where he was as they rushed past: the human race, he thought, sinned against as well as sinning.

Stooping, he helped a heifer free herself from under a fallen beam. She cantered away to the grazing land. She would have to take her chance when and if the stoats came.

As he turned back toward his house, a shot – it sounded like Mole's revolver – came from the direction of the stone bridge. It was echoed by another. Starlings clattered up from the roof-tops and soared for safety in the trees across the river. Greybeard quickened his pace, doubled through the straggling plot that was the garden of his house, and peered around the corner of it.

By the bridge, a group of villagers was struggling. A low afternoon mist tinted the scene, and the towering trees behind dwarfed it, but through a gap in a collapsing garden wall Greybeard had a clear enough view of what was going on.

The second boat from Grafton floated down the river just as the Sparcot boat was launching itself across stream. It was laden with a motley collection of whiteheads, most of whom were now waving their arms with gestures that distance rendered puppet-like. The Sparcot boat was heavily overloaded with the more aggressive members of the community, who had insisted on being on the first ferry trip. Through imcompetence and stupidity on both sides, the boats collided.

Jim Mole stood on the bridge, pointing his revolver down into the melee. Whether or not he had hit anyone with his first two shots it was impossible for Greybeard to see. As he strained his eyes, Martha came up beside him.

'Mole ever the bad leader!' Greybeard exclaimed. 'He's brutal enough, but he has no sense of how to restore discipline – or if he had, he's in his dotage now and has forgotten. Firing at people in the boats can only make matters worse.'

Someone was shouting hoarsely to get the boat to the bank. Nobody obeyed, and abandoning all discipline, the two crews fought each other. Senile anger had overwhelmed them again. The Grafton boat, a capacious old motor launch, tipped danger-ously as the villagers piled in upon its unlucky occupants. To add

27

to the clamor, others were running up and down the bank, crying advice or threats.

'We're all mad,' Martha said. 'And our bag is packed.'

He flashed her a brief look of love.

With three overlapping splashes, three ancient Graftonites fell or were knocked overboard into the water. Evidently there was some half-formed scheme to appropriate their boat for use as a second ferry; but as the two craft drifted downstream, the motor launch capsized.

White heads bobbed amid white water. A great stupid outcry went up from the bank. Mole fired his revolver into the confusion.

'Damn them all to hell!' Greybeard said. 'These moments of unreason – they overcome people so easily. You know that that packman who was through here last week claimed that the people of Stamford had set fire to their houses without cause. And the population of Burford cleared out overnight because they thought the place had been taken over by gnomes! Gnomes – old Jeff Pitt has gnomes on his brain! Then there are all these reports of mass suicides. Perhaps this will be the end – general madness. Perhaps we're witnessing the end!'

On the stage of the world it was rapidly growing darker. The average age of the population already stood high in the seventies. Each succeeding year saw it rise higher. In a few more years . . . An emotion not unlike exhilaration filled Greybeard, a sort of wonderment to think he might be present at the end of the world. No: at the end of humankind. The world would go on; man might die, but the earth still yielded up its abundance.

They went back into the house. A suitcase – incongruous item in pigskin that had made a journey down the years to a ruined world – stood on the dry side of the hall.

He looked around him, looked around the room at the furniture they had salvaged from other houses, at Martha's roughly drawn calendar on one wall, with its year, 2029, written in red, at the fern she grew in an old pot. Eleven years since they arrived here from Cowley with Pitt, eleven years of padding around the perimeter to keep the world out.

'Let's go,' he said, adding as an afterthought, 'do you mind leaving, Martha?'

'I don't know what I'm letting myself in for, do I? You'd better just take me along.'

'At least there's a measure of safety here. I don't know what I'm letting you in for.'

'No weakness now, Mr Greybeard.' On impulse, she added, 'May I get Charley Samuels if he is in? He'd miss us most. He ought to come with us.'

He nodded, reluctant to have anyone share his plan, yet reluctant to say no to Martha. She was gone. He stood there, heavy, feeling the weight of the past. Yes, Charley ought to come with them, and not only because the two of them had fought side by side almost thirty years ago. That old battle brought back no emotion; because it belonged to a different age, it cauterized feeling. The young soldier involved in that conflict was a different being from the man standing in this destitute room; he even went by a different name.

A log still smoldered in the grate; but in the hall and on the stairs, which creaked in the long nights as if gnomes were more reality than legend, the smell of damp was as thick as twilight. They would leave this dwelling, and soon it would all decompose like a man's body, into its separate glues and dusts.

Now he could understand why people set fire to their own homes. Fire was clean; cleanliness was a principle that man had otherwise lost. An angry pleasure roused in him at the thought of moving on, though as ever he showed little of what he felt.

He went briskly to the front door. Martha was stepping over the bricks that marked the old dividing line between their garden and the next. With her was Charley Samuels, his muffler of grey wool around his head and throat, his coat tied tight, a pack on his back, the fox Isaac straining at its leash. His face was the scaly yellow color of a boiled fowl, but he looked resolute enough. He came up to Greybeard and gripped his hand. Frosty tears stood in his eyes.

Anxious to avoid an emotional scene, Greybeard said, 'We need you with us, Charley, to deliver sermons at us.'

29

But Charley only shook his hand the harder.

'I was just packing. I'm your man, Greybeard. I saw that criminal sinner Mole shoot poor old Betty from the bridge. His day will dawn, his day will dawn.' His words came thickly. 'I vowed on that instant that I'd dwell no more in the tents of the unrighteous.'

Greybeard thought of old Betty, nodding over the guardroom fire so recently; by now her stew would be spoiled.

The fox whined and pranced with impatience.

'Isaac seems to agree with you,' Greybeard said, with something of his wife's attempt at humor. 'Let's go, then, while everyone's attention is distracted.'

'It won't be the first time we've worked together,' Charley said.

Nodding in agreement, Greybeard turned back into the hall; he did not particularly want any sentimentalizing from old Charley.

He picked up the suitcase his wife had packed. Deliberately, he left the front door of their house open. Martha shut it. She fell into step behind him, with Charley and the dog-fox. They walked down the relapsed road eastward, and out into the fields. They marched parallel with the riverbank, in the general direction of the horns of the old ruined bridge.

Greybeard took it at a good pace, deliberately not easing up for the older Charley's sake; Charley might as well see from the start that only in one aspect was this an escape; like every escape, it was also a new test. He drew up sharply when he saw two figures ahead, making for the same break in the thicket as he was.

The sighting was mutual. The figures were those of a man and a woman; the man knotted up his face, snaring his eyes between brow and cheek to see who followed him. Recognition too was mutual.

'Where are you off to, Towin, you old scrounger?' Greybeard asked when his party had caught up. He looked at the wispy old man, cuddling his cudgel and wrapped in a monstrous garment composed of blanket, animal hide, and portions of half a dozen old coats, and then regarded Towin's wife, Becky. Becky Thomas, in her mid-seventies, was possibly some ten years younger than her husband. A plump, birdlike woman, she carried two small sacks and was dressed in a garment as imposingly disorganized as her husband's. Her ascendancy over her husband was rarely disputed, and she spoke first now, her voice sharp. 'We might ask you lot the same thing. Where are you going?'

'By the looks of things, we're off on the same errand as you,' Towin said. 'We're getting out of this moldy concentration camp while we've still got legs on us.'

'That's why we're wearing these things we've got on,' Becky said. 'We've been preparing to leave for some time. This seemed a good opportunity, with old Mole and the major busy. But we'd never thought you might be hopping it, Greybeard. You're well in with the major, unlike us folk.'

Ignoring the jibe, Greybeard looked them over carefully.

'Towin's about right with his "concentration camp." But where are you thinking of going?'

'We thought we might sort of head south and pick up the old road toward the downs,' Becky said.

'You'd better join us,' Greybeard said curtly. 'We don't know what conditions we may meet. I've got a boat provisioned and hidden below the weir. Let's get moving.'

Hidden in the thicket, drawn up from the river's edge, sheltered in the remains of a small byre, lay a sixteen-foot clinker-built dinghy. Under Greybeard's instruction, they lifted it down into the water. Charley and Towin held it steady while he piled their few possessions into it. A previous owner had equipped the craft with a canopy, which they erected. The bows were decked in; the canopy covered most of the rest of the length. Three pairs of paddles lay on the planking of the boat, together with a rudder and tiller. These latter Greybeard fitted into place.

They wasted no time. Their nearness to the settlement was emphasized by the shouting they could still hear upstream.

Martha and Becky were helped into seats. The men climbed in; Greybeard let down the centerboard. Under his direction, Becky took the steering while the rest of them paddled – awkwardly and with a certain amount of guarded cursing from Towin, who took off his beloved broken wrist-watch before

31

getting down to work. They maneuvered themselves into mid-stream, the current took them, and they began to move.

Over against the farther bank, a patch of color bobbed. A body was trapped between two chunks of masonry carried down from the broken bridge. Its head was submerged beneath an ever-breaking wave from the little weir; but the orange, green, red, and yellow stripes of the shirt left them in no doubt that it was Sam Bulstow.

An hour later, when they were well clear of Sparcot, Martha began to sing. The song came quietly at first, then she gave her notes words.

> ' "Here shall he see
> No enemy
> But winter and rough weather . . ." '

'Towin, you're right with your remark about concentration camps,' she broke off to say. 'Everything at Sparcot was getting so worn and – overused, grimy and overused. Here, it could never be like that.' She indicated the growth drooping over the bank of the river.

'Where are you planning that we should go?' Charley asked Greybeard.

That was something he had never thought of fully. The dinghy had represented no more than his store of hope. But without cogitation he said, 'We will make our way down the Thames to the estuary. We can improvise ourselves a mast and a sail later, and get to the sea. Then we will see what the coast looks like.'

'It would be good to see the sea again,' Charley said soberly.

'I had a summer holiday at – what was the name of the place? It had a pier – Southend,' Towin said, snugging down into his collar as he paddled. 'I'd think it would be pretty sharpish cold at this time of the year – it was bad enough then. Do you think the pier could still be standing? Very pretty pier it was.'

'You daft thing, it will be tumbled down years ago,' his wife said.

The fox stood with its paws on the side of the boat, its sharp muzzle picking up scents from the bank. It looked ready for anything.

Nobody mentioned Scots or gnomes or stoats. Martha's brief song was still with them, and they dared be nothing but optimistic.

After half an hour, they were forced to rest. Towin was exhausted, and they all found the unaccustomed exercise tiring. Becky tried to take over the paddle from Martha, but she was too unskilled and impatient to wield it effectively. After a while Charley and Greybeard shared the work between them. The sound of blade meeting water hung heavily between the bushes that fringed the river, and mist began to veil the way before them. The two women huddled together on the seat by the tiller.

'I'm still a townswoman at heart,' Martha said. 'The lure of the countryside is strongest when I'm away from it. Unfortunately, the alternatives to the countryside are growing fewer. Where are we going to stop for the night, Algy?'

'We'll be pulling in as soon as we sight a good spot,' Greybeard said. 'We must get well away from Sparcot, but we don't want to overtake Gypsy Joan's crew from Grafton. Keep a good heart. I've some provisions stored in the boat, as well as what we've brought with us.'

'You're a deep one,' Towin said. 'You ought to have shot Jim Mole and taken over Sparcot, man. The people would have backed you.'

Greybeard did not reply.

The river unfolded itself with a series of bends, a cripple in a rack of sedges making its way eastward to liberty. When a bridge loomed ahead, they ceased paddling and drifted toward it. It was a good Georgian structure with a high arch and sound parapet; they snuggled into the bank on the upstream side of it. Greybeard took up his rifle.

'There should be habitation near a bridge,' he said. 'Stay here while I go and look around.'

'I'll come with you,' Charley said. 'Isaac can stay in the boat.'

He gave the anxious beast's leash to Martha, who fondled the fox to keep it quiet. The two men stepped out of the boat. They climbed up the bank and crouched among rotting plants.

Behind them, an overripe winter's sun blinked at them from among trees. Except for the sun, distorted by the bare trunks through which it shone, all else was told in tones of gray. A mist like a snowdrift hung low across the land. Before them, beyond the littered road that crossed the bridge, was a large building. It seemed to stand on top of the mist without touching the ground. Under a muddle of tall chimney stacks, it lay ancient and wicked and without life; the sun was reflected from an upper window-pane, endowing it with one lusterless eye. When nothing moved but a scatter or rooks winging overhead, the men heaved themselves up onto the road, and crossed to the cover of a hedgerow.

'Looks like an old public house,' Charley said. 'No sign of life about it. Deserted, I should say.'

As he spoke, they heard a cough from beyond the hedgerow.

They crouched, peering among the haws that hung there, scanning the field beyond. The field ran down to the river. Though it was drenched in mist, its freedom from weed and other growth indicated the presence of some sort of ruminative life. Their breath steamed in the brush as they scanned the place. The cough came again.

Greybeard pointed silently. In the corner of the field closest to the house, a shed stood. Clustered against one side of it were sheep, four or five of them.

'I thought sheep had died out long ago,' Charley muttered.

'It means there's someone in the house.'

'We don't want an argument with them. Let's pull farther upstream. We've an hour more daylight yet.'

'No, let's look over this place. They're isolated here; they may be glad of company, if we can convince them we're friendly.'

It was impossible to overcome the feeling that they might be covered by one or more guns from the silent building. Keeping their gaze on the vacant windows, they moved forward. In front of the house, with ample cover nearby, stood a car of dejected appearance. It had long since slumped into a posture of defeat, its tires sagged onto the ground. They ran to it, crouching behind it to observe the house. Still no sign of movement. They saw that most of the windows were boarded up.

'Is there anyone there?' Greybeard called.

No answer came.

As Charley had guessed, it was a public house. The old inn sign lay rotting nearby, and a name board had curled away from over the front door and lay across the well-worn steps. On a downstairs window they read the word ALES engraved there. Greybeard took in the details before calling again. Still there was no answer.

'We'll try around the back,' he said, rising.

'Don't you think we'd be all right in the boat for one night?'

'It will be cold later. Let's try the back.'

At the rear of the building, a track led from the back door toward the sheep field. Standing against the damp brickwork, Greybeard with his rifle at the ready, they called again. Nobody replied. Greybeard leaned forward and stared quickly into the nearest window. A man was sitting just inside, looking at him.

His heart gave a jerk. He fell back against Charley, his spine suddenly chill. When he had control of his nerves, he thrust his gun forward and rapped on a windowpane.

'We're friends,' he called. Silence.

'We're friends, you bastard!' This time he shattered the pane. The glass fell, then silence again. The two men looked at each other, their faces close and drawn.

'He must be sick or dead or something.' Charley said. Ducking past Greybeard and under the window, he reached the back door. With a shoulder against it, he turned the handle and charged in. Greybeard followed.

The face of the seated man was as grey as the daylight at which he stared with such fixity. His lips were ravaged and broken as if by a powerful poison. He sat upright in an old chair facing the sink. In his lap, still not entirely empty, lay a can of pesticide.

Charley crossed himself. 'May he rest in peace. There's provocation enough for anyone taking their own life these days.'

Greybeard took the can of pesticide and hurled it out into the bushes.

'Why did he kill himself? It can't have been for want of food, with his sheep still out there. We'll have to search the house, Charley. There may be someone else here.'

Upstairs, in a room into which the dying sun still gleamed, they found her. She was wasted to nothing under the blankets. In a receptacle by her bedside was a pool of something that might have been clotted soup. She had died of an illness, that much was obvious; that she had been dead longer than the man downstairs was also apparent, for the room was thick with the odor of death.

'Probably cancer,' Greybeard said. 'Her husband had no reason to go on living once she'd gone.' He had to break the silence, though breathing in the room was difficult. Pulling himself together, he said, 'Let's get them both outside and hidden in the bushes. Then we can move in here for the night.'

'We must give them burial, Algy.'

'It takes too much energy. Let's get settled in and be thankful we found a safe place so easily.'

'We may have been guided here to give these poor souls decent burial.'

Greybeard looked slantingly at the brown object rotting on the pillow.

'Why should the Almighty want that back, Charley?'

'You might as well ask why He wants us here.'

'By God, I often do ask it, Charley. Now, don't argue; let's get the corpses hidden where the women won't see them, and perhaps in the morning we'll think about burial.'

With as good a grace as he could muster, Charley helped in the dreary business. The best place of concealment turned out to be the shed in the field. They left the corpses there, with the sheep – there proved to be six of them – looking on. They saw to it that the sheep had water, wrenched open a couple of windows to air the house, and went to get the rest of the party. When the boat was safely moored, they all moved into the house.

Down in the cellars where barrels of beer had once stood, they found a smoked joint of meat hanging on a hook to be out of the reach of rats – of those there was plenty of evidence. They found a lamp that contained sheep fat and stank villainously, though it burned well. And Towin found five bottles of gin in a crate hidden in an unused grate.

'Just what I need for my rheumatics, then!' he said, opening a bottle. Placing his sharp nose over the mouth, he inhaled eagerly and then took a swig.

The women piled wood into a range in the kitchen and prepared a meal, disguising the high taste of the mutton with some of the herbs that lay in jars in the larder. Their warmth came back to them. Something like the elderly brother of a party spirit revived between them, and when they had eaten, they settled down for sleep in a cheerful frame of mind.

Martha and Greybeard bedded down in a small parlor on the ground floor. Since it was evident by many signs that the dead couple had not lived in a state of siege, Greybeard saw no reason for them to keep a guard; under Mole's regime they had grown obsessed with such precautions. After all, as every year went by, man should have less to fear from his fellow men, and this house seemed to be far from any other settlement . . .

All the same, he was not easy. He had said nothing to the others, but before leaving the boat he had felt in the lockers under the decking to get the two bayonets he had stored there; he wished to arm Towin and Charley with them; but the bayonets were missing, together with other things he had stowed there. The loss meant but one thing: somebody else had known of the whereabouts of his boat.

When Martha was asleep, he rose. The mutton-fat light still burned, though he had shielded its glow from the window. He stood, letting his mind become like a landscape into which strange thoughts could wander. He felt the frost gathering outside the house, and the silence, and turned away to close his mind again. The light stood on an old chest of drawers. He opened one of the drawers at random and looked in. It contained family trinkets, a broken clock, some pencil stubs, an ink bottle empty of ink. With a feeling of wrongdoing, he pocketed the two longest bits of pencil and opened the neighborhood drawer. Two photograph albums of an old-fashioned kind lay there. On top of them was the framed picture of a child.

37

The child was a boy of about six, a cheerful boy whose smile showed a gap in his teeth. He was holding a model railway engine and wore long tartan trousers. The print had faded somewhat. Probably it was a boyhood photograph of the man now stacked carelessly out in the sheep shed.

Sudden tears stood in Greybeard's eyes. Childhood itself lay in the rotting drawers of the world, a memory that could not stand permanently against time. Since that awful – accident, crime, disaster, in the last century, there had been no more babies born. There were no more children, no more boys like this. Nor, by now, were there any more adolescents, or young men, or young women with their proud style; not even the middle-aged were left now. Of the seven ages of man, little but the last remained.

'The fifties group are still pretty youthful,' Greybeard told himself, bracing his shoulders. And despite all the hardships, and the ghastliness that had gone before, there were plenty of spry sixty-year-olds about. Oh, it would take a few years yet before . . . But the fact remained that he was one of the youngest men on earth.

No, that wasn't quite true. Persistent rumor had it that an occasional couple was still bearing children; and in the past there had been cases . . . There had even been the pathetic instance of Eve, in the early days at Sparcot, who had borne a girl to Major Trouter and then disappeared. A month later, both she and her baby were found dead by a wood-gathering expedition . . . But apart from that, you never saw anyone young. The accident had been thorough. The old had inherited the earth.

Mortal flesh now wore only the Gothic shapes of age. Death stood impatiently over the land waiting to count his last few pilgrims.

And from all this, I do derive a terrible pleasure, Greybeard admitted, looking down at the impaled smile in the photograph. They could tear me apart before I'd confess, but somewhere it is there, a little stoaty thing that makes of a global disaster a personal triumph. Perhaps it's this fool's attitude I've always taken that any experience can be of value. Perhaps it's the reassurance to be derived from knowing that even if you live to be a hundred, you'll never be an old fogy: you'll always be the younger generation.

He beat out the silly thought that had grown in him so often. Yet it remained smoldering. His life had been lucky, wonderfully lucky, for all mankind's ill luck.

Not that mankind suffered alone. All mammals were nearly as hard hit. Dogs had ceased to whelp. The fox had almost died out; its habit of rearing its young in earths had doubtless contributed to its ultimate recovery – that and the abundance of food that came its way as man's grip on the land slackened. The domestic pig had died out even before the dogs, though perhaps as much because it was everywhere killed and eaten recklessly as because it failed to litter. The domestic cat and the horse proved as sterile as man; only its comparatively large number of offspring per litter had allowed the cat to survive. It was said to be multiplying in some districts again; peddlers visiting Sparcot spoke of plagues of feral cats here and there.

Bigger members of the cat tribe had also suffered. All over the world, the story in the early nineteen-eighties had been the same: the creatures of the world were incapable of reproduction. The earth – such was the apocalyptic nature of the event that it was easy even for an agnostic to think of it in biblical terms – the earth failed to bring forth its increase. Only the smaller creatures that sheltered in the earth itself had escaped wholly unscathed from that period when man had fallen victim of his own inventions.

Oh, it was an old tale now, and nearly half a century separated the milk teeth smiling in the photograph from the corrupt grin that let in frost out in the sheep shed.

Greybeard shut the drawer with a slam.

Something had disturbed the sheep. They were bleating in fright.

He had a superstitious picture of the dead walking, and blocked it off. Some sort of animal predator would be a more likely explanation of the disturbance. He went into the kitchen and peered through the window. The sky was lighter than he had expected. A chip of moon shone, giving frail shape to the nearby trees. Putting an ear to the draft pouring through the broken pane, Greybeard could hear the sheep trotting in their field. Frost glittered on the pinched sedges outside the door; as he looked at its tiny lost reflections, he heard the creak-crunch of footsteps moving across a stretch of grass. He raised his rifle. It was impossible to get out without making a noise opening the back door.

The footsteps came nearer; a man, all shadow, passed the window.

'Halt or I fire!' Greybeard called. Though the man had disappeared from his line of sight, he reckoned on the shock of discovery freezing him still.

'Is that you, Greybeard?' The voice came hollow from outside. 'Is that you, Greybeard? Keep your itchy finger off that trigger.'

Even as he recognized the voice, Martha came to his side, clutching her coat about her. He thrust the rifle into her hands.

'Hold this and keep me covered,' he whispered. Aloud, he said, 'Come in front of the window with your hands up.'

A man appeared in silhouette, his fingers stretched as if to rake the sky. He gave a cackling laugh. Martha swung the rifle to cover him. Greybeard flung open the door and motioned the man in, stepping back to let him pass. The old poacher, Jeff Pitt, walked into the kitchen and lowered his arms.

'You still want to buy that beaver, Greybeard?' he asked, grinning his old canine grin.

Greybeard took his gun and put an arm around Martha's frail shoulders. He kicked the door shut and surveyed Pitt unsmilingly.

'It must be you who stole the provisions from my boat. Why did you follow us? Have you a boat of your own?'

'I didn't swim, you know!' Pitt's gaze ran restlessly about the room as he spoke. 'I'm better at hiding my little canoe than you were! I've watched you for weeks, loading up your boat. There isn't much goes on at Sparcot I don't know about. So today, when you did your flit, I thought I'd chance running into the gnomes and come and see how you were all getting on.'

'As you see, we survive, and you nearly got yourself shot. What are you planning to do now you're here, Jeff?'

The old man blew on his fingers and moved over to the range, where some heat still lingered. As his custom was, he looked neither of them straight in the face.

'I thought I might come with you as far as Reading, if you were going that far. And if your good lady wife would have my company.'

'If you come with us, you must give any weapons you possess to my husband,' Martha said sharply.

Cocking an eyebrow to see if he surprised them, Pitt drew an old service revolver from his coat pocket. Deftly, he removed the shells from it and handed it across to Greybeard.

'Since you're so mad keen on my company, the pair of you,' he said, 'I'll give you some of my knowledge as well as my gun. Before we all settle down to a cosy night's rest, let's be smart and drive those sheep in here, out of harm's way. Don't you know what a bit of luck you've chanced on? Those sheep are worth a fortune apiece. Farther down river, at somewhere like Reading, we should be little kings on account of them – if we don't get knocked off, of course.'

Greybeard slipped the revolver into his pocket. He looked a long time at the wizened face before him. Pitt gave him a wet-chinned grin of reassurance.

'You get back into bed, sweet,' Greybeard said to Martha. 'We'll get the sheep. I'm sure Jeff has a good idea.'

She could see how much it went against the grain for him to acknowledge the worth of an idea he felt he should have thought of himself. She gave him a closed-eye look and went through into the other room as the men left the house. The mutton fat spluttered in the lamp. Wearily, as she lay down again on the improvised bed – it might have been midnight, but she guessed that in a hypothetical world of clocks it would be accounted not yet nine P.M. – the face of Jeff Pitt came before her.

It was a face that had been molded until it expressed age as much as personality; it had been undermined by the years, until with its wrinkled cheeks and ruined molars it became a common face, closely resembling, say, Towin Thomas's, and many another countenance that had survived the same storms. These old men, in a time bereft of proper medical and dental care, had taken on a

41

facial resemblance to other forms of life, to wolves, to apes, or to the bark of trees. They seemed, Martha thought, to merge increasingly with the landscape they inhabited.

It was difficult to recall the less raggle-taggle Jeff Pitt she had known when their party first established itself at Sparcot. Perhaps he had been less cocky then, under the fever of events. His teeth had been better, and he wore his army uniform. He had been a gunman, if an ineffectual one, not a poacher. Since then, how much he had changed!

But perhaps they had all changed in that period. It was eleven years, and the world had been a very different place.

2
Cowley

They had been lucky ever to get to Sparcot. During those last few days in Cowley, the factory suburb of Oxford, she had not thought they would escape at all. For that was the autumn of the dusty year 2018, when cholera lent its hand to the other troubles that plagued mankind.

Martha was almost a prisoner in the Cowley flat in which she and Greybeard – but in those days he was simply the forty-three-year-old Algernon Timberlane – had been forcibly installed.

They had driven to Oxford from London, after the death of Algy's mother. Their truck had been stopped on the borders of Oxfordshire; they found martial law prevailing, and a Commander Croucher in charge, with his headquarters in Cowley. Military police had escorted them to this flat; although they were given no choice in the matter, the premises proved to be satisfactory.

For all the trouble sweeping the country and the world, Martha's chief enemy was boredom. She sat doing endless jigsaws of farms at blossomtime, trappers in Canada, beaches at Acapulco, and listening to the drizzle of light music from her handbag radio; throughout the sweltering days she waited for Algy to return.

Few vehicles moved along the Iffley Road outside. Occasionally one would growl by with an engine note that she thought was familiar. She would jump up, often to stand staring out of the window for a long time after she realized her mistake.

Martha looked out on an unfamiliar city. She smiled to think how they had been buoyed with the spirit of adventure on the

43

drive down from London, laughing, and boasting of how young they felt, how they were ready for anything – yet already she was surfeited with jigsaws and worried about Algy's increasingly heavy drinking.

When they were in America, he drank a lot, but the drinking there with Jack Pilbeam, an eager companion, had a gaiety about it that was lacking now. Gaiety! The last few months in London had held none. The government enforced a strict curfew; Martha's father had disappeared into the night, presumably arrested without trial; and as the cholera spread, Patricia, Algy's feckless old mother, deserted by her third husband, had died in agony.

She ran her fingers over the windowsill. They came away dirty and she looked at them.

She laughed her curt laugh at an inner thought, and returned to the table. With an effort, she forced herself to go on building the sunlit beach of Acapulco.

The Cowley shops opened only in the afternoon. She was grateful for the diversion they offered. When she went into the street, she deliberately made herself unattractive, wore an old bonnet and pulled coarse stockings over her fine legs, despite the heat, for the soldiers had a rough way with women.

This afternoon, she noticed fewer uniforms about. Rumor had it that several platoons were being driven east, to guard against possible attack from London. Other rumor said the soldiers were confined to their barracks and dying like flies.

Standing in line by the white-tiled fishmonger's shop in the Cowley Road, Martha found that her secret fears accepted this latter rumor the more readily. The overheated air held a taste of death. She wore a handkerchief over her nose and mouth, as did most of the other women. Rumor of plague becomes most convincing when strained through dirty squares of fabric.

'I told my husband I'd rather he didn't join up,' the woman next to Martha told her. 'But you can't get Bill to listen if he don't want to. See, he used to work at the garage, but he reckons they'll lay him off sooner or later, so he reckons he'd be better in the army. I told him straight, I said, I've had enough of war if you

44

haven't, but he said, This is different from war, it's a case of every man for himself. You don't know what to do for the best, really, do you?'

As she trudged back to the fiat with her ration of dried and nameless fish, Martha echoed the woman's words.

She went and sat at the table, folded her arms on it, and rested her head on her arms. In that position, she let her thoughts ramble, waiting all the while for the sound of that precious truck which would herald Timberlane's return.

When finally she heard the truck outside, she went down to meet Timberlane. As he opened the door, she clung to him, but he pushed her off.

'I'm dirty, I'm foul, Martha,' he said. 'Don't touch me till I've washed and got this jacket off.'

'What's the matter? What's been happening?'

He caught the overwrought note in her voice.

'They're dying, you know. People, everywhere.'

'I know they're dying.'

'Well, it's getting worse. It's spread from London. They're dying in the streets now, and not getting shifted. The army's doing what it can, but the troops are no more immune to the infection than anyone else.'

'The army! You mean Croucher's men!'

'You could have worse men ruling the Midlands than Croucher. He's keeping order. He understands the necessity for running some sort of public service; he's got hygiene men out. Nobody could do more.'

'You know he's a murderer. Algy, how can you speak well of him?'

They went upstairs. Timberlane flung his jacket into a corner.

He sat down with a glass and a bottle of gin. He added a little water, and began to sip at it steadily. His face was heavy; the set of his mouth and eyes gave him a brooding look. Beads of sweat stood on his bald head.

'I don't want to talk about it,' he said. His voice was tired and stony: Martha felt her own slip into the same cast. The shabby

45

room was set solid with their discomfort. A fly buzzed fitfully against the windowpane.

'What do you want to talk about?'

'For God's sake, Martha, I don't want to talk about anything. I'm sick of the stink of death and fear, and people talking of nothing but death and fear. I've been going around with my recorder all day, doing my bloody stuff for DOUCH(E). I just want to drink myself into a stupor.'

Although she had compassion for him, she would not let him see it.

'Algy – your day has been no worse than mine. I've spent all day sitting here doing these jigsaw puzzles till I could scream. I've spoken to no one but a woman at the fish shop. For the rest of the time the door has been locked and bolted as you instructed. Am I just expected to sit here in silence while you get drunk?'

'Not by me you're not. You haven't got that amount of control over your tongue.'

She went over to the window, her back to him. She thought: I am not sick; I am vital in my senses; I can still give a man all he wants; I am Martha Timberlane, born Martha Broughton, forty-three years of age. She heard his glass shatter in a far corner.

'Martha, I'm sorry. Murdering, getting drunk, dying, living, they're all reduced to the same dead level . . .'

Martha made no answer. With an old magazine she crushed the fly buzzing against the window. She closed her eyes to feel how hot her eyelids were. At the table, Timberlane went on talking.

'I'll get over it, but to see my poor dear silly mother panting out her last – well, I'm full of sentimental stuff I've not felt for years, recalling how I loved her as a kid. Ah . . . Get me another glass, love – get two. Let's finish this gin. Sod the whole rotten system. How much longer are people going to be able to take this?'

'This what?' she asked, without turning around.

'This lack of children. This sterility. This creeping paralysis. What else do you think I mean?'

'I'm sorry, I've got a headache.' She wanted his sympathy, not his speeches, but she could see that something had upset him, that

46

he was going to have to talk, and that the gin was there to help him talk. She got him another glass.

'What I'm saying is, Martha, that it's finally sinking in on people that the human race is not going to produce any more young. Those little bawling bundles we used to see outside shops in prams are gone for good. Those little girls that used to play with dolls and empty cereal packets are things of the past. The knot of teen-agers standing on corners or bellowing by on motorbikes have had it forever. They aren't coming back. Nor are we ever going to see a nice fresh young twenty-year-old girl pass us like a blessing in the street, with her little bum and tits like a banner. Where are all your young sportsmen? Remember the cricket teams, Martha? Football, eh? What about the romantic leads of television and the cinema? Where are the pop singers of yester-year?'

'Stop it, Algy. I know we're all sterile as well as you do. We knew that when we got married, seventeen years ago. I don't want to hear it once more.'

When he spoke, his voice was so changed that she turned and looked at him.

'Don't think I want to hear it again, either. But you see how every day reveals the wretched truth all over again. The misery always comes hot and new. We're over forty now, and there's scarcely anyone younger than we. You only have to walk through Oxford to see how old and dusty the world is getting. And it's now that youth is passing that the lack of replenishment is really being felt – in the marrow.'

She gave him another measure of gin, and set a glass down on the table for herself. He looked up at her with a wry smile.

'Perhaps it's the death of my mother makes me talk like this. I'm sorry, Martha, particularly when we don't know what's become of your father. All the while I've been so busy living my life, Mother's been living hers. You know what her life's been like! She fell in love with three useless men, my father, Keith Barratt, and this Irishman, poor woman! Somehow I feel we should have done more to help her.'

47

'You know she enjoyed herself in her own way. We've said all this before.'

. He wiped his brow and head on a handkerchief; his smile was more relaxed.

'Maybe that's what happens when the mainspring of the world snaps: everyone is doomed forever to think and say what they thought and said yesterday.'

'We don't have to despair, Algy. We've survived years of war, we've come through waves of puritanism and promiscuity. We've got away from London, where they are in for real trouble, now that the last authoritarian government has broken down. I know Cowley isn't any bed of roses, but Croucher is only a local phenomenon; if we can survive him, things may get better, become more settled. Then we can get somewhere permanent to live.'

'I know, my love. We seem to be going through an interim period. The trouble is, there have been a number of interim periods already, and there will be more. I can't see how stability can ever be achieved again. There's just a road leading downhill.'

'We don't have to be involved in politics. DOUCH(E) doesn't require you to mix in politics to make your reports. We can just find somewhere quiet and reasonably safe for ourselves, surely?'

He laughed. He stood up and looked genuinely amused. Then he stroked her hair with its grey and brown streaks and drew his chair closer.

'Martha, I'm mad about you still! It's a national failing to think of politics as something that goes on in Parliament. It isn't; it's something that goes on inside us. Look, love, the United National Government has broken apart, and thank God for it. But at least its martial law kept things going and wheels turning. Now it has collapsed, millions of people are saying, "I have nothing to save for, no sons, no daughters. Why should I work?" and they've stopped work. Others may have wanted to work, but you can't carry on industry like that. Disorganize one part effectively, and it all grinds to a halt. The factories of Britain stand empty. We're making nothing to export. You think America and the Commonwealth and the other countries are going to go on sending us food free? Of course not, especially when a lot of them are harder hit than we are! I know food is short at present, but next year, believe me, there's going to be real famine. Your safe place won't exist then, Martha. In fact, there may only be one safe place.'

'Abroad?'

'I meant working for Croucher.'

She turned away frowning, not wishing to voice again her distrust of the local dictator.

'I've got a headache, Algy. I shouldn't be drinking this gin. I think I must go and lie down.'

He took her wrist.

'Listen to me, Martha. I know I'm a devil to live with just now, and I know you don't want to sleep with me just now, but don't stop listening to me or the last line of communication will be cut. We may be the final generation, but life's still precious. I don't want us to starve. I have made an appointment to see Commander Croucher tomorrow. I'm offering to cooperate.'

'What?'

'Why not?'

'Why not? How many people did he massacre in the center of Oxford last week? Over sixty, wasn't it? And the bodies left lying there for twenty-four hours so that people could count and make sure. And you—'

'Croucher represents law and order, Martha.'

'Madness and disorder!'

'No. The commander represents as much law and order as we have any right to expect, considering the horrible outrage we have committed on ourselves. There's a military government in the Home Counties centered on London, and one of the local gentry has set up a paternalistic sort of community covering most of Devon. Apart from them and Croucher, the country is slipping rapidly into anarchy. Have you thought what it must be like farther up in the Midlands, and in the North, in the industrial areas? What do you think is going to happen up there?'

'They'll find their own little Crouchers soon enough.'

'Right! And what will their little Crouchers do? March 'em down south as fast as they can.'

'And risk the cholera?'

'I only hope the cholera stops them! Quite honestly, Martha, I hope this plague wipes out most of the population. If it doesn't stop the North, then Croucher had better be strong, because he'll have to be the one to stop them. Have another gin. Here's to Bonnie Prince Croucher! We'll have to defend a line across the Cotswolds from Cheltenham to Buckingham. We should be building our defenses tomorrow. It would keep Croucher's troops busy *and* out of the center of population where they can spread infection. He's got too many soldiers; the men join his army rather than work in the car factories. They should be put on defense at once. I shall tell Croucher when I see him . . .'

She lurched away from the table and went to swill her face under the cold tap. Without having dried it, she rested by the open window, looking at the evening sun trapped in the shoddy suburban street.

'Croucher will be too busy defending himself from the hooligans in London to guard the north,' she said. She didn't know what either of them was saying. The world was no longer the one into which she had been born; nor was it even the one in which – ah, but they had been young and innocent then! – they had married; for that ceremony was distant in space as well as time, in a Washington they idealized because they had then been idealists, where they had talked a lot of being faithful and being strong . . . . No, they were all mad. Algy was right when he said they had committed a horrible outrage on themselves. She thought about the expression as she stared into the street, no longer listening as Timberlane embarked on one of the long speeches he now liked to make.

Not for the first time, she reflected on how people had grown fond of making rambling monologues; her father had fallen into the habit in recent years. In a vague way, she could analyze the reasons for it: universal doubt, universal guilt. In her own mind the same monologue rarely stopped, though she guarded her speech. Everyone spoke endlessly to imaginary listeners. Perhaps they were all the same imaginary listener.

It was really the generation before hers that was most to blame, the people who were grown-up when she was born, the millions who were adults during the nineteen-sixties and seventies. They had known all about war and destruction and nuclear power and radiation and death – it was all second nature to them. But they never renounced it. They were like savages who had to go through some fearful initiation rite. Yes, that was it, an initiation rite, and if they had come through it, then perhaps they might have grown up into brave and wise adults. But the ceremony had gone wrong. Too frenzied by far, it had not stopped short at circumcision; the whole organ had been lopped off. Though they wept and repented, the outrage had been committed: all they could do was hop about with their deformity, alternately boasting about and bemoaning it.

Through her misery, peering between the seams of her headache, she saw a windrush with Croucher's yellow X on its sides swing around the corner and prowl down the street. Windrushes were the locally manufactured variety of hovercraft, a family-sized model now largely appropriated by the military. A man in uniform craned his neck out of the blister, staring at house numbers as he glided down the street. When it drew level with the Timberlane flat, the machine stopped and lowered itself to the ground in a dying roar of engines.

Frightened, Martha summoned Timberlane over to the window. There were two men in the vehicle, both wearing the yellow X on their tunics. One climbed out and walked across the street.

'We've nothing to fear,' Timberlane said. He felt in his pocket for the little 7.7 mm. automatic with which DOUCH(E) had armed him. 'Lock yourself in the kitchen, love, just in case there's trouble. Keep quiet.'

'What do they want, do you think?'

There was a heavy knocking on the door.

'Here, take the gin bottle,' he said, giving her a taut grin. The bottle passed between them, all there was time to exchange. He patted her behind as he pushed her into the kitchen. The knocking was repeated before he could get down to the door.

A corporal was standing there; his mate leaned from the blister of the windrush, half whistling and rubbing his lower lip on the protruding snout of his rifle.

'Timberlane? Algernon Timberlane? You're wanted up at the barracks.'

The corporal was an undersized man with a sharp jaw and patches of dark skin under his eyes. He would be only in his early fifties – youngish for these days. His uniform was clean and pressed, and he kept one hand near the revolver at his belt.

'Who wants me? I was just going to have my supper.'

'Commander Croucher wants you, if you're Timberlane. Better hop in the windrush with us.' The corporal had a big nose, which he rubbed now in a furtive fashion as he summed up Timberlane.

'I have an appointment with the commander tomorrow.'

'You've got an appointment with him this evening, mate. I don't want any argument.'

There seemed no point in arguing. As he turned to shut the door behind him, Martha appeared. She spoke direct to the guard.

'I'm Mrs Timberlane. Will you take me along too?'

She was an attractive woman, with a rich line to her, and a certain frankness about her eye that made her appear younger than she was. The corporal looked her over with approval.

'They don't make 'em like you anymore, lady. Hop up with your husband.'

She silenced Timberlane's attempt at protest by hurrying ahead to climb into the windrush. Impatiently, she shook off the corporal's hand and swung herself up without aid, ignoring the man's swift, instinctive glance at the thigh she showed.

They toured by an unnecessarily long way to the Victorian pseudocastle that was Croucher's military headquarters. On the first part of the way she thought in anguish to herself, Isn't this one of the archetypal situations of the last century – and the twentieth really was the Last Century – the unexpected peremptory knocking at the door, and the going to find someone there in uniform waiting to take you off somewhere, for reasons unknown? Who invented the situation, that it should be repeated so often? Perhaps this is what happens after an outrage – unable to regenerate, you just have to go on repeating yourself. She longed to say some of this aloud; she was generalizing in the rather pretentious way her father had done, and generalizing is a form of relief that gains its maximum effect from being uttered aloud; but a look at Timberlane's face silenced her. She could see he was excited.

She saw the boy in his face as well as the old man.

Men! she thought. There was the seat of the whole sickness. They invented these situations. They needed them – torturer or tortured, they needed them. Friend or enemy, they were united in an algolagnia beyond woman's cure or understanding.

The instant that imperious knocking had sounded at the door, their hated little flat had turned into a place of refuge; the dripping kitchen tap, whistling into its chipped basin, had turned into a symbol of home, the littered pieces of jigsaw a sign of a vast intellectual freedom. She had whispered a prayer for a safe return to the fragmented beach of Acapulco as she hastened down to join her husband.

Now they moved three feet above ground level, and she tasted the chemistries of tension in her bloodstream.

In the September heat the city slept. But the patient was uneasy in its slumber. Old cartons and newspaper heaved in the gutters. A battery-powered convertible lay with its nose nestling in a shattered shop front. At open windows, people lolled, heavy sunlight filling their gasping mouths. The smell of the patient showed that blood poisoning had set in.

Before they had gone far, their expectation of seeing a corpse was satisfied, doubly. A man and woman lay together in unlikely attitudes on the parched grass of St Clement's roundabout. A group of starlings fluttered around their shoulders.

Timberlane put an arm about Martha and whispered to her as he had when she was a younger woman.

'Things will be a lot worse before they're better,' the beak-nosed corporal said to nobody in particular. 'I don't know what'll happen to the world, I'm sure.' Their passage sent a wave of dust washing over the houses.

At the barracks they sailed through the entrance gate and disembarked. The corporal marched them toward a distant arch-way. The heat in the central square lay thick; they pressed through it, in at a door, along a corridor, and up into cooler quarters. The corporal conferred with another man, who summoned them into a farther room, where a collection of hot and weary people waited on benches, several of them wearing cholera masks.

They sat there for half an hour before being summoned. Finally they were led into a spacious room furnished in a heavy way that suggested it had once been used as an officers' mess. Occupying one half of it were a mahogany table and three trestle tables. Men sat at these tables, several of them with maps and papers before them; only the man at the mahogany table had nothing but a notebook before him; he was the only man who did not seem idle. The man at the mahogany table was Commander Peter Croucher.

He looked solid, fleshy, and hard. His face was big and unbeautiful, but it was the face of neither a fool nor a brute. His sparse grey hair was brushed straight back in furrows; his suit was neat, his whole aspect businesslike. He was little more than ten years older than Timberlane; fifty-three or four, say. He looked at the Timberlanes with a tired but appraising look.

Martha knew his reputation. They had heard of the man even before the waves of violence had forced them to leave London. Oxford's major industry was the production of cars and GEMs (Ground Effect Machines), particularly the windrush. Croucher had been personnel manager at the largest factory. The United National Government had made him Deputy District Officer for Oxfordshire. On the collapse of the government, the district officer had been found dead in mysterious circumstances, and Croucher had taken over the old controls, drawing them in tighter.

He spoke without moving. He said, 'No invitation was issued for you being here, Mrs Timberlane.'

'I go everywhere with my husband, Commander.'

'Not if I say not. Guard!'

'Sir.' The corporal marched forward with a parody of army drill.

'It was an infringement, you bringing this woman in here,

Corporal Pitt. Supervise her immediate removal at once. She can wait outside.'

Martha started to protest. Timberlane silenced her, pressing her hand, and she allowed herself to be led away. Croucher got up and came around his table.

'Timberlane, you're the only DOUCH(E) man in the territory under my control. Dissuade your mind that my motives toward you are ulterior. That's the reverse of the truth. I want you on my side.'

'I shall be on your side if you treat my wife properly.'

Croucher gestured to show how poorly he regarded the remark. 'What can you offer me in any way advantageous to me?' he asked. The involved semiliteracy of his speech added to his menace, in Greybeard's estimation.

'I'm well informed, Commander. I have an idea that you must defend Oxfordshire and Gloucestershire from the Midlands and the North, if your forces are strong enough. If you could lend me a map . . .'

Croucher held up a hand.

'Look, I'd better cut you down to size a bit, my friend. Just for the record, I don't need any half-baked intellectual ideas from self-styled pundits like yourself. See these men here, sitting at these tables? They have the mutual benefit of performing my thinking for me, thus utilizing advantageously one of the advantages of having a terra firma in a university city like Oxford. The old Town versus Gown battle has been fought and decided, Mr Timberlane, as you'd know if you hadn't been knocking about in London for so long. I decided and implemented it. I rule all Oxford for the benefit of one and all. These blokes are the cream of the colleges that you are seeing here, all very high-flown intellects. See that gink at the end, with the shaky hands and the cracked specs? He's the University Chichele Professor for War, Harold Biggs. Down there, that's Sir Maurice Rigg, one of the all-time greats at history, I'm told. So kindly infer that I'm asking you about DOUCH(E), not how you'd run operations if you were in my shoes.'

'Not doubt one of your intellectual ginks can tell you about DOUCH(E).'

'No, they can't. That's why it was compulsory that you come here. You see, all the data I've got about DOUCH(E) is that it's some sort of an intelligence unit with its headquarters in London. London organizations are suspect with me just now, for obvious reasons. Unless you wish to be mistaken for a spy, et cetera, perhaps you ought to set my mind in abeyance about what you intend doing here.'

'I think you misunderstand my attitude, sir. I wish to inform you about DOUCH(E); I am no spy. Although I was brought to you like a captive, I had an appointment through the patrols to see you tomorrow and offer you what help I could.'

'I am not your dentist. You do not make an appointment with me – you crave an audience.' He rapped his knuckles on the table. 'I cavil at your phony attitude! Get wise to the reality of the situation – I can have you shot anywhere in the curriculum if I find you unconstructive.'

Timberlane said nothing to that. In a more reasonable voice, Croucher said, 'Now then, let's have the lowdown what exactly DOUCH(E) is and how it functions.'

'It is simply an academic unit, sir, although with more power behind it than academic units usually have. Can I explain in private? The nature of the unit's work is confidential.'

Croucher looked at him with raised eyebrows, turned and surveyed the jaded men at the trestle tables, flicked an eye at two guards.

'I should not cavil at a change of scenery. I work long hours.'

They moved into the next room. The guards came too. Although the room was small and hot, it was a relief to get away from the idle faces sitting by the tables. When Croucher gestured to one of the guards, the man opened a window.

'What exactly is this "confidential work," precisely?' Croucher asked.

'It's a job of documentation,' Timberlane said. 'As you know, it was in 1981 that the Accident occurred which sterilized man and most of the higher mammals. The Americans were first to realize the full implications of what was happening. In the nineties, various foundations collaborated in setting up DOUCH in Washington. There it was decided that in view of the unprecedented global conditions, a special emergency study group should be established. This group was to be equipped to function for seventy-five years, whether man eventually recovered his ability to procreate or whether he failed to do so and became extinct. Members were enlisted from all over the world and trained to interpret their country's agonies objectively and record them permanently.

'The group was called Documentation of Universal Contemporary History. The bracketed E means I'm one of the English wing. I joined the organization early, and was trained in Washington in '01. Back in those days, the organization tried to be as pessimistic as possible. Thanks to their realistic thinking, we can go on functioning as individuals even when national and international contacts have broken down.'

'As has now happened. The President was eliminated by a bunch of crooks. The United States is in a state of anarchy. You know that?'

'Britain too.'

'Not so. We have no anarchy here, don't know the meaning of the word. I know how to keep order, of that you can be quite convicted. Even with this plague on, we have no disorder and British justice prevails.'

'The cholera is only just hitting its stride, Commander Croucher. And mass executions are not a manifestation of order.'

Angrily, Croucher said, 'Manifestations, hell! Tomorrow everyone in the Churchill Hospital will be shot. No doubt you will cry out about that also. But you do not understand. You must expunge the erroneous misapprehension. I have no wish to kill. All I want is to keep order.'

'You must have read enough history to know how hollow that rings.'

'It's true! Chaos and civil war are absolutely deterrent to me! Listen to me, what you tell me of DOUCH(E) confirms what I had already been informed. You were not lying to me. So . . .'

'Why should I lie to you? If you are the benefactor you claim to be, I have nothing to fear from you.'

'Because if I was the madman you take me for, my main objective would be to kill any objective observers of my regime. The reverse is true – I visualize my job as to keep order, only that. Consequentially, I can utilize your DOUCH(E) setup. I want you here, recording. Your testimony is going to vindicate me and the measures I am forced to implement.'

'Vindicate you before whom? Before posterity? There is no posterity. They died in addled sperm, if you remember.'

They were both sweating freely. The guard behind them shuffled weary feet. Croucher brought a tube of peppermints from his pocket and slipped one into his mouth.

He said, 'How long do you keep on persevering with this DOUCH(E) job, Mr Timberlane?'

'Till I die or get killed.'

'Recording?'

'Yes, recording and filming.'

'For posterity?'

After a moment of silence, Timberlane said, 'All right, we both think we know where duty lies. But I don't have to shoot all the poor old wrecks in the Churchill Hospital.'

Croucher crunched his peppermint. The eyes in his ugly face stared at the floor as he spoke.

'Here's a nodule of information for you to record. For the last ten years, the Churchill has been devoted to one line of research and one only. The doctors and staff there include some expert biochemists. Their project and endeavor is trying to prolong life. They are not just studying ger—what do you call it, geriatrics; they are looking for a drug, a hormone; I am no medical special-ist, and I don't differentiate one from the other, but they are looking for a way to enable people such as me and you to live to be two hundred or two thousand years old. Impossible baloney! Waste an organization chasing phantoms! I can't let that hospital run to waste, I want to utilize it for more productive purposes.'

'The government subsidized the hospital?'

'They did. The corrupt politicians of Westminster aspired to discover this elixir of life and immortality and perpetuate it for their own personal advantage. With that kind of nonsense we aren't going to be bothered with. Life's too short.'

They stared at each other.

'I will accept your offer,' said Timberlane, 'though I cannot see how it will benefit you. I will record whatever you do at the Churchill. I would like documentary evidence that what you say about this longevity project is true.'

'Documents! You talk like one of these clever fool dons in the other room. I respect learning, but not pedantry, get that straight. Listen, I'm evacuating the whole bunch of crooks out of that hospital, them and their mad ideas; I don't believe in the past – I believe in the future.'

To Timberlane it sounded only like an admission of madness. He said, 'There is no future, remember? We killed it stone dead in the past.'

Croucher unwrapped another peppermint; his thick lips took it from the palm of his hand.

'Come to me tomorrow and I will show you the future. The sterility was not entirely total, you know. There was, there still are, a minimal trickle of children being born in odd corners of the world – even in Britain. Most of them are defectives – monstrosities beyond your conception.'

'I know what you mean. Do you remember the Infantop Corps during the war years? It was the British equivalent of the American Project Childsweep. I was on that. I know all about monstrosities. My feeling is that it would be sane to kill most of them at birth.'

'A percentage of the local ones are not killed at birth, motherly love being such as it is.' Croucher turned to the guards, who were whispering behind him, and irritably ordered them to be silent. He continued, 'I'm rounding up all these creatures, whatever they look like. Some of them are limbless. Sometimes they are without intelligence and unspeakably stupid. Sometimes they are born inside out, and then they die by degrees. Though we have got one boy who survives despite his whole digestive system – stomach, intestines, anus – being on the outside of his body in a sort of bag.

It's a supremely gruesome sight. Oh, we've got all sorts of miscellaneous half-human creatures. They will be incarcerated in the Churchill, for supervision. They are the future.' When Timberlane did not speak, he added, 'Admitted, a frightening future, but it may be the only one. We must labor under the assertion that when these creatures reach adulthood, they will breed normal infants. We shall keep them and make them breed. Assure yourself it's better a world populated by freaks than a dead world.'

Croucher eyed Timberlane challengingly, as if expecting him to disagree with this proposition. Instead, Timberlane said, 'I'll come and see you in the morning. You will place no censorship on me?'

'You will have a guard with you to ensure security. Corporal Pitt, whom you met, has been detailed for the task. I do not want your reports falling into hostile hands.'

'Is that all?'

'No. I have to consider your own hands as hostile hands. Till you prove them otherwise, your wife will live here in these barracks as a token of your good will. You will billet here too. You'll find the comfort will be more considerable than your flat was. Your belongings are already undergoing transportation to here from the flat.'

'So you are just a dictator, like all the others before you!'

'Be careful – I cannot stomach a stubborn mind! You will soon learn otherwise of me – you'd better! I want you as my conscience. Get that point clarified in your brain with all just momentum. You have seen I have surrounded myself with the intelligentsia; unfortunately, they superficially do what I say – at least to my face. Such a creed revolts me to my skin! I don't want that from you; I want you to do what you have been trained for. Damn it, why should I bother with you at all when there's plenty else to worry about? You must do as I say.'

'If I am to be independent, I must retain my independence.'

'Don't go all highbrow on me! You must do as I say. I ask you to sleep here tonight, and that's an order. Think this conversation over, talk with your wife. I saw immediately she was a fairly hirsute type. Remember, I offer you security, Timberlane.'

'In this insanitary fort?'

'You will be sent for in the morning. Guard, take this man away. Give him into Corporal Pitt's keeping.'

As they came up in a businesslike way to take Timberlane, Croucher coughed into a handkerchief, wiped his hand across his brow, and said, 'One concluding point, Timberlane. I hope friendship will originate between us, as far as that's possible. But if you cogitate trying to escape, I had better inform you that from tomorrow new restrictive orders are in operation throughout the area in my jurisprudence. I will stamp out the spread of plague at all costs. Anybody caught trying to move from Oxford in future will be shot, no questions asked. Barriers will be erected around the city at dawn. All right, guard, remove him. And expedite me a secretary and a pot of tea immediately.'

Their quarters in the barracks consisted of one large room. It contained a washbasin, a gas ring, and two army beds with a supply of blankets. Their belongings arrived in fits and starts from a lorry downstairs. Other commandeered property arrived spasmodically, until they grew tired of the echo of army boots.

A senile guard sat on a chair in the doorway, fingering a light machine gun and staring at them with the stony curiosity of the bored.

Martha lay on one of the beds with a damp towel across her forehead. Timberlane had given her a full account of the talk with Croucher. They remained in silence, he sitting on his bed, resting his head heavily on his elbow, sinking slowly into a sort of lethargy.

'Well, we've more or less got what we wanted,' Martha said. 'We're working for Croucher with a vengeance. Is he to be trusted?'

'I don't think that's a question you can ask. He can be trusted as far as circumstances allow. He had a way of not seeming to take in all that I was saying – as if his mind was working all the time on another problem. Perhaps I got a glimpse of that problem when he visualized a world populated by monsters. Perhaps he felt he must have someone to rule over, even if it was only a – a collection of abnormalities.'

His wife's thoughts returned to a point they had reached earlier in the day.

'Everyone is obsessed with the Accident, even if they do not show it immediately. We're all sick with guilt. Perhaps that's Croucher's trouble, and he has to live with a vision of himself ruling over a twilight world of cripples and deformed creatures.'

'His grip on the present seems stronger than that would imply.'

'How strong is anyone's grip on the present?'

'It's a pretty fleeting grip, as the cholera reminds us, but . . .'

'Our society, our biosphere, has been sick for forty years now. How can the individual remain healthy in it? We may all be madder than we know.'

Not liking the note in her voice, Timberlane went over and sat on the edge of her bed, saying strongly, 'Anyhow, our immediate concern is with Croucher. It will suit the DOUCH scheme if we cooperate with him, so that's what we will do. But I still can't see why, at a time like this, he should want to encumber himself with me.'

'I can think of a reason. He doesn't want you. He's after the truck.'

He squeezed her hand. 'It could be that. He might think that as we have come from London, I have recorded information he could use. Indeed I may have done. London is his best-organized enemy at present. I wonder how long they will leave the truck where it is now?'

The DOUCH(E) truck was a valuable piece of equipment. When national governments broke down, as foreseen by the Washington foundation, the trucks became in themselves small DOUCH HQs. They contained full recording equipment, stores, and sundry supplies; they were fully armored; an hour's work would convert them into tracked vehicles; they ran on the recently perfected charge-battery system, and had an emergency drive that worked on petrol or any of the current petrol substitutes. This neat packet of technology, or rather Timberlane's sample of it, had been left in its garage, below the flat in Iffley Road.

'I have the keys still,' Timberlane said, 'and the vehicle is shuttered down. They haven't asked me for the keys.'

Martha's eyes were closed. She heard him, but she was too tired to reply.

'We're well placed here to observe contemporary history,' he said. 'What DOUCH did not consider was that the vehicles might be an attraction to the history-makers. Whatever happens, we must not let the truck pass out of our control.'

After a minute of silence, he added, 'The vehicle must be our first concern.'

With the sudden energy of fury she sat up on the bed. 'Damn and blast the bloody vehicle,' she said. 'What about me?'

She slept fitfully throughout that stuffy night in the barracks. The silence was fractured by army boots stamping across a parade ground, by shouts, by the close vibrations of a mosquito, or by the surge of a windrush coming home. Her bed rumbled like an empty stomach when she turned in it.

Night, it seemed to her, was a padded pin cushion – she almost had it in her hand, so closely did its warmth match the humidity of her palm – and into it, an infinite number of pins, went the sound effects of militant humanity. But each pin pierced her as well as the cushion. Toward morning the noises grew less frequent, though the heat bowl of the square outside remained unemptied. Then from a different quarter came the faint ring, long continued, of an alarm clock. Distantly, a cock crowed. She heard a town clock – Magdalen? – chime five. Birds quarreled over the dawn in their guttering. Army noises slowly took over again. The clang of buckets and iron utensils from the cookhouse proclaimed that preparations for breakfast had begun. She slept, fading out on a tide of despair.

Her sleep was deep and restorative.

Timberlane was sitting, grey and unshaven, on the edge of his bed when she awoke. A guard came in with a breakfast tray, set it down, and departed.

'How are you feeling, my love?'

'I'm better this morning, Algy. But what a noise there was in the night.'

'A lot of stretcher parties, I'm afraid,' he said, glancing out of the window. 'We're in one of the centers of infection here. I am prepared to give Croucher guarantees about my conduct if he'll let us live away from here.'

She went over to him, cupping his stubbly jaws in her hands. 'You've come to a decision, then?'

'I had last night. We took on a job with DOUCH(E). We are after history, and history is now being made here. I think we must trust Croucher; so we remain in Cowley to cooperate with him.'

'You know I don't question your decisions, Algy. But can we trust a man in his position?'

'Let's just say that a man in his position does not seem to have any reason to shoot us out of hand,' he said.

'Perhaps a woman looks at these things differently, but let's not allow DOUCH to take precedence over our safety.'

'Look at it this way, Martha. In Washington we didn't just take on obligations; we took on a way of thinking that makes sense when most human activities no longer do. That may have a lot to do with the way we have survived as a pair in London while all around us personal relationships were going to pot. We have a mission; we must serve it, or it won't serve us.'

'You put it like that and it sounds fine. Just let's not fall into the trap of putting ideas before people, eh?'

They turned their attention to the breakfast. It looked like soldiers' rations; because tea was scarce, there was weak beer to drink; to eat, there were the inevitable vitamin pills that had established themselves as a national food since domestic animals were stricken, a grainy bread, and some fillets of a brown and nameless fish. Because whales and seals had almost vanished from the sea, and freak radiation effects seemed to have encouraged the growth of plankton and minute Crustacea, fish had multiplied. Many farmers in coastal areas throughout the world had been forced to take to the seas when their livestock dwindled; so there was still a strip of fish to stretch across the cracked plates of the world.

64

As they ate, Martha said, 'This Corporal Pitt who is acting as combined jailer and bodyguard is a nice sort of man. If we must have someone sitting over us all the time, perhaps we could have him. Ask Croucher about it when you see him.'

They were swallowing the vitamin pills down with the last of the beer when Pitt came in with another guard. On his shoulder tabs Pitt wore the insignia of a captain.

'It looks as if we have to congratulate you on a good and swift promotion,' said Martha.

'You needn't be funny,' Pitt said sharply. 'There happens to be a shortage of good men around these parts.'

'I was not trying to be funny, Mr Pitt, and I can see from the number of stretchers busy outside that men are growing scarcer all the while.'

'It doesn't do to try and make jokes about the plague.'

'My wife was attempting to be pleasant,' Timberlane said. 'Just watch how you answer her, or there will be complaints in.'

'If you have any complaints, address them to me,' Pitt said.

The Timberlanes exchanged glances. The unassuming corporal of the night before had disappeared; this man's voice was ragged and his whole manner highly strung. Martha went over to her mirror and sat down before it. How the hollows crept on in her cheeks! She felt stronger today, but the thought of the trials and heat that lay before them gave her no reassurance. She felt in the springs of her menstruation a dull pain, as if her infertile and unfertilizable ovaries protested their own sterility. Laboriously, from her pots and tubes, she endeavored to conjure into her face a life and warmth she felt she would never again in actuality possess.

As she worked, she studied Pitt in the glass. Was that nervous manner simply a result of sudden promotion, or was there another reason for it?

'I am taking you and Mrs Timberlane out on a mission in ten minutes,' he told Timberlane. 'Get yourself ready. We shall proceed to your old flat in Iffley Road. There we shall pick up your recording van, and go up to the Churchill Hospital.'

'What for? I have an appointment with Commander Croucher. He said nothing to me about this yesterday.'

'He told me he did tell you about it. You said you wanted documentary evidence of what has been going on up at the hospital. We are going up there to get it.'

'I see. But my appointment—'

'Look, don't argue with me, I've got my orders, see, and I'm going to carry them out. You don't have appointments here, anyway – we just have orders. The commander is busy.'

'But he told me—'

Captain Pitt tapped his newly acquired revolver for emphasis.

'Ten minutes, and we are going out. I'll be back for you. You are both coming with me to collect your vehicle.' He turned on his heel and marched noisily out. The other guard, a big slack-jawed fellow, moved ostentatiously to stand by the door.

'What's it mean?' Martha asked, going to her husband. He put his arms about her waist and gave her a worried frown.

'Croucher must have changed his mind in some way. Yet it may be perfectly okay. I did ask to see the Churchill records, so perhaps he is trying to show he will cooperate with us.'

'But Pitt is so different, too. Last night he was telling me about his wife, and how he had been forced to take part in this massacre in the center of Oxford . . .'

'Perhaps his promotion has gone to his head . . .'

'Oh, it's the uncertainty, Algy, everything's so – nothing's definite, nobody knows what's going to happen from day to day . . . Perhaps they are just after the truck.'

She stood with her head against his chest, he stood with his arms around her, neither saying more until Pitt returned. He beckoned to them and they went down into the square, the new captain leading and the slack-mouthed guard following.

They climbed into a windrush. Under Pitt's control, the motor faltered and caught, and they moved slowly across the parade ground and through the gates with a wave at the sentries.

The new day had brought no improvement in Oxford's appearance. Down Hollow Way, a row of semidetacheds burned in a devitalized fashion, as though a puff of wind might extinguish the blaze; smoke from the fire hung over the area. Near the old motor works there was military activity, much of it disorganized.

They heard a shot fired. In the Cowley Road, the long straggling street of shops that pointed toward the ancient spires of Oxford, the façades were often boarded or broken. Refuse lay deep on the pavements. By one or two of the shops old women queued for goods, silent and apart, with scarves around their mouths despite the growing heat. Dust eddying from the underthrust of the windrush blew around their broken shoes. They ignored it, in the semblance of dignity that abjection brings.

Throughout the journey Pitt's face was like brittle leather. His nose, like the beak of a falcon, pointed only ahead. None of the company spoke. When they arrived at the flat, he settled the machine to a poor landing in the middle of the road. Martha was glad to climb out; their windrush was full of stale male odors.

Within twenty-four hours their flat had become a strange place. She had forgotten how shabby and unpainted it looked from outside. They saw a soldier sitting at what had been their living-room window. He commanded a line of fire onto the garage door. At present, he was leaning out of the flat window shouting down to a ragged old man clad in a pair of shorts and a mackintosh. The old man stood in the gutter clutching a bundle of newspapers.

'*Oxford Mail!*' the old man croaked. As Timberlane went to buy one, Pitt made as if to stop him, muttered 'Why not?' and turned away. Martha was the only one to see the gesture.

The paper was a single sheet peppered with literals. A prominently featured leader rejoiced in being able to resume publication now that law and order had been restored; elsewhere it announced that anyone trying to leave the city boundaries without permission would be shot; it announced that the Super Cinema would give a daily film show; it ordered all men under the age of sixty-five to report within forty-eight hours to one of fifteen schools converted into emergency military posts. Clearly, the newspaper had fallen under the commander's control.

'Let's get moving. We haven't got all day,' Captain Pitt said.

Timberlane tucked the paper into his hip pocket and moved toward the garage. He unlocked it and went in. Pitt stood close by his side as he squeezed along the shuttered DOUCH(E) truck and fingered the combination lock on the driver's door. Martha watched the captain's face; over and over, he was moistening his dry lips.

The two men climbed into the truck. Timberlane unlocked the steering column and backed slowly out into the road. Pitt called to the soldier in the window to lock up the flat and drive his wind-rush back to the barracks. Martha and the slack-mouthed guard were told to climb aboard the truck. They settled themselves in the seats immediately behind the driver. Both Pitt and his sub-ordinate sat with revolvers in their hands, resting them on their knees.

'Drive toward the Churchill,' Pitt said. 'Take it very slowly. There's no hurry at all.' He cleared his throat nervously. Sweat stood out on his forehead. He rubbed his left thumb up and down the barrel of his revolver without ceasing.

Giving him a searching glance, Timberlane said, 'You're sick, man. You'd better get back to barracks and have a doctor ex-amine you.'

The revolver jerked. 'Just get her rolling. Don't talk to me.' He coughed, and ran a hand heavily over his face. One of his eyelids developed a nervous flutter and he glanced over his shoulder at Martha.

'Really, don't you think—'

'Shut up, woman!'

With Timberlane hugging the wheel, they crawled down a little dead side street. Two Cowley Fathers in black habits were carrying a woman between them, moving with difficulty under her weight; her left hand trailed against the pavement. They stood absolutely still as the truck came level with them and did not move until it had gone past. The dead vacant face of the woman gaped at Martha as they growled by. Pitt swallowed spittle audibly.

As if coming to a resolution, he raised his revolver. As the point swung toward Timberlane, Martha screamed. Her husband trod on the brake. They rocked back and forth, the engine died, they stopped.

Before Timberlane could heave himself around, Pitt dropped

the gun and hid his face in his hands. He was weeping and raving, but what he said was indistinguishable.

The slack-mouthed fellow said, 'Keep still! Keep still! Don't run away! We don't none of us want to get shot.'

Timberlane had the captain's revolver in his hand. He knocked Pitt's arms down from his face. Seeing how his weapon had changed owners sobered Pitt.

'Shoot me if you must – think I'd care? Go on, better get it over with. I shall be shot anyhow when Croucher finds I let you escape. Shoot us all and be done with it!'

'I never done no one any harm – I used to be a postman. Let me get out! Don't shoot me,' the slack-mouthed guard said. He still nursed his revolver helplessly on his lap. The sight of his captain's breakdown had completely disorganized him.

'Why should I shoot either of you?' Timberlane asked curtly. 'Equally, why should you shoot me? What were your orders, Pitt?'

'I spared your life. You can spare mine. You're a gentleman! Put the gun away. Let me have it again. Shut it in a locker.' He was recovering again, still confused, but cocky and casting his untrustworthy eye about. Timberlane kept the gun aimed at his chest.

'Let's have that explanation.'

'It was Croucher's orders. He had me in front of me – I mean in front of him – this morning. Said that this vehicle of yours should be in his hands. Said you were just an intellectual trouble-maker, a spy maybe, from London. Once you'd got the truck moving, I was to shoot you and your lady wife. Then Studley here and me was to report back to him with the vehicle. But I couldn't do it, honest, I'm not cut out for this sort of thing. I had a wife and family – I've had enough of all this killing – if my poor old Vi—'

'Cut out the ham acting, Mr Pitt, and let us think,' Martha said. She put an arm over her husband's shoulder. 'So we couldn't trust friend Croucher after all.'

'He couldn't trust us. Men in his position may be fundamentally liberal, but they have to remove random elements.'

'You got that phrase from my father. Okay, Algy, so we're random elements again – now what do we do?'

69

To her surprise, he twisted around and kissed her. There was a hard gaiety in him. He was the man in command. He removed the revolver from the unprotesting Studley, and slipped it into a locker.

'In the circumstances we have no alternatives. We're getting out of Oxford. We'll head west toward Devon. That would seem to be the best bet. Pitt, will you and Studley join us?'

'You'll never get out of Oxford and Cowley. The barricades are up. They were put up during the night across all roads leading out of town.'

'If you want to throw in your lot with us, you take orders from me. Are you going to join us? Yes or no?'

'But I'm telling you, the barricades are up. You couldn't get out of town, not if you were Croucher you couldn't,' Pitt said.

'You must have a pass or something to permit you to be driving around the streets. What was that thing you flashed at the guard as we left the barracks?'

Pitt brought a pass sheet out of his tunic pocket, and handed it over.

'I'll have your tunic, too. From now on you are demoted to private. Sorry, Pitt, but you didn't exactly earn your promotion, did you?'

'I'm no murderer, if that's what you mean.' His manner was steadier now. 'Look, I tell you we'll all get killed if you attempt to drive through the barricades. They've established these big concrete blocks everywhere. They stop traffic and tip up GEMs.'

'Get that tunic off before we talk.'

The Cowley Fathers came level with the truck. They stared in before laboring into a public house with their burden.

As Timberlane passed his jacket over to Martha and slipped on Pitt's tunic – it creaked at its rotten seams as he struggled into it – he said, 'Food must be still coming into the town, mustn't it? Food, stores, ammunition – God knows what. Don't tell me Croucher isn't intelligent enough to organize that. In fact he's probably looting the counties all around for his supplies.'

Unexpectedly, Studley leaned forward and tapped Timberlane on the shoulder. 'That's right, sir, and there's a fish convoy coming up from Southampton due here this morning, 'cause I heard that Transport Sergeant Tucker say so when we signed for the windrush earlier on.'

'Good man! The barriers will have to go down to let the convoy through. As the convoy enters, we go out. Which way will it be coming from?'

As they trundled south through the devouring sunlight, the sound of an explosion came to them. Farther up the road, they saw by a pall of smoke to their right that Donnington Bridge had been blown up. A way out of the city had been cut off. Nobody spoke. Like the cholera, the desolation in the streets was contagious.

At Rose Hill, the blocks of flats set back from the road were as blank as cliffs. The only alleviation to the stark nudity of the thoroughfare was an ambulance that crawled from a service road, its blue light revolving. All its windows were blanketed. It mounted the grass verge, crossed the main road only a few yards ahead of the DOUCH(E) vehicle, and stopped on the opposite verge with a final shudder. As they passed it, they caught sight of the driver sprawled across the wheel . . .

Farther on, among private houses, it was less like death. In several front gardens old men and women were burning bonfires. And what superstition did that represent, Martha wondered.

When they reached a roundabout, soldiers with slung rifles came out from a check point to meet them. Timberlane leaned out of the window and flashed the pass without stopping. The soldiers waved him on.

'How much farther?' Timberlane asked.

'We're nearly there. The roadblock we want is at Littlemore Railway Bridge. Beyond that it's just country,' Pitt said.

'Croucher has a long boundary to defend.'

'That's why he wants more men. This blocking of roads was a bright idea of his. It helps keep strangers out as well as us in. He doesn't want deserters getting away and setting up an opposition, does he? The road takes a right bend here toward the bridge, and there's a road joins it from the right. Ah, there's that pub, the Marlborough – that's on the corner!'

'Right, do what I told you. Take a tip from that ambulance we passed. All right, Martha, my sweet? Here we go!'

As they rounded the bend, Timberlane slumped over the wheel, trailing his right hand out of the window. Pitt slumped beside him; the other two lolled back in their seats. Steering carefully, Timberlane negotiated their vehicle in a drunken line toward the public house Pitt had mentioned. He let it mount the pavement, then twisted the wheel and released the clutch while remaining in gear. The truck shuddered violently before stopping. They were facing Littlemore Bridge, a mere two hundred yards up the road.

'Good, keep where you are,' Timberlane said. 'Let's hope the Southampton convoy is on time. How many vehicles is it likely to consist of, Studley?'

'Four, five, six. Hard to tell. It varies.'

'Then we ought to aim to get through after the second truck.'

As Timberlane spoke, he was scanning ahead. The railway line lay hidden in its cutting. The road narrowed into two traffic lanes by the bridge. It was concealed beyond the bridge by the rise of the land, but fortunately the roadblock had been set up on this side of the bridge, and so was visible from where they waited. It consisted of a collection of concrete blocks, two old lorries, and wooden poles. A small wooden building nearby had been taken over by the military; it looked as if it might house a machine gun. Only one soldier could be seen, leaning by the door of the building and shading his eyes to look down the road at them.

A builder's lorry stood near the barrier. A man was standing in it, throwing bricks down to another man. They appeared to be strengthening the defenses, and to judge by their clumsy movements, they were unused to the job.

Minutes passed. The whole scene was nondescript; this dull stretch of road was neither town nor country. Not only did the sunlight drain it of all its pretensions; it had perhaps never been surveyed as purposefully as Timberlane surveyed it now. The slothful movements of the men handling bricks took on a sort of dreamlike persistence. Flies entered the DOUCH(E) truck, droning their way fruitlessly about the interior. Their noise reminded

Martha of the long summer days of her girlhood, when into her happiness, to become an inseparable part of it, had entered the realisation that a wrong like a curse hung over her and over her parents and over her friends – and over everyone. She had seen the effects of the curse spread wider and wider, like the sand in a desert sandstorm that erodes the sky. Wide-eyed, she stared at the hunched back of her husband, indulging herself in a little horror fantasy that he was dead, really dead of the cholera. She succeeded in frightening herself.

'Algy—'

'Here they come! Watch it now! Lie flat, Martha; they're bound to shoot as we go through.'

He sent them rolling forward, bumping back onto the road. A first lorry, a big furniture lorry plastered in dust, humped itself over the narrow bridge from the other side. One soldier came to attend to it; he drew back part of the wooden barricade to allow the lorry through. It growled forward through the narrow opening. As it moved down the road toward the DOUCH(E) vehicle, a second lorry – this one an army lorry with a torn canopy – appeared over the bridge.

Their timing had to be good. Rolling steadily ahead, the DOUCH(E) truck had to pass that second lorry as close to the bridge as possible. Timberlane pressed his foot down harder. Elms by the roadside, tawdry from dust, scattered sunlight red and white across his vision. They passed the first lorry. The driver called something. They sped toward the army lorry. It was coming through the concrete blocks. The driver saw Timberlane, gestured, accelerated, swung his wheel to the near side. The sentry ran forward, swinging up his rifle. His mouth flapped. His words were lost in the sound of engines. Timberlane drove straight at him.

They roared past the army lorry without touching it, all four of them instinctively watching and yelling. Their offside headlight struck the soldier before he could turn. His rifle went flying. Like a bag of cement, he was flung against one of the concrete blocks. Something screamed as they scraped past the barrier: steel on stone. As they lurched across the bridge, the third vehicle in the convoy loomed up ahead of them.

From the wooden sentry post they had passed, a machine gun woke into action. Bullets clattered against the grating across the back of their truck, making the inside ring like a steel drum. The windscreen of the vehicle ahead shattered; new rips bloomed sharp across its old canvas. With a whistle of tires, it slewed off to one side. The driver flung open his door, but fell back into the cab as it canted to the other side. Bumping and jarring, it smashed through railings down the embankment toward the railway line below.

Timberlane had swerved in the other direction to avoid hitting the lorry. Only the accident that overtook it enabled him to get past it. They lurched forward again, and the road was clear ahead. The machine gun was still barking, but the lie of the land sheltered them from it.

If Studley had not collapsed at that point, and had to be rested in a deserted village called Sparcot, where other refugees were gathering, they might have made it down to Devon. But Studley had the cholera; and a paranoiac called Mole arrived to turn them into a fortified outpost; and a week later severe rains washed out a host of opportunities. The halt at Sparcot lasted for eleven long grey years.

Looking back to that time, Martha reflected on the way in which the nervous excitement of their stay at Cowley had embalmed it in memory, so that it all came back easily. The years that followed were less clear, for they had been dulled by misery and monotony. The death of Studley; the deaths of several others of that original bunch of refugees; the appearance of Big Jim Mole, and the quarrels as he distributed them among the deserted houses of the village; the endless struggle, the fights over women; the abandonment of hope, convention, and lipstick; these were now like figures in a huge but faded tapestry to which she would not turn again.

One event in those days (ah, but the absence of children had been a sharper wound in her mind then!) remained with her clearly, because she knew it still fretted her husband. That was

74

their bartering of the DOUCH(E) truck, during the second winter at Sparcot, when they were all lightheaded from starvation. They exchanged it for a cartload of rotting fish, parsnips, and vitamin pills belonging to a one-eyed wandering hawker. She and Algy had haggled with him throughout one afternoon, to watch him in the end drive away into the dusk in their truck. In the darkness of that winter, their miseries had reached their deepest point.

Several men, among them the ablest, had shot themselves. It was then that Eve, who was mistress to Trouter, bore a child with no deformity. She had gone mad and run away. A month later her body and the baby's were found in a wood nearby.

In that vile winter Martha and Greybeard had organized lectures, not entirely with Mole's approval. They had spoken on history, on geography, on politics, on the lessons to be learned from life; but as all their subject matter was necessarily drawn from an existence that died even as they spoke, the lectures were a failure. To the hunger and deprivation had been added something more sinister: a sense that there was no longer a place on earth for mind.

Someone had invented a brief-lived phrase for that feeling: 'the brain curtain.' Certainly the brain curtain had descended that winter with a vengeance.

In January, the fieldfares brought their harsh song of Norway to Sparcot. In February, cold winds blew and snow fell every day. In March, the sparrows mated on the crusted and dirty piles of ice. Only in April did a softer air return.

During that month Charley Samuels married Iris Ryde. Charley and Timberlane had fought together in the war, years earlier, when both had formed part of the Infantop Corps. It had been a good day when he arrived at the motley little village. When he married, he moved his bride into the house next to Martha and Algy. Six years later, Iris died of the cancer that, like sterility, was an effect of the Accident.

That had been an ill time. And all the while they had labored under Mole's fears, hardly aware of the imposition. To get away was like a convalescence: one looks back and sees for the first time how ill one has been. Martha recalled how eagerly they had conspired with nature, encouraging the roads to decay, sealing them off from the dangerous world outside, and how anxiously they guarded Sparcot against the day when Croucher's forces moved to overwhelm them.

Croucher never came to Sparcot. He died from the pandemic that killed so many of his followers and converted his stronghold into a morgue. By the time the disease had run its course large organizations had gone the way of large animals; the hedges grew, the copses heaved their shoulders and became forests; the rivers spread into marshland; and the mammal with the big brain eked out his dotage in small communities.

3
The River: Swifford Fair

Both human beings and sheep coughed a good deal as the boats sailed downstream. The party had lost its first sense of adventure. They were too old and had seen too much wrong to entertain high feeling for long. The cold and the landscape also had a hand in subduing them: bearded with rime like the face of an ancient spirit, the vegetation formed part of a scene that patently had come about and would continue without reference to the stray humans crossing it.

In the sharp winter's air their breath steamed behind them. The dinghy went first, followed by Jeff Pitt rowing his little boat, with two sheep in a net lying against his tattered backside. Their progress was slow; Pitt's pride in his rowing was greater than his ability.

In the dinghy, Charley and Greybeard rowed most of the time, and Martha sat at the tiller facing them. Becky and Towin Thomas remained sulkily at one side; Becky had wished to stay at the inn where the sheep were until the liquor and the winter ran out, but Greybeard had overruled her. The rest of the sheep now lay between them on the bottom of the boat.

Once, tired of having a man sit idle beside her, Becky had ordered Towin to get into Jeff Pitt's boat and help him row. The experiment had not been successful. The boat had almost capsized. Pitt had cursed continuously. Now Pitt rowed alone, thinking his own thoughts.

His was, in its sixty-fifth year of existence, a strange, spiky face. Although his nose still protruded, a gradual loss of teeth and a

77

drying of flesh had brought his jawline and chin also into prominence.

Since his arrival at Sparcot, when he had been happy enough to get away from Greybeard, the ex-captain of Croucher's guard had led a solitary life. That he resented the existence into which he was forced was clear enough; though he never confided, his air was the air of a man long used to bitterness; the fact remained that he, more effectively than anyone else, had taken to a poacher's ways.

Though he had thrown in his lot with the others now, his unsociable disposition still lingered; he rowed with his back to the dinghy, gazing watchfully at the ruffled winter landscape through which they journeyed. He was with them, but his manner suggested he was not necessarily for them.

Between low banks scourged tawny and white by the frost, their way crackled continuously as ice shattered under their bows. On the second afternoon after leaving the inn where they found the sheep, they smelled woodsmoke and saw its haze ahead of them, heavy over the stream. Soon they reached a place where the ice was broken and a fire smoldered on the bank. Greybeard reached for his rifle, Charley seized his knife, Martha sat alertly watching; Towin and Becky ducked out of sight below the decking. Pitt rose and pointed.

'My God, the gnomes!' he exclaimed. 'There's one of them for sure!'

On the bank, dancing near the fire, was a little white figure, flexing its legs and arms. It sang to itself in a voice like a creaking bough. When it saw the boats through the bare shanks of a bush, it stopped. Coming forward to the edge of the bank, it clasped hands over the black fur of its crotch and called to them. Though they could not understand what it was saying, they rowed, mesmerized, toward it.

By the time they reached the bank the figure had put on some clothes and looked more human. Behind it they saw, half hidden in an ash copse, a tarred barn. The figure was jigging and pointing to the barn, talking rapidly at them as he did so.

He was a lively octogenarian, judging by appearances, a

sprightly grotesque with a tatter of red and violet capillaries running from one cheekbone to another over the alp of his nose. His beard and topknot formed one continuous conflagration of hair, tied bottom and top below jaw and above crown, and dyed a deep tangerine. He danced like a skeleton and motioned to them.

'Are you alone? Can we put in here?' Greybeard called.

'I don't like the look of him – let's press on,' Jeff Pitt called, laboring his boat up through the panes of ice. 'We don't know what we're letting ourselves in for.'

The skeleton cried something unintelligible, jumping back when Greybeard climbed ashore. He clutched some red and green beads that hung around his neck.

'Sirrer vine daver zwimmin,' he said.

'Oh – fine day for swimming! You have been swimming? Isn't it cold? Aren't you afraid of cutting yourself on the ice?'

'Warreryer zay? Diddy zay zomminer bout thize?'

'He doesn't seem to understand me any better than I can understand him,' Greybeard remarked to the others in the boats. But with patience he managed to penetrate the skeleton's thick accent. His name appeared to be Norsgrey, and he was a traveler. He was staying with his wife, Lita, in the barn they saw through the ash trees. He would welcome the company of Greybeard and his party.

Like Charley's fox, the sheep were all on tethers. They were made to jump ashore, where they immediately began cropping the harsh grasses. The humans dragged their boats up and secured them. They stood stretching themselves, to force the chill and stiffness from their limbs. Then they made toward the barn, moving their legs painfully. As they became used to the skeleton's accent, what he had to say became more intelligible, though in content his talk was wild.

His preoccupation was with badgers.

Norsgrey believed in the magical power of badgers. He had a daughter, he told them, who would be nearly sixty now, who had run off into the woods ('when they was a-seeding and a-branching themselves up to march forth and strangle down the towns of man') and she had married a badger. There were badger men

79

in the woods now who were her sons, and badger girls her daughters, black and white in their faces, very lovely to behold.

'Are there stoats around here?' Martha asked, cutting off what threatened to be a long monologue.

Old Norsgrey paused outside the barn and pointed into the lower branches of a tree.

'There's one now, a-looking down at us, Mrs Lady, sitting in its wicked little nest as cute as you like. But he won't touch us 'cause he knows as I'm related to the badgers by mattterrimony.'

They stared and could see only the pale grey twigs of ash thrusting black-capped into the air.

Inside the barn, an ancient reindeer lay in the half-dark, its four broad hoofs clumped together. Becky gave a shriek of surprise as it turned its ancient sullen face toward them. Hens clucked and scattered at their entrance.

'Don't make a lot of row,' Norsgrey warned them. 'Lita's asleep, and I don't want her wakened. I'll turn you out if you disturb her, but if you're quiet, and give me a bite of supper, I'll let you stay here, nice and warm and comfortable – and safe from all those hungry stoats outside.'

'What ails your wife?' Towin asked. 'I'm not staying in here if there's illness.'

'Don't you insult my wife. She's never had an illness in her life. Just keep quiet and behave.'

'I'll go and get our kit from the boat,' Greybeard said. Charley and the fox came back to the river with him. As they loaded themselves, Charley spoke with some show of embarrassment, looking not at Greybeard but at the cool grey landscape.

'Towin and his Becky would have stayed at the place where the dead man sat in his kitchen,' he said. 'They didn't care to come any farther, but we persuaded them. That's right, isn't it, Greybeard?'

'You know it is.'

'Right. What I want to ask you, then, is this. How far are we going? What are you planning? What have you got in mind?'

Greybeard looked at the river.

'You're a religious man, Charley. Don't you think God might have something in mind for us?'

Charley laughed curtly. 'That would sound better if you believed in God yourself. But suppose I thought He had in mind for us to settle down here, what would you do? I don't see what you are aiming on doing.'

'We're not far enough from Sparcot to stop yet. They might make an expedition and catch us here.'

'You know that's nonsense as well as I do. Truth of the matter is, you don't really know where you want to go, or why, isn't that it?'

Greybeard looked at the solid face of the man he had known for so long. 'Each day I become more sure. I want to get to the mouth of the river, to the sea.'

Nodding, Charley picked up his equipment and started to trudge back toward the barn. Isaac led the way. Greybeard made as if to add something, then changed his mind. He did not believe in explaining. To Towin and Becky, this journey was just another hardship; to him, it was an end in itself. The hardship of it was a pleasure. Life was a pleasure; he looked back at its moments, many of them as much shrouded in mist as the opposite bank of the Thames. Objectively, many of them held only misery, fear, confusion; but afterward, and even at the time, he had known an exhilaration stronger than the misery, fear, or confusion. A fragment of belief came to him from another epoch: *Cogito ergo sum*. For him that had not been true; his truth had been: *Sentio ergo sum*. I feel, so I exist. He enjoyed this fearful, miserable, confused life, and not only because it made more sense than nonlife. He could never explain that to anyone. He did not have to explain it to Martha; she knew, she felt as he did in that respect.

Distantly, he heard music.

He looked about him with a tingle of unease, recalling the tales Pitt and others told of gnomes and little people, for this was a little music. But he realized it came to him over a long distance. Was it – he had almost forgotten the name of the instrument – an accordion?

He went thoughtfully back to the barn, and asked Norsgrey

about it. The old man, sprawling with his back to the reindeer's flank, looked up keenly through his orange hair.

'That would be Swifford Fair. I just come from there, done a bit of trading. That's where I got my hens.' As ever, it was hard to make out what he was saying.

'How far's Swifford from here?'

'Road will take you quicker than the river. A mile as the crow flies. Two miles by road. Five by your river. I'll buy your boat from you, give you a good price.'

They did not agree to that, but they gave the old man some of their food. The sheep they had killed ate well, cut up into a stew and flavored with some herbs that Norsgrey supplied from his little cart. When they ate meat, they took it in the form of stews, for stews were kindest to old teeth and tender gums.

'Why doesn't your wife come and eat with us?' Towin asked. 'Is she fussy about strangers or something?'

'She's asleep like I told you, behind that blue curtain. You leave her alone – she's done you no harm.'

The blue curtain was stretched across one corner of the barn, from the cart to a nail on the wall. The barn was now uncomfortably full, for they brought the sheep in with them at dusk. They made uneasy bedfellows with the hens and the old reindeer. The glow of their lamps hardly reached up to the rafters. Those rafters had ceased to be living timber two and a half centuries before. Other life now took refuge in them: grubs, beetles, larvae, spiders, chrysalises slung to the beams with silken threads, fleas and their pupae in swallows' nests, awaiting their owners' return in the next unfailing spring. For these simple creatures, many generations had passed since man contrived his own extinction.

'Here, how old was you reckoning I was?' Norsgrey asked, thrusting his colorful countenance into Martha's face.

'I wasn't really thinking,' Martha said sweetly.

'You was thinking about seventy, wasn't you?'

'I really was not thinking. I prefer not to think about age; it is one of my least favorite subjects.'

'Well, think about mine, then. An early seventy you'd say, wouldn't you?'

'Possibly.'

Norsgrey let out a shriek of triumph, and then looked apprehensively toward the blue curtain.

'Well, let me tell you that you'd be wrong, Mrs Lady – ah, oh dear, yes, very wrong. Shall I tell you how old I am? Shall I? You won't believe me.'

'Go on, how old are you?' Towin asked, growing interested. 'Eighty-five, I'd say you were. I bet you're older than me, and I was born in 1945, the year they dropped that first atomic bomb. I bet you were born before 1945, mate.'

'They don't have years with numbers attached anymore,' Norsgrey said with immense scorn, and turned back to Martha. 'You won't believe this, Mrs Lady, but I'm close on two hundred years old, very close indeed. In fact you might say that it was my two-hundredth birthday next week.'

Martha raised an ironical eyebrow. She said, 'You look well for your age.'

'You're never two hundred, no more than I am,' Towin said scornfully.

'That I am. I'm two hundred, and what's more I shall still be knocking around the old world when all you buggers are dead and buried.'

Towin leaned forward and kicked the old man's boot angrily. Norsgrey brought up a stick and whacked Towin smartly over the shin. Yelping, Towin heaved himself up on his knees and brought his cudgel down at the old man's flaming cranium. Charley stopped the blow in mid-swing.

'Give over,' he said sternly. 'Towin, leave the poor old chap his delusions.'

' 'Tisn't no delusion,' Norsgrey said irritably. 'You can ask my wife when she wakes up.'

Throughout this conversation and during the meal, Pitt had said hardly a word, sitting withdrawn into himself, as he so often did in the Sparcot days. Now he said, mildly enough, 'We'd 'a done better if you'd listened to what I said and stayed on the river rather than settle down in this madhouse for the night. All the world to choose from and you had to choose here!'

83

'You can get outside if you don't like the company,' Norsgrey said. 'Your trouble is you're rude as well as stupid. Praise be, you'll die! None of you lot know anything of the world – you've been stuck in that place wherever-it-was you told me about. There are strange new things in the world you've never heard of.'

'Such as?' Charley asked.

'See this red and green necklace I got around my neck? I got it from Mockweagles. I'm one of the few men who've actually been to Mockweagles. I paid two young cow reindeer for it, and it was cheap at half the price. Only you have to call back there once every hundred years to renew, like, or one morning as you open your eyelids on a new dawn – phutt!, you crumble into dust, all but your eyeballs.'

'What happens to them?' Becky asked, peering at him through the thick lamp glow.

Norsgrey laughed.

'Eyeballs never die. Didn't you know that, Mrs Taffy? They never die. I seen them watching out of thickets at night. They wink at you to remind you what will happen to you if you forget to go back to Mockweagles.'

'Where is this place, Mockweagles?' Greybeard asked.

'I shouldn't be telling you this. There aren't any eyeballs looking, are there? Well, there's this place Mockweagles, only it's secret, see, and it lies right in the middle of a thicket. It's a castle – well, more like a sort of skyscraper than a castle, really. Only they don't live on the bottom twenty floors; those are empty. I mean, you've got to go right up to the top floor to find them.'

'Them, who are them?'

'Oh, men, just ordinary men, only one of them has got a sort of second head with a sealed-up mouth coming out of his neck. They live forever because they're immortals, see. And I'm like them, because I won't ever die, only you have to go back there once every hundred years. I've just been back there now, on my way south.'

'You mean this is your second call there?'

'My third. I went there first of all for the treatment, and you have to go to get your beads renewed.' He ran his fingers through the orange curtain of his beard and peered at them. They were silent.

Towin muttered, 'You can't be that old. It isn't all that time since things fell apart and no more kids were born. Is it?'

'You don't know what time is. Aren't you a bit confused in your mind? Mind you, I'm saying nothing. All I'm saying is I just come from there. There's too many vagabonds wandering around like you lot, moving about the country. It'll be better next time I go there, in another hundred years. There won't be any vagabonds then. They'll all be underground, growing toadstools. I shall have the whole world to myself, just me and Lita and those things that twitter and fry in the hedges. How I wish they'd stop that bloody old twittering and frying all the time. It's going to be hell with all them in a few thousand years or so.' Suddenly he put his paws over his eyes; big senile tears came spurting through his fingers; his shoulders shook. 'It's a lonely life, friends,' he said.

Greybeard laid a hand on his shoulder and offered to get him to bed. Norsgrey jumped up and cried that he could look after himself. Still sniveling, he turned into the gloom, scattering hens, and crawled behind the blue curtain. The others sat looking at each other.

'Daft old fool!' Becky said uncomfortably.

'He seems to know a lot of things,' Towin said to her. 'In the morning, we'd better ask him about your baby.'

She rounded angrily on him.

'Towin, you useless clot you, letting our secrets out! Didn't I tell you over and over you wasn't to mention it till people saw the state I'm in? Your stupid old clacking tongue! You're like an old woman—'

'Becky, is this true?' Greybeard asked 'Are you pregnant?'

'Ah, she's gravid as a rabbit,' Towin admitted, hanging his head. 'Twins. I'd say it is, by the feel.'

Martha looked at the plump little woman; phantom pregnancies were frequent in Sparcot, and she did not doubt this was another such. But people believed what they wanted to believe; Charley clasped his hands together and said earnestly, 'If this be true, God's name be praised! It's a miracle, a sign from Heaven!'

'Don't give us any of that old rubbish,' Towin said angrily. 'This was my doing and no one else's.'

'The Almighty works through the lowest among us, Towin Thomas,' Charley said. 'If Becky is pregnant, then it is a token to us that He will after all come down in the eleventh hour and replenish the earth with His people. Let us all join in prayer – Martha, Algy, Becky—'

'I don't want any of that stuff,' Towin said. 'Nobody's praying for my offspring. We don't owe your God a brass farthing, Charley boy. If He's so blessed powerful, then He was the one that did all this damage in the first place. I reckon old Norsgrey was right – we don't know how long ago it all happened. Don't tell me it was only eleven years we was at Sparcot! It seemed like centuries to me. Perhaps we're all a thousand years old, and—'

'Becky, may I put my hand on your stomach?' Martha asked.

'Let's all have a feel, Beck,' Pitt said, grinning, his interest momentarily roused.

'You keep your hands to yourself,' Becky told him. But she allowed Martha to feel beneath her voluminous clothes, looking into space as the other woman gently kneaded the flesh of her stomach.

'Your stomach is certainly swollen,' Martha said.

'Ah ha! Told you!' Towin cried. 'Four years gone, she is – I mean, four months. That's why we didn't want to leave that house where the sheep were. It would have made us a nice little home, only Clever Dick here would shove off down his beloved river!'

He bared his stubbly wolf visage in a grin toward Greybeard.

'We'll go to Swifford Fair tomorrow, and see what we can fix up for you both,' Greybeard said. 'There should be a doctor there who will examine Becky and give her advice. Meanwhile, let's follow the ginger chap's example and settle down for some sleep.'

'You mind that old reindeer don't eat Isaac during the night,' Becky told Charley. 'I could tell you a thing or two about them animals, I could. They're crafty beasts, reindeer.'

'It wouldn't eat a fox,' Charley said.

'We had one ate our cat now, didn't we, Tow? Tow used to

86

trade in reindeer, whenever it was they first came over to this country – Greybeard'll know, no doubt.'

'Let's see, the war ended in 2005, when the government was overthrown,' Greybeard said. 'The Coalition was set up the year after, and I believe they were the people who first imported reindeer into Britain.'

The memory came back like a blurred newspaper photo. The Swedes had discovered that, alone among the large ruminants, the reindeer could still breed normally and produce living fawns. It was claimed that these animals had acquired some immunity against radiation because the lichen they ate contained a high degree of fallout contamination. In the nineteen-sixties, before Greybeard was born, the contamination in their bones was on the order of a hundred to two hundred strontium units – between six and twelve times above the safety limit for humans.

Since reindeer made efficient transport animals as well as providing good meat and milk, there was a great demand for them throughout Europe. In Canada the caribou became equally popular. Herds of Swedish and Lapp stock were imported into Britain at various times.

'It must have been about '06,' Towin confirmed. ' 'Cause it was then my brother Evan died. Went just like that he did, as he was supping his beer.'

'About this reindeer,' Becky said. 'We made a bit of cash out of it. We had to have a license for the beast – Daffid, we called it. Used to hire it out for work at so much a day.

'We had a shed out the back of our little shop. Daffid was kept in there. Very cosy it was, with hay and all. Also we had our old cat, Billy. Billy was real old and very intelligent. Not a better cat anywhere, but of course we wasn't supposed to keep it. They got strict after the war, if you remember, and Billy was supposed to go for food. As if we'd give Billy up!

'Sometimes that Coalition would send police around and they'd come right in – not knock or nothing, you know. Then they'd search the house. It's ungodly times we've lived through, friends!

'Anyhow, this night, Tow here comes running in – been down

the boozer, he had – and he says the police are coming around to make a search.'

'So they were!' Towin said, showing signs of an old discomfiture.

'So he says,' Becky repeated. 'So we has to hide poor old Billy or we'd all be in the cart. So I run with her out into the shed, where old Daffid's lying down just like this ugly beast here, and tucks Billy under the straw for safety.

'Then I goes back into our parlor. But no police come, and Tow goes off fast asleep, and I nod off too, and at midnight I know the old fool has been imagining things.'

'They passed us by!' Towin cried.

'So out I went into the shed, and there's Daffid standing there chewing, and no sign of Billy. I get Towin and we both have a search, but no Billy. Then we see his tail hanging out bloody old Daffid's mouth.'

'Another time, he ate one of my gloves,' Towin said.

As Greybeard settled to sleep by a solitary lantern, the last thing he saw was the gloomy countenance of Norsgrey's reindeer. These animals had been hunted by Paleolithic man; they had only to wait a short while now and all the hunters would be gone.

In Greybeard's dream, there was a situation that could not happen. He was in a chromium-plated restaurant dining with several people he did not know. They, their manners, their dress, were all very elaborate, even artificial; they ate ornate dishes with involved utensils. Everyone present was extremely old – centenarians to a man – yet they were sprightly, even childlike. One of the women there was saying that she had solved the whole problem: that just as adults grew from children, so children would eventually grow from adults, if they waited long enough.

And then everyone was laughing to think the solution had not been reached before. Greybeard explained to them that it was as if they were all actors performing their parts against a lead curtain that cut off forever every second as it passed – yet as he spoke he was concealing from them, for reasons of compassion, the harsher truth that the curtain was also barring them from the seconds and all time *before* them. There were young children all around them (though looking strangely grown-up), dancing and throwing some sticky substance to each other.

He was trying to seize a strand of this stuff when he woke. In the ancient dawn light Norsgrey was harnessing his reindeer. The animal held its head low, puffing into the stale cold. Huddled under their wrappings, the rest of Greybeard's party bore as much resemblance to human forms as a newly made grave.

Wrapping one of his blankets around him, Greybeard got up, stretched, and went over to the old man. The draft he had been lying in had stiffened his limbs, making him limp.

'You're on your way early, Norsgrey.'

'I'm always an early mover. Lita wants to be off.'

'Is she well this morning?'

'Never mind about her. She's tucked safe under the canopy of the cart. She won't speak to strangers in the mornings.'

'Are we not going to see her?'

'No.' Over the cart, a tatty brown canvas was stretched, and tied with leather thongs back and front so that nobody could see within. The cockerel crowed from beneath it. Norsgrey had already gathered up his chickens. Greybeard wondered what of their own equipment might not be missing, seeing that the old fellow worked so quietly.

'I'll open the door for you,' he said. Weary hinges creaked as he pushed the door forward. He stood there scratching his beard, taking in the frost-becalmed scene before him. His company stirred as cold air entered the barn. Isaac sat up and licked his sharp muzzle. Towin squinted at his defunct watch. The reindeer started forward and dragged the cart into the open.

'I'm cold and stiff. I'll walk with you a minute or two to see you on your way,' Greybeard said, wrapping his blanket more tightly about him.

'As you will. I'd be glad of your company as long as you don't talk too much. I like to make an early start when the frying's not so bad. By midday, it makes such a noise you'd think the hedges were burning.'

'You still find roads you can travel?'

'Ah, lots of roads still open between necessary points. There's more traveling being done again lately; people are getting restless. Why they can't sit where they are and die off in peace, I don't know.'

'This place you were telling us about last night . . .'

'I never said nothing last night; I was drunk.'

'Mockweagles, you called it. What sort of treatment did they give you when you were there?'

Norsgrey's little eyes almost disappeared between folds of his fibrous red and mauve skin. He jerked his thumb into the bushes through which they were pushing their way.

'They're in there waiting for you, my bearded friend. You can hear them twittering and frying, can't you? They get up earlier than us and they go to bed later than us, and they'll get you in the end.'

'But not you?'

'I go and have this injection and these beads every hundred years . . .'

'So that's what they give you . . . You get an injection as well as those things around your neck. You know what those beads are, don't you? They're vitamin pills.'

'I'm saying nothing. I don't know what you're talking about. Any case, you mortals would do best to hold your tongues. Here's the road, and I'm off.'

They had come out at a sort of crossroads, where their track crossed a road that still boasted traces of tarmac on its rutted surface. Norsgrey beat at his reindeer with a stick, goading it into a less dilatory walk.

He looked over his shoulder at Greybeard, his misty breath entangled with the bright hairs of his cheeks. 'Tell you one thing – if you get to Swifford Fair, ask for Bunny Jingadangelow.'

'Who's he?' Greybeard asked.

'I'm telling you, he's the man you should ask for at Swifford Fair. Remember the name – Bunny Jingadangelow.'

Wrapped in his blanket, Greybeard stood looking at the disappearing cart. He thought the canvas at the back stirred, and that he glimpsed – no, perhaps it was not a hand but his imagination.

He stood there until the winding track carried Norsgrey and his conveyance out of sight.

As he turned away, he saw in the bushes close by a broken-necked corpse pinned to a post. It had the cocky, grinning appearance achieved only by those successfully long dead. Its skull was patched with flesh like dead leaves. Thin though the corpse's jacket was, its flesh had worn still thinner, had shriveled and parted like moisture drying off a stretch of sand, leaving the bars of rib salt beneath.

'Left dead at the crossroads as a warning to wrongdoers . . . Like the Middle Ages . . . the old-aged Middle Ages . . .' Grey-beard muttered to himself. The eye sockets stared back at him. He was overtaken less by disgust than by a pang of longing for the DOUCH(E) truck he had parted with years ago. How people had underestimated the worth of mechanical gadgetry! The urge to record was on him; someone should leave behind a summary of earth's decline, if only for visiting archeologists from other possible worlds. He trotted heavily back down the track toward the barn, saying to himself as he went, 'Bunny Jingadangelow, Bunny Jingadangelow . . .'

Nightfall came that day to the sound of music. They could see the lights of Swifford across the low flood. They rowed through a section of the Thames that had burst its banks and spread over the adjoining land, making water plants of the vegetation. Soon there were other boats near them, and people calling to them; their accents were difficult to understand, as Norsgrey's had been at first.

'Why don't they speak English the way they used?' Charley asked angrily. 'It makes everything so much harder.'

'P'raps it isn't only the time that's gone funny,' Towin suggested. 'P'raps distances have gone wrong too. P'raps this is France or China, eh, Charley? I'd believe anything, I would.'

'More fool you,' Becky said.

They came to where a raised dike or levee had been built. Behind it were dwellings of various kinds, huts and stalls, most of them of a temporary nature. Here was a stone bridge built in imposing fashion, with a portly stone balustrade, some of which had tumbled away. Through its span they saw lanterns bobbing, and two men walked among a small herd of reindeer, tending them and seeing they were watered for the night.

'We shall have to guard the boats and the sheep,' Martha said, as they moored against the bridge. 'We don't know how trust-worthy these people are. Jeff Pitt, stay with me while the others go to look about.'

'I suppose I'd better,' Pitt said. 'At least we'll be out of trouble here. Perhaps you and I might split a cold lamb cutlet between us while the others are gone.'

Greybeard touched his wife's hand.

'I'll see how much the sheep will fetch while I'm about it,' he said.

They smiled at each other and he stepped up the bank, into the activity of the fair, with Charley, Towin, and Becky following. The ground squelched beneath their feet; smoke rolled across it from the little fires that burned everywhere. A heartening savor of food being cooked hung in the air. By most of the fires were little knots of people and a smooth talker, a vendor offering something for sale, whether a variety of nuts or fruits – one slab-cheeked fellow offered a fruit whose name Greybeard recalled only with difficulty from another world: peaches – or watches or kettles or rejuvenation elixirs. The customers were handing over coin for their acquisitions. In Sparcot currency had almost disappeared; the community had been small enough for a simple exchange of work and goods to be effective.

'Oooh, it's like being back in civilization again,' Towin said, rubbing his wife's buttocks. 'How do you like this, eh, missus? Better than cruising on the river, wouldn't you say? Look, they've even got a pub! Let's all get a drink and get our insides warm, wouldn't you say?'

He produced a bayonet, hawked it to two dealers, set them bidding against each other, and handed over the blade in exchange for a handful of silver coin. Grinning at his own business acumen, Towin doled some of the money out to Charley and Greybeard.

'I'm only lending you this, mind. Tomorrow we'll flog one of the sheep and you can repay me. Five percent's my rate, lads.'

They pushed into the nearest liquor stall, a framework hut with wooden floor. Its name, Potsluck Tavern, stood above the door in curly letters. It was crowded with ancient men and women, while behind the bar a couple of massive gnarled men like diseased oaks presided over the bottles. As he sipped a mead, Greybeard listened to the conversation about him, insensibly letting his mood expand. He had never thought it would feel so good to hear money jingle in his pocket.

Impressions and images fluttered in on him. It seemed as if, in leaving Sparcot, they had indeed escaped from a concentration camp. Here the human world went on in a way it had not managed at Sparcot. It was fatally wounded perhaps; in another half-century it would be rolled up and put away; but till then there was business to be made, life to be transacted, the chill and heat of personality to be struck out. As the mead started its combustion in his blood, Greybeard rejoiced to see that here was humanity, rapped over the knuckles for its follies by Whatever-Gods-May-Be, but still totally unregenerate.

An aged couple sat close by him, both of them wearing ill-fitting false teeth that looked as if they had been hammered into place by the nearest blacksmith; Greybeard drank in the noisy backchat of their party. They were celebrating their wedding. The man's previous wife had died a month before of bronchitis. His playful scurries at his new partner, all fingers under the table, all lopsided teeth above, had about it a smack of the Dance of Death, but the earthy optimism of it all went not ill with the mead.

'You aren't from the town?' one of the knotty barmen asked Greybeard. His accents, like those of everyone else they met, were difficult to understand at first.

'I don't know what town you mean,' Greybeard said.

'Why, from Ensham or Ainsham, up the road a mile. I took you for a stranger. We used to hold the fair there in the streets, where it was comfortable and dry, but last year they reckoned we brought the flu bugs with us, and they wouldn't have us in this year. That's why we're camped here on the marsh, developing rheumatics. Now they walk down to us – no more than a matter of a mile it is, but a lot of them are so old and lazy they won't come this far. That's why business is so bad.'

Although he looked like a riven oak, he was a gentle enough man. He introduced himself as Pete Potsluck, and talked with Greybeard between servings.

Greybeard began to tell him about Sparcot; bored by the subject, Becky and Towin and Charley, the latter with Isaac in his arms, moved away and joined in conversation with the wedding party. Potsluck said he reckoned there were many communities like Sparcot buried in the wilderness. 'Get a bad winter, such as we've not had for a year or two, and some of them will be wiped out entirely. That'll be the eventual end of all of us, I suppose.'

'Is there fighting anywhere? Do you hear rumors of an invasion from Scotland?'

'They say the Scots are doing very well, in the Highlands anyhow. There was so few of them in the first place; down here, population was so high it took some years for plagues and famines to shake us down to a sort of workable minimum. The Scots probably dodged all that trouble. But why should they bother us? We're all getting too long in the tooth for fighting.'

'There are some wild-looking sparks at this fair.'

Potsluck laughed. 'I don't deny that. Senile delinquents, I call them. Funny thing, without any youngsters to set the pace, the old ones get up to their tricks – as well as they're able.'

'What has happened to people like Croucher, then?'

'Croucher? Oh, this Cowley bloke you mentioned! The dictator class are all dead and buried, and a good job too. No, it's getting too late for that sort of strong-arm thing. I mean, you just find laws in the towns, but outside of them, there is no law.'

'I didn't so much mean law as force.'

'Well now, you can't have law without force, can you? There's a level where force is bad, but when you get to the sort of level we are down to, force becomes strength, and then it's a positive blessing.'

'You are probably right.'

'I'd have thought you would have known that. You look the kind who carries a bit of law about with him, with those big fists and that bushy great beard.'

Greybeard grinned. 'I don't know. It's difficult to judge what one's own character is in unprecedented times like ours.'

'You haven't made up your mind about yourself? Perhaps that's what's keeping you looking so young.'

Changing the subject, Greybeard changed his drink, and got himself a big glass of fortified parsnip wine, buying one for Potsluck also. Behind him, the wedding party became tuneful, singing the ephemeral songs of a century back, which had oddly developed a power to stick – and to stick in the gullet, Greybeard thought – as they launched into

> ' "If you were the only girl in the world,
> And I were the only boy . . ." '

'It may come to that yet,' he said, half laughing, to Potsluck. 'Have you seen any children around? I mean, are any being born in these parts?'

'They've got a freak show here. You want to go and look in at that,' Potsluck said. Sudden bleakness eclipsed his good humor, and he turned sharply away to arrange the bottles behind him. In a little while, as if feeling he had been discourteous, he turned back and began to talk on a new tack.

'I used to be a hairdresser, back before the Accident and until that blinking Coalition government closed my shop. Seems years ago now, but then so it is – long years, I mean. I was trained up in my trade by my dad, who had the shop before me; and I always used to say when we first heard about this radiation scare that as long as there were people around they'd still want their hair cut – as long as it didn't all fall out, naturally. I still do a bit of cutting for the other traveling men. There are those that still care for their appearance, I'm glad to say.'

Greybeard did not speak. He recognized a man in the grip of reminiscence. Potsluck had lost some of his semirustic way of speech; with a genteel phrase like 'those that still care for their appearance,' he revealed how he had slipped back half a century to that vanished world of toilet perquisites, hair creams, before- and after-shave lotions, and the disguising of odors and blemishes.

'I remember once, when I was a very young man, having to go around to a private house – I can picture the place now, though I daresay it has fallen down long since. It was very dark going up the stairs, and I had to take the young lady's arm. Yes, that's right and I went there after the shop had shut, I remember. My old dad sent me; I can't have been more than seventeen, if that.

'And there was this dead gentleman laid out upstairs in his coffin, in the bedroom. Very calm and prosperous he looked. He'd been a good customer, too, in his lifetime. His wife insisted that his hair was cut before the funeral. He was always a very tidy gentleman, she told me. I spoke to her downstairs afterward – a thin lady with earrings. She gave me five shillings. No, I don't remember – perhaps it was ten shillings. Anyhow, sir, it was a generous sum in those days – before all this dreadful business.

'So I cut the dead gentleman's hair. You know how the hair and the fingernails keep on growing on a man after death, and his had got rather straggly. Only a trim it needed really, but I cut it as reverently as I could. I was a churchgoer in those days, believe it or not. And this young lady that showed me upstairs, she had to hold his head up under the neck so that I could get at it with my scissors; and in the middle of it she got the giggles and dropped the dead gentleman. She said she wanted me to give her a kiss. I was a bit shocked at the time, seeing that the gentleman was her father. . . . I don't know why I should be telling you this. Memory's a rare, funny thing. I suppose if I'd had any sense in those days, I'd have screwed the silly little hussy on the spot, but I wasn't too familiar with life then – never mind death! Have another drink on me?'

'Thanks, I may come back later,' Greybeard said. 'I want to have a look around at the fair now. Do you know of anyone called Bunny Jingadangelow?'

'Jingadangelow? Yes, I know of him. What do you want with him? Go over the bridge and up the road toward Ensham, and you'll come to his stall; it's got the words "Eternal Life" above it. You can't mistake it. Okay?'

Looking around at the party of singers, Greybeard caught Charley's eye. Charley rose, and they walked out together, leaving Towin and Becky singing 'Any Old Iron' with the wedding party.

'The fellow who's just got married again is a reindeer breeder,' Charley said. 'It seems they're still the only big mammal unaffected by the radiation. Do you remember how people said they'd never do over here when they were first imported, because the climate was too wet for their coats?'

'It's too wet for my coat too, Charley. It's less cold than it was, and by the look of the clouds there's rain about. What sort of shelter are we going to find ourselves for the night?'

'One of the women back in the bar said we might get lodgings up this way, in the town. We'll look out. It's early yet.'

They walked up the road, taking in the bustle at the various pitches.

Isaac yipped and snuffled as they passed a cage of foxes, and next to it a run full of weasels. There were also hens for sale, and a woman wrapped in furs tried to sell them powdered reindeer antler as a charm against impotence and ill health. Two rival quacks sold purges and clysters, charms against rheumatism, and nostrums for the cramps of age; the few people who stood listening to them seemed skeptical. Trade was dropping off at this time of evening; people were now after entertainment rather than business, and a juggler drew appreciative crowds. So did a fortuneteller – though that must be a limited art now, Greybeard thought, with all dark strangers turned to grey and no possible patter of tiny feet.

They came to the next stall, which was little more than a wooden platform; above it fluttered a banner with the words ETERNAL LIFE on it.

'This must be Jingadangelow's pitch,' Greybeard said.

Several people were here; some were listening to the man speaking from the platform, while others jostled about a fallen figure that was propped against the platform edge, with two aged crones weeping and croaking over it. To see what was happening was difficult in the flapping light of unguarded torches, but the words of the man on the platform made things clearer.

This speaker was a tall raven figure with wild hair and a face absolutely white except for quarries of slaty grey under his eyes. He spoke in the voice of a cultured man, with a vigor his frame seemed scarcely able to sustain, conducting time to his phrases with a pair of fine wild hands.

'Here before us you see evidence of what I am saying, my friends. In sight and hearing of us all, a brother has just departed this life. His soul burst out of his ragged coating and left us. Look at us – look at us, my dearly loved brethren, all dressed in our ragged coating on this cold and miserable night somewhere in the great universe. Can you say any one of you in your hearts that it would not be better to follow our friend?'

'To hell with that for a lark!' a man called, clasping a bottle. He drew the speaker's accusing finger.

'For *you* it might not be better, I agree, my friend – for you would go as our brother here did, loaded before the Lord with liquor. The Lord's stood enough of our dirty nonsense, brethren; that's the plain truth. He's had more than He can stand. He's finished with us, but not with our souls. He's cut us off, and manifestly He will disapprove if we persist till our graves in perpetuating the follies we should have left behind in our youth.'

'How else are we to keep warm on these mucking winter nights?' the jolly man asked, and there was a murmur of approval about him. Charley tapped him on the shoulder and said, 'Would you mind keeping quiet while this gentleman speaks?'

The jolly man swung around on Charley. Though age had withered him like a prune, his mouth was spread red and large across his face as if it had been plastered there by a fist. He worked this ample mouth now, realized that Charley was stronger than he was, and relapsed into silence. Unmoved, the parson continued his oration.

'We must bow before His will, my friends, that's what we must do. Soon we shall all go down on our knees here and pray. It will be fitting for us all to go together into His presence, for we are the last of His generations, and it is meet that we should bear ourselves accordingly. What have we to fear if we are righteous, ask yourselves that? Once before He swept the earth clean with a flood because of the sins of man. This time He has taken from our generative organs the God-given power to procreate. If you think that to be a more terrible punishment than the flood, then the sins of our century, the twenty-first century, are more terrible sins. He can wipe the slate clean as many times as He will, and begin again.

'So we do not weep for this earth we are to leave. We are born to vanish as the cattle we once tended have already vanished, leaving the earth clean and new for His further works. Let me recall to you, my brethren, before we sink upon our knees in prayer, the words of the Scriptures concerning this time.'

He put his fluttering hands together and peered into the darkness to recite: ' "For that which befalleth the sons of men befalleth beasts; even one thing befalleth them. As the one dieth, so dieth the other; yea, they have all one breath. So that a man hath no pre-eminence above a beast; for all is vanity. All go unto one place, all are of the dust, and all turn again to dust. Wherefore I perceive that there is nothing better than that a man should rejoice in the Lord's works, for that is his portion. And who shall bring him to see what shall be after him?" '

'My old missus will be after me, if I don't get home,' the jolly man said. 'Good night to thee, parson.' He began to straggle up the road, supported by a crony. Greybeard shook Charley's arm and said, 'This man isn't Bunny Jingadangelow, for all that he advertises eternal life. Let's move on.'

'No, let's hear a bit more yet, Greybeard. Here's a man speaking truth. In how many years have I heard someone so worth listening to?'

'You stay here, then; I'll go on.'

'Stay and listen, Algy – it'll do you good.'

But Greybeard moved up the road. The parson was again using the dead man near his platform for his text. Perhaps that had been one of the ineradicable faults of mankind – for even a convinced atheist had to admit there were faults – that it was never content with a thing as a thing; it had to turn things into

99

symbols of other things. A rainbow was not only a rainbow, a storm was a sign of celestial anger, and even from the puddingy earth came forth dark chthonian gods. What did it all mean? What an agnostic believed and what the willowy parson believed were not only irreconcilable systems of thought: they were equally valid systems of thought, because somewhere along the evolutionary line, man, developing this habit of thinking of symbols, had provided himself with more alternatives than he could manage, more systems of alternatives than he could manage. Animals moved in no such channel of imagination – they copulated and they ate. But to the saint, bread was a symbol of life, as the phallus was to the pagan. The animals themselves were pressed into symbolic service – and not only in medieval bestiaries, by any means.

Such a usage was a distortion, although man seemed unable to ratiocinate without it. That had been the trouble right from the beginning. Perhaps it had even been the beginning, back among those first men that man could never get clearly defined (for the early men, being also symbols, had to be either lumbering brutes, or timid noble savages, or undergo some other interpretation). Perhaps the first fire, the first tool, the first wheel, the first carving in a limestone cave, had each possessed a symbolic rather than a practical value, had each been pressed to serve distortion rather than reality. It was a sort of madness that had driven man from his humble sites on the edges of the woods into towns and cities, into arts and wars, into religious crusades, into martyrdom and prostitution, into dyspepsia and fasting, into love and hatred, into this present cul-de-sac. It had all come about in pursuit of symbols. In the beginning was the symbol, and darkness was over the face of the earth.

Greybeard abandoned this line of thought as he came to the next pitch along the road. He found himself looking at another banner reading ETERNAL LIFE.

The banner hung across the front of a garage standing drunkenly beside a dilapidated house. Its doors had fallen off but were propped inside to screen off the back half of the garage. A fire burned behind this screen, throwing the shadows of two people across the roof. In front of the screen, nursing a lantern in chilled hands, was a shrivel-gummed old girl perched on a box. She called to Greybeard in a routine fashion, 'If you want Eternal Life, here's the place to find it. Don't listen to the parson! His asking price is too high. Here, you don't have to give anything, you don't have to give anything up. Our kind of eternal life can be bought by the syringe-full and paid for without any trouble over your soul. Walk in if you want to live forever!'

'Shot in the arm or shot in the dark, I don't know that I entirely trust you or the parson, old lady.'

'Come in and get reborn, you bag of bones!'

Not relishing this mode of address, even if delivered by rote, Greybeard said sharply, 'I want to speak to Bunny Jingadangelow. Is he here?'

The old witch coughed and sent a gob of green phlegm flapping toward the floor.

'*Dr* Jingadangelow ain't here. He's not at everyone's beck and call, you know. What do you want?'

'Can you tell me where he is? I want to speak to him.'

'I'll fix you an appointment if you want a rejuvenation or the immortality course, but I tell you he ain't here.'

'Who's behind the screen?'

'My husband, if you must know, and a client, as if it's any of your business. Who are you, anyway? I never seen you before.'

One of the shadows flopped more widely across the roof, and a high voice said, 'What's the trouble out there?'

Next moment, a youth appeared.

The effect on Greybeard was like a shock of cold water. Through the toils of the years he had arrived at the realization that childhood was now no more than an idea interred within the crania of old men, and that young flesh was an antiquity in the land. If you forgot about rumors, he was himself all that the withered world had left to offer in the way of a youngster. But this – this stripling, dressed merely in a sort of tunic, wearing a red and green necklace like Norsgrey's, exposing his frail white legs and arms, regarding Greybeard with wide and innocent eyes . . .

'My God,' Greybeard said. 'Then they are still being born!'

The youth spoke in a shrill, impersonal voice. 'You see before you, sir, the beneficial effects of Dr Jingadangelow's well-known combined Rejuvenation and Immortality Course, respected and recommended from Gloucester to Oxford, from Banbury to Berks. Enroll yourself here for a course, sir, before you are too late. You can be like me, friend, after only a few trial doses.'

'I believe you no more than I believed the parson,' Greybeard said, still slightly breathless. 'How old are you, boy? Sixteen, twenty, thirty? I forget the young ages.'

A second shadow flapped across the roof, and a shabby grotesque with a plantation of warts on his chin and forehead hobbled into view. He was bent so double that he could scarcely peer up at Greybeard through his tangled eyebrows.

'You want the treatment, sir? You want to become lovely and beautiful again, like this fine young attractive fellow?'

'You're not a very good advertisement for your own preparation, are you?' Greybeard said, turning again to regard the youth. He stepped forward to peer at him more closely. As the stunning first effects wore off, he saw that the youth was in fact a flabby and poor specimen with a pasty countenance.

'Dr Jingadangelow developed his wonderful treatments too late to help me, sir,' said the grotesque. 'I run up against him too late in life, you might say, but he could help you, as he did our young friend here. Our young friend is actually one hundred and ninety-five years old, sir, though you'd never think it to see him. Why, bless him, he's in the full bloom of youth, as you could be.'

'I never felt better in my life,' the youth said, in his curious high voice. 'I'm in the full bloom of youth.'

Suddenly Greybeard grasped his arm and swung him so that the light from the crone's lantern gleamed directly onto the boy's face. The boy cried out in sudden hurt. The innocence in his eyes was revealed as vacancy. Thick powder on his face furrowed up into tracks of pain; he opened his mouth and exposed black fangs behind a frontal layer of white paint. Slipping away, he kicked Greybeard fiercely on the shin, cursing as he did so.

'You rogue, you filthy little swindler, you're ninety years old –

you've been castrated!' Greybeard swung angrily on the ancient man. 'You've no right to do such a thing!'

'Why not? He's my son.' He shrank back with raised arm in front of his face. He showed his twisted and pocked jaw, champing with fury. The 'boy' started to scream. As Greybeard turned, he shrieked, 'Don't touch my dad! Bunny and I thought of the idea. I'm only earning an honest living. Do you think I want to spend my days haggard and starved like you? Help, help, murderer! Thieves! Fire! Help, friends, help!'

'Shut your—' Greybeard got no further. The crone moved, leaping from behind him. She swung her lantern down across the side of his face. As he twisted around, the old man brought a thick stick down on his neck, and he tumbled toward the crumbling concrete floor.

Again, for him a situation that could not happen. There were young women sitting at tables, scantily clad, entertaining antique men with physiognomies like ill-furled sails. Their lips were red, their cheeks pink, their eyes dark and lustrous. The girl nearest Greybeard wore stockings of a wide mesh net that climbed up to the noble eminence of her crotch; here they met red satin knickers, frilled at the edges, as though to conceal a richer rose among their petals, and matching in hue the brief tunic, set off with inviting brass buttons, that partially bid a bosom of such splendor that it made its possessor's chin appear undershot

Between this spectacle and Greybeard were a number of legs, one pair of which he identified as Martha's. The act of recognition made him realize that this was far from being a dream and that he was near to being unconscious. He groaned, and Martha's tender face came down to his level; she put a worn hand to his face and kissed him.

'My poor old sweetheart, you'll be all right in a minute.'

'Martha . . . Where are we?'

'They were mobbing you for laying hands on that eunuch at the garage. Charley heard them and fetched Pitt and me. We came as soon as we could. We're going to stay here for the night, and you'll be all right by morning.'

Prompted by this remark, he recognized two of the other pairs of legs now; both sprouted mud and marsh grass; one pair was Charley's, one Jeff Pitt's. He asked again, more strongly, 'Where are we?'

'Lucky you didn't get yourself killed,' Pitt grunted.

'We're next door to the garage where they attacked you,' Martha said. 'It's a house – to judge by its popularity – of rather good repute.'

He caught the fleeting smile on her face. His heart opened up to her, and he pressed her hand to show how he cherished a woman who could make even an unpleasant pleasantry. Life flowed back into him.

'Help me up, I'm mended,' he said.

Pitt and Charley took hold of him under his arms. Only the pair of legs he had not recognized did not move. As he rose his gaze traveled up these solid shanks and up the extravagant territory of a coat fashioned from rabbit skins. The skins preserved the heads of these lagomorphs, teeth, ears, whiskers, and all; the eyes had been replaced with black buttons; some of the ears, improperly preserved, were decaying, and a certain effluvium – probably encouraged by the warmth of the room – was radiated; but the effect of the whole was undeniably majestic. As Greybeard's eyes came level with those of the coat's wearer, he said, 'Bunny Jingadangelow, I presume?'

'Dr Bunny Jingadangelow at your service, Mr Timberlane,' the man in the coat said, flexing his sacrolumbar regions sufficiently to indicate a bow. 'I'm delighted that my ministrations have had such excellent and speedy effect on your injuries – but we can discuss the state of your indebtedness to me later. First, I think you should exercise your circulation by taking a turn about the room. Allow me to assist you.'

He took a purchase on Greybeard's arm, and began to walk him between the tables. For the moment, Greybeard offered no opposition as he studied the man in the rabbit-skin coat. Jingadangelow looked to be scarcely out of his fifties – perhaps no more than six years older than Greybeard, and a young man as men went these days. He wore a twirling moustache and sideburns, but the rotundity of his chin attained a smoothness now seldom seen or attempted. There was over his face such a settled look of blandness that it seemed no metoposcopy could ever decide his true character.

'I understand,' he said, 'that before you tried to attack one of my clients you were seeking me out to ask my help and advice.'

'I did not attack your client,' Greybeard said, freeing himself from the man's embrace. 'Though I regret that in a moment of anger I seized hold of one of your accomplices.'

'Tosh, man, young Trotty is an advertisement, not an accomplice. The name of Dr Jingadangelow is known throughout the Midlands, you understand, as that of a great humanitarian – a human humanitarian. I'd give you one of my bills if I had one on me. You should realize before you start feeling pugilistic that I am one of the great figures of the – er, where are we now – of the twenty-twenties.'

'You may be widely known. I'm not arguing about that. I met a poor mad fellow, Norsgrey, and his wife, who had been to you for treatment—'

'Wait, wait. Norsgrey, Norsgrey . . . What kind of name is that? Not on my books . . .' He stood with his head raised and one finger planted in the middle of his forehead. 'Oh, yes, yes, yes, indeed. Mention of his wife had me baffled for a moment. Strictly between you and me . . .' Jingadangelow maneuvered Greybeard into a corner; he leaned forward and said confidentially, 'Of course, the complaints of one's patients are both private and sacred, but poor old Norsgrey hasn't really got a wife, you know, any more than this table has; it's a she-badger that he's rather too fond of.' He tapped his forehead again with an ample finger. 'Why not? Thin blood needs a little warmth abed these chilly nights. Poor fellow nutty as a walnut tree . . .'

'You are broad-minded.'

'I forgive all human faults and follies, sir. It's part of my calling. We must mitigate this vale of tears what way we can. Such understanding is, of course, part of the secret of my wonderful curative powers.'

'Which is a way of saying you leech a living out of old madmen like Norsgrey. He is under the delusion that you have made him immortal.'

During this conversation Jingadangelow seated himself and beckoned to a woman who hobbled over and set down two drinks before them. The doctor nodded and waved a pair of plump fingers at her in thanks. To Greybeard he said, 'How strange to hear ethical objections again after all these years— quite takes me back . . . You must lead a secluded life. This old chap Norsgrey, you understand, is dying. He gets noises like frying in his head; it's a fatal dropsy. So – he mistakes the hope I have given him for the immortality I promised him. It's a comfortable error, surely? I travel, if I may for a moment indulge in a personal confidence, without any such hope; therefore Norsgrey – and there are many like him, luckily – is more fortunate than I in spirit. I console myself by being more fortunate in worldly possessions.'

Greybeard set down his drink and looked about. Although his neck still ached, good humor filled him.

'Do you mind if my wife and friends join us?'

'Not at all, not at all, though I trust you are not bored with my company already. I hoped some talk of this and that might precede any business we might do together. I thought I had recognized a kindred spirit in you.'

Greybeard said, 'What made you think that?'

'Mainly the intuitive feeling with which I am richly endowed. You are uncommitted. You don't suffer as you should in this blighted time; though life is miserable, you enjoy it. Is this not so?'

'How do you know this? Yes, yes, you are correct, but we have only just met—'

'The answer to that is never entirely pleasing to the ego. It is that, although all men are each unique, all men are also each much the same. You have an ambivalence in your nature; many men have an ambivalence. I only have to talk with them for a minute to diagnose it. Am I making sense?'

'How do you diagnose *my* ambivalence?'

'I am not a mind reader, but let me cast about.' He expanded his cheeks, raised his eyebrows, gazed into his glass, and made a very judicious face indeed. 'We need our disasters. You and I have weathered, somehow, the collapse of a civilization. We are survivors after shipwreck. But for us two, we feel something deeper than survival – triumph! Before the crash came, we willed it, and so disaster for us is a success, a victory for the raging will. Don't look so surprised! You're not a man, surely, to regard the recesses of the mind as a very salubrious place. Have you thought of the world we were born in, and what it would have grown into had not that unfortunate little radiation experiment run amok? Would it not have been a world too complex, too impersonal, for the likes of us to flourish in?'

'You are doing my thinking for me,' Greybeard said.

'It is a wise man's role, but so is listening.' Jingadangelow quaffed his drink and leaned forward over the empty glass. 'Is not this ragtaggle present preferable to that other mechanized, organized, deodorized present we might have found ourselves in, simply because in this present we can live on a human scale? In that other present that we missed by a neutron's breadth, had not megalomania grown to such a scale that the ordinary simple richness of an individual life was stifled?'

'Certainly there was a lot wrong with the twentieth-century way of life.'

'There was everything wrong with it.'

'No, you exaggerate. Some things—'

'Don't you think that if everything spiritual was wrong with it, *everything* was wrong with it? It's no good getting nostalgic. It wasn't all drugs and education. Wasn't it also the need for drugs and the poverty of education? Wasn't it the climax and orgasm of the Machine Age? Wasn't it Mons and Belsen and Bataan and Stalingrad and Hiroshima and the rest? Didn't we do well to get flung off the roundabout?'

'You only ask questions,' Greybeard said.

'They are themselves answers.'

'That is double talk. You are giving me double talk. No, wait – look, I wish to talk more with you. I can pay you. This is an important conversation . . . Let me get my wife and friends here.'

Greybeard rose. His head ached. The drink had been powerful, the room was noisy and hot, he was overexcited. It was seldom anyone talked about anything but toothache and the weather. He looked about for Martha and could not see her.

He walked through the room. There were stairs leading to the rooms above. He saw that the painted women were neither so voluptuous nor so busy as he had at first imagined. Though they were padded and painted, their skins were stamped with the liver marks and whorls of age, their eyes were rheumy. Bizarrely smiling, they reached out hands to him. He stumbled through them. They were full of liquor, they coughed and laughed and trembled as he went by. The room was full of their motions, like a cage of captive jackdaws.

The women waved – had he once dreamed of them? – but he took no notice. Martha had gone. Charley and old Pitt had gone. Seeing that he was all right, they must have returned to guard the boats. And Towin and Becky – no, they had not been here . . . He remembered what he had been seeking Bunny Jingadangelow for; instead of leaving, he turned back to the far corner, where another drink awaited him and the doctor sat with an octogen-arian hussy on his knee. This woman sat with one hand about his neck and with the other stroked the rabbit heads on his coat.

'Look, Doctor, I came here to seek you not for myself, but for a couple who are of my party,' Greybeard said, leaning over the table. 'There's a woman, Becky; she claims that she is with child, though she must be over seventy. I want you to examine her and see if what she says is true.'

'Sit down, friend, and let us discuss this expectant lady of yours,' Jingadangelow said. 'Drink your drink, since I presume you will be paying for this round. The delusions of elderly ladies is a choice topic for this time of night, eh, Jean? No doubt neither of you would recall that little poem – how does it go now? "Looking in my mirror to see my wasted skin," and yes—

> ' "But time, to make me grieve,
> Part steals, part lets abide,
> And shakes my fractured frame at eve
> With throbbings of noontide."

'Touching, eh? I fancy your lady has a few throbbings left, nothing more. But I shall come and see her, of course. It is my duty. I shall naturally assure her that she is in the family way, if that is what she desires to hear.' He folded his fleshy hands together and frowned.

'There's no chance she might really be about to bear a child?'

'My dear Timberlane – if you will pardon my not using your somewhat inane sobriquet – hope springs as eternal to the human womb as to the human breast, but I am surprised to find you seem to share her hope.'

'I suppose I do. You said yourself that hope was valuable.'

'Not valuable: imperative. But you must hope for yourself – when we hope for other people we are invariably disappointed. Our dreams have jurisdiction only over ourselves. Knowing you as I do, I see that you really came to me for your own sake. I rejoice to see it. My friend, you love life, you love this life with all its blemishes, with all its tastes and distastes – you also desire my immortality cure, do you not?'

Resting his throbbing head on his hand, Greybeard quaffed down more drink and said, 'Many years ago I was in Oxford – in Cowley, to be accurate – when I heard of a treatment, it was just a rumor, a treatment that might prolong life, perhaps for several hundred years. It was something they were developing at a hospital there. Is it possible this could be done? I'd want scientific evidence before I believe.'

'Of course you do, naturally, undeniably, and I would expect nothing less of a man like you,' Jingadangelow said, nodding so vigorously that the woman was almost dislodged from his lap. 'The best scientific evidence is empirical. You shall have empirical evidence. You shall have the full treatment – I'm absolutely convinced that you could afford it – and you shall then see for yourself that you never grow a day older.'

Squinting at him cunningly, Greybeard said, 'Shall I have to come to Mockweagles?'

'Ah ha, he's clever, isn't he, Ruthie? He's prepared the way for himself nicely. That's the sort of man I prefer to deal with. I—'

'Where is Mockweagles?' Greybeard asked.

'It's what you might call my research headquarters. I reside there when I am not traveling the road.'

'I know, I know. You have few secrets from me, Dr Jinga-dangelow. It's twenty-nine stories high, more like a castle than a skyscraper . . .'

'Possibly your informants have been slightly exaggerating, Timberlane, but your general picture is of course amazingly accurate, as Joan will tell you, eh, my pet? But first we should get a few details straight; you will want your lovely wife to undergo the treatment too?'

'Of course I will, you old fool. I can quote poetry too, you know; to be a member of DOUCH(E) you have to be educated. "Let me not to the marriage of two minds omit impediment . . ." How does it go? Shakespeare, Doctor, Shakespeare. Ever make his acquaintance? First-class scholar . . . Oh, there is my wife! Martha!'

He staggered to his feet, knocking over his glass. Martha hurried toward him, anxiety in her face. Charley Samuels was close behind, carrying Isaac in his arms.

'Oh, Algy, Algy, you must come at once. We've been robbed!'

'What do you mean, robbed?' He stared stupidly at her, resenting the interruption of his train of thought.

'While we were bringing you in here after you were attacked, thieves got into the boats and took everything they could lay their hands on.'

'The sheep!'

'They've all been taken, and our supplies.'

Greybeard turned to Jingadangelow and made a loose gesture of courtesy.

'Be seeing you, Doctor. Got to go – den of thieves – we've been robbed.'

'I always mourn to see a scholar suffer, Mr Timberlane,' Jingadangelow said, bowing his massive head toward Martha, without otherwise moving.

As he hurried into the open with Martha and Charley, Grey-beard said brokenly, 'Why did you leave the boats?'

'You know why! We had to leave them when we heard you

were in trouble. We heard they were beating you up. Everything's gone except the boats themselves.'

'My rifle!'

'Luckily Jeff Pitt had your rifle with him.'

Charley put the fox down, and it pulled on ahead. They pushed through the dark, down the uneven road. There were few lights now. Greybeard realized how late it was; he had lost the idea of time. Potsluck Tavern had its single window boarded up. The bonfires were mere smoldering cones of ash. One or two stalls were being shut by their owners; otherwise, the place was silent. A thin chip of moon, high overhead, shone on the expanse of flood water that threaded its way through the darkness of the land. Breathing the sharp air steadied the pulse in Greybeard's head.

'That Jingadangelow's behind all this,' Charley said savagely. 'He has these traveling people in the power of his hand, from what I've seen and heard. He's a charlatan. You shouldn't have had anything to do with him, Greybeard.'

'Charlatans have their ambivalences,' Greybeard said, recognizing the preposterousness of the words as soon as they were out. Hurriedly he said, 'Where are Becky and Towin?'

'They're down by the river with Jeff now. We couldn't find them first off, then they turned up. They were busy celebrating.'

As they came off the road and padded over soggy ground, they saw the trio huddled by the riverbank near the dinghy, carrying a couple of lanterns. They all stood together, not saying much. The celebration was over. Isaac padded unhappily in the mud until Charley took pity on him and lifted him into his arms.

'It would be best if we leave this place straight away,' Greybeard said, when examination proved that though the two boats were indeed all that was left to them, they were intact. 'This is not the place for us, and I am ashamed of my part in this evening's events.'

'If you'd taken my advice, you'd never have left the boat in the first place,' Pitt said. 'They're just a lot of crooks here. It's the loss of the sheep that grieves me.'

'You could have stayed by the boat as you were told,'

Greybeard pointed out sharply. Turning to the others, he said, 'My feeling is that we'll be better off on the river. It is a fine night; I have alcohol in my system to row off. By tomorrow we can reach Oxford and get work and shelter there. It will be a very different place from what it was when Martha and I were last there, however many years ago that was. Do you all agree to leaving this thieves' den now?'

Towin coughed, shifting his lantern from hand to hand.

'Actually, me and the missus was thinking of staying here, like. We made some great friends, see, called Liz and Bob, and we thought we'd join forces with them – if you had no particular objection. We aren't much set on this idea of going down the river, as you know.' In the moonlight, he smiled his injured wolf's grin and shuffled his feet.

'I need rest in my condition,' Becky said. She spoke more boldly than her husband, glaring at them through the sickly light. 'I've had enough of being in that little leaking boat. We'd be better off with these friends of ours.'

'I'm sure that's not true, Becky,' Martha said.

'Why, I should catch my death of cold in that boat, me in my condition. Tow agrees with me.'

'He always has to,' Pitt observed.

There was a silence as they stood together but separate in the dark. Much lay between them they could never express, currents of liking and resentment affinity and aversion – vague but not the less strong for that.

'All right, if you've decided, we'll continue without you,' Greybeard said. 'Watch your belongings, that's all I say.'

'We don't like leaving you, Greybeard,' Towin said. 'And you and Charley can keep that bit of money you owe me.'

'It's entirely your choice.'

'That's what I said,' Becky said. 'We're about old enough to take care of ourselves, I should reckon.'

As they were shaking hands all around, bidding each other good-bye, Charley started to hop about and scold.

'This fox has picked up all the fleas in Christendom. Isaac, you're letting them loose on me, you villain!'

Setting the fox down, he ordered it toward the water. The fox understood what was required of it. It moved backward into the flood, slowly, slowly, brush first and then the rusty length of its body, and finally its head. Pitt held a lantern so that they could see it better.

'What's he doing? Is he going to drown himself?' Martha asked anxiously.

'No, Martha, only humans take their own lives,' Charley said. 'Animals have got more faith. Isaac knows fleas don't like cold water. This is his way of getting rid of them. They climb right up his body onto his muzzle, see, to avoid a soaking. You watch him now.'

Only part of the fox's head was above the water. He sank down until his muzzle alone was showing. Then he ducked under completely. A circle of little fleas was left struggling on the surface. Isaac came up a yard away, bounded ashore, shook himself, and raced around in circles before returning to his master.

'I never saw a smarter trick,' Towin said to Becky, nodding his head, as the others climbed into the boats. 'It must be something like that that the world's doing to human beings, when you work it out – shaking us off its snout.'

'You're talking a lot of rubbish, Towin Thomas,' she said.

They stood waving as the boats moved slowly away, Towin with his cheeks screwed up to see the particular outline merge with the general gloom.

'Well, there they go,' Charley said, pulling on his paddle. 'She's a sharp-tongued one, but I'm sorry to leave them in such a thieves' den.'

They were towing Jeff Pitt's little boat, so he could be in with them. He said, 'Who's the thieves? It might have been Jinga-dangelow's men took our property. On the other hand, I reckon it might just as well have been old Towin. I never did trust him, crafty old blighter.'

'Whoever it was, the Lord will provide for us,' Charley said. He bent his back and guided his paddle deeper into the sedgey waters.

4
Washington

In the first dreary days at Sparcot, when the rabble cast up there were forming into a community and the disease-ridden summer broke into a rain-swept autumn, Charley Samuels had not realized for some while that he knew the big man with the high bald head and growing beard. It was a time when everyone was more alert for enemies than friends.

Charley arrived at Sparcot some days after the Timberlanes, and in a dejected state of mind.

His father had owned a small bookshop in a South Coast town. Ambrose Samuels was a man of gloom and tempers. When he was in his most smiling mood, he would read aloud to Mrs Samuels, the boy Charley, and his two sisters, Ruth and Rachel. He read to them from the thousands of obsolete theological books with which the second floor of the old shop was stocked, or from the works of obsolete and morose poets that sold no better than the theology.

Much of this dead stock thus inevitably passed into Charley's mind. He could quote it at any later time of life, without knowing who wrote it or when, remembering only that it came from what his father had designated as 'a gilt-tooled thirty-two-mo' or a 'tree'd calf octavo.'

> 'All men think all men mortal but themselves;
> Themselves, when some alarming shock of fate
> Strikes through their wounded hearts the sudden dread.
> But their hearts wounded, like the wounded air,
> Soon close; where passed the shaft, no trace is found.

As from the wing no scar the sky retains;
The parted wave no furrow from the keel;
So dies in human hearts the thought of death.
Even with the tender tear which Nature sheds
O'er those we love, we drop it in their grave.'

It was a lie. When Charley was eleven, an alarming shock of fate set the thought of death in his heart forever. In his eleventh year came the radiation sickness – the result of that deliberate act men called the Accident. His father died of cancer a year later.

The shop was sold. Mrs Samuels took her children to live in her home town, where she got a secretarial job. Charley went to work when he was fifteen. His mother died three years later.

He took a series of unskilled jobs while trying to act as father to his sisters. That had been in the late eighties and early nineteen-nineties. Compared with what was to come, it was – morally and economically – a fairly stable time. But work became harder to get. He saw his sisters established in good jobs while he was un-employed.

It was the outbreak of war that had the final shaping of him. He was twenty-nine. This madness added to madness, as nations bled themselves fighting over the few children who survived, decided him that there had to be something higher than man if all creation was not a mockery. Only in religion, it seemed to him, lay an antidote to despair. He had himself baptized into the Methodist Church – a step that would have enraged his father.

To avoid being called to fight in the war, Charley joined the Infantop Corps, a semi-international branch of Child-sweep, dedicated to saving life rather than taking it. At once he had been swept away from Rachel and Ruth and plunged into the thick of the global struggle. It was then he met Algy Timberlane.

With the revolution and Britain's withdrawal from the war in 2005, Charley returned to look after his sisters again. He found to his horror that Ruth and Rachel had taken to prostitution and were prospering. It was all done very discreetly, and they still worked in the afternoon at a nearby shop. Charley closed down part of his mind, settled in with them, and defended them where and when he could.

He became the glorified chucker-out of their thriving establishment. For under the Coalition and later the United governments, hard times came with a vengeance. The world was crumbling into senescence and chaos. But what the sisters supplied remained a necessity. They flourished until the cholera stalked through England.

Charley prized his sisters away from their stricken town and headed into the country with them. Rachel and Ruth did not protest; they had seen enough from their vantage point to scare them. A client dying on the stairs precipitated them into the little car Charley bought with his war savings.

Outside the town, the car expired. They found a nylon stocking rammed into the oil sump. They began to walk, carrying their bundles on their backs on a road that led – though they did not know it – to Sparcot. Many other refugees went by that way.

It was a gruesome exodus. Among the genuine travelers were bandits who set upon their fellows, cut their throats, and took their belongings. Another robber went that way; it crept through the blood, burst out on the brow, was interested only in taking life. It stole up on Ruth in the first night and on Rachel in the third, and left them face upward in the mounds of humus over which Charley raised crosses made with sticks from the dusty hedgerows.

When he limped into the doubtful shelter of Sparcot (helping a woman called Iris, whom he would find strength to marry eighteen months later), Charley was a man turned in on himself. He had no wish to interest himself in the world again. In his wounded heart the sudden dread had found a permanent billet.

Both he and Timberlane had changed so much that it was not surprising recognition was only gradual. In that first Sparcot year of 2019, they had not seen each other for almost twenty years – since 2001, when the war still engulfed the world and they were both in the Infantop Corps. Then they had been operating overseas, combing the shattered valleys of Assam . . .

Of their patrol, only two survived. Those two, from old habit, walked in single file. The man in the rear, Corporal Samuels, carried a natterjack, the light nuclear gun, various packs filled with provisions, and a can of water. He walked somnambulistically, stumbling as they walked down the wooded hillside.

Before him a child's head jogged, hanging upside down and regarding him with a sightless eye. The child's left arm swung against the thigh of the man over whose broad back it lay. This was a boy child, a child of the Naga tribe, delicately built, shaven of head, and perhaps nine years old. He was unconscious; the flies that buzzed incessantly about his eyes and about the wound on his thigh did not trouble him.

He was carried by Sergeant Timberlane, a bronzed young man of twenty-six. Timberlane wore a revolver, had various pieces of equipment strapped about him, and carried a tall stick with which he helped himself along as he followed the sandy path leading down to the valley bottom.

The dry season ruled Assam. The trees, which were no more than nine feet high, stood as if dead, their leaves limp. The river in the valley bottom had dried out, leaving a sandy chaung along which wheeled vehicles and GEMs could move. The dust the vehicles had disturbed had settled on the trees on either side of the chaung, whitening them until they bore the appearance of a disused indoor television lot. The chaung itself dazzled in the bright sun.

Where the trees ceased to grow, Timberlane stopped, hoisting the wounded child more firmly onto his shoulder. Charley bumped into him.

'What's the matter, Algy?' he asked, coming back into weary wakefulness. As he spoke, he stared at the child's head. Because it had been shaved, the hair showed only as fine bristles; little flies crawled like lice among the bristles. The boy's eyes were as expressionless as jelly. Upside down, a human face is robbed of much of its meaning.

'We've got visitors.' The tone of Timberlane's voice brought Charley instantly back onto the alert.

Before they went over the mountain, they had left their sectional hovercraft below a small cliff, hidden from the air under a camouflage net. Now a tracked ambulance of American design was parked below the cliff. Two figures stood beside it, while a third investigated the hovercraft.

This tiny tableau, embalmed in sunlight, was broken by the sudden chatter of a machine gun. Without thinking, Timberlane and Charley went flat on their stomachs. The Naga boy groaned as Timberlane rolled him aside and swept binoculars up to his eyes. He ranged his vision along the shabby hillside to their left, where the shots had come from. Crouching figures sprang into view, their khaki dark against dusty white shrubs, their outlines hardening as Timberlane got them in focus.

'There they are!' Timberlane said. 'Probably the same bastards we ran into on the other side of the hill. Get the natterjack up, Charley, and let's settle them.'

Beside him, Charley was already assembling their weapon. Down in the chaung, one of the three Americans had been hit by the first burst of machine-gun fire. He sprawled in the sand. Moving painfully, he pulled himself along into the shadow of the ambulance. His two companions were concealed behind bushes. Of a sudden, one of them burst from cover and ran toward the ambulance. The enemy gun opened up again. Dust flicked around the running figure. He swerved, tumbled head over heels, and pitched out of sight among the dusty foliage.

'Here goes!' Charley muttered. The dust on his face, most of it turned into mud by sweat, crinkled as he slapped the barrel of the natterjack into place. He gritted his teeth and pulled the firing lever. A little nuclear shell went whistling over the scrubby hillside.

'And another, fast as you can,' Timberlane muttered, kneeling over the natterjack and feeding in a magazine. Charley switched over to automatic, and kept the lever squeezed for a burst. The shells squeaked like bats as they headed for the target. On the hillside, little brown figures scampered for safety. Timberlane brought up his revolver and aimed at them, but the range was too great for accuracy.

They lay and watched the pall of smoke settle across the slope. Someone out there was screaming. It looked as if only two of the enemy had escaped, beating a retreat over the brow of the hill.

'Can we chance going down?' Charley asked.

'I don't think they'll bother us. They'll have had enough.'

They dismantled the gun, shouldered up the child, and continued warily down the slope. As they approached the waiting vehicles, the surviving American came to meet them. He was a willowy man of no more than thirty, with dark eyebrows that almost met in the middle and fair hair cropped close. He came forward with a pack of cigarettes extended toward them.

'You boys came along in the nick of time. Thanks for the neat way you received my reception committee.'

'It's a pleasure,' Timberlane said, shaking the man's hand and taking a cigarette. 'We first got acquainted with that little section over the other side of the hill, at Mokachandpur, where they shot up the rest of our fellows. They're very personal enemies. We were only too glad to have the chance of another pot at them.'

'You're English, I guess. My name's Jack Pilbeam, Special Detachment attached to Fifth Corps. I was on my way through when we saw your craft and stopped to see if everything was okay.'

They introduced themselves all around, and Timberlane laid the unconscious boy in the shade. Pilbeam beat the dust out of his uniform and went with Charley to look to his companions.

For a moment Timberlane squatted by the boy, laying a leaf over his thigh wound, wiping the dust and tears from his face, brushing the flies away. He looked at the thin brown body, felt its pulse. The fold of his mouth grew ugly, and he seemed to stare through the fluttering rib cage, through the earth, into the bitter heart of life. He found no truth there, only what he recognized as an egotistical lie, born of his own heart: I alone loved children dearly enough!

Aloud he said, speaking mainly to himself, 'There were three of them over the hill. The other two were a pair of girls, sisters. Pretty kids, wild as mountain goats, no abnormalities. Girls got killed when the shells were slinging about, blown to bits before our eyes.'

'More are getting killed than saved,' Pilbeam said. He was kneeling by the crumpled figure in the shadow of the ambulance.

'My two buddies are both done for – well, they weren't really buddies. I'd only met the driver today, and Bill was just out from the States, like me. But that doesn't make it hurt any less. This stinking war, why the hell do we fight when the world's way down on its reservoir of human life already? Help me get 'em into the agony wagon, will you?'

'We'll do more than that,' Timberlane promised. 'If you're going back to Wokha, as I assume you must be, we'll act as escort to each other, just in case there are any more of these happy fellows perched up on the ridges.'

'Done. You've got yourself some company, and don't think I don't need company myself. I'm still trembling like a leaf. Tonight you must come on over to the PX and we'll drink to life together. Suit you, Sergeant?'

As they loaded the two bodies, still warm, into the ambulance, Pilbeam lit himself another cigarette. He looked Timberlane in the eyes.

'There's one consolation,' he said. 'This one really is a war to end war. There won't be anyone left to fight another.'

Charley was the first to arrive in the PX that evening. As he entered the low building, exchanging the hum of insects for the hum of the refrigeration plant, he saw Jack Pilbeam sitting over a glass at a corner table. The American rose to meet him. He was dressed now in neatly pressed olive drabs, his face shone, he looked compact and oddly more ferocious than he had done standing by the dying jungle. He eyed Charley's Infantop flash with approval.

'What can I get you to drink – Charley, isn't it? I'm way ahead of you.'

'I don't drink.' He had long since learned to deliver the phrase without apology; he added now, with a sour smile, 'I kill people, but I don't drink.'

Something – perhaps the mere fact that Jack Pilbeam was American, and Charley found Americans easier to talk to than his own countrymen – made him add the explanation that carried its own apology. 'I was eleven when your nation and mine detonated those fatal bombs in space. When I was nineteen, shortly after my mother died – it was a sort of compensation, I suppose – I got engaged to a girl called Peggy Lynn. She wasn't in good health and she had lost all her hair, but I loved her. . . We were going to be engaged. Well, of course we got medically examined and were told we were sterilized for life, like everyone else . . . Somehow that killed the romance.'

'I know what you mean.'

'Perhaps it was just as well. I had two sisters to look after anyway. But from then on, I started not to want anything . . .'

'Religious?'

'Yes, though it's mainly a sort of self-denial.'

Pilbeam's were clear and bright eyes that looked more attractive than his rather tight mouth. 'Then you should get through the next few decades okay. Because there's going to be a lot of self-denial needed. What happened to Peggy?'

Charley looked at his hands. 'We lost touch. One fine spring day she died of leukemia. I heard about it later.'

After drinking deep, Pilbeam said, 'That's life, as they always say about death.' His tone robbed the remark of any facetiousness it might have had.

'Although I was only a kid, I think the – Accident sent me quietly mad,' Charley said, looking down at his boots. 'Thousands – millions of people were mad, in a secretive way. Some not so secret, of course. And they've never got over it, though it's twenty years ago. I mean, though it's twenty years ago, it's still present. That's why this war's being fought, because people are mad . . . I'll never understand it: we need every young life we can get, yet here's a global war going on . . . Madness!'

Pilbeam somberly watched Charley draw out a cigarette and light it; it was one of the new tobacco-free brands and it crackled, so fiercely did Charley draw on it.

'I don't see the war like that,' Pilbeam said, ordering up another Kentucky bourbon. 'I see it as an economic war. This may be because of my upbringing and training. My father – he's dead now – be was senior sales director in Jaguar Records, Inc., and I could say "consumer rating" right after I learned to say

"Mama." The economy of every major nation is in flux, if you can have a one-way flux. They are suffering from a fatal malady called death, and up to now it's irremediable – though they're working on it. But one by one, industries are going bust, even where there's the will to keep them going. And someday soon, the will is going to fail.'

'I'm sorry,' Charley said. 'I don't quite grasp what you mean. Economics is not my field at all. I'm just—'

'I'll explain what I mean. God, I may as well tell you: my old man died last month. He didn't die – he killed himself. He jumped from a fifty-second-floor window of Jaguar Records, Inc. in LA.' His eyes were brighter; he drew down his brows as if to hood them, and put one clenched first with slow force down on the table. 'My old man, he was part of Jaguar. He kept it going, it kept him going. In a way, I suppose he was a very American sort of man – lived for his family and his job, had a great range of business associates . . . To hell with that. What I'm trying to say – God, he wasn't fifty! Forty-nine, he was.

'Jaguar went broke; more than broke – obsolete. Suddenly wilted and died. Why? Because their market was the adolescent trade. It was the kids, the teens, that bought Jaguar records. Suddenly – no more kids, no more teens. The company saw it coming. It was like sliding toward a cliff. Year after year, sales down, diminishing returns, costs up . . . What do you do? What in hell can you do, except sweat it out?

'There are other industries all around you just as badly hit. One of my uncles is an executive with Park Lane Confectionery. They may hang on a few more years, but they're getting pretty shaky. Why? Because it was the under-twenties that consumed most of their candies. Their market's dead – unborn. A technological nation is a web of delicately balanced forces. You can't have one bit rotting off without the rest going too. What do you do in a case like that? You do what my old man did – hang on for as long as you can, then catch a downdraft from the fifty-second floor.'

Charley said gently, envying Pilbeam his slight drunkenness as he sipped his bourbon, 'You said something about someone's will going to fail.'

'Oh, that. Yup, my father and his pals, well, they go on fighting while there's a chance left. They try and salvage what's salvage-able for their sons. But *us* – we don't have sons. What's going to happen if this curse of infertility doesn't wear off *ever?* We aren't going to have the will to work if there's nobody to—'

'Inherit the fruits of our labors? I've already thought of that. Perhaps every man has thought of it. But the genes must recover soon – it's twenty years since the Accident.'

'I guess so. They're telling us in the States that this sterility will wear off in another five or ten years' time.'

'They were saying the same thing when Peggy was alive . . . It's a cliché of the British politicians, to keep the voters quiet.'

'The American manufacturers use it to keep the voters buying. But all the time the industrial system's going to pot under them. So we have to have a war, keep up falling production, explain away shortages, conceal inflation, deflect blame, tighten con-trols . . . It's a hell of a world, Charley! Look at the guys in here – all buying death on the credit system and richly, ripely aware of it . . .'

Charley gazed about the colorful room, with its bar and its groups of smiling, greying soldiers. The scene did not appear to him as grim as Pilbeam made it sound; all the same, it was even betting that in each man's heart was the knowledge of an anni-hilation so greedy that it had already leaped forward and swal-lowed up the next generation. The irony was that over this sterile soldiery hung no threat of nuclear war. The big bombs were obsolete after only half a century of existence; the biosphere was too heavily laden with radiation after the Accident of 1981 for anyone to chance sending the level higher. Oh, there were the armies' strategic nuclear weapons, and the neutrals protested about them all the time, but wars had to be fought and they had to be fought with something, and since the small nuclear weapons were in production, they were used. What were several fewer species of animals compared with a hundred-mile advance and another medal on another general?

He cut off his thoughts, ashamed of their easy cynicism. Oh Lord, though I die, let me live!

He had lost the thread of Pilbeam's discourse. It was with relief that he saw Algy Timberlane enter the canteen.

'Sorry I'm late,' Timberlane said, gratefully accepting a bourbon and ginger on ice. 'I went into the hospital to look at that kid we brought in from Mokachandpur. He's in a feverish coma. Colonel Hodson has pumped him full of mycetinin, and will be able to tell if he will pull through by morning. Poor little fellow is badly wounded – they may have to amputate that leg of his.'

'Was he all right otherwise? I mean, not mutated?' Pilbeam asked.

'Physically, in normal shape. Which will make it all the worse if he dies. And to think we lost Frank, Alan, and Froggie getting him. It's a damn shame the two little girls got blown to bits.'

'They would probably have been deformed if you had got hold of them,' Pilbeam said. He lit a cheroot after the two Englishmen had refused them. His eyes looked more alert now that Timberlane had joined the party. He sat with his back straighter and talked in a more tightly controlled way. 'Ninety-six point four percent of the children we have picked up on Operation Child-sweep have external or internal deformities. Before you came in, Charley and I were on the stale old subject of the madness of the world. There's the brightest and best example this last twenty years affords us – the Western world spent the first fifteen years of it legally killing off all the little monstrosities born of the few women who weren't rendered out-and-out sterile. Then our quote advanced thinkers unquote got the idea that the monstrosities might, after all, breed and breed true, and restore a balance after one generation. So we go in for kidnapping on an international scale.'

'No, no, you can't say that,' Charley exclaimed. 'I'd agree that the legal murder of – well, call them monstrosities—'

'*Call* them monstrosities? Without arms or legs, without eye-holes in their skulls, with limbs like those bloated things in those old Picasso paintings!'

'They were still of the human race, their souls were still

immortal. Their legal murder was worse than madness. But after that we did come to our senses and start free clinics for the children of backward races, where the poor little wretches would get every care—'

Pilbeam laughed curtly. 'Apologies, Charley, but you're telling me history I had a hand – a finger in. Sure, you have the propaganda angle down pat. But these so-called backward races – they were the ones who didn't do the legal murder! They loved their horrors and let them live. So we came around to thinking we needed their horrors, to prop our future. I told you, it's an economic war. The democracies – and our friends in the Communist community – need a new generation, however come by, to work in their assembly lines and consume their goods . . . Hence this stinking war, as we quarrel over what's left! Hell, a mad world, my masters! Drink up, Sergeant! Let's have a toast – to the future generation of consumers, however many heads or assholes they have!'

As Timberlane and Pilbeam laughed, Charley rose.

'I must be going now,' he said. 'I've a guard duty at eight tomorrow morning, and I have to get my kit cleaned. Good night, gentlemen.'

The other two filled up their glasses when he had gone, instinctively settling more closely together.

'Kind of a weeping Jesus, isn't he?' Pilbeam asked.

'He's a quiet fellow,' Timberlane said. 'Useful to have around when there's any trouble, as I discovered today. That's one thing about these religious boys – they reckon that if they are on God's side, then the enemy must be on the devil's, and so they have no qualms about giving it to 'em hot and strong.'

Pilbeam regarded him, half smiling through a cloud of cigarette smoke.

'You're a different type.'

'In some ways, *I'm* trying to forget there will be a funeral service for our boys tomorrow – Charley's trying to remember.'

'There'll be a burial in our lines for my buddy and the driver. It'll delay my getting away.'

'You're leaving?'

'Yup, going back to the States. Get a GEM down to Kohima, then catch an orbit jet home to Washington, D.C. My work here is done.'

'What is your work, Jack, or should I not ask?'

'Right now, I'm on detachment from Childsweep, recruiting for a new worldwide project.' He stopped talking and focused more sharply on Timberlane. 'Say, Algy, would you mind if we took a turn outside and got a little of that Assamese air into my sinuses?'

'By all means.'

The temperature had dropped sharply, reminding them that they were almost ten thousand feet above sea level. Instinctively they struck up a brisk pace. Pilbeam threw down the end of his cheroot and ground it into the turf. The moon hung low in the sky. One night bird emphasized the stillness of the rest of creation.

'Too bad the Big Accident surrounded the globe with radiations and made space travel almost impossible,' Pilbeam said. 'There might have been a way of escape from our earth-born madness in the stars. My old man was a great believer in space travel, used to read all the literature. A great optimist by nature – that's why failure came so hard to him. I was telling your friend Charley, Dad killed himself last month. I'm still trying to come to terms with it.'

'It's always a hard thing, to get over a father's death. You can't help taking it personally. It's a – well, a sort of insult, when it's someone that was dear to you and full of life.'

'You sound as if you know something about it.'

'Something. Like thousands of other people, my father committed suicide too. I was a child at the time. I don't know whether that makes it better or worse . . . You were close to your old man?'

'No. Maybe that's why I kick against it so hard. I could have been close. I wasted the opportunity. To hell with it, anyway.'

A katabatic wind was growing, pouring down from the higher slopes above the camp. They walked with their hands in their pockets.

In silence, Pilbeam recalled how his father had encouraged his idealism.

'Don't come into the record business, Son,' he had said. 'It'll get by without you. Join Childsweep, if yon want to.'

Pilbeam joined Childsweep when he was sixteen, starting somewhere near the bottom of the organization. Childsweep's greatest achievement was the establishment of three Children's Centers, near Washington, Karachi, and Singapore. Here the world's children born after the Accident were brought, where parental consent could be won, to be trained to live with their deformities and with the crisis-ridden society in which they found themselves.

The experiment was not an unqualified success. The shortage of children was acute – at one time, there were three psychiatrists to every child. But it was an attempt to make amends. Pilbeam, working in Karachi, was almost happy. Then the children became the subject of an international dispute. Finally war broke out. When it developed into a more desperate phase, both the Singapore and the Karachi Children's Centers were bombed from orbital automatic satellites and destroyed. Pilbeam escaped and flew back to Washington with a minor leg wound, in time to learn of his father's suicide.

After a minute's silence Pilbeam said, 'I didn't drag you out into the night air to mope but to make a proposition. I have a job for you. A real job, a lifetime job. I have the power to fix it with your commanding officer if you agree—'

'Hey, not so fast!' Timberlane cried, spreading his hands in protest. 'I don't want a job. I've got a job – saving any kids I can find lurking in these hills.'

'This is a real job, not a vacation for gun-toting nursemaids. The most responsible job ever thought up. I back my hunches, and I'm certain you're the sort of guy we're looking for. I can fix it so you fly back to the US with me tomorrow.'

'Oh no, I've got a girl in England I'm very fond of, and I'm due for leave at the end of next week. I'm not volunteering, thanks all the same for the compliment.'

Pilbeam stopped and faced Timberlane.

'We'll fly your girl out to Washington. Money's no problem, believe me. At least let me tell you about the deal. You see, sociologically and economically, we live in very interesting times, provided you can be detached enough to view things in that light. So a university group with corporation and government backing has been set up to study and record what goes on. You won't have heard of the group – it's new and it's being kept out of the news. It calls itself Documentation of Universal Contemporary History – DOUCH for short. We need recruits to operate in all countries. Come back to my billet and meet Bill Dyson, who's in charge of the project for Southeast Asia, and we'll give you the dope.'

'This is crazy. I can't join. You mean you'd fly Martha out of England to meet me?'

'Why not? You know the way England is going – way back into the darkness, under this new government and wartime conditions. You'd both be better off in America for a while, while we trained you. That's a big consideration, isn't it?' He caught the look on Timberlane's face and added, 'You don't have to make up your mind right away.'

'I can't . . . How long do I have to think about it?'

Pilbeam looked at his watch and scratched his skull with a fingernail. 'Till we've got another drink down our throats, shall we say?'

On the dusty airstrip at Kohima, two men shook hands.

'I feel bad about leaving like this, Charley.'

'The CO must feel even worse.'

'He took it like a lamb. What sort of blackmail Pilbeam used, I'll never know.'

A moment of awkward silence, then Charley said, 'I wish I was coming with you. You've been a good friend.'

'Your country needs you, Charley, don't kid yourself.' But Charley only said, 'I might have been coming with you if I'd been good enough.'

Embarrassed, Timberlane climbed the steps to the plane and turned to wave. They took a last look at each other before he ducked inside.

The orbit jet blasted off through the livid evening, heading on a transpolar parabola for the opposite side of the globe. For a long while the sun bumped over the western lip of the world, while far below them the land was tawny with a confusion of dark and light.

Jack Pilbeam, Algy Timberlane, and Bill Dyson sat together, talking very little at first. Dyson was a thick-set individual, as tough-looking as Pilbeam was scholarly, with a bald head and a genial smile. He was as relaxed as Pilbeam was highly strung. Although no more than ten years senior to Timberlane, he gave the impression of being a much older man.

'It's our job, Mr Timberlane, to be professional pessimists in DOUCH,' be said. 'With reference to the future, we may only permit ourselves to be hardheaded and dry-eyed. You have to face the fact that if vital genes have been knocked out of the human reproductive apparatus, the rest of the apparatus may never have the strength to build them back up again. In which case, young men like you and this reprobate Pilbeam represent the ultimate human generation. That's why we need you; you'll record the death throes of the human race.'

'Sounds to me as if you want journalists,' Timberlane said.

'No, sir, we require steady men with integrity. This is not a scoop, it's a way of life.'

'Way of death, Bill,' Pilbeam corrected.

'Bit of both. As the Good Book reminds us, in the midst of life we are in death.'

'I still don't see the object of the project if the human race is going to become extinct,' Timberlane said. 'Whom will it help?'

'Good question. Here's what I hope's a good answer. It will help two sorts of people. Both groups are purely hypothetical. It will help a small group we might imagine in, say, America thirty or forty years from now, when the whole nation may have broken up in chaos. Suppose they establish a little settlement and find that they are able to bear children? Those children will be almost savages – feral children, severed from the civilization to which they rightly belong. DOUCH records will be a link for them between their past and their future, and will give them a chance to think along right lines and construct a socially viable community.'

'And the second group?'

'I imagine you are not a very speculative man, Mr Timberlane. Has it ever crossed your mind that we are not alone in this universe? I don't mean just the Creator; it's difficult to imagine He would make any human company except Adam. I mean the other races who live on the planets of other stars. They may one day visit earth, as we have visited the moon and Mars. They will seek an explanation for our "lost civilization," just as we wonder about the Martian lost civilization of which Leatherby's expedition found traces. DOUCH will leave them an explanation. If the explanation also packs a moral they can use, so much the better.'

'There's a third hypothetical group,' Pilbeam said, leaning forward. 'That's the one that sends the prickles down my spine. Maybe I read too much of my father's science fiction at too early an age. But if man is going to tumble off his ecological niche, maybe some creature lurking around right now will climb up and take his place in a couple of hundred years – when the place is properly aired.'

He laughed. With quiet humor, Dyson said, 'Could be, Jack. Statistics on how the Big Accident affected the larger primates are hard to come by. Maybe the grizzlies or the gorillas have already started along a favorable mutational line.'

Timberlane was silent. He did not know how to join in this sort of conversation. The whole thing was still unreal to him. When he had said good-bye to Charley Samuels, the look of dismay on his friend's face had shaken him almost as much as the CO's instant cooperation with Childsweep. He peered down through the window. Far below, cumulus made a tumbled bed of the earth. He was in Cloud Cuckoo Land.

Down below in that tenebrific world, a million years' doubtful dynasty was coming to an end, with the self-immolation of the reigning house. He was not sure how he would relish recording its death throes.

There was mild autumnal sunshine and a military escort to greet them at Bolling Field. Half an hour – to Pilbeam's sore irritation – passed in the inspection block before Health and Security checks cleared them. They were driven with their kit by electric truck to a little grey private bus that awaited them outside. On its side were painted the letters DOUCH.

'Looks good,' Timberlane exclaimed. 'Now for the first time I believe I'm not the victim of some elaborate hoax.'

'Didn't think you'd find yourself putting down in Peking, did you?' Dyson said, grinning his comfortable grin.

'And be sure never to climb into a bus labeled OICH or DUCA, however canned you are,' warned their military escort, helping Timberlane with his bags. 'They stand for Oriental Integration and Cultural Habitation or something like it, and DUCA is a flamboyant organization run by the *Post* and standing for Department of Unified Child Assistance. They keep awful busy, even without any actual children to assist. Washington is a rash of initials and organizations – and disorganization – right now. It's like living up to here in alphabet soup. Jump in, fellows, and we'll go see a traffic jam or two.'

But somewhat to Timberlane's disappointment, they kept to the east of the grey river he had glimpsed as they came in to land, and crawled into the part of town Pilbeam informed him was Anacostia. They pulled up in a trim street of new white houses before a block he was told was home. It proved to be swarming with decorators and echoing with the sound of carpenters.

'New premises,' Pilbeam explained. 'Up to a month ago this was a home for mentally deranged juvenile delinquents. But that's one problem this so-called Accident has abolished entirely. We've run clean out of delinquents! It'll make us a good HQ, and when you see the swimming pool, you'll realize why delinquency in this country was almost a profession!'

He flung open the door of a spacious room. 'You've got bedroom and toilet off through that door there. You share shower facilities with the guy next door, who happens to be me. Right down the corridor is the bar, and by God if they don't have that to rights by now, and with a pretty girl at the alert behind it, there's going to be hell raised. See you across a Martini in ten minutes, hey?'

*

The DOUCH training course was planned to last for six weeks. Although it was in a high degree of organization, the system remained chaotic, because of the disorder of the times.

Internally, all big cities were in the toils of labor problems; the conscription of strikers into the armed forces had served only to spread trouble to those bodies. The war was not a popular one, and not only because the enthusiasm of youth was missing.

Externally, the cities were under enemy bombardment. The so-called 'Fat Choy' raids were the enemy's specialty: detection-baffled missiles that dropped in from spatial orbits, disintegrating above ground and scattering 'suitcases' of explosive or incendiaries. It was the first time the American population had experienced aerial attack on their home ground. While many city dwellers evacuated themselves to smaller towns or country areas – only to straggle back later, preferring the risk of bombardment to an environment with which they had little sympathy – many country folk entered the cities in search of higher wages. Industry complained loudly; but as yet it was agriculture that was hardest hit, and Congress was busily passing laws that would enable it to order men back to the land.

The one happy feature of the whole war was that the enemy's economy was a deal more insecure than America's; the number of Fat Choys had noticeably decreased over the last six months. As a result, the feverish night life of the wartime capital had accelerated.

Timberlane was able to see a good deal of this night life. The DOUCH officials had good contacts. Within a day he was supplied with all necessary documents enabling him to survive in the local rat race: stamped passport, visa, alien curfew exemptions, police file card, clothing purchase permit, travel warrant within the District of Columbia, and vitamin, meat, vegetable, bread, fish, and candy ration cards. In every case except that of the travel warrant, the restrictions seemed liberal to all but the local inhabitants.

Timberlane was a man who only rarely indulged in self-examination. So he never asked himself how strongly his decision to throw in his lot with DOUCH was influenced by their promise to reunite him with his girl friend. It was a point on which he never had to press Dyson.

Within four days, Martha Broughton was flown out of the little besieged island off the continent of Europe and delivered to Washington.

Martha Broughton was twenty-six, Timberlane's age. Not only because she was among the youngest of the world's women but because she carried her good looks with an easy air, she attracted attention wherever she went. At this time she boasted a full crop of fine ash-blond hair, which she wore untamed to shoulder length. One generally had to be well acquainted with her to notice that her eyebrows were painted on; she had no eyebrows of her own.

At the time of what Washington circles referred to euphemistically as the Big Accident, Martha was six. She had fallen ill with the radiation sickness; unlike many of her little contemporaries, she survived. But her hair had not; and the baldness that accompanied her throughout her schooldays, in subjecting her to taunts against which she had readily defended herself, had been instrumental in sharpening her wit. By her twenty-first birthday, a fuzz covered her skull; now her beauty would not have been despised in any age. Timberlane was one of the few people outside her family who knew of the internal scars that were the unique mark of her own age.

Pilbeam and Timberlane showed her to a women's hostel a couple of blocks from the new DOUCH headquarters.

'You're having an effect on Algy already,' Martha told Pilbeam. 'His long English a's are eroding. What's next to go?'

'Probably the English middle-class inhibition against kissing in public,' Timberlane said.

'My God, if you call me public, I'm getting out of here,' Pilbeam said good-naturedly. 'I can take a hint as well as anyone – and a drink. You'll find me down in the bar when you want me.'

'We won't be long, Jack.'

'We won't be very long, Jack,' Martha amended.

As the door closed, they put their arms about each other and stood with their lips together, each feeling the other's warmth through mouth and body. They remained like that, kissing and talking, for some while. Finally he stood back on the other side of the room, cupped his chin in his hand in a judicious gesture, and admired her legs.

'Ah, the cute catenary curve of your calves!' he exclaimed.

'Well, what a lovely transatlantic greeting,' Martha said. 'Algy, this is wonderful! What a marvelous thing to happen! Isn't it exciting? Father was furious that I so much as contemplated coming – preached me a long sermon in his deeeepest voice about the flightiness of young womanhood—'

'And no doubt admires you madly for sticking to your guns and coming! Though if he suspects the American male will be after you, he's right.'

She opened her night bag, setting bottles and brushes out on the dressing table, and never taking her eyes off him. As she sat down to attend to her face, she said, 'Any fate is better than death! And what is going on here? And what is DOUCH, and why have you joined, and what can I do to help?'

'I'm being trained here for six weeks. All sorts of courses – boy, these fellows really know how to work! Contemporary history, societies, economy, geopolitics, a new thing they call existentietics, functional psychology – oh, and other things, and practical subjects, such as engine maintenance. And twice a week we drive out to Rock Creek Park for lessons joying it. There's a dedicated feeling about here that gives in self-defense from a judo expert. It's tough, but I'm en-everything meaning. I'm out of the war, too, which means life again makes a little sense.'

'You look well on it, honey. And are you going to practice self-defense on me?'

'Other forms of wrestling, perhaps, not that. No, I suspect you are out here for one very good reason. But we'll ask Jack Pilbeam about that. Let's go and join him – he's a hell of a good chap; you'll like him.'

'I do already.'

Pilbeam was in one corner of the hostel bar, sitting close with an attentive redhead. He broke away reluctantly, swung his raincoat off the back of a chair, and came toward them, saluting as he did so.

'All play and no work makes Jack a dull boy,' he said. 'Where do we take the lady now, and is it anywhere we can take a friendly redhead?'

'Having restored the ravages of travel, I'm in your hands,' Martha said.

'And she doesn't mean that literally,' Timberlane added.

Pilbeam bowed. 'I have the instructions, the authority, and the inclination to take you anywhere in Washington, and to wine and dine you as long as you are here.'

'I warn you, darling, they play hard as well as work hard. DOUCH will do its best for us before dumping us down to record the end of the world.'

'I can see you need a drink, you grumpy man,' Pilbeam said, forcing his smile a little. 'Let me just introduce the redhead, and then we will move along to a show and a bottle. Maybe we can fight our way into the Dusty Dykes show. Dykes is the slouch comedian.'

The redhead joined the party without too great a show of reluctance, and they moved into town. The blackouts that had afflicted the cities of other nations in earlier wars did not worry Washington. The enemy had the city firmly in its missile sights, and no lighting effects would change the situation. The streets were a blaze of neon as the entertainment business boomed. Flashing signs lit the faces of men and women with the stigmata of illness as they pushed into cabarets and cafés. Black-market food and drink were plentiful; the only shortage seemed to be parking spaces.

These evenings became part of a pattern of fierce work and relaxation into which the DOUCH personnel fitted. On her third night in Washington, when they were sitting in the Trog and watching the cabaret that included Dusty Dykes, Martha managed to put her question to Pilbeam.

'Jack, you give us a wonderful time. I wish I could seem to do something in return. Is there something I can do? I don't see really why I was invited out here.'

Without ceasing to caress the wrist of the dark and green-eyed beauty who was his date for the night, Pilbeam said, 'You were invited to keep one Algy Timberlane company – not that he deserves any such good fortune. And you have sat in on several of his lectures. Isn't that enough? Relax, enjoy yourself. Have another drink. It's patriotic to over-consume.'

'I am enjoying myself. I'd just like to know if there is anything I can *do*.'

Pilbeam winked at his green-eyed friend. 'You'd better ask Algy that, honey baby.'

'I'm terribly persistent, Jack. I do want an answer.'

'Go and ask Bill Dyson, it's really his pigeon. I'm just the DOUCH playboy – Warm Douche, they call me. And I may have to be off on my travels again, come Wednesday.'

'Oh, lambie pie, but you said—' the green-eyed girl protested. Pilbeam laid a cautionary finger on her lustrous lips.

'Shhh, sweetie – your Uncle Sam must come before your Uncle Jack. But tonight, believe me, Uncle Jack comes first – metaphorically speaking, you understand.'

The lights dimmed; there was a drum roll followed by an amplified hiccup. As silence fell, Dusty Dykes floated in on an enormous dollar bill and climbed down onto the floor. He was an almost menacingly ordinary little man, wearing a creased lounge suit. He spoke in a flat, husky voice.

'You'll see I've abandoned my old gimmick of not having a gimmick. It's not the first time this country's economy has taken me for a ride. Good evening, ladies and gentiles, and I really mean that – it may be your last. In New York, where I come from – and you know state tax is so high there I needed a parachute to get away – they are very fond of World End parties. You rub two moralities together: the result's a bust. You rub two busts together: the result is always a titter. The night Senator Mulgravy went, it was a twitter.' At this, there was a round of applause. 'Oh, some of you have heard of senators? Friends told me when I arrived – friends are the people who stand you one drink and one afternoon – they told me Washington, DC, was politically uneducated. Well, they didn't put it like that, they just said nobody went to photograph the African bronzes in the White House anymore. I said, remember, it isn't the men of the state that counts, it's the state of the men. At least they're no poorer than a shareholder in the contraceptive industry.'

'I can't hear what he's saying – or else I can't understand it,' Martha whispered.

'It doesn't sound particularly funny to me either,' Timberlane whispered.

With his arm around his girl friend's shoulder, Pilbeam said, 'It's not meant to be *funny*. It's meant to be *slouch*, as they call it.' Nevertheless, he was grinning broadly, as were many other customers. Noticing this, Dusty Dykes shook a cautionary finger. It was his only gesture. 'Smiling won't help it,' he said. 'I know you're all sitting there naked under your clothes, but you can't embarrass me – I go to church and hear the sermon every Sunday. We are a wicked and promiscuous nation, and it gives me as much pleasure as the preacher to say so. I've no objection to morality, except that it's obsolete.

'Life gets worse every day. In the high court in California, they've stopped sentencing their criminals to death – they sentence them to life instead. Like the man said, there's no innocence anymore, just undetected crime. In the state of Illinois alone, there were enough sex murders last month to make you all realize how vicarious your position is.

'The future outlook for the race is black, and that's not just a pigment of my imagination. There were two sex criminals talking over business in Chicago the other day. Butch said, "Say, Sammy, which do you like best, murdering a woman or thinking about murdering a woman?" "Shucks, I don't know, Butch, which do you prefer?" "Thinking about murdering a woman, every time!" "Why's that?" "That way you get a more romantic type of woman."'

For some minutes more the baby-faced little man stood there under the spot in his slept-in suit, making his slept-in jokes. Then the light cut off, he disappeared, and the house lights rose to applause.

'More drinks!' Pilbeam said.

'But he was awful!' Martha exclaimed. 'Just blue!'

'Ah, you have to hear him half a dozen times to appreciate him – that's the secret of his success,' Pilbeam said. 'He's the voice of the age.'

'Did *you* enjoy him?' Martha asked the green-eyed girl.

'Well, yes, I guess I did. I mean, well, he kind of made me feel at home.'

Twice a week they went over to a small room in the Pentagon, where a blond young major taught them how to program and service a POLYAC computer. These new pocket-sized computers would be fitted in all DOUCH recording trucks.

Timberlane was setting out for one of the POLYAC sessions when be found a letter from his mother awaiting him in his mail slot. Patricia Timberlane wrote irregularly. This letter, like most of them, was mainly filled with domestic woes, and Timberlane scanned it without a great deal of patience as his taxi carried him over the Potomac. Near the end he found something of more interest.

'It's nice for you to have Martha over there in Washington with you. I suppose you will marry her – which is romantic, because it is not often people marry their childhood sweethearts. But *do make sure*. I mean, you're old enough to know that I made a great mistake marrying your stepfather. Keith has his good points, but he's terribly faithless, sometimes I wish I was dead. I won't go into details.

'He blames it on the times, but that's a too easy get-out. He says there's going to be a revolution here. I dread to think of it. As if we haven't gone through enough, what with the Accident and this awful war, revolution I dread. There's never been one in this country, whatever other countries have done. Really it's like living in a perpetual earthquake.'

It was a telling phrase, Timberlane thought soberly. In Washington, the perpetual earthquake ground on day and night, and would grind, until all was reduced to dust, if the gloomy DOUCH predictions were fulfilled. It revealed itself not only in the constant economic upheavals, the soup queues downtown, and the crazy sales as the detritus of fallen financial empires was thrown onto the market, but in the wave of murders and sexual crimes that the law found itself unable to check. This wave rose to engulf Martha and Timberlane.

The morning after the letter from Patricia Timberlane arrived, Martha appeared early in Timberlane's room. Clothes lay scattered over the carpet – they had been out late on the previous evening, attending a wild party thrown by an Air Strike buddy of Bill Dyson's.

Wearing his pajama trousers, Timberlane stood shaving himself in semigloom. Martha went over to the window, pulled the curtains back, and turned to face him. She told him about the flowers that had been delivered to her at the hostel.

He squinted at her and said, 'And you say you got some yesterday morning, too?'

'Yes, just as many – crates full of orchids, the same as this morning. They must have cost hundreds of thousands of dollars.'

He clicked off the spiteful buzz of his razor and looked at her. His eyes were dull and his face pale.

'Kind of slouch, eh? I didn't send them to you.'

'I know that, Algy. You couldn't afford them. I have looked at the price of flowers in the shops – they're dear in the first place, and they carry state tax, entry tax, purchase tax, and what the hostel matron calls GDT, General Discouragement Tax, and goodness knows what else. That's why I destroyed yesterday's lot – I mean, I knew they weren't from you, so I burned them and meant to say no more about it.'

'You burned them? How? I've not seen a naked flame on anything bigger than a cigar lighter since I got here.'

'Don't be so dumb, darling. I pushed them all down the disposal chute, and anything that goes down there gets burned in the basement of the hostel. Now, this morning, another lot, again with no message.'

'Maybe the same lot, with love from the fellow in the basement.'

'For God's sake, don't go slouch on me, Algy!'

They laughed. But next morning, another bank of flowers

arrived at the hostel for Miss Martha Broughton. Timberlane, Pilbeam, and Martha's matron came to look at them.

'Orchids, roses, violets – whoever he is, he can afford to get very sentimental,' Pilbeam said. 'Let me assure you, Algy, old man, I didn't send these to your girl friend. Orchids is one thing you can't slap on a DOUCH expense account.'

'I am frankly worried, Miss Broughton, honey,' the matron said. 'You have to be careful, especially seeing you're a stranger to this country. Remember now, there are no more girls under twenty around. That was the age older men used to go for. Now it's the twenties-thirties group must watch out. Those older men, who are the rich men, have always been used to – well, to making hay while the sun shines. Now that the sun is going down – they will be more anxious to get at the last of the hay. If you know what I mean.'

'Dusty Dykes himself couldn't have put it better. Thanks for the warning, Matron. I'll watch my step.'

'Meanwhile, I'll phone a florist,' Pilbeam said. 'There's no reason why you shouldn't pick up a cool couple of thousand from this slob's amorousness. Small change is mighty useful.'

Pilbeam was due to leave Washington the next day. The order had come through Dyson for him to go to another theater of war – this time, central Sarawak. As he put it himself, he could use the rest. During the afternoon he was down in town collecting more kit and an inoculation when the Fat Choy alert sounded. He phoned through to Timberlane, who was then attending a lecture on propaganda and public delusion.

'Thought I'd tell you I'm likely to be delayed by this raid, Algy,' Pilbeam said. 'You and Martha better go on to the Thesaurus without me and get the drinks moving, and I'll meet you there as soon as I can. We can eat there if we have to, though the Babe Lincoln down the block gives you less synthetics.'

'It's chiefly calorie intake I'm having to watch,' Timberlane said, patting his waistline.

'See how your sensuality output reacts this evening – I've met a real scorcher here, Algy, name of Coriander and as plastic as Silly Putty.'

'I can't wait. Is she married or single?'

'With her energy and talent, could be both.'

They winked at each other's images in the vision screens and cut off.

Timberlane and Martha caught a prowling taxi cab into town after dark. The enemy attack consisted of two missiles, one of which broke into suitcases over the now almost derelict slaughter and marshaling yards, while the other, causing more damage, broke over the thickly populated Cleveland Park suburb. On the sidewalks police uniforms seemed to predominate over service uniforms; the Choy had served to make a lot of people stay at home, and as a result the streets were clearer than usual.

At the Thesaurus, Timberlane climbed out and inspected the façade of the club. It was studded with groups of synonyms in bas-relief: Chosen Few, Prime, Picked Bunch, Crême of the Cream, Elite, Salt of the Earth, Top Drawer, Pick of the Pops, Best People. Smiling, he turned to pay the cabbie.

'Hey, you!' he yelled.

The taxi, with Martha in it, swerved out into traffic, squealed around a private car, and sped down a side street. Timberlane ran into the road. Brakes and tires whined behind him. A big limousine bucked to a stop inches from his legs, and a red face was thrust from the driver's window and began to curse him. A crunching noise sounded from behind, and the red face turned toward the rear to curse even more ferociously. As a cop came running up, Timberlane grabbed his arm.

'My girl's been kidnapped. Some chap just drove off with her.'

'Happens all the time. You sure have to watch them.'

'She was made away with!'

'Go and tell it to the sergeant, Mac. Think I don't have troubles? I have to get this tin real estate rolling again.' He jerked a thumb at an approaching prowl car. Biting his lip, Timberlane made his way toward it.

At eleven o'clock that night, Dyson said, 'Come on, Algy, we're doing no good here. The police'll phone us if they get a lead. Let's find a bite to eat before my stomach falls apart.'

'It must have been that devil that sent her the flowers,' Timberlane said, by no means for the first time. 'Surely the flower shop could give the police a lead.'

'They got no change from the manager of the flower store. If only you recalled the taxi number.'

'All that I can remember is that it was mauve and yellow, with the words "Antelope Taxis" across the boot. Hell, you're right, Bill, let's go and get a bite to eat.'

As they left the police station, the superintendent said sympathetically, 'Don't worry, Mr Timberlane. We'll have your fiancée tracked down by morning.'

'What makes the man so confident?' Timberlane asked grumpily as they climbed into Dyson's car. Although both Dyson and Jack Pilbeam, who had been down at the station earlier, had done all they could, he felt unfairly eager to annoy them. He felt so vulnerable in what was, however much he liked it, a strange country. Trying to button down his emotions, he remained silent as he and Dyson went to a nearby all-night stall and wolfed down hamburgers with chilis and mustard; the hamburgers were synthetic but good.

'Thank God for chilis,' Dyson said. 'They could put a bit of fire into sawdust. I've often wondered if chilis aren't the things the scientists are really looking for in all their megabuck's worth of research into a way of restoring our poor old shattered genes.'

'Could be,' Timberlane assented. 'Bet you they invent synthetic chilis first.'

He got to bed after a final nightcap and fell asleep at once. When he woke next morning, he phoned the police station straightaway, but they had nothing new to offer him. Moodily, he washed and dressed for breakfast, and went down the hall to collect his mail from the mail slot.

A hand-delivered letter awaited him in the rack. He tore it open to find a sheet of paper bearing the words:

'If you want your girl back, take a look in God's Sufferance Press. Go alone, for her sake. Then call off the cops.'

Suddenly, he wanted no breakfast. He almost ran to the hall phone booth and thumbed through the appropriate volume of the phone directory. There it was, under an old-style nonvision number: God's Sufferance Press, and its address. Should he ring first or go straight around? He hated the feeling of indecision that flooded him. He dialed and got the disconnected tone.

Hurrying back to his room, he wrote a hasty note to Pilbeam, giving the address to which he was going, and left it on the pillow of his unmade bunk. He pocketed his revolver.

He walked down to the end of the street, picked up a taxi from the regular rank, and told the driver to take it as fast as he could. Once over the Anacostia Bridge, they hit tight traffic as the capital moved in to do its day's work. Even swamped as it was by wartime congestion, Washington kept its beauty; as they filtered past the Capitol, the sward about it now peppered with emergency office buildings, and swung westward along Pennsylvania Avenue, the white stone caught a flush from the clear sky. The permanence and proportion of the buildings gave Timberlane a little reassurance.

Later, as they headed north, the impression of dignity and justice was broken. Here the unsettlement of the times found expression. Name and sign altering was in full swing. Property changed hands rapidly; office furniture vans and military lorries delivered or removed furniture. And there were other buildings standing unaccountably silent and empty. Sometimes a whole street seemed deserted, as if its inhabitants had fled from a plague. In one such street, Timberlane noticed, stood the travel offices of overseas airlines and the tourist bureaus of Denmark, Finland, Turkey. The shutters were up; private travel had closed down for the duration, and the big airliners were under United Nations' charge, flying medical aid to war victims.

Some districts showed evidence of suitcase damage, though an attempt had been made to cover the desolation with large advertisement hoardings. Like all the great cities of the world, this one, behind its gay smile, revealed the rotting cavities that nobody was able to fill.

'Here's your destination, bud, but it don't look like anybody's at home,' the taxi driver said. 'Do you want me to wait around?'

'No, thank you.' He paid the man, who saluted and drove off.

*

The home of the God's Sufferance Press was a drably pretentious five-story building dating from the turn of the previous century. For-sale notices were plastered over its windows. The iron folding gates giving access to the main swing door were secured in place with a strong chain and padlock. By the name plates on the porch, Timberlane saw how the Press had occupied itself. It was mainly a religious publisher catering to children, issuing such periodicals as *The Children's Sunday Magazine, The Boys' Bugle, Girls' Guidance*, more popular lines such as *Bible Thrills, Gospel Thrills, Holy Adventures*, and the educational line, *Sufferance Readers*. A torn bill slid across the porch and wrapped itself around Timberlane's leg. He turned away. On the opposite side of the road a large apartment house rose. He surveyed the windows, trying to see if anyone was watching him. As he stood there, several people hurried by without looking at him.

There was a side alley flanked by a high wall. He went down it, treading through rubbish. He slid one hand to his revolver, and held it ready for action in his pocket. With pleasure he felt a primitive ferocity grow in his chest; he wanted to smash somebody's face in. The alley led to a waste lot at the back. In the middle distance, framed between two shoulders of wall, an old black man with round shoulders flew a kite, leaning dangerously back to watch its course over the rooftops.

Before Timberlane reached the lot, he came upon a side door into the Press. It had been broken open; two of the little squares of glass in its upper half were shattered, and it stood ajar. He paused against the wall, remembered procedure for army house-to-house fighting, kicked the door open, and ran through it for cover.

In the gloom, he peered cautiously about. Not a movement, or a whisper of movement. Silence. The Big Accident had decimated the rat population. It had been almost as hard on cats, and human hunger for meat had probably accounted for most of the rest of the feline population; so that if rats came back, they would be more difficult than ever to check. But as yet this gaunt building obviously needed no cat.

He was in a broken-down store. An ancient raincoat on a peg

spoke mutely of desertion. Piles of children's religious reading stood about gathering dust, their potential purchasers either dead or forever unborn and unconceived. Only the footsteps across the floor to an inner passage were new.

He followed the prints across the room, into the passage, and along it to the main hall, conscious of the sound of his own footsteps. Above grimy swing doors, through which dim figures could be seen passing in the street, was a bust and an inscription in marble: 'Suffer the Little Children and Let Them Come to Me.'

'They suffered all right,' Timberlane said to himself.

He started a search downstairs, growing less cautious as he went along. Stagnation lay here like a malediction. Standing under the blind eyes of the founder, he looked up the stairs.

'I'm here, you bastards. Where are you?' he shouted. 'What have you done with Martha?' The noise of his own voice shocked him. He stood frozen as it echoed up the elevator shaft into the regions above. Then he took the steps two at a time, gun out before him, with the safety catch off.

At the top he paused. Still the silence. He walked reverberatingly down the corridor and threw open a door. It slammed back on its hinges, knocking over an ancient blackboard and easel. This was some kind of editorial room, by the look of it. He stared out of the window down onto the waste lot; he looked for the old Negro flying a kite, recalling him almost as one recalls a friend. The old man had gone, or could not be seen. Nobody could be seen, not a human, not a dog.

God, this is what it's like to be left alone in the world, he subvocalized. And another thought followed: Better get used to it now, youngster; one day you may be left alone in the world.

He was not a particularly imaginative man. Although for almost all the years of his life he had been confronted with the knowledge of the extinction mankind had unleashed upon itself, the optimism of youth helped him to believe either that conditions would right themselves naturally (nature had recovered from so many outrages before) or that one of the lines of research being pursued in a score of countries would turn up a restorative (surely

145

a multibillion-dollar-a-year program could not be entirely wasted). The levelheaded pessimism of the DOUCH project had brought his wishful thinking to a standstill.

He saw in sober fact that his kind might have reached the end of its time. Year by year, as the living died, the empty rooms about him would multiply, like the cells of a giant hive that no bees visited, until they filled the world. The time would come when he would be a monster, alone in the rooms, in the tracks of his search, in the labyrinth of his hollow footsteps.

Over the room, as over the face of an inquisitor, was written his future. Its wound was inescapable, for he had found it for himself. He opened his mouth, to cry or suck in air, as though someone had flung him under a cascade. Only one thing, one person, could make that future tolerable.

He ran out into the corridor, flaying the echoes again.

'It's me – Timberlane! Is anyone here, for God's sake?'

And a voice near at hand called, 'Algy, oh, Algy!'

She lay in a composing room among a litter of broken and discarded flongs. Like the rest of the building, it bore every sign of a long desertion. Her captors had tied her to the supports of a heavy metal bench on which lay discarded galleys of lead type, and she had been unable to break free. She estimated she had been lying there since midnight.

'You're all right? Are you all right?' Timberlane kept asking, rubbing her bruised arms and legs after he had wrenched apart the plastic straps that bound her.

'I'm perfectly all right,' Martha said, beginning to weep. 'He was quite a gentleman, he didn't rape me! I suppose I am very lucky. He didn't rape me.'

Timberlane put his arms around her. For minutes they crouched together on the littered floor, glad in the sensible warmth and solidity of each other's bodies.

After a while, Martha was able to tell her story. The taxi driver who had whipped her away from the front of the Thesaurus Club had driven her only a few blocks into a private garage. She thought she might be able to identify the spot. She remembered that the garage had a motorboat stored overhead. She was frightened, and fought the taxi driver when he tried to pull her out of the car. Another man appeared, wearing a white handkerchief over his face. He carried a chloroform-impregnated pad. Between them, the men forced the pad over Martha's nose and mouth, and she became unconscious.

She roused to find herself in another car, a larger one. She thought they were traveling through a suburb or semi-country; there were trees and low-lying houses flashing by outside, and another girl lying inertly by her side. Then a man in the front seat saw she was rousing, leaned over, and forced her to breathe more chloroform.

When Martha woke again, she was in a bedroom. She was sprawled over a bed, lying against the girl who had been in the car with her. They both roused and tried to pull themselves together. The room they were in was without windows; they thought it was a large room partitioned into two. A dark woman entered and led Martha into another room. She was brought before a man in a mask, and allowed to sit on a chair. The man told her that she was lucky to be chosen, and that there was no need to be frightened. His boss had fallen in love with her, and would treat her well if she would live with him; the flowers had been sent to her as a token of the honesty of his intentions. Angry and frightened though she was, Martha kept quiet at this point.

She had then been taken to the 'boss,' in a third room. He wore a domino. His face was thin, and deficient in chin. His jaw looked grey in the bright light. He rose when Martha entered, and spoke in a gentle, husky voice. He told her he was rich and lonely, and needed her company as well as her body. She asked how many girls he required to overcome his loneliness; he said huffily that the other girl was for a friend of his. He and his friend were shy men, and had to resort to this method of introduction; he was not a criminal, and he had no intention of harming her.

Very well, Martha had said, let me go. She told him she was engaged to be married.

The man sat in a swivel chair behind a table. Chair and table stood on a dais. The man moved very little. He looked at her for a long while in silence, until she became very sick and scared. What chiefly scared her was her belief that this man was in an obscure way scared of her, and would go to considerable lengths to alter this situation.

'You should not get married,' he said at last. 'You can't have babies. Women don't have babies anymore, now that radiation sickness is so fashionable. Men used to hate those little bawling ugly brats so much, and now their secret dreams have been fulfilled, and women can be used for nice things. You and I could do nice things.

'You're lovely, with those legs and breasts and eyes of yours. But you're only flesh and blood, like me. A little thing like a scalpel could cut right into you and make you unfit for nice things. I often say to my friends, "Even the loveliest girl can't stand up to a little scalpel." I'm sure you'd rather do nice things, a girl like you, eh?'

Martha repeated shakily that she was going to get married.

Again he sat in silence, not moving. When he spoke again it was with less interest, and on a different tack.

He said he liked her attractive foreign accent. He had a large bomb-proof shelter underground, stocked with a two-year supply of food and drink. He had a private plane. They could winter in Florida, if she would sign an agreement with him. They could do nice things.

She told him he had ugly thumbs and fingers. She would have nothing to do with anyone with hands like that.

He rang a bell. Two men ran in and seized Martha. They held Martha while the man in the domino came down off his dais and kissed her and ran his hands under her clothes and over her body. She struggled and kicked his ankle. His mouth trembled. She called him a coward. He ordered her taken out. The two men dragged her back into the bedroom and held her down on the bed, while the other girl cried in a corner. In outrage, Martha screamed as loudly as she could. The men put her out with another chloroformed pad.

When she came back to her senses, it was the cold air of night

148

that roused her. She was being hustled into the deserted Sufferance Press building and tied to the bench.

She had been frightened and sick all night. When she heard someone below, she had not dared to call out until Timberlane had uttered his name, fearing the kidnappers had come back for her.

'That vile, loathsome creature! I'd tear his throat out if I got hold of him. Darling – you're sure that's all he did to you?'

'Yes – in an obscure way, I felt he'd got the thrill he was after – something in my fear he needed – I don't know.'

'He was a maniac, whoever he was,' Timberlane said, pressing her close to him, running his hands through her hair. 'Thank God he was mad the way he was and did you no real harm. Oh, my darling, it's like a miracle to have you again. I'll never let you go.'

'All the same, I shouldn't stay too close, love, until I've had a bath,' she said, laughing shakily. Having told her tale, something of her normal composure was back. 'You must have been in a state when you saw the taxi speeding away with me, poor darling.'

'Dyson and Jack were a great help. I left a note for Jack at the billet in case I ran into trouble. The police'll get this slimy little pervert. The details you have should be enough to track him down.'

'Do you think so? I'm sure I'd be okay on an identification parade, if they'd let me look at their thumbs. I keep wondering – I've been wondering all night – whatever happened to the other girl? What happens if you give in to a man like that, I don't know.'

Suddenly she burst into tears and wrapped her arms about Timberlane's waist. He helped her to her feet, and they sat side by side on frames in which leaden sentences were set backward and upside down. He put his arm around her and wiped her face with his handkerchief. Her painted eyebrows had come off, smeared across her forehead; licking the handkerchief, he cleaned their remains away.

Having her so close, seeing her, helping her restore herself, he broke into a flurry of words.

'Listen, Martha, when I was kicking my heels down at the police station last night, I put your question to Bill Dyson – you know, about why they had gone to the trouble of flying you over here from England. At first he tried to kid me that it was just because he and Jack were sentimentalists. I wouldn't wear that, so he came out with the truth. He said it was a DOUCH regulation. At the end of this course, they're going to put me back in England, and if things get as bad as they expect, I shall be on my own, cut off from their support.

'Currently, they're predicting the rise of authoritarian regimes in Britain and America at the cessation of hostilities. They think international communications will soon be a thing of the past. Survival will be tough, and will grow steadily tougher, as Bill pointed out with some relish. So DOUCH require me – and the Japanese, German, Israeli, and other operators in training – to be married to what they call "a native" – a girl who has been brought up in the local ways, and will therefore have inbred knowledge of local conditions. As Dyson put it, "Environmental know-how is a survival factor."

'There's a lot more to it, but the essence of it is that they wanted you around so that I would not get too interested in any girl I met here and wreck my bit of the project. If I married an American girl, I would be dropped like a hot potato.'

'We always knew they were thorough.'

'Sure. While old Bill was talking, I saw what the future was going to be like. Have you ever *really* looked ahead, Martha? I never have. It's a lack of courage, perhaps – just as I've heard Mother say her generation never looked ahead when they heard more nuclear bombs were being made and detonated. But these Americans have looked ahead. They have seen how difficult survival is going to be. They have survival broken down into figures, and the figures for Great Britain show that if present trends continue, in fifteen or twenty years only fifty percent of the population will still be living. Britain's particularly vulnerable, because we are so much less self-supporting than the States. The point is, all my DOUCH training is directed toward setting me with the DOUCH truck in that doubtfully privileged fifty percent. And in their materialistic way, they've grasped something that I'm sure my religious pal Charley Samuels in Assam would endorse – that the one possible thing that will make that funereal future tolerable is the right sort of partner.' He broke off. Martha was laughing with a sound like suppressed sobs.

'Algernon Timberlane, you poor lost soul, this is a dickens of a place to propose to a girl!'

Nettled, he said, 'Am I really so damned funny?'

'Men always have to spell things out to themselves. Don't worry, it's something I love. You remind me of Father, honey, except that you're sexy. But I'm not laughing at your conclusions, really I'm not. I came to the same conclusion long ago in my heart.'

'Martha, I love you desperately, I need you desperately. I want to marry you just as soon as possible, and I never want us to be apart again, whatever happens.'

'My sweet, I love you and need you just as much. Why else do you think I came out to America? I'll never leave you, never fear.'

'I do fear. I fear mightily! When I thought I was alone in this morgue just now, I had a vision of what it will be like to grow old in a world grown old. We can't stop growing old, but at least let's do it together and make it tolerable.'

'We will, we will, darling! You're upset. Let's get out of here. I think I can walk now, if you give me your arm.'

He held away from her, grinning, with his hands behind his back.

'Are you sure you don't want a good look at my thumbs first, before you commit yourself?'

'I'll take a rain check on them, as Jack would say. Walk me as far as the window just to see how I make out. Oh, my legs – I thought I'd die, Algy . . .'

As she hobbled across the dirty floor on Timberlane's arm, Fat Choy sirens began to scream across the city. Their hollow voices came distantly, but from all around. The world was making itself felt again. Mingling with them came the lower note of police-car sirens. They got to the window, cobwebbed behind narrow bars. Timberlane wrestled it open and peered out his face tight between twin lances of iron.

He was in time to see two police cars slide up to the sidewalk below. Doors opened, uniformed men poured out. Among them, stepping from the rear car, was Jack Pilbeam. Timberlane shouted and signaled. The men looked up.

'Jack!' he bellowed down. 'Can you put off your travels for twenty-four hours? Martha and I need a best man!'

Right thumb raised above his head, Pilbeam disappeared from view. Next moment, the sound of his footsteps came echoing up the forsaken stairwell.

5
The River: Oxford

They had raised a mast and a sheet, and were carried forward by a light wind. Since their night flight from Swifford Fair, their progress had been slow. They had been hindered at an old and broken lock; a boat had foundered there and blocked the navigable stream, and no doubt would continue to do so until the spring floodwater broke it up. They unloaded the boats there, pushing or carrying them and their few possessions to a point where they could safely launch them again.

The country here was particularly wild and inhospitable. Pitt thought he saw gnomes peering at them from bushes. All four of them thought they saw stoats climbing in the trees, finally deciding that the animals were not stoats but pine martens, an animal hardly ever seen in those parts since the Middle Ages. With bow and arrow they killed two of the creatures that afternoon, eating their flesh and preserving their fine pelts, when they were forced to make a camp in the open, under trees. Wood for burning lay about in plenty, and they huddled together between two fires; but it was an ill night for them all.

Next day, when they were under way again, they were fortunate enough to see a peddler fishing on the bank. He bought Pitt's little rowing boat from them, giving them money and two sails, one of which they used that night to make themselves a tent. The peddler offered them tinned apricots and pears, but since these must have been at least a dozen years old, and were very expensive, they did not buy. The little old man, made garrulous by solitude, told them he was on his way to join Swifford Fair, and that he had some medicines for Dr Bunny Jingadangelow.

After they left the peddler, they came to a wide sheet of water, patched with small islands and banks of rushes. Under the drab sky, it appeared to stretch on forever, and they could not see their proper course through it. This lake was a sanctuary for wild life; dippers, moor hens, and an abundance of duck moved over or above its surface. In the clear waters beneath their centerboard, many shoals of fish were visible.

They were in no mood to appreciate the natural attractions. The weather had turned blustery; they did not know in which direction they should sail. Rain, galloping over the face of the water, sent them scurrying for shelter under the spare sail. As the showers grew heavier and the breeze failed, Greybeard and Charley rowed to one of the islands, and there they made camp.

It was dry under the sail, and the weather had turned milder, but a sense of depression settled on them as they watched shawls of water and cloud embrace the landscape. Greybeard husbanded a small fire into life, which set them all coughing, for the smoke would not disperse. Their spirits recovered only when Pitt appeared, shrunken, withered, weathered, but triumphantly bearing a pair of fine beavers on his back. One of the beavers was a giant, four feet long from whiskers to tail. Pitt reported a colony of them only a hundred yards away; the few that were about had shown no fear of him.

'I'll catch another pair in the morning for breakfast,' he said. 'If we've got to live like savages, let's live as well as savages.'

Although he was not a man ever to grumble extensively, Pitt found few consolations in their way of life. Whatever his success as a trapper of animals – and he derived satisfaction from outwitting and slaying them – he saw himself as a failure. Ever since he had proved himself unable to kill Greybeard, a dozen years before, he had lived an increasingly solitary life; even his gratitude to Greybeard for sparing him was tempered with the thought that but for him he might now be controlling his own body of soldiers, the remains of Croucher's command. He nourished this grievance inside himself, though he knew there was no real substance in it. Earlier experience should have convinced him that he could never fulfill the proper duty of a soldier.

*

As a child, Jeff Pitt used to make his way through the outskirts of the great city in which he lived to a stretch of common land beyond the houses. This land merged with moorland, and was a fine place for a boy to roam. From the tops of the moors, where only an occasional hawk rode the breezes, you could look down onto the maze of the city, with its chimneys, its slaty factory roofs, and the countless little millipedes that were its houses. Jeff used to take his friend Dicky onto the common; when the weather was fine, they would go there every day of their school holidays.

Jeff owned a large, rusty bike, inherited from one of his elder brothers; Dicky had a white mongrel dog called Snowy. Snowy enjoyed the common as much as the boys did. All this was in the early nineteen-seventies, when they were in short trousers and the world was at peace.

Sometimes Jeff and Dicky played soldiers, using bits of stick for rifles. Sometimes they tried to capture lizards with their cupped hands; these were little brown lizards that generally escaped, leaving their wriggling bloody tails in the boys' palms. Sometimes they wrestled.

One day they wrestled with such absorption that they rolled down a bank and into a luxuriant bed of nettles. They were both badly stung. However much it hurt, Jeff would not cry before his friend. Dicky blubbered all the way home. Even a ride on Jeff's bike could not silence him completely.

The boys grew up. The steel-cowled factories swallowed young Jeff Pitt, as they had swallowed his brothers. Dicky obtained a job in an estate office. They found they had nothing in common and ceased to seek each other's company.

The war came. Pitt was conscripted into the air force. After some hazardous adventures in the Middle East, he deserted, together with several of his fellows. This was like a token to other units in the area, where dissatisfaction with the cause and course of the war was already rife. Mutiny broke out. Some of the mutineers seized a plane at the Teheran airport and flew it back to Britain. Pitt was on the plane.

In Britain, revolution was gathering momentum. In a few

months the government would collapse and a hastily established people's government sue for peace with the enemy powers. Pitt found his way home and joined the local rebels. One moonlit night, a pro-government group attacked their headquarters, which was in a big Victorian house in the suburbs. Pitt found himself positioned behind a concrete bench, his heart hammering dreadfully, firing at the enemy.

One of his mates in the house brought a searchlight into play. Its beam picked up Dicky, wearing the government flash and coming toward Pitt's position at a run. Pitt shot him.

He regretted the shot even before – as if by magic – a wound burst over Dicky's shirt and he spun around and pitched onto the gravel. Pitt crawled forward to him, but the shot had been a true one; his friend was almost dead.

Since that time, he could never nerve himself to kill anything much bigger than a beaver.

Cramped in the tent, they ate well and slept well that night. Sailing throughout the next day, they saw no living person. Man had gone, and the great interlocking world of living species had already knitted over the space he once occupied. Moving without any clear sense of direction, they had to spend another two nights on islands in the lake; but since the weather continued mild and the food plentiful, they raised very little complaint, beyond the unspoken one that beneath their rags and wrinkles they regarded themselves still as modern man, and modern man was entitled to something better than wandering through a Pleistocene wilderness.

The wilderness was punctuated now and again by memorials of former years, some of them looking all the grimmer and blacker for lingering on out of context. The dinghy bore them to a small railway station, which a board still announced as Yarnton Junction. Its two platforms stood above the flood, while the signal box, perched on its brick tower, served as a lookout across the meads.

In the broken and ruined waiting room they found a reindeer and calf. In the lookout lived a hideously deformed old hermit, who kept them covered with a homemade bomb, held menacingly above his head, while he spoke to them. He told them that the lake was formed by a conflux of overflowing streams, among them the Oxford Canal and the Evenlode. Only too keen to get rid of them, the old fellow gave them their general direction, and once more the party moved forward, aided by a light and steady wind. After some two hours Charley stood up in the dinghy and pointed toward the southeast.

'There they are!'

Martha, Timberlane, and old Jeff Pitt rose too, peering where Charley pointed across the lake. Isaac the fox paced up and down the tiller seat. The reassuring spread of Oxford's spires could be seen through the trees. They stood, as many of them had stood for centuries, beckoning toward the traditions of learning and piety, now broken at their feet, that had given them birth. The sun rolled from behind rain clouds and lit them. There was no one in the boat who did not feel his heart beat faster at the sight.

'We could stay here, Algy – at least for the rest of the winter,' Martha said.

He looked at her face, and was touched to find tears in her eyes. 'I'm afraid it's mainly an illusion,' he said. 'Oxford too will have changed. We may find only deserted ruins.'

She shook her head without speaking.

'I wonder if old Croucher has still got a warrant out for our arrest,' Pitt said. 'I wouldn't want to get shot as soon as we stepped ashore.'

'Croucher died of the cholera, and I don't doubt that Cowley proceeded to turn itself first into a battleground and then a cemetery, leaving only the old city,' Greybeard said. 'Let's hope we get a friendly welcome from whoever's left. A roof over our heads tonight would be a change for the better, wouldn't it?'

The scenery became less imposing as they drifted south toward the city. Rows of poor houses stood in the flood, their desolation only emphasized by the sunlight. Their roofs had caved in; they resembled the carcasses of enormous Crustacea cast up on a primeval beach. Dwarfed by them, an ancient creature swathed in furs watered a couple of reindeer. Farther on, the stir they made on the water threw wavering reflections onto the roofs of empty timber yards. The heavy silence was broken a little later by the crunch of a vehicle. Two old women, as broad as they were long, bundled together to drag a cart behind them, its wheels grinding up the sunlight as they pulled it along a quayside. The quayside ended by a low bridge.

'This I recognize,' Greybeard said, speaking in a hushed voice. 'We can tie up here. This is Folly Bridge.'

As they climbed ashore, the two old women came up and offered the hire of their cart. As always when they met strangers, Greybeard's party had difficulty in understanding their accent. Pitt told the crones they had nothing worth carrying, and the crones told them they would find shelter for the night at Christ Church, 'up the road.' Leaving Charley behind with Isaac to guard the boat, Martha, Greybeard, and Pitt set out along the broken track that led over the bridge.

The fortresslike walls of the ancient college of Christ Church loomed over one of the southern approaches of the city. From the top of the walls a knot of bearded men watched the newcomers walk up the road. They approached warily, half expecting a challenge, but none came. When they reached the great wooden gates of the college, they paused. Untended, the college walls were crumbling. Several windows had fallen out or were boarded up, and the shattered stone lying at the foot of the walls spoke of the action of heat and frost and the elements. Greybeard shrugged his shoulders and marched under the tall archway.

In contrast to the ruination through which they had passed, here was habitation, the bustle of people, the color of market stalls, the smell of animals and foods. The newcomers' spirits rose. They found themselves in a great quad, which had housed many past generations of undergraduates; wooden stalls had been set up, several of them forming small enclosed buildings from which a variety of goods was being sold. Another part of the quad was railed off, and here reindeer stood, surveying the scene from under their antlers with their customary look of morose humor.

A bald-headed shred of manhood with a nose as thin as a needle skipped out of the lodge at the gate and asked them, as they were strangers, what they wanted. They had a deal of difficulty making him understand, but eventually he led them to a portly fossil of a man with three chins and a high complexion who said they could rent, for a modest fee, two small basement rooms in Killcanon. They entered their names in a register and showed the color of their money.

Killcanon turned out to be a small square within Christ Church, and their rooms a larger room subdivided. But the needle-nosed messenger told them they might burn firewood in their grates, and offered them fuel cheap. Mainly from weariness, they accepted the offer. The messenger lit the fires for them, while Jeff Pitt walked back to collect Charley and the fox and make arrangements for the boat.

Once the fire was burning cheerfully, the messenger showed signs of lingering, squatting by the flame and rubbing his nose, trying to listen to what Martha and Greybeard said to each other. Greybeard stirred him with a toe.

'Before you go out, Chubby, tell me if this college is still used for learning as it used to be.'

'Why, there's nobody to learn anymore,' the man said. It was plain that he intended his verb to be transitive, whatever a legion of vanished grammar books might have said. 'But the Fellows own the place, and they seem to learn each other a bit still. You'll see them going about with books in their pockets, if you watch out. For a tip, I'd introduce you to one of them.'

'We'll see. There may be time for that tomorrow.'

'Don't leave it too long, sir. There's a local legend that Oxford is sinking into the river, and when it's gone under, a whole lot of little naked people what now live under the water will come swimming up like eels and live here instead.'

Greybeard contemplated the ruin of a man. 'I see. And do you give this tale much credence?'

'What you say, sir?'

'Do you believe this tale?'

The old man laughed, casting a shuffling side glance at Martha. 'I ain't saying I believe it and I ain't saying I don't believe it, but I know what I've heard, and they do say that for every woman as dies, one more of these little naked people is born under water. And this I do know because I saw it with my own eyes last Michaelmas – no, the Michaelmas before last, because I was behind with my rent this Michaelmas. There was an old woman of ninety-nine died down at Grandpont, and very next day a little two-headed creature all naked floated up at the bridge.'

'Which was it you saw?' Martha asked. 'The old lady dying or the two-headed thing?'

'Well, I'm often down that way,' the messenger said confusedly. 'It was the funeral and the bridge I mainly saw, but many men told me about all the rest and I have no cause to doubt 'em. It's common talk.'

When he had gone, Martha said, 'It's strange how everyone believes in something different.'

'They're all a bit mad.'

'No, I don't think they're mad – except that other people's beliefs always seem mad, just as their passions do. In the old days, before the Accident, people were more inclined to keep their beliefs to themselves, or else confide only in doctors and psychiatrists. Or else the belief was widespread, and lost its air of absurdity. Think of all the people who believed in astrology, long after it was proved to be a pack of nonsense.'

'Illogical, and therefore a mild form of madness,' Greybeard said.

'No, I don't think so. A form of consolation, rather. This old fellow with a nose like a knitting needle nurses this crazy dream about little naked things taking over Oxford; it in some way consoles him for the dearth of babies. Charley's religion is the same sort of consolation. Your recent drinking companion, Bunny Jingadangelow, had retreated into a world of pretense.'

She sank wearily down onto the bed of blankets and stretched. Slowly she removed her battered shoes, massaged her feet, and then stretched full length, with her hands under her head. She regarded Greybeard, whose bald pate glowed as he crouched by the fire.

'What are you thinking, my venerable love?' she asked.

'I was wondering if the world might not slip – if it hasn't

already – into a sort of insanity, now that everyone left is over fifty. Is a touch of childhood and youth necessary to sanity?'

'I don't think so. We're really amazingly adaptable, more than we give ourselves credit for.'

'Yes, but suppose a man lost his memory of everything that happened to him before he was fifty, so that he was utterly cut off from his roots, from all his early achievement – wouldn't you classify him as insane?'

'It's only an analogy.'

He turned to her and grinned. 'You're a bugger for arguing, Martha Timberlane.'

'After all these years we can still tolerate each other's fatheaded opinions. It's a miracle!'

He went over to her, sitting on the bed beside her and stroking her thigh.

'Perhaps that's our bit of madness or consolation or whatever – each other. Martha, have you ever thought . . .' He paused, and then went on, screwing his face into a frown of concentration. 'Have you ever thought that that ghastly catastrophe fifty years ago was, well, was lucky for us? I know it sounds blasphemous; but mightn't it be that we've led more interesting lives than the perhaps rather pointless existence we would otherwise have been brought up to accept as life? We can see now that the values of the twentieth century were invalid; otherwise they wouldn't have wrecked the world. Don't you think that the Accident has made us more appreciative of the vital things, like life itself, and like each other?'

'No,' Martha said steadily. 'No, I don't. We would have had children and grandchildren by now, but for the Accident, and nothing can ever make up for that.'

Next morning, they were roused by the sound of animals, the crowing of cocks, the pad of reindeer hoofs, even the bray of a donkey. Leaving Martha in the warm bed, Greybeard rose and dressed. It was cold. Drafts flapped the rug on the floor and had spread the ashes of the fire far and wide during the night.

Outside, it was barely daylight and the puddingy Midland sky rendered the quad in cold tones. But there were torches burning, and people on the move, and their voices sounding – cheerful sounds, even where their owners were toothless and bent double with years. The main gates had been opened, and many of the animals were going forth, some pulling carts. Greybeard saw not only a donkey but a couple of horses that looked like the descendants of hunters, both fine young beasts and pulling carts. They were the first he had seen or heard of in over a quarter century. One sector of the country was now so effectively insulated from another that widely different conditions prevailed.

The people were on the whole well clad, many of them wearing fur coats. Up on the battlements a pair of sentries clouted their ribs for warmth and looked down at the bustle below.

Going to the lodge, where candles burned, Greybeard found the treble-chinned man off duty. His place was taken by a plump fellow of Greybeard's age, who proved to be a son of the triple chins; he was as amiable as his father was fossilized, and when Greybeard asked if it would be possible to get a job for the winter months, he became talkative.

They sat over a small fire, huddled against the chill blowing in through the big gate from the street. Speaking against the rumble and clatter of the traffic passing his cabin, the plump fellow chatted of Oxford.

For some years the city had possessed no central governing body. The colleges had divided it up and ruled it indifferently. Such crime as there was, was treated harshly; but there had been no shootings at Carfax for over a twelve-month.

Christ Church and several of the other colleges now served as a cross between a castle, a hostel, and a manor house. They provided shelter and defense when defense was needed, as it had been in the past. The bigger colleges owned most of the town about them. They remained prosperous, and for the past ten years had lived peaceably together, developing agriculture and rearing livestock. They did what they could to provide drainage to fight the nearby floods, which rose higher every spring. And in one of the colleges at the other end of the town, Balliol by name, the

Master was looking after three children who were shown ceremonially to the population twice a year.

'What age are these children? Have you seen them?' Greybeard asked.

'Oh yes, I've seen them all right. Everyone's seen the Balliol children. I wouldn't miss them. The girl's a little beauty. She's about ten, and was born of an imbecile woman living at Kidlington, which is a village away in the woods to the north. The two boys, I don't know where they come from, but one had a hard time before he got here, and was displayed by a showman in Reading, I heard tell.'

'These are genuine, normal children?'

'One of the boys has got a withered arm, a little arm that finishes off with three fingers at his elbow, but you wouldn't call that a proper disfigurement and the girl has no hair and something a bit funny with her ear, but nothing really wrong, and she waves very pretty to the crowd.'

'And you've actually seen them?'

'Yes, I've seen them in The Broad, where they parade. The boys don't wave so much, because they're older, but they're nice fresh young chaps, and it's certainly good to see a bit of smooth flesh.'

'You're sure they're real? Not old men disguised, or anything like that?'

'Oh no, no, no, nothing like that. They're small, just like children in old pictures, and you can't mistake young skin, can you?'

'Well, you have horses here. Perhaps you have children.'

They changed the topic then, and after some discussion, the porter's son advised Greybeard to go and speak to one of the college Fellows, Mr Norman Morton, who was responsible for employing people in the college.

Martha and he made a frugal meal of some tough cold beaver and a hunk of bread that Martha had bought from one of the stalls the previous evening; then she and Greybeard told Charley and Pitt where they were going, and headed for Norman Morton's rooms.

In Peck, the farthest quadrangle of the college, a fine two-story stable had been built, with room to house beasts and carts. Morton had his suite of rooms facing this stable. In some of these rooms he lived; in others he kept animals.

He was a tall man, broad-shouldered and stooped, with a nervous nod to his head and a countenance so lined it looked as if it had been patiently assembled from bits of string. Greybeard judged him to be well into his eighties, but he showed no sign of intending to give up good living yet awhile. When a servant ushered Martha and Greybeard into his presence, Mr Norman Morton was engaged with two cronies in sipping a hot spiced wine and demolishing what looked like a leg of mutton.

'You can have some wine if you talk interestingly,' he said, leaning back in his chair and pointing a patronizing fork at them. 'My friends and I are always happy to be entertained by the tales of travelers, lies though they generally are. If you're going to lie, have the kindness to make them big 'uns.'

'In my childhood,' Martha said, nodding gravely to the other gentlemen, whose mouths worked busily as they returned the gesture, 'hosts were expected to entertain visitors, not vice versa. But in those days, seats of learning housed courtesy rather than cattle.'

Morton raised a pair of feathery eyebrows and put down his glass.

'Madam,' he said, 'forgive me. If you dress like a cowherd's woman, you must be used to being mistaken for a cowherd's woman, don't you know. To each his or her own eccentricity. Allow me to pour you a little of this negus, and then we will talk together as equals – at least until it is proved otherwise.'

The wine was good enough to take off some of the sharpness of Morton's speech. Greybeard said as much.

'It drinks well enough,' one of the Fellows agreed carelessly. He was a tallowy man, addressed as Gavin, with a yellow face and a forehead from which he constantly wiped sebum. 'It's only a homegrown wine, unfortunately. We finished off the last of the college cellars the day the Dean was deposed.'

The three men bowed their heads in mock-reverence at mention of the Dean.

'What is your story, then, strangers?' Morton asked, in a more unbuttoned fashion.

Greybeard spoke briefly of their years in London, of their brush with Croucher in Cowley, and of their long withdrawal at Sparcot. However much the Fellows regretted the absence of palpable lies, they expressed interest in the account.

'I remember this Commander Croucher,' Morton said. 'He was not a bad chap as dictators go. Fortunately, he was the sort of illiterate who preserves an undue respect for learning. Perhaps because his father, it was rumored, was a college servant, his attitude to the university was astonishingly respectful. We had to be inside college by seven P.M., but that was no hardship. I recall that even at the time we regarded his regime as one of historical necessity. It was after he died that things became really intolerable. Croucher's soldiery turned into a rabble of looters. That was the worst time in our whole miserable half-century of decline.'

'What happened to these soldiers?'

'Roughly what you'd expect. They killed each other, and then the cholera got the rest of them, thank heaven, don't you know. For a year, this was a city of the dead. The colleges were closed. Nobody about. I took over a cottage outside the city. After a time, people started drifting back. Then, that winter or the next, the flu hit us.'

'We missed serious flu epidemics at Sparcot,' Greybeard said.

'You were fortunate. You were also fortunate in that the flu missed very few centers of population, by all accounts, so you were spared armed bands of starving louts roving the country and pillaging.'

The Fellow addressed as Vivian said, 'At its best, this country could support only half the populace by home agriculture. Under worsening conditions it might support under a sixth of the number. In normal times the death rate would be about six hundred thousand per year. There are of course no accurate figures available, but I would hazard that at the time of which we speak, about twenty-twenty or a little earlier, the population shrank from about twenty-seven million to twelve million. One can easily calculate that in the decade since then the population must have shrunk to a mere six million, estimating by the old death rate. Given another decade—'

'Thank you, no more statistics, Vivian,' Morton said. To his visitors, he added, 'Oxford has been peaceful since the flu epidemic. Of course, there was the trouble with Balliol.'

'What happened there?' Martha asked, accepting another glass of the homemade wine.

'Balliol thought it would like to rule Oxford, don't you know. There was some paltry business about trying to collect arrears of rent from their city properties. The townspeople appealed to Christ Church for assistance. Fortunately we were able to give it.

'We had a rather terrible artillery man, a Colonel Appleyard, taking refuge with us at the time. He was an undergraduate of the house – plowed, poor fellow, and fit for nothing but a military life – but he had a couple of mortars with him. Trench mortars, don't you know. He set them up in the quad and began to bombard – to mortar, I suppose one should say, if the verb can be used in that application – Balliol.'

Gavin chuckled and added, 'Appleyard's aim was somewhat uncertain, and he demolished most of the property in between Balliol and here, including Jesus College; but the Master of Balliol ran up his white flag, and we have all lived equably ever after.'

The three Fellows were put in a good humor by this anecdote, and ran over the salient points of the campaign among themselves, forgetting their visitors. Mopping his forehead, Gavin said, 'Some of the colleges are built like little fortresses; it is pleasant to see this aspect is to some extent functional.'

'Has the lake we sailed over to reach Folly Bridge any particular history?' Greybeard inquired.

'Particular meaning pertaining to? Why, yes and no, although nothing so dramatic – nothing so full of human interest, shall we say – as the Balliol campaign,' Morton said. 'The Meadow Lake, as our local men know it, covers ground that was always liable to flood, even in the palmy days of the Thames Conservancy, rest their souls. Now it is a permanent flood, thanks to the work of undermining the banks carried out by an army of coypus.'

'Coypu is an animal?' Martha asked.

'A rodent, madam, of the echimyidae family, hailing from South America, now as much a native of Oxford as Gavin or I – and I fancy will continue to be so long after we are put to rest, eh, Gavin? You might not have seen the creature on your travels, since it is shy and conceals itself. But you must come and see our menagerie, and meet our tame coypus.'

He escorted them through several odorous rooms, in which he kept a number of animals in cages. Most of them ran to him and appeared glad to see him.

The coypus enjoyed a small pool set in the stone slabs of a ground-floor room. They looked like a cross between a beaver and a rat. Morton explained how they had been imported into the country back in the twentieth century to be bred on farms for their nutria fur. Some had escaped, to become a pest throughout much of East Anglia. In several concentrated drives, they had been almost exterminated; after the Accident, they had multiplied again, slowly at first and then, hitting their stride like so many other rapid-breeding creatures, very fast. They spread westward along rivers, and it now seemed as if they covered half the country.

'They will be the end of the Thames,' Morton said. 'They ruin any watercourse. Fortunately, they more than justify their existence by being both very good to eat and to wear! Fricaseed coypu is one of the great consolations of our senility, eh, Vivian? Perhaps you have observed how many people are able to afford their old bones the luxury of a fur coat.'

Martha mentioned the pine martens they had seen.

'Eh, very interesting! *They* must be spreading eastward from Wales, which was the only part of Britain where they survived a century ago. All over the world there must be far-reaching changes in animal behavior and habitat; if only one could have another life in which to chart it all . . . Ah, well, that's not a fruitful thing to wish, is it?'

Morton finished by offering Martha a job as an assistant to his menagerie keeper, and advising Greybeard to see a Farmer Flitch, who was wanting a man for odd jobs.

Joseph Flitch was an octogenarian as active as a man twenty years his junior. He needed to be. He supported a house full of nagging women: his wife, his wife's two hoary old sisters, their mother, and two daughters, one prematurely senile, the other permanently crippled with arthritis. Of this unhappy crew of harridans, Mrs Flitch was, perhaps because the rule in her household was the survival of the fiercest, undoubtedly the fiercest. She took an instant spite to Greybeard.

Flitch led him around to an outhouse, shook his hand, and engaged him for what Norman Morton had said would be a fair price. 'Oi knows as you will be a good man by the way the missus took against you,' he declared, speaking in a broad Oxfordshire that at first barely escaped incomprehensibility.

He was – not unnaturally in the circumstances – a morose man. He was also a shrewd and enterprising man, as Greybeard saw, and ran an expanding business. His farm was at Osney, on the edge of Meadow Lake, and he employed several men on it. Flitch had been one of the first to take advantage of the changing natural conditions, and used the spreading reed beds as a supply of thatch materials. No brick or tile was made in the locality; but several of the better houses thereabouts were handsomely covered in a deep layer of Farmer Flitch's thatch.

It was Greybeard's job to row himself about the lake harvesting armful after armful of the reeds. Since he used his own boat for this, Flitch, a fair dealer, presented him with a gigantic, warm, and waterproof nutria coat, which had belonged to a man who died in debt to him. Snug in the coat, Greybeard spent most of his daylight hours working slowly about the lake, feeling himself absorbed between the flat prospect of water and marsh and the mold of sky. It was a period of quiet punctuated by the startlements of water birds; sometimes he filled the dinghy with an abundance of reed, and could then spend half an hour fishing for his and Martha's supper. On these occasions, he saw many different sorts of rodent swimming in and out of the swampy places: not only water rats but the larger animals, beaver, otter, and the coypu, in whose skin he was clad. Once he saw a female coypu with young being suckled as they swam along.

Although he accepted that hard-worked time among the reeds, he did not forget the lesson he had gained at Sparcot, that serenity came not from the external world but from within. If he needed reminding, he had only to cut reeds in his favorite bay. From there he had a view of a large burial place, to which almost every day a grey knot of mourners came with a coffin. As Flitch dryly remarked when Greybeard commented on the graveyard, 'Ah, they keep a-planting of 'em, but there ain't any more of 'em growing up.'

So he would then go home to Martha, often with his beard coated with frost, back to the drafty room in Killcanon that she had succeeded in turning into a home. Both Charley and Pitt lived outside Christ Church, where they had secured cheaper and more tumbledown lodgings; Charley, whom they saw most days, had secured a job of sorts in a tannery; Pitt had returned to his old game of poaching and made little attempt to seek out their company. Greybeard saw him once along the south bank of the lake, a small and independent old figure.

On the darkest mornings Greybeard was at the great college gate at six, waiting for it to be opened to go to work. One morning, when he had been working for Flitch for a month, a bell in the ruinous Tom Tower above his head began to toll.

It was New Year's Day, which the inhabitants of Oxford held in festival.

'I don't expect any work off you today,' Flitch said when Greybeard showed himself at the little dairy. 'Life's short enough as well as being long enough – you're a young man, you are, go and enjoy yourself.'

'What year is it, Joe? I've lost my calendar and forgotten where we are.'

'What's it matter where we are? I barely keep the score of my own years, never mind the world's. You go on home to your Martha.'

'I'm just thinking. Why wasn't Christmas Day celebrated?'

Flitch straightened up from the sheep he was milking and

regarded Greybeard with an amused look. 'You mean why should it be celebrated? I can tell you're no sort of a religious man, or you wouldn't ask that. Christmas was invented to celebrate the birth of God's Son, wasn't it? And the Fellows in Christ Church reckon as it aren't in what you might call good taste to celebrate birth any more.' He moved his stool and pail to a nanny goat and added, ' 'Course, if you were under tenancy to Balliol or Magdalen, now they do recognize Christmas still.'

'Are you a religious man, Joe?'

Flitch pulled a face. 'I leaves that sort of thing to women.'

Greybeard tramped back through the miry streets to Martha. He saw by the look in her face that there was some excitement brewing. She explained that this was the day when the children of Balliol were displayed in The Broad, and she wanted to go and see them.

'We don't want to see children, Martha. It'll only upset you. Stay here with me, where it's cozy. Let's look up Tubby at the gate and have a drink with him. Or come and meet old Joe Flitch – you don't have to see his womenfolk. Or—'

'Algy, I want to be taken to see the children. I can stand the shock. Besides, it's a sort of social event, and they're few and far enough between,' She tucked her hair inside her hood, eyeing him in a friendly but detached way. He shook his head and took her by the arm.

'You were always a stubborn woman, Martha.'

'Where you are concerned, I'm always as weak as water, and you know it.'

Along the path known as The Corn, presumably from a plowed-up strip of wheatland along one side of it, many people were flocking. Their appearance was as grey and seamed as that of the ruined buildings below which they shuffled; they sucked their gums against the cold and did not chatter much. They gave way falteringly to a cart pulled by reindeer. As the cart creaked level with Martha and Greybeard, someone called her name.

Norman Morton, with a scholastic gown draped over a thick array of furs, rode in the cart, accompanied by some of the other Fellows, including the two Greybeard had spoken with already, the tallowy Gavin, the silent Vivian. He made the driver stop the cart, and invited the two pedestrians to climb up. They stepped up on the wheel hubs and were helped in.

'Are you surprised to find me participating in the common pleasure?' Morton asked. 'I take as much interest in Balliol's children as I do in my own animals. They make a pretty display as pets and reflect a little much-needed popularity onto the Master. What will happen to them when they are grown-up, as they will be in a few years, is a matter beyond the power of the Master to decide.'

The cart trundled to a convenient position before the battered fortress of Balliol, with its graceless Victorian façade. The ultimate effectiveness of Colonel Appleyard's mortar fire was apparent. The tower had been reduced to a stump, and two large sections of the façade were patched rather clumsily with new stone. A sort of scaffold had been erected outside the main gate and the college flag hung over it.

The crowd here was as large as those Martha and Greybeard had seen in earlier years. Although the atmosphere was more solemn than gay, hawkers moved among the numbers assembled, selling scarves and cheap jewelry and hats made of swans' feathers and hot dogs and pamphlets. Morton pointed to one man who bore a tray full of broadsheets and books.

'You see – Oxford continues to be the home of printing, right to the bitter end. There is much to be said for tradition, don't you know. Let's see what the rogue has to offer, eh?'

The rogue was a husky, broken-mouthed man with a notice pinned to his coat saying 'Bookseller to the University Press,' but most of his wares were intended, as Morton's friend Gavin remarked, turning over an ill-printed edition of a thriller, for the rabble.

Martha bought a four-page pamphlet produced for the occasion, and headed, HAPPY NEW YEAR OXFORD 2030!! She turned it over and handed it to Greybeard.

'Poetry seems to have come back into its own. Though this is mainly nursery-pornographic. Does it remind you of anything?'

He read the first verse. The mixture of childishness and smut did seem familiar.

> 'Little man Blue,
> Come rouse up your horn,
> The babies all bellow,
> They aren't getting born.'

'America . . .' he said. The names of everything had deserted him over almost thirty years. Then he smiled at her. 'Our best man – I can see him so clearly – what was it he called this sort of stuff? "Slouch"! By golly, how it takes you back!' He wrapped his arm around her.

'Jack Pilbeam,' she said. They both laughed, surprised by pleasure, and said simultaneously, 'My memory is getting so bad . . .'

Momentarily, both of them escaped from the present and the festering frames and rotten breath of the crowd about them. They were back when the world was cleaner, in that heady Washington they had known.

One of Bill Dyson's wedding presents to them was a permit for them to travel throughout the States. They took part of their honeymoon in Niagara, rejoicing in the hackneyed choice, pretending they were American, listening to the mighty fall of waters.

While they were there they heard the news. Martha's kidnapper was found and arrested. He proved to be Dusty Dykes. The news of the arrest made headlines everywhere; but next day there was a mighty factory fire in Detroit to fill the front pages.

That world of news and event was buried. Even in their memories it lived only flickeringly, for they formed part of the general disintegration. Greybeard closed his eyes and could not look at Martha.

The parade began. Various dignitaries, flanked by guards, marched from the gates of Balliol. Some mounted the scaffold, some guarded the way. The Master appeared, old and frail, his face a dead white against his black gown and hat. He was helped up the steps. He made a speech as brief as it was inaudible, subsiding into a fit of coughing, after which the children emerged from the college.

The girl appeared first, walking pertly and looking about her as she went. At the cheer that rose from the crowd, her face lit; she climbed the platform and waved. She was completely hairless, the structure of her skull knobbly through her pale skin. One of her ears, as Greybeard had been warned, was swollen until it was no more than a confused mess of flesh. When she turned so that it was toward the spectators, she resembled a goblin.

The crowd was delighted by the sight of youth. Many people clapped.

The boys appeared next. The one with the withered arm looked unwell; his face was pinched and bluish; he stood there apathetically, waving but not smiling. He was perhaps thirteen. The other boy was older and healthier. His eye as he regarded the crowd was calculating; Greybeard watched him with sympathy, knowing how untrustworthy a crowd is. Perhaps the boy felt that those who cheered so easily today might by next year be after his blood, if the wind but changed direction. So he waved and smiled, and never smiled with his eyes.

That was all. The children went in amid cries from the crowd, among which were many wet eyes. Several old women wept openly, and hawkers were doing a beneficial business in handkerchiefs.

'Extremely affecting,' said Morton harshly.

He spoke to the driver of their cart, and they began to move off, maneuvering with difficulty through the crowds. It was obvious that many of the spectators would hang about yet awhile, enjoying each other's company.

'There you have it,' Gavin said, pulling a handkerchief from a pocket to mop his sebaceous brow. 'So much for the miracle, the sign that under certain conditions the human race might renew itself again. But it is less easy for humans to build up from scratch than it is for most of our mammals. You only need a pair of Morton's stoats or coypus or rabbits, and in five years, given moderate luck, you have a thriving little horde of them, eh, Morton? Human beings need a century to reach anything like similar numbers. And then they need more than moderate luck. Rodents and lesser animals do not kill each other as does Homo sapiens. Ask yourself how long it is before that girl we've seen comes of rapable age, or the older boy, out after a bit of fun, gets set on by a group of coffin-bearers and beaten to death with stinking crutches.'

'I suppose the purpose of this yearly exhibition is to make people familiar with the children, so that they are less likely to be harmed?' Martha said.

'The psychological effect of such actions is frequently the very opposite of that intended,' Gavin said severely.

After that, they rode silently down The Corn and St Aldates and in through the tall gate of Christ Church. As they dismounted, Greybeard said, 'Would you ban the demonstration outside Balliol, Fellow Morton, if it were within your power?'

The old man looked at him slyly.

'I'd ban human nature if I could. We're a bad lot, don't you know.'

'Just as you've taken it upon yourself to ban Christmas?'

The stringy old countenance worked into something like a smile. He winked at Martha.

'I ban what I see fit – I, and Gavin, and Vivian here. We exercise our wisdom, you see, for the common good. We have banned many things more important than Christmas, let me tell you.'

'Such as?'

'The Dean for one,' Fellow Vivian said, displaying false teeth in a rare grin.

'You ought to have a look in the cathedral,' Morton said. 'We have converted it into a museum, where we keep a lot of banned things. How about it, gentlemen, shall we take a turn around our museum, since the day is fine?'

The other two Fellows assented, and the little party made their way across to the east side of the market quad, where the cathedral formed a part of the college.

'Wireless – the radio, don't you know – is one of the things we do not like in our quiet little gerontocracy,' Morton said. 'It could not profit us, and might upset us, to have news of the outside world. Who wishes to learn the death rate in Paris, or the extent of famine in New York? Or even the state of the weather in Ireland?'

'You have a wireless station here, then?' Greybeard asked.

'Well, we have a truck that broadcasts—' He broke off, fiddling with a large key in the cathedral door. Pushing together, he and Vivian got the door open.

They entered together into the gloom of the cathedral.

There, standing close to the door, was their DOUCH(E) truck.

'This truck belongs to me!' Greybeard exclaimed, running forward, and pressing his gloved hands over the bonnet. He and Martha stared at it in a sort of amazed ecstasy.

'Forgive me, but it is not yours,' Morton said. 'It is a possession of the Fellows of this house.'

'They've done no damage to it,' Martha said, her cheeks flushed, as Greybeard opened the driver's door and looked in. 'Oh, Algy, doesn't this take you back! I never thought to see it again! How did it get here?'

'Looks as if some of the tapes on which we recorded have gone. But the film's all here, filed as we left it! Remember how we hurtled across Littlemore Bridge in this bus? We must have been mad in those days. What a world ago it all is! Jeff Pitt will be interested.' He turned to Norman Morton and the other Fellows. 'Gentlemen, this truck was issued to me as a solemn obligation by a group whose motives would immediately win your sympathy – a study group. I was forced to exchange it for food at a time when we and the rest of Sparcot were starving. I must ask you to be good enough to return it to me for my further use.'

The Fellows raised eyebrows and exchanged looks.

'Let us go through to my rooms,' Morton said. 'There perhaps we can discuss the matter, and draw up agreements if need be. You understand there is no question of your receiving the truck as a gift?'

'Quite so. I am asking for its return as my right, Mr Morton.'

Martha squeezed Greybeard's arm as they made their way out of the cathedral and locked the door. 'Try to be tactful, darling,' she whispered.

As they walked along, Gavin said, 'You are newcomers here, but you will have observed the guard we keep posted along the walls. The guard is perhaps hardly necessary; certainly it is hardly efficient. But those old men are pensioners; they come here when there is nowhere else for them to go, and we are bound in all charity to take them in. We make them earn their keep by doing guard duty. We are not a charity, you understand; our coffers would not allow us to be, whatever our hearts said. *Everyone*, Mr Greybeard, everyone would come here and live at our expense if we let them. No man wishes to labor once he is past his half-century, especially if he has no future generations who may profit by his labors.'

'Precisely so, Gavin,' Vivian agreed, tapping his stick along the worn flags. 'We have to make this place pay its way in a manner quite foreign to our predecessors and our founders. Cardinal Wolsey would have died the death . . . That is why we run the place as a mixture of tavern, auction room, cattle market, and bawdy house. One cannot escape the cash nexus.'

'I get the message,' Greybeard said as they turned into Morton's chambers, where the same sharp-nosed fellow they had met on their first day in the college hurriedly put a stopper back in one of his master's bottles and disappeared into the adjoining rooms. 'You expect me to pay for what is mine.'

'Not necessarily,' Morton said, bending before a bright fire and stretching out thin hands toward it. 'We could, if the point were conceded that it was your vehicle, charge you a parking fee . . . A garaging fee, don't you know. Let me see. The bursar would have a record somewhere, but we must have kept the vehicle in our luxurious ecclesiastical garage for seven or eight years now . . . Say a modest fee of three shillings per diem – er, Vivian, you are the mathematician . . .'

'My head isn't what it was.'

'As we are aware . . .'

'It would be a sum of approximately four hundred pounds.'

'That's absurd!' Greybeard protested. 'I could not possibly raise that amount, or anything like it. How did you acquire the vehicle, I would like to know.'

'Your laboring pursuits are telling on you somewhat, Mr Greybeard,' Morton said. 'We raise glasses but never voices in this room. Will you drink?'

Martha stepped forward.

'Mr Morton, we would be delighted to drink.' She placed a coin on the table. 'There is payment for it.'

Morton's lined face straightened and achieved such a considerable length that his chin was lost inside his coat.

'Madam, a woman's presence does not automatically make of this room a tavern. Kindly pocket money you are going to need.'

He poked his tongue around his upper gum, smiled sourly, raised his glass, and said in a more reasonable voice than he had used before, 'Mr Greybeard, it was in this manner that the vehicle in which you are so interested came into our possession. It was driven here by an aged hawker. As friend Gavin will remember, this hawker boasted one eye and multitudinous lice. He thought he was dying. So did we. We had him taken in, and looked after him. He lingered through the winter – which was something a good many stronger men failed to do – and recovered after a fashion in the spring. He had a species of palsy and was unfit even for guard duty. To pay for his keep, he handed over his truck. Since it was worthless to us, he got good value for his money. He died after a drinking bout some months ago, cursing – as I heard the story – his benefactors.'

Moodily, Greybeard swigged his wine.

'If the truck is valueless to you, why not simply give it to me?'

'Because it is one of our assets – we hope an asset about to be realized. Suppose the garaging dues to be roughly as Vivian has estimated, four hundred pounds; we would let you take it away for two hundred pounds. How's that?'

'But I'm broke! It would take me – you know how little I earn with Joe Flitch – it would take me four years to put that amount by.'

'We could allow you reduced garage rates for the period, could we not, Gavin?'

'If the bursar were agreeable we might, yes.'

'Precisely. Say a shilling a day for four years . . . Vivian?'

'My head is not what it was. An additional seventy-five pounds, do I make it?'

Greybeard broke into an account of DOUCH(E)'s activities. He explained how often he had reproached himself for letting the truck go to the hawker, although the exchange had saved half of Sparcot from starving. The Fellows remained unmoved; Vivian, in fact, pointed out that since the vehicle was so valuable, and since he had not clearly established his ownership, they really ought to sell it to him for a thousand pounds. So the discussion closed, with the college men firm in their demand for money.

Next day Greybeard went to see the venerable bursar, and signed an agreement to pay him so much every week until the garage fee was settled.

He sat in their room that night in a gloomy mood. Neither Martha nor Charley, who had come around with Isaac to see them, could raise his spirits.

'If everything goes well, it will take us all but five years to clear the debt,' he said. 'Still, I do feel honor-bound to clear it. *You* see how I feel, don't you, Martha? I took on the DOUCH job for life, and I'm going to honor my obligations. When a man has nothing, what else can he do? Besides, when the truck is ours again, we can get the radio working and we may be able to raise other trucks. We can learn what has been happening all over the world. I care about what's going on, if the old fools who rule this place don't. Wouldn't it be wonderful if we could get in touch with old Jack Pilbeam in Washington?'

'If you really feel that way, Algy,' Martha said, 'I'm sure five years will soon go.'

He looked her in the eye.

'That's what I'm afraid of,' he said.

The days yielded one to another. The months went by. Winter gave way to spring, and spring to summer. That summer gave way to another winter, and that winter to a second summer. The earth renewed itself; only men grew older and were not replenished. The trees grew taller, the rookeries noisier, the graveyards fuller, the streets more silent. Greybeard embarked upon the

Meadow Lake in most weathers, drawing the swathes of green reed into his boat, taking each day as it came, not fretting that a time would soon come when people would no longer have the energy to thatch or want thatch.

Martha worked on among the animals, helping Norman Morton's assistant, the gnarled and arthritic Thorne. The work was interesting. Most mammals were now bringing forth normal young, though the cows, of which they possessed only a small herd, still threw miscarriages as often as not. As healthy beasts were reared, they were auctioned in the quad market alive, or slaughtered and sold as meat.

To Martha it seemed that a kind of eclipse overtook Greybeard's spirit. When he came back from Joe Flitch's in the evening, he rarely had much to say, though he listened with interest to her store of gossip about the college, acquired through Thorne. They saw less of Charley Samuels, and very little of Jeff Pitt. At the same time, they were slow to make new friends. Their putative friendship with Morton and the other Fellows withered directly the financial deal was struck.

Martha let this altered situation make no difference to her relationship with her husband. They had known each other too long, and through too many stresses. To strengthen her purpose, she thought of their love as the lake on which Algy labored day in, day out; the surface mirrored every change of weather, but below was a deep, undisturbed place. Because of this, she let the days run away and kept her heart open.

She returned to their rooms – they had moved to better rooms on the first floor in Peck – one golden summer evening, to find her husband there before her. He had washed his hands and freshly combed his beard.

They kissed each other.

'Joe Flitch is having a row with his wife. He sent me home early so that he could get on with it in peace, so he said. And there's another reason why I'm back – it's my birthday.'

'Oh, darling, and I've forgotten! I hardly ever think of the date – just the day of the week.'

'It's June the seventh, and I am fifty-six, and you look as beautiful as ever.'

'And you're the youngest man in the world!'

'Still? And still the handsomest?'

'Mmm, yes, though that's a very subjective judgment. How shall we celebrate? Are you going to take me to bed?'

'For a change, I'm not. I thought you'd like a little sail in the dinghy, as the evening's fine.'

'Darling, haven't you had enough of that dinghy, bless you? Yes, I'd love to have a sail, if you want to.'

He stroked her hair and looked down at her dear lined face. Then he opened his left hand and showed her the bag of money there. She stared questioningly at him.

'Where did you get it, Algy?'

'Martha, I've done my last day's reed-cutting. I've been mad this last year and a half, just slaving my life away. And what for? To earn enough money to buy that bloody obsolete truck stuck in the cathedral.' His voice broke. 'I've expected so much of you . . . I'm sorry, Martha, I don't know why I did it – or why you didn't hit me for it – but now I've forgotten the crazy idea. I've withdrawn my money from the bursar, the best part of two years' savings. We're free to go, to leave this dump altogether!'

'Oh, Algy, you . . . Algy, I've been happy here. You know I've been happy – we've been happy, we've been quiet together. This is home.'

'Well, now we're going to move on. We're still young, aren't we, Martha? Tell me we're still young! Let's not rot here. Let's complete our old plan and sail down the river and go on until we get to its mouth and the clean sea. You would like to, wouldn't you? You can, can't you?'

She looked beyond him, through the dazzling light at the window to the roofs of the stables visible beyond, and the blue evening sky above the roofs. At last in a grave voice she said, 'This is the dream in your heart, Algy, isn't it?'

'Oh, my love, you know it is, and you will like it too. This place is like – oh, some sort of a materialist trap. There will be other communities by the sea that we can join. It will be all different there . . . Don't weep, Martha, don't weep, my creature!'

It was almost dusk before their possessions were packed and they slipped through the tall college gateway for the last time, heading back down the hill toward the boat and the river and the unknown.

6
London

To her surprise, Martha found her limbs tremble with delight in the freedom of being once more upon the river. She sat in the dinghy clutching her knees, and smiled and smiled to see Greybeard smiling. His decision to move on was not so spontaneous as he represented it. Their boat was well provisioned and fitted with a better sail than previously. With deep pleasure, Martha found that Charley Samuels was coming along too. He had aged noticeably during their time in Oxford; his cheeks were shrunken and as pale as straw. Isaac the fox had died a couple of months before, but Charley was as much a dependable man as ever. They did not see Jeff Pitt to say good-bye to; he had vanished into the watery mazes of the lake a week before, and nobody had seen him since. Whether he had died there or gone off to seek new trapping grounds remained a mystery.

For Greybeard, to have river water flowing beneath his keel again was a liberation. He whistled as they sailed downstream, passing close to the spot where, back in Croucher's day, Martha and he had shared a flat and bickered and worried and been taken to Cowley barracks. His mood was entirely different now, so much that he had difficulty in remembering the person he then was. Much nearer to his heart – ah, and clearer in the memory! – was the little boy he had been, delighting in trips on the sunny Thames, in those months of 1982 when he was recovering from the effects of radiation illness.

As they sailed south, the new freedom took him back to that old freedom of childhood.

But it was only memory that represented that time as freedom.

The child he had been was less free than the sunburned man with bald head and grey beard who sat by his wife in his boat. The child was a prisoner, a prisoner of his weakness and lack of know-ledge, of his parents' whims, of the monstrous fate unleashed so recently on the world that the world had yet to grasp its full power. The child was a pawn.

Moreover, the child had a long road of sorrow, perplexity, and struggle before him. Why then could the man look back down the perspective of forty-nine years and regard that little boy boxed in by events with an emotion more like envy than compassion?

As the car stopped, Jock Bear, the teddy bear in tartan pajamas, rolled off the rear window ledge and onto the car seat. Algy picked him up and put him back.

'Jock must be sick too, Mummy. He's rolling about like any-thing back here.'

'Perhaps he'll feel better when we've looked at the house,' Patricia Timberlane said. She raised what was left of her eye-brows at her friend Venice, who was sitting in the front with her. 'I know I shall,' she said.

She climbed out and opened the rear door, helping her son to the ground. He was tall for a boy of seven, but the sickness had left him thin and lifeless. His cheeks were sallow, his skin rough. With nursing him and being ill herself, she felt as bad as he looked. But she smiled encouragingly and said, 'I suppose Jock wouldn't like to look round the new house?'

'I just told you, Mum, he's sick. Gosh, when you're sick, you don't want to do a thing except die, like the way Frank did. So if it's all the same to you, he'll hang around in the car.'

'As you wish.' It still hurt to be reminded of the death of her older boy Frank after many months of the sickness.

Venice came to her rescue.

'Wouldn't you like to play outside, Algy, while Mummy and I look over the house? There's an exciting-looking garden here. Only don't fall in the Thames, or you'll get awfully wet.'

Mayburn was a quiet house, set on the river not too far from the suburb of London where the Timberlanes lived. It had stood empty for six weeks, and the estate agent who gave Patricia the keys assured her that now was the time to buy, since the bottom had fallen out of the property market. This was her second visit to the property; on the first occasion, she had come with her husband, but this time she wanted someone slightly more receptive to see it. Arthur was all very well, but he had these money troubles.

The attraction of the house was that it was small, yet had a fairly long strip of ground behind, which led down to the river and a little landing stage. The place would suit them both; Arthur was a keen gardener, she loved the river. It had been so lovely, earlier in the summer, when both she and Algy were feeling a little better, to bundle up in warm clothes and sail on one of the pleasure steamers from Westminster Pier, up or down the river, watching the city slide past. On the river, the feebleness of convalescence had taken on almost a spiritual quality.

She unlocked the front door and moved in, with Venice behind her. Algy trotted off around the back of the house.

'Of course, it looks a bit ghastly at present,' Patricia said as they walked through the echoing rooms. 'The last owners were nuts on white paint – so colorless! But when it's redecorated, it'll be a different proposition. I thought we might knock this wall down – nobody wants a breakfast room nowadays – and then there would be this lovely view down to the river. Oh, I can't tell you how glad I'll be to get out of Twickenham. It's a bit of London that gets worse every year.'

'Arthur still seems to like it,' Venice said, observing her friend closely as Patricia peered out of a window.

'Arthur's . . . Well, I know that we're closer to the factory than we should be here. Oh, of course times are difficult, Venice, and this beastly radiation sickness has left everyone a little depressed, but why doesn't Arthur buck up a bit? It may sound awful, but he *bores* me so much nowadays. He's got this new young partner now, Keith Barratt, to cheer him up . . .'

'Oh, I know you're sweet on Keith,' Venice said, smiling. Patricia turned to her friend. She had been beautiful before her illness and before Frank died; now that her vivacity had fled, it was noticeable that most of her beauty had resided in that quality.

'Does it show? I've never said a thing to a soul. Venny, you've been married longer than me, Are you still in love with Edgar?'

'I'm not the demonstrative type that you are. Yes, I love Edgar. I love him for many things. He's a nice man – kind, intelligent, doesn't snore. I also love him because he goes away a lot, and that eases the relationship. Which reminds me, he'll be back from his medical conference in Australia this evening. We mustn't be too long here. I must get back and do something for dinner.'

'You do change the subject, don't you?'

Through the kitchen window, they had a glimpse of Algy running in long grass, on a pursuit no one else would ever know about. He ran behind a lilac tree and studied the fence which divided this garden from the next. The strangeness of the place excited him; he had spent too long in the familiar enclosure of his bedroom. The fence was broken at one point, but he made no attempt to get into the next garden, though he thought to himself how beautiful it would be if all the fences fell down in every garden and you could go where you liked. He ran a stick experimentally along the fence, liked the result, and did it again. A small girl of about his own age appeared on the other side of the gap.

'You knock it down better by pushing it,' she said.

'I don't want to knock it down.'

'What are you doing, then?'

'You see, my daddy's going to buy this house.'

'What a moldy shame! Then I shan't be able to creep into the garden and play anymore. I bet your moldy old father will mend the fence.'

Leaping to his father's defense, Algy said, 'He won't, because he can't mend fences. He's not a handyman at all. He's completely useless.' Catching a clearer glimpse of her through the bushes, he said, 'Gosh, you're bald. What's your name?'

'My name is Martha Jennifer Broughton, and my hair will all grow on again by the time I'm a big girl.'

He edged closer to the fence, dropping the stick to stare at her. She wore a blouse and a pleated skirt, both red, and her face was open and friendly; but the dome of her head was utterly naked.

'Gosh, you aren't *half* bald!'

'Dr MacMichael says my hair will grow again, and my dad says he's the best doctor in the world.'

Algy was put on his mettle by small girls who claimed to be authorities on medical matters.

'I know that. We have Dr MacMichael too. He had to come to see me every day because I've been at Death's Door.'

The girl came closer to her side of the fence.

'Did you actually *see* Death's Door?'

'Jolly nearly. It was very boring on the whole. It uses up your resources.'

'Did Dr MacMichael say that?'

'Yes. Often. That's what happened to my brother Frank. His resources got used up. He went right through Death's Door.'

They laughed together. In a mood for confidences, Martha said, 'Aren't Dr MacMichael's hands cold?'

'I didn't mind. After all, I'm seven.'

'That's funny, I'm seven too!'

'Lots of people are seven. I ought to tell you my name's Algernon Timberlane, only you can call me Algy, and my father owns a factory where they make toys. Shall we have to play together when I come to live here? My brother Frank who got buried says girls are stupid.'

'What's stupid about me? I can run so fast that nobody catches me.'

'Huh, I bet! I bet I could catch you!'

'I tell you what, then – I'll come in your garden, 'cause it's a good one; it hasn't got flowers and things like ours has, and we'll play catch.'

She climbed through the broken fence, lifting her skirts daintily, and stood in his garden looking at him. He liked her face. He could smell the sweet smell of the afternoon; he saw the pattern of sunlight and shadow fall across her head, and was moved.

'I'm not supposed to run fast,' he said, 'because I've been ill.'

'I thought you looked pretty awful. You ought to have some cream on your cheeks like I do. Let's play hide-and-seek then. You've got a smashing old summerhouse to hide in.'

She took his hand.

'Yes, let's play hide-and-seek,' he said. 'You can show me the summerhouse, if you like.'

Patricia had finished measuring the windows for curtains, and Venice was smoking a cigarette and waiting to go.

'Here comes your devoted hubby,' she announced, catching sight of a car turning in at the drive.

'He promised he'd be here half an hour ago. Arthur's always late these days. I want his advice on this primitive brute of a cooker. Is Keith driving him?'

'Your luck's in, my girl: yes, he is. You go and let them in and I'll slip out and collect Algernon. We really ought to be off.'

Venice let herself out of the back door and called Algy's name. Her own children were older than the Timberlanes', and had escaped most of the effects of the sickness; Gerald, in fact, had suffered no more than a seeming cold, which was all the external evidence of the sickness most adults showed.

Algy did not answer her call. As she walked over the unkept lawn, a little girl in a red outfit ran before her and disappeared behind a lilac tree. Half in fun, Venice ran after her; the girl wriggled through a gap in the fence and stood there gazing challengingly at Venice.

'I shan't hurt you,' Venice said. She suppressed an exclamation at the sight of the child's bald head. It was not the first she had met. 'Have you been playing with Algy? Where is he? I can't see him.'

'That's because he drowned in the river,' the girl said, clasping her hands behind her back. 'If you won't be cross, I'll come back and show you.'

She was trembling violently. Venice held out a hand to her.

'Come through quickly and show me what you're talking about.'

The girl was back through the gap in an instant. Shyly, she took Venice's hand, looking up to judge her reaction to the move.

'My nails weren't affected, only my head,' she said, and led the way down to a landing stage that jutted into the river along the end of the garden. Here her courage failed her, and she broke into a storm of tears. For a while she could not speak, until from the barricade of Venice's arms she pointed a finger at the dark stream.

'That's just where Algy drowned. If you look, you can see his face looking up at you under the water.'

In alarm, Venice held the child tightly and peered down through the willow tree into the stream. Clinging around a root half submerged and moving gently against the current was something that did vaguely resemble a human face. It was a sheet of newspaper.

Patiently, she cajoled Martha into looking and seeing her mistake for herself. Even then the girl continued to cry, for the shape of the paper was sinister.

'Now you run along home to tea,' Venice said. 'Algy can't be far away. I will find him – perhaps he ran round to the front garden and went indoors – and perhaps in a little while you will be able to play with him again. Would you like that?'

The girl looked into her face with immense swimming eyes, nodded, and dashed away toward the hole in the fence. As Venice straightened up and began to walk back toward the house, Patricia Timberlane came out of the back door with two men. One of the men was her husband, Arthur, a man who at forty-odd gave all the appearance of having forgotten his more youthful years. Venice, who liked him – but she was far less choosy than Patricia with her likes and dislikes, and tended to be friendly to anyone who seemed friendly to her – had to admit that Arthur cut a glum figure; he was a man saddled with troubles who had never decided to meet them either stoically or with a sense of defiance.

Patricia held her husband's arm, but it was toward the other man that she most frequently glanced. Keith Barratt, Arthur Timberlane's co-director, was a personable man with a too-shallow jaw and tawny hair brushed back untidily. Keith was only five years younger than Arthur, but his manner – particularly his manner with Pat, Venice thought cattily – was more youthful, and he dressed more like a man-about-town.

As Venice went toward them, answering their greetings, she saw a glance like a bird of sweet ill-omen fly between Patricia and

Keith. She saw in it – heavily, for there was pain enough – that trouble was nearer than she had thought.

'Venice likes the house, Arthur,' Patricia said.

'I'm afraid of damp with the river so close,' Arthur said to Venice. He put his hands in his trouser pockets and stared down toward the river as if expecting to see it rise and engulf them. It seemed to be with reluctance that he swung his eyes around to look at her as he asked, 'Is Edgar getting back early tonight? Good. Why don't you both come round for a drink with us? I'd like to hear what he makes of the situation in Australia. Things look very black, very black indeed.'

'Art, you old pessimist!' Keith said. He spoke in a tone of laughing reproach that pronounced his partner's name Ah-ha-hart. 'Come off it! A lovely afternoon like this and you talk like that. Wait till you get that MR report and see if things aren't just as bad for everyone. Come Christmas, trade will improve.' In explanation, he said to Venice, 'We've had Moxan, the market research people, in, to find out what exactly has hit our trade; their report should be with us tomorrow.' He pulled a funny face and slit his throat with a knife-edged forefinger.

'The report should have been in today,' Arthur said. He stood with his hands in his pockets and his shoulders hunched, looking about at surroundings and sky as he spoke, as if tired of talk. 'There's a touch of autumn in the afternoons already. Where's Algy, Pat? Let's be getting home.'

'I want you to have a look at the boiler before we go, darling,' Patricia said.

'We'll talk about the boiler later. Where's Algy? The boy's never about when you want him.'

'He's hiding somewhere,' Venice said. 'He's been playing games with the little girl from next door. Why don't you two look for him? I really ought to be getting along, or I'll never be ready for Edgar. Keith, be a darling and give me a lift home, will you? It's not much off your route.'

'But enchanted,' Keith said, and made an effort to look as though he meant it. They said their farewells and went around to the front drive. Keith's car had brought him and Arthur over from the factory, as Patricia had the Timberlane car. When Venice settled in beside him, Keith drove away in silence; though far from being a sensitive man, he lost some of his assurance with her, knowing that she did not greatly approve of him.

Between Arthur and Patricia a silence also fell, which he covered by saying, 'Well, let's look for the child, if we must. Perhaps he's down in the summerhouse. Why didn't you keep an eye on him?'

Ignoring this opening for a quarrel – of all her tricks, that one annoyed him most – Patricia said, as they turned toward the bottom of the garden, 'The last owners let this place become a wilderness. There's more work here than you will be able to tackle alone; we shall have to have a gardener. We must have this row of bushes out and perhaps just leave that peony where it is.'

'We haven't bought the place yet,' Arthur said morosely. His reluctance to disappoint her made him speak more grudgingly than he intended. She did not seem to be able to understand that their business slipped nearer disaster every day.

What Arthur most resented was that this trouble, into which his firm slipped more deeply even as he spoke, should come as a barrier between Pat and him. He had seen clearly, a while ago, that they failed to make a very united couple; at first he had almost welcomed the financial crisis, hoping it would bring them more closely together, for Patricia had listened sympathetically enough to his woes before they married. Instead, there seemed something deliberate in her lack of understanding.

Of course, the miserable business with the boys had upset her. But after all, she knew Sofftoys and its workings. She had been a secretary in the firm before Arthur married her, a little irresponsible slip of a thing with a good figure and twinkling eyes. Even now, he could recall his surprise when she agreed to marry him. He told himself he was not like most men: he did not forget the good or the bad things in his past life.

It was the good things that sharpened his present miseries.

Plodding through the grass, he shook his head and repeated, 'We haven't bought the place yet.'

They reached the summerhouse, and he pushed the door

open. The summerhouse was a tiny semirustic affair with an ornamental bargeboard hanging low enough to catch a tall man's head and one window set in its riverside wall. It contained two folded garden chairs leaning across one corner, a rotted awning of some kind, and an empty oil drum. Arthur glanced round it in distaste, closed the door again, and leaned against it, looking at Patricia.

Yes, for him she was attractive still, even after her illness and the death of Frank and eleven years of marriage to him. He felt an awful complex thing rise in his breast, and wanted to tell her all in one breath that she was too good for him, that he was doing his best, that she ought to see that ever since those bloody bombs were let off the world was going to hell in a bucket, and that he knew she was a bit sweet on Keith and was glad for her sake if it made her happy, provided she just didn't leave him—

'I hope Algy hasn't fallen in the river and drowned,' she said, dropping her eyes before his gaze. 'But perhaps he's gone back to the house. Let's go back and see.'

'Pat, never mind about the boy. Look, I'm sorry about all this – I mean about life and things being difficult lately. I love you very much, darling. I know I'm a bit of a duffer, but the times we live in—'

She had heard him use that phrase 'I know I'm a bit of a duffer' in apology before, as if apology was the same as reform. She lost track of what he was saying under a memory of the Christmas before last, when she had induced him to give a party for some of their friends and business acquaintances. It had not been a success. Arthur had sensed it was not succeeding, and – to her dismay – had produced a pack of cards and said to a knot of his junior employees and their wives, with a host's hollow geniality, 'Look, I can see the party's not going too well – perhaps you'd like to see a few card tricks.'

Standing there in the cool afternoon, she blushed dull red again at her embarrassment and his. There were no shames like social shames, suffered before people who would always try to smile. He was pathetic to think that naming the truth altered it in any way.

'Are you listening, Pat?' Arthur said. He still leaned against the door, as if trying to keep something trapped inside. 'You don't seem to listen to me these days. You know I love you. What I'm trying to say is this – we can't buy Mayburn, not at present. Business is too bad. It would be unwise. I saw my bank manager today, and he said it wouldn't be wise. You know we have an overdraft already. He said times were going to be worse before they were better. Very much worse.'

'But it was all arranged! You promised!'

'The bank manager explained—'

'Damn the bank manager, and damn you! What did you do, show him a new card trick? You promised me when Frank died that we—'

'Patty, dear, I know I promised, but I just can't. We're not children. Don't you understand, we haven't got the money?'

'What about one of your life insurances—' she began, then checked herself. He had moved toward her and then stopped, afraid he would be repulsed if he came nearer. His suit looked shabby and needed pressing. The set of his face was unfamiliar to her. Her anger left her. 'Are you telling me we're *bankrupt?*'

He wetted his lips.

'It's not as bad as that, of course. You know we have Moxan looking into matters. But last month's figures are very poor indeed.'

At this she looked angry.

'Well, are things bad or aren't they, Arthur? Why not come out with it and tell me the truth? You treat me like a child.'

He looked painfully at her, his face puffy, wondering which of half a dozen things would be best to say to her. That he loved her for her streak of childishness? That although he wanted her to share his troubles, he did not want her hurt? That he needed her understanding? That it made him miserable to quarrel in this ugly strange garden?

As always, he had a sense of missing in what he said the complexity he felt.

'I'm just saying, Pat, last month's figures are very bad – very bad indeed.'

'Do you mean nobody is buying Sofftoys anymore?'

'That's about it, yes.'

'Not even Jock Bear?'

'No, my dear, not even little Jock Bear.'

She took his arm, and they walked together toward the empty house without speaking.

When they found Algy was not in the house, other troubles were temporarily forgotten as they began to worry about the boy. They called continuously through the bare and echoing rooms. No answer came back.

Patricia ran out from the house, still calling, running through the bushes, down toward the river, full of a fright she dared not name. She was level with the summerhouse when a voice called 'Mummy!' As she swerved toward it, Algy was standing there in the gloom with the door half open; like a small projectile, he came flying to her, weeping.

Clutching him tightly, she asked him why he had remained in hiding when they had looked for him before.

He had no way of explaining, though he blurted out something about a girl and a game of hide-and-seek.

It had been a game; when his father opened the summer-house door and looked in, it remained a desperate game. He wanted his father to find him and embrace him. He did not know why he crouched behind the garden chairs, half fearing discovery.

Stiff with pins and needles, he remained where he was when the door closed again. He had overheard the conversation between his parents, a secret conversation more terrible for being mainly incomprehensible. It told him that there existed a tremendous threatening world with which no one – not even his father – could come to terms; and that they lived not among solid and certain things but in a crumbling pastry world. Guilty and afraid, he hid from his knowledge behind the chairs, anxious to be found, scared of the finding.

'It was naughty and cruel of you, Algy, do you hear? You knew I would be worried with the river so near. And you are not to play with strangers – I told you before, they sometimes have sicknesses about which you know nothing. You heard us calling you – why didn't you come out immediately?'

He answered only with sobs.

'You frightened Mummy very much, and you are a naughty boy. Why don't you say something? You're never going to play here again, do you understand? Never!'

'I shall see Martha Broughton again, shan't I?'

'No. We're not going to live here, Algy. Daddy's not going to buy the house, and you're coming home and going straight to bed. Do you understand?'

'It was a game, Mummy!'

'It was a very nasty game.'

Only when they were in the car and driving back to Twickenham did Algy cheer up and lean over from the back seat to stroke his father's head.

'Daddy, when we get home, would you do some of those card tricks to cheer us up with?' he asked.

'You're going to bed as soon as you get home,' Arthur Timberlane said, unmoved.

While Patricia was upstairs, seeing that Algy got into bed as soon as possible, Arthur walked moodily about before the television. The color reception was bad this evening, giving the three gentlemen sitting round a BBC table the genial hues of apoplectics. They were all, one of them with considerable pipemanship, being euphoric about world conditions.

Their bland voices only infuriated Arthur. He had no faith in the present government, though it had replaced, less than a year ago, the previous pro-bomb government. He had no faith in the people who supported the government. The shuffle only demonstrated people's fatuous belief in a political cure for a human condition, Arthur thought.

Throughout the nineteen-sixties and seventies, a period representing most of his adult life, Arthur had prided himself on remaining unscared by the dangers of nuclear warfare. 'If it comes to the point – well, too bad, but worrying isn't going to stop it coming': that had been his commonsense man-in-the-street approach to the whole thing. Politicians, after all, were paid to worry about such matters; he was better occupied fighting his way up Sofftoys Ltd., which he joined in the sixties as a junior traveler.

The bomb tests were on and off in turn, as the Communist countries and the Western ones played their incomprehensible game of ideology; nobody kept count of the detonations, and one grew bored with the occasional scares about increasing radiation in the northern hemisphere and overdoses of strontium in the bones of Lapp reindeer or the teeth of St. Louis schoolchildren.

With a sort of rudimentary space travel developing in the sixties and seventies, and Mars, Venus, Mercury, and Jupiter being examined, it had seemed only natural that the two leading powers should announce that they were conducting a series of 'controlled' nuclear detonations in space. The American 'rainbow bomb' in the early sixties proved to be the first of many. People – even scientists – grumbled, but the grumbles went unheeded. And most people felt it must be safer to activate the bombs beyond Earth's atmosphere.

Well, it had not been safer. Man had acted in ignorance before; this time the ignorance exacted a high price. The van Allen belts, those girdles of radiation encircling the Earth, and in some parts much wider than the diameter of the Earth, were thrown into a state of violent activity by the nuclear blasts, all of which were in the multimegaton range. The belts had pulsated, contracting and then opening again, and then again contracting to a lesser degree. Visually, the effect of this perturbation was small, apart from some spectacular displays of aurorae boreales and australies down into even equatorial latitudes. Vitally, the disturbance was much greater. The biosphere received two thorough if brief duckings in hard radiation.

Long-term results of this ducking could not as yet, barely a year later, be predicted. But the immediate results were evident. Although most of the world's human population went down with something like a dose of influenza and vomiting, most of them recovered. Children suffered most severely, many of them – depending on how much they had been exposed – losing their hair or their nails, or dying, as Frank Timberlane died. Most of the women pregnant at the time of the disturbance had suffered miscarriages. Animals, and in particular those mammals most exposed to an open sky, had suffered similarly. Reports from the dwindling game reserves of Africa suggested that the larger wild animals had been severely hit. Only the musk-ox of Greenland and the hardy reindeer of Scandinavia's north (where earlier generations of the creature had presumably reached some sort of immunity to cosmic and other fast-traveling particles) seemed to be almost entirely unaffected. A high percentage – some authorities put the figure at 85 percent – of domestic dogs and cats had been stricken; they developed mange or cancer, and had to be destroyed.

All of which pointed to a moral that they should have learned long before, Arthur thought: Never trust a bunch of lousy politicians to do your thinking for you. Obviously they should have had sense enough to explode their ruddy bombs on the moon.

As he bent down and switched the wall TV set off, letting the three bland men whirl away into darkness, Patricia came down into the room. She carried a shirt and a pair of pants due for a dip in the washing machine.

'Algy's miserable. I've got him into bed but he wants you to go up and see him,' she said.

'I'm not going up to see him. I've had enough of him for today.'

'He wants you, Arthur. He loves you.'

'I'm angry with him still, hiding from me like that. No, I'm not particularly angry. But you've been at him, haven't you, upsetting him and telling him we wouldn't be going to live at Mayburn?'

'Someone had to tell him sometime, Arthur. I didn't think you'd have the courage to.'

'Oh, don't let's bicker like this, Patty darling. You know I'm upset still about poor little Frank dying.'

'First it's the firm, then it's Frank! Really, Arthur, you must think I don't fret about the same things, but someone has to keep the house and things going.'

'Don't let's quarrel. Everything's miserable enough as it is.'

'I'm not quarreling, I'm telling you.'

He looked forlornly at her, pursed up his face, and shook his head, uncertain whether to be pathetic or defiant, and achieving an ineffectual mixture of the two. 'I only wanted a bit of comfort, else I wouldn't have spoken.'

'Pity you did, then,' she said sharply. 'I can't bear you when you make that foolish face at me, Arthur, I really can't.' She walked over to the wall and switched the big screen on again. 'Why don't you go up and say good night to Algy? He wants a bit of comfort too.'

'I'm going out. I'm sick of everything.'

He marched into the hall and struggled into his heavy blue serge overcoat. She turned her eyes away from the pathos of his struggle, thinking that anything she said would only provoke an argument. As he opened the front door, she called, 'Don't forget that Edgar and Venice will be round in about half an hour.'

'I'll see you later,' he said. She had no reason not to believe him.

Lying on top of the desk, sprawling over a chaotic bed of papers, brochures, and files, was a teddy bear. It was a special teddy bear. It wore a black eyeshade and a wee tartan kilt and sporran. It carried bagpipes under one arm. It was a Jock Bear, the best-selling line of Sofftoys – in the days when Sofftoys sold.

Ignoring the malevolence of its one-eyed gaze, Arthur Timberlane swept the bear onto the floor and picked a bunch of letters from his desk. He sat in the deserted factory reading them, huddled in his little office on the ground floor, while outside the lorries rumbled along the Staines road toward central London. He did not remove his overcoat.

All the letters told the same story. The one that hit hardest came from his most valued representative, old Percy Pargetter, who had traveled for the firm since the late forties and worked on sales commission alone before Arthur changed that. Percy was a good representative. He was coming to see Arthur in the morning; meanwhile, he made the situation clear. Nobody was buying his toys; the retailers and the wholesale trade had cut purchases to absolute zero because their outlets were clogged; the customer was not interested in Sofftoys anymore. Even his oldest friends in the trade now winced when they saw Percy's face at the door. Percy thought some dreaded rival must somehow have scooped the market in baby toys.

'But who, who?' Arthur asked himself in anguish. From the trade and financial papers, he knew that conditions in the toy trade were bad generally. That was all he knew. Finance and industry fluctuated between boom and slump, but there was nothing new in that, except that the fluctuations had become more violent in the last six months. He spread the letters back on his desk, shaking his head over them.

He had done all that could be done, at least until Moxan came up with their wretched report. Working with Keith, he had cut production to a minimum, had postponed until nearer Christmas the puppet-film series that would advertise Jock Bear on ICV, had canceled deliveries, had squeezed creditors, had cut overtime, had killed the contract with Straboplastics, had shelved their plans for the Merry Mermaid Rattle. And had dropped the idea of moving house . . .

He went to a metal file and turned up the last letter from Moxan, checking the name of Gaylord K. Cottage – not, he thought sourly, that it was a name one would normally forget; Cottage was the bright young man who was in charge of Moxan's investigation into the reasons for Sofftoys' slump. Arthur looked at his watch. No, it was not late. He might still catch Cottage at his desk.

The phone rang at Moxan's end for some while. Arthur sat listening to it and to the traffic beyond his office. Finally a grumpy voice came onto the line and asked what Arthur wanted. The vision cleared and a shabby round face peered out at Arthur. It was the night porter; at Arthur's insistence, he agreed to ring Cottage's extension number and switch the call through.

Cottage came on the line almost at once. He sat at a desk in an empty room with his jacket off. A hank of hair swung over his brow; his tie sagged under one ear. Arthur hardly took in his appearance beyond realizing that he looked less debonair than on his visits to Sofftoys. When he spoke, to Arthur's relief he sounded less the unsympathetic and chromium-plated young man than he had done at their last meeting.

'Your report's up in Process, Mr Timberlane,' he said. 'The slight delay was beyond our control. I am full of apologies that we didn't get it to you earlier, but you see – oh God, the thing's a bloody bust! Look, Mr Timberlane, I must talk to someone about this. You'd better listen before complete government censorship clamps down.'

He stared keenly at Arthur. Either the color on the line was bad or he was very pale.

Inside his blue serge coat, Arthur felt small and cold.

'I'm listening, but I don't know what you mean about censorship, Mr Cottage. Of course I feel very sympathetic about your personal troubles, but—'

'Oh, this isn't just personal, friend, not by a long chalk. Look, let me light a cigarette . . .' He reached for a pack on his desk, lit up and inhaled, then said, 'Look, your firm's bust, flat, finished! You can't have it plainer than that, can you? Your fellow director, Keith Barratt was it, was all wrong when he said he thought you'd been scooped by another toy firm. We've done our research, and you're all in the same boat, every firm from the biggest to the smallest. The figures prove it. The fact is, nobody's buying kiddy toys.'

'But these summer season slumps come and—'

Cottage waved a hand in front of him, sneering as he did so.

'Take it from me, this is no seasonal slump, Mr Timberlane, nothing approaching it. This is something much bigger. I've spoken to some of the other chaps here. It isn't only the toy industry. Know Johnchem, the firm that specializes in a whole range of infant products from prepared strained foods to skin powders? They're customers of ours. Their figures are worse than yours, and they've got ten times your overhead! Radiant, the pram and baby carriage people – they're in the same boat.'

Arthur shook his head as if doubling the truth of what he heard. Cottage leaned forward until his nose blurred out of focus.

'You know what it means,' he said, pressing his cigarette down into an ashtray, billowing smoke from his lungs into the screen. 'It means one thing – ever since that accident with the van Allen belts a year ago last May, there haven't been any kids born at all. You can't sell because you've got no consumers.'

'I don't believe it! I can't believe it!'

Cottage was fumbling stupidly in his pocket and playing with his cigarette lighter.

'Nobody will believe it until they get it officially, but we've checked with the General Register Office at Somerset House, and with the General Registry up in Edinburgh. They haven't given a thing away – but from what they didn't say, our figures help us to draw the correct conclusions. Our overseas connections all report the same thing. Everywhere it's the same thing – no kids!'

He spoke almost gloatingly, leaning forward with his eyes slitted against the lights of the visiphone.

Arthur switched off the vision. He could not bear to look at Cottage or to let Cottage see him. He held his head in his hands, dimly aware of how cold he was, of how he trembled.

'It's a general bust,' he said. 'The end of the world.'

He felt the coarseness of his cheeks.

'Not quite as bad as that,' Cottage said from the blank screen. 'But I'll bet you a fiver that we'll not see normal trading conditions again till 1987.'

'Five years! It's as bad as the end of the world. How can I keep afloat for five years? I've got a family. Oh, what can I do? Jesus Christ . . .' He switched off as Cottage began to launch into another dose of bad news, and sat staring at the litter on the desk without seeing it. 'It's the end of the bloody lousy world. Oh Christ . . . Bloody failure, bloody . . .'

He felt in his pocket for cigarettes, found only a pack of cards, and sat staring hopelessly at it. Something rose in his throat like a physical blockage; a salt tingle made him screw up his eyes. Dropping the cards onto the floor beside Jock Bear, he made his way out of the factory and around to his car, without bothering to drop the latch of the door behind him. He was crying.

A convoy of military vehicles rumbled along the Staines road. He threw the car into gear and grasped the steering wheel as it bounded forward toward the road.

Patricia had hardly poured Venice and Edgar their first drink when the front doorbell sounded. She went through to find Keith Barratt smiling on the doorstep. He bowed gallantly to her.

'I was driving by the factory and saw Arthur's car parked in the yard, so I thought you might like a bit of company, Pat,' he said. 'This bit of company, to be exact.'

'Venny and Edgar Harley are here, Keith,' she said, using a loud voice so that what she said could be heard in the living room. 'Do come in and join us.'

Keith winced, spread his hands in resignation, and said in exaggeratedly refined tones, 'Oh, but absolutely delighted, Mrs Timberlane.'

When he had been provided with a drink, he raised it and said to the company, 'Well, here's to happier days! The three of you look a bit gloomy, I must say. Have a bad trip, Edgar?'

'There is some reason for gloom, I should say,' Edgar Harley said. He was a tubby man, the sort of man on whom tubbiness sits well. 'I've been telling Venny and Pat about what I turned up in Australia. I was in Sydney dining next to Bishop Aitken the night before last, and he was complaining about a violent wave of ir-religion sweeping Australia. He claimed that the churches had only christened a matter of seven children – seven! – during the last eighteen months, in the whole of Australia.'

'I can't say that makes me feel too desperately suicidal,' Keith said, smiling, settling himself on the sofa next to Patricia.

'The bishop had it wrong,' Venice said. 'At this conference Edgar went to, they told him the real reason for the lack of chris-tenings. You'd better tell Keith, Ed, since it affects him and there will be an official announcement anyway at the weekend.'

With a solemn face, Edgar said, 'The bishop had no babies to christen simply because there are no babies. The contraction of the van Allen belts brought every human being in contact with hard radiation.'

'We knew that, but most of us have survived,' Keith said. 'How do you mean this affects me personally?'

'Governments have kept very quiet, Keith, while they try to

sort out just what damage this – er, accident has caused. It's a tricky subject for several reasons, the chief one being that the effects of exposure to different types of radioactive emissions are not clearly understood, and that in this case, the exposure is still going on.'

'I don't understand that, Ed,' Venice said. 'You mean the van Allen belts are still expanding and contracting?'

'No, they appear to be stable again. But they made the whole world radioactive to some extent. There are different sorts of radiation, some of which entered our bodies at the time. Other sorts, long-lived radio-isotopes of strontium and cesium, for example, are still in the atmosphere, and soak into our bodies through the skin, or when we eat or drink or breathe. We cannot avoid them, and unluckily the body takes these particles in and builds them into our vital parts, where they may cause great damage to the cells. Some of this damage may not yet be apparent.'

'We ought to all be living in shelters in that case,' Keith said angrily. 'Edgar, you put me off this drink. If this is true, why doesn't the government do something, instead of just keeping quiet?'

'You mean why doesn't the United Nations do something,' Patricia said. 'This is a worldwide thing.'

'It is too late for anyone to do anything,' Edgar said. 'It was always too late, once the bombs were launched. The whole world cannot go underground, taking its food and water with it.'

'So what you're saying is that we're not going to have just this temporary dearth of kids around, but we're going to have lots of cases of cancer and leukemia, I suppose?'

'That, yes, and possibly also a shortening of individual lives. It's too early to tell. Unfortunately we know much less about the subject than we have pretended to know. It is a very complex one.'

Keith smoothed his unruly hair and looked ruefully at the women.

'Your husband has come back with a cheery bag of news,' he said. 'I'm glad old Arthur isn't here to listen in – he's depressed enough as it is. I can see us having to give Jock Bear the push and turn to making crucifixes and coffins instead, eh, Pat?'

Edgar had pushed his drink aside and sat on the edge of his armchair, his eyes and stomach both rather prominent, as if he was winding himself up to say more. He looked about the comfortable, commonplace room, with its Italian cushions and Danish lamps, and said, 'The effects of radiation must always strike us as freakish, particularly in the present case, when we have been subjected to a wide spectrum of radiations of comparatively mild dosage. It is our misfortune that mammals have proved most susceptible to them, and of mammals, man.

'Obviously it won't mean anything to you if I go into it too deeply, but I'll just say that just as the destructive force of radio-active material may concentrate on one kind or phylum of life, so its full fury may focus on a single organ – because, as I said, bodies have efficient mechanisms for capturing some of these materials. The human body captures radioactive iodine and uses it as natural iodine in the thyroid gland. A sufficient dosage will thus destroy the thyroid gland. Only in the present case, it is the gonads which are destroyed.'

'Sex rearing its ugly head,' Keith exclaimed.

'Perhaps for the last time, Keith,' Edgar said quietly. 'The gonad, as you seem to know, is an organ that produces sex cells. The stillbirths, miscarriages, and monstrosities born since May last year show that the human gonads have collectively sustained serious damage from the radiation to which we have been and are still subjected.'

Venice stood up and began walking about the room.

'I feel as if I were going mad, Edgar. Are you sure of your facts? I mean this conference . . . You mean to say that no more babies will be born anywhere?'

'We can't say yet. And the situation could improve in some unforeseen way next year, I suppose. The figures are hardly likely to be one hundred percent. Unfortunately, of the seven Australian children mentioned by Bishop Aitken, six have died since christening.'

'This is terrible!' Venice stood in the middle of the room,

clasping her forehead. 'What seems so crazy to me is to think that half a dozen rotten bombs could do anything so – so catastrophic. It isn't as if they let them off on Earth! How can these damned van Allen layers be so unstable?'

'A Russian Professor Zilinkoff suggested at the conference that the belts may indeed be unstable and easily activated by slight radioactive overloads from either the sun or the Earth. He suggested that the same contractions that have hit us now also took place at the end of the Cretaceous Era; it's a bit fanciful, but it would explain the sudden extinction of the ancient orders of land, sea, and air dinosaurs. They died off because their gonads were rendered ineffective, as ours are now.'

'How long before we recover? I mean, we will recover?' Venice said.

'I hate to think I'm like a dinosaur,' Patricia said, conscious of Keith's gaze upon her.

'There's one ray of comfort,' Keith said brightly, holding up a finger of promise to them. 'If this sterility stunt is going on all over the world, it won't half be a relief to countries like China and India. For years they've been groaning about their population multiplying like rabbits! Now they'll have a chance to thin the ranks a bit. Five years – or let's be generous and say ten years – without any more kids born, and I reckon that a lot of the world's troubles can be sorted out before the next lot start coming!'

Patricia sprawled on the sofa beside him, clutching his lapel.

'Oh, Keith darling,' she sobbed, 'you're such a comfort always!'

They were so engrossed in talk that they did not hear Dr MacMichael's knock at the front door. He hesitated there a moment, hearing their voices within and reluctant to enter. Keith Barratt had left the door slightly ajar. He pushed it open and stepped dubiously into the hall.

On the stairs, half hidden in the darkness, a small figure in pajamas confronted him.

'Hello, Toad, what are you doing there?' the doctor asked affectionately. As he went over to Algy, the boy retreated a step or two and held up a warning finger.

'Ssh, don't make a noise, Doctor! They're talking very seriously in there. I don't know what it's about but I should think it's about me. I did something awful today.'

'You'd better get up to bed, Algernon. Come on, upstairs with you! I'll come too.' He clutched the child's hand and they went up the rest of the stairs together. 'Where's young Jock Bear? Is he creeping round the house without a dressing gown too?'

'He's already in bed, for all the good he is. I thought you were Daddy. That's why I crept downstairs. I was going to say I was sorry to him for what I did wrong.'

MacMichael stared at the toes of his shoes. 'I'm sure he'd forgive you, Toad, whatever it was – and I don't suppose it was anything too terrible you did.'

'Daddy and I think it was pretty terrible. That's why it's important for me to see him. Do you know where he is?'

The old doctor did not reply for a moment, as he stood by the boy's bed watching him climb between the sheets with the bear in tartan pajamas. Then he said, 'Algernon, you are getting a big lad. So you mustn't mind too much if you don't see your father for – well, for a little while. There will be other men about, and we will help you if we can.'

'All right – but I must see him again soon, because he's going to teach me to do the Four Ace trick. I'll teach you when I've learned, if you like.'

Algy snuggled himself down between the sheets until there was little more than a tuft of hair, a nose, and a pair of eyes showing. He looked hard at the doctor, standing there anxious and familiar in an old raincoat.

'You know I'm your friend, Algernon, don't you?'

'You must be, I suppose, because I heard Mummy tell Aunt Venny that you saved my life. I almost ran out of resources, didn't I? But would you like to do something real important for me?'

'Tell me what it is, and I'll try.'

'Would you think I was mad if I whispered?'

Dr MacMichael went close to the bed and bent his head over the pillow.

'Shoot pal,' he said.

'You know that bald girl, Martha Broughton? We were going to live next to her till I mucked things up. Do you think you could make Daddy have her round here so that I could play with her?'

'I promise I'll do that, Algy. I promise.'

'She's awfully bald – I mean *realty* bald, but I like her. Perhaps girls are better without hair.'

Gently, the doctor said, 'I'll see she comes round here before the end of the week, because I like her very much too.'

'Gosh, you're a pretty good doctor. I'll show you I'm grateful – I won't bust any more of your thermometers.'

Dr MacMichael smoothed the hair on the boy's head and left the room. He waited at the top of the stairs to master his emotions, straightened his tie, and then went down to tell the others about the car crash.

7

The River: The End

Wild life swarmed back across the earth as abundantly as it had ever done. In its great congress, there were a few phyla absent; but in numbers the multitude was as rich as it had ever been.

The earth had great powers of replenishment, and would have as long as the sun maintained its present output of energy. It had supported many different kinds of life through many different ages. As far as that outcast spit of the European mainland called the British Isles was concerned, its flora and fauna had never entirely regained the richness they enjoyed before the Pleistocene. During that period, the glaciers descended over much of the Northern Hemisphere, driving life southward before them. But the ice retreated again; life followed it back toward its northern strongholds. Toward the end of the Pleistocene, like the opening of a giant hand, a stream of life poured across the lands that had recently been barren. The ascendancy of man had only momentarily affected the copiousness of this stream.

Now the stream was a great tide of petals, leaves, fur, scales, and feathers. Nothing could stem it, though it contained its own balances. Every summer saw its weight increasing as it followed paths and habits established, in many cases, in distant ages before Homo sapiens made his appearance.

The summer nights were brief. They retained something of the translucence of the day, losing the last of their warmth only as light seeped once more across the landscape, so that the sigh of cool air that brought dawn ruffled the pelts of animals and the feathers of innumerable birds as they woke to one more day of living.

The rousing of these creatures provided the first sounds to be heard every morning in a tent pitched so near the water that it was reflected on the surface.

When Greybeard and Martha and Charley Samuels rose at this time, it was to find themselves on the edge of a widening Thames dissolved in mist. The new day drew from the land a haze into which a myriad ducks scattered. As the day advanced, the mist became orange-tinted before it thinned, to reveal the ducks flying overhead or sailing in convoy on the burnished water.

Before the mists cleared, wings whispering overhead suggested the gathering of an invisible host. Geese, heading for their feeding grounds, moved over, with a hollow sound that contrasted with the clat of flying swans. Smaller birds flew at higher levels. There were birds of prey, too, eagles and falcons that were comparative strangers to the region.

Some of these birds had traveled over vast tracts of land to feed here, from the little teal to the shelduck, strutting with his striking plumage through the mud. Many of the migrants had been forced here by adamant necessity: their little warm-blooded morsels of fledglings, with a high metabolic rate to sustain, would starve to death if left without food for eight hours; so their parents had flown to more northerly latitudes, where the hours of daylight at this time of the year lingered long over the feeding grounds.

The humans were of all the living things in this region of mist and water the least bound to such natural necessities. But they, unlike the proliferating bird life about them, had no instinctual means of determining their direction, and within three days of leaving Oxford, their journey toward the river mouth was snared in a maze of waterways.

Their way might be difficult to find, but a sense of leisure filled them, and they felt no compulsion to get out of an area so abundantly stocked with food. Herons, geese, and duck went into a series of soups and stews at which Martha excelled herself. Fish seemed to ask only to be pulled from the river.

In these activities they had few human rivals. Those few came mostly from the north side of the flood, from the settlements that still remained outside Oxford. They saw stoats hunting again, though not in packs, and an animal they took to be a polecat, making off through reeds with a mallard in its jaws. They saw otter and coypu and, at the place where they camped on the third night, the spoor of some sort of deer that had come down to the water's edge to drink.

Here, next morning, Greybeard and Martha stood over their fire poaching fish with mint and cress, when a voice behind them said, 'I'm inviting myself in for breakfast!'

Floating toward them over the water, his oars raised and dripping water from the rowlocks, was Jeff Pitt in a much-mended rowing boat.

'Fine friends you turn out to be,' he said across the intervening water. 'I go out on a little hunting expedition with some friends. When I come back to Oxford, I find old Charley's gone and his landlady's heartbroken. I go up to Christ Church, and you two have disappeared. It's a fine way to treat me!'

Embarrassed by the sense of grievance they felt behind his words, Martha and Greybeard went to the water's edge to greet him. When he had found that they had actually left Oxford, Pitt had guessed the direction they would take; he told them that as a sign of his own cleverness as they helped secure his boat. He climbed stiffly out and shook them both by the hand, which he managed to do without looking them straight in the face.

'You can't leave me behind, you know,' he said. 'We belong together. It may be a long time ago, Greybeard, but I've not forgotten you could have killed me that time when I was supposed to shoot you.'

Greybeard laughed. 'The idea never even entered my head.'

'Ah, well, it's because it didn't that I'm shaking your hand now. What you cooking there? Now I'm with you, I'll see you don't starve.'

'We were intending to fob off starvation with salmon this morning, Jeff,' Martha said, hitching her skirt to squat over the open stove. 'These must be the first salmon caught in the Thames for two hundred years.'

Pitt folded his tattered arms and looked askance at the fish. 'I'll catch you bigger 'uns than that Martha. You need me about the place – older we get, more we need friends. Where's old Holy Joe Samuels, then?'

'Just taking a morning walk. He'll be back, and horrified to see you standing here, no doubt.'

When Charley returned and finished slapping Pitt on the back, they sat down to eat their meal. Slowly the heat mist thinned, revealing more and more of their surroundings. The world expanded, showing itself full of sky and reflections of sky.

'You see, you could be lost here easy enough,' Pitt said. Now the first pleasure of reunion was over, he lapsed into his customary grumbling tone. 'Some of the lads I know back in Oxford used to be freebooters and sort of water-highwaymen around this region, until they became too old and turned to a bit of quiet poaching instead. They still talk about the old days, and they were telling me that there was a lot of fierce fights went on here some years back. They call this the Sea of Barks, you know.'

'I heard them speak of it in Oxford,' Charley said. 'They say it's still spreading, but there are fewer folk to chart it now.'

Pitt wore two old jackets and a pair of trousers. He felt in one of the pockets of the inner jacket and produced a square of paper, which he unfolded and handed to Greybeard. Greybeard recognized the paper; it was one of the broadsheets distributed during the last exhibition of the Balliol children. On its back, a map was drawn in ink.

'It shows you what this region's like now, according to these pals of mine, who explored most of it,' Pitt said. 'Can you understand it?'

'It's a good map, Jeff. Although there are names missing here, it's easy to identify the old features. Barks must be a corruption of the old Berkshire.'

Martha and Charley peered at the map with him. Marked on the southern tip of the Sea of Barks was Goring. There, on either side of the old river, two ranges of hills, the Chilterns and the Berkshire Downs, met. The river had become blocked at that point and, rising, had flooded all the land north of it where a sort of triangular trough was formed between the two ridges of bills and the Cotswolds.

Charley nodded. 'Although it's far from being a sea, it's easily twenty miles across from east to west and perhaps fifteen the other way. Plenty of room to get lost on it.'

Martha traced the edge of the so-called sea with a finger and said, 'A lot of towns must have been submerged in it, Abingdon and Wallingford among them. This makes Meadow Lake appear a mere pond! If the water level is still rising, I suppose in time the two stretches of water will meet, and then Oxford itself will sink.'

'Don't things change fast when they're under God's care rather than man's,' Charley said. 'I've been reckoning up. It must be about fourteen years since I arrived at Sparcot, and before then the country was getting a bit run-down and tatty – but now it's a different country altogether.'

'Now it's only us that's getting tattier,' Pitt said. 'The land's never looked better. I wish I were younger again, Charley, don't you? Both of us young rips of eighteen, say, with a couple of nice young bits of stuff to keep us company! I'd see I had a better life than the one I have had.'

As Pitt expected, Charley would not agree to the young bits of stuff. 'I wish I had my sisters with us, Jeff. They'd be happier in this place than they were, poor things. We've lived through desperate times! Now you can't call this England anymore – it's reverted to God. It's His country now, and it's the better for it.'

'Nice of Him to put up with us,' Pitt said sarcastically. 'Though He won't have to do that much longer, will He?'

'It's terribly anthropocentric of me, but I can't help feeling He'll find it the slightest bit dull when we've all gone,' Martha said.

They moved off after their meal. As they had done a couple of years before, they all traveled in the dinghy and towed Pitt's boat. The wind was hardly strong enough to move them over the silent waters.

They had been traveling only a brief while before they saw in the hazy distance the spires and roofs of a half-drowned town. The church steeple stood out cleanly, but most of the roofs were concealed by plants that had taken root in their blocked gutters. This vegetation would presumably be an important factor in causing the buildings to slide beneath the surface. For a while the steeple would remain; then the slow crumbling of its foundations would cause it too to disappear, and the finger of man would no longer be evident on the scene.

Pitt hung over the side of the dinghy, and peered into the 'sea.'

'I was wondering what happened to the people that used to live down there,' he said uneasily, 'and wondering if they might perhaps still be carrying on their life under the water, but I don't see any of them looking up at us.'

'Here, Jeff, that reminds me,' Charley said. 'What with you arriving, it went clean out my mind, but you know you used to reckon there was goblins in the woods.'

'Goblins and gnomes,' said Pitt, regarding him unblinkingly. 'What of it? Have you been seeing them too, a religious man like you, Charley?'

'I saw something.' Charley turned to Greybeard. 'It was first thing this morning, when I was going to see if there was anything in our snares. As I knelt over one of them, I looked up, and there were three faces staring at me through the bushes.'

'Ah, I told you – gnomes without a doubt! I seen 'em. What did they do?' Pitt asked.

'Fortunately, they were across a little brook from me and couldn't get at me. And I stuck my hand out and made the sign of the cross at them and they disappeared.'

'You ought to have loosed an arrow at them – they'd have gone faster,' Pitt said. 'Or p'raps they thought you were going to give 'em a sermon.'

'Charley, you can't believe they really were gnomes,' Greybeard said. 'Gnomes were things we used to read about as children, in fairy tales. They didn't really exist.'

'P'raps they come back like the polecat,' Jeff Pitt said. 'Those books were only telling you what *used* to be in the times before men grew so civilized.'

'You're sure these weren't children?' Greybeard demanded.

'Oh, they weren't children, though they were small like children. But they'd got – well, it was difficult to see, but they seemed to have muzzles like old Isaac's, and cat's ears, and fur on their heads, though I thought they had hands like us.'

There was silence in the boat.

Martha said, 'Old Thorne, with whom I worked in Christ Church, was a learned man, though a bit soft in the head. He used to claim that as man was dying off, a new thing was coming up to take his place.'

'A Scotsman, perhaps!' Greybeard said, laughing, recalling how Towin and Becky Thomas had believed that the Scots would invade from the north.

'Thorne was vague as to what this new thing would be, though he said it might look like a shark with the legs of a tiger. He said there would be hundreds of it, and it would be very grateful to its creator as it moved in and discovered all the little people provided for its fodder.'

'We've got enough trouble from our own Creator without worrying about rival ones,' Pitt said.

'That's blasphemy,' Charley said. 'You're getting too old to talk like that, Jeff Pitt. Anyhow, if there was a thing like that, I should think it would prefer to eat duck to us lot. Look at us!'

That evening, they took care to select a site for the night where they would not be too easily taken by surprise.

Next day saw them sailing south, rowing when the freshets failed. The wooded hills that had been visible all the previous day sank slowly out of sight, and the only landmark was a two-humped island ahead. They made this by late afternoon, when the shadow of the boat hung away to one side, and tied up beside a boat already moored in a crudely made inlet.

Much of this land bore signs of cultivation, while farther up the slopes they saw poultry and ducks confined in runs. Some old ladies who had been standing among the poultry came down to the water to inspect the new arrivals, told them this was called Wittenham Island, and grudgingly agreed that they could stay where they were for the night if they made no trouble. Most of the women had tame otters with them, which they said they had trained to catch fish and fowl for them.

They became slightly more friendly when they realized that Greybeard's party had only peaceful intentions, and proved eager to gossip. It soon emerged that they were a religious community, believing in a Master who appeared among them occasionally and preached of a Second Generation. They would have tried to make converts had not Martha tactfully changed the subject by asking how long they had lived on the island.

One woman told Martha that they came from a town called Dorchester, retreating to these bills with their menfolk when their homes and land were besieged by the rising waters some seven years earlier. Now their old home lay completely under the Sea of Barks.

Much of what this old woman had to say was difficult to understand. It was as if the mist that spread over the water at this season had also spread between human comprehensions; but it was not hard to understand that small groups cut off from their neighbors should increasingly develop an accent and a vocabulary peculiar to themselves. What was surprising was the rate at which this process operated.

Martha and Greybeard discussed the phenomenon when they were between their blankets that night.

'Do you remember that old fellow we met on our way to Oxford, the one that you said had a badger for a wife?' Martha asked.

'It's a long time ago. Can't say I do.'

'I remember we slept in a barn with him and his reindeer. Whatever his name was, he was getting treatment from that weird man at that fair – oh, my memory!'

'Bunny Jingadangelow?'

'That's it, your friend! The old man talked some nonsense about the years speeding by; he reckoned he was two hundred years old, or some such age. I've been thinking about him lately, and at last beginning to understand how he felt. There's been so much change, Algy, I begin to wonder quite seriously if we haven't been living for centuries.'

'It's a change in pace. We were born into a fevered civilization; now there's no civilization left, and the pace has slowed.'

'Longevity's an illusion?'

'Man's the thing that's stopped, not death. Everything else but us – the whole bag of tricks – goes on unabated. Now let's get to sleep, sweet. I'm tired after the rowing.'

After a moment she said, 'I suppose it's not having any children. I don't mean just not having them myself, but not seeing any around me. It makes a life terribly bare . . . and terribly long.'

Greybeard sat up angrily.

'For God's sake, woman, shut up about not having kids. I know we can't have kids – we're too old for it anyhow, by now. It's the cardinal fact of my life as much as it is yours, but you don't have to go on about it!'

'I don't go on about it, Algy! I doubt if I mention it once a year.'

'You do mention it once a year. It's always about this time, late summer, when the wheat's ripening. I wait for you to say something.'

In a moment he had repented his anger, and took Martha in his arms.

'I didn't mean to snap,' he said. 'Sometimes I'm scared at my own thoughts. I wonder if perhaps the dearth of children hasn't caused a madness we don't identify because it's unclassified. Is it possible to be sane in a world where only your own senility greets you on every side?'

'Darling, you're young yet, young and strong. We still have many years together.'

'No, but you see what I mean: you should be able to renew your youth in the generation that follows yours. In your thirties your sons keep you nimble and laughing. In your forties they keep you worried and attached to the world. In your fifties you may have grandchildren to play with. You can live till your grandchildren come along to see your creaking smiles and your card tricks . . . They replenish you. If everyone's cut off from all that – who's to wonder if time goes wrong, or if poor old Charley gets some crazy idea about seeing gnomes?'

'Perhaps a woman looks at it differently. What I regret most is the reservoir of something in me – love, I suppose – that I sense has never found its object.'

He stroked her hair tenderly and answered, 'You're the most loving person who has ever lived. Now, do you mind if I go to sleep?'

But it was Martha who slept. Greybeard lay there for a while, listening to the distant sounds of night-feeding birds. Restlessness took him. He pulled the end of his beard gently from under Martha's shoulder, slipped his shoes on, unlatched the tent flap, and climbed stiffly outside. His back was not so flexible these days.

Because of its impenetrability, the night seemed more stifling than it was. He could not explain his unease. He seemed to hear the sound of an engine – he could only visualize the steamer that his mother had taken him on from Westminster Pier in his early childhood, before his father had died. But that was impossible. He indulged himself by thinking about the past and about his mother. It was wonderful how vivid some of the memories seemed. He wondered if his mother's life – she must have been born – so long ago! – in the nineteen-forties – had not been more thoroughly ruined by the Accident than was his own. He could hardly recall the days before the Accident happened, so that he existed only within the context of the Accident and its aftermath, and was adapted to it. But how could a woman adapt? He thought rather owlishly, as if it were a discovery: Women are different.

The steamer's engine was heard again; the sound might have been sailing to him across time and probability.

He went and woke Charley, and they stood together down by the water's edge, listening.

'It's some sort of steamer right enough,' Charley said. 'After all, why not? There must still be supplies of coal lying about here and there.'

The sound faded. They stood there thinking, waiting, peering at blankness. Nothing else happened. Charley shrugged and went back to bed. After a little while, Greybeard climbed back into his blankets too.

'What's the matter, Algy?' Martha asked, wakening.

'There was a steamer somewhere out on the pond.'

'We may see it in the morning.'

'It sounded like the ones Mother used to take me on. Standing there looking out into nothing, I thought how I've wasted my life, Martha. I've had no faith—'

'Sweetie, I don't think this is a good time for an inquest on your life. Daylight in say twenty years' time would be more suitable.'

'No, Martha, listen, I know I'm an imaginative and an introspective sort of chap, but—'

Her small laugh stopped him. She sat up in bed, yawned, and said, 'You are one of the least introspective men I ever knew, and I have always rejoiced that your imagination is so much more prosaic than mine. May you always have such illusions about yourself – it's a sure sign of youth.'

He leaned over toward her, feeling for her hand.

'You're a funny creature, Martha. Sometimes you make me wonder how much two people can ever know each other, if you know me so little. It's amazing how you can be so blind when you've been such a wonderful companion for thirty years or three hundred years or however long it really is. You're so admirable in many ways, whereas I've been such a flop.'

She lit the lamp by their bed and said gravely, 'At the risk of getting chewed to death by mosquitoes, I must put on a light and look at you. I can't stomach disembodied miseries. Love, what is this you're saying about yourself? Let's have it before we settle down.'

'You must have seen clearly enough. It is not as if I chose to marry a foolish woman, as some men chose to do. I've been a flop all through my life.'

'Examples?'

'Well, look at the way I've got us more or less lost now. And far bigger things. Like the war. I ought to have refused to go – you know I was morally convinced of its wrongness. But I compromised, and joined the Infantop. Then there was the business of joining DOUCH. You know, Martha, I think that was the slobbiest thing I ever did. Those DOUCH fellows, old Jack and the others, they were dedicated men. I never believed in the project at all.'

'You're talking nonsense, Algy. I remember how hard you worked, in Washington and London.'

He laughed. 'Know why I joined? Because they offered to fly you out to Washington to join me! That was it! My interest in DOUCH was purely subsidiary to my interest in you.

'It's true I did the job fairly well during the after-war years, when the government collapsed and the United National Government made peace with the enemy. But look at the chance I missed when we were in Cowley. If I hadn't been so concerned about us, we could have been in on an important bit of history.

'Instead, we nipped off and vegetated all those dreary years at Sparcot. And what did I do there? Why, I flogged the DOUCH track just because our bellies were a bit empty. And when I might have redeemed myself at Christ Church by retrieving the truck, I just couldn't bear to stick out another couple of years' hard work. Hearing that engine throb out there on the pond, I thought of that bloody truck, and how it stands for all I might have been or had.'

Martha hit at a moth that circled around her face and turned gleamingly to him.

'People who have been betrayed often see themselves as betrayers. Don't do that, Algy. You're thinking rubbish tonight. You're too big a man to puddle about in silly self-deception. Don't you see that what you've just told me is a potted history of your integrity?'

'The lack of it, you mean.'

'No, I don't. You spent the war first trying to save children, then trying to do something constructive about the future. You married me, when you might have been having the sort of debauches most men of your age were enjoying all over the world. And I suspect you have remained faithful to me ever since. I don't think that shows any lack of character.

'As for your feebleness at Cowley, you can go and ask old Jeff what he thinks to that one! You sold the DOUCH(E) truck after infinite painful debate with yourself, and saved the whole community at Sparcot from starving. As for getting it back again, why should you? If there is a future for any humans, they'll be looking ahead, not back. DOUCH was a great idea when it was conceived in the year two thousand. Now we can see it's irrelevant.

'But what's never been irrelevant to you is other people – me, among others. You've always put me first. I've seen it; as you say, I'm not a fool. You put me before your job in Washington and in Cowley. Do you think I minded? If more people had put their fellow human beings before abstractions last century, we shouldn't be where we are now.' She stopped abruptly. 'That's all, I think. End of lecture. Feeling better, Greybeard?'

He pressed his lips to her veined temple.

'Darling, I tell you we're all suffering from some form of madness. After all this time – I've discovered yours!'

When he woke again, it was light, and Pitt was shaking him. Even before the old trapper spoke, he heard the throb of the steamer again.

'Better get your gun in case it's pirates, Greybeard,' Pitt said. 'The women say the boat's coming in here.'

Pulling on his trousers, Greybeard moved out barefoot over the dew-soaked grass. Martha and Charley stood peering into the mist; Greybeard went behind them, laying a hand on his wife's shoulder. This morning the mist was thick as milk. Behind them, the hillside was lost. Summoned by the throbbing of the engine, the women of the religious community were materializing and shuffling down to line the bank.

'The Master is coming! The Master is coming!' they cried.

The throbbing engine stopped. The sound of it died across the water. They strained their eyes to see.

A phantom river steamer appeared, gliding forward in silence. It seemed to have no substance, to exist merely in outline. On its deck, people stood motionless, staring over the sea. The old women on shore, those of them that were capable of it, sank to arthritic knees and cried, 'The Master comes to save us!'

'I suppose there must still be depots of coal about, if you know where to look,' Greybeard said to Martha. 'Presumably there's not a coal mine left in action. Or maybe they fuel it with wood.

219

We'd better be wary, but it hardly looks as if its intentions are hostile.'

'I know now how savages feel when the missionaries turn up with a cargo of Bibles,' Martha said. She was looking at a long banner draped along the steamer's railings, which bore the words REPENT – THE MASTER COMES! And beneath, in smaller letters, 'The Second Generation Needs Your Gifts and Prayers. Donations Wanted to Further Our Cause.'

'Looks as if the Bibles have a price tag,' Greybeard observed.

A group of people on the steamer came forward and removed a section of rail; they lowered a small boat into the water, obviously with the intention of coming ashore. At the same time, a loud-hailer opened up with a preliminary rasp and began to address the women ashore.

'Ladies of Wittenham Island, the Master calls you! He greets you and he will deign to see you. But this time he will not leave his holy vessel. If you want to speak with him, you'd better come aboard. We're putting out a boat to ferry you and your gifts over. Remember, it costs only a dozen eggs to get you into his presence, and for a chicken you can have a word with him.'

The rowing boat put out from the steamer and labored toward the shore. Two women rowed it, bent double over the oars, coughing and gasping as if on the verge of thrombosis. They became less insubstantial as, emerging from the mist they reached the bank and climbed ashore.

Martha clutched Greybeard's hand.

'Do you recognize one of those women? The one spitting into the water now?'

'It can't be! It looks like old – what was her name?'

'We left her at whatever that place was – Becky! It is, it's Becky Thomas!'

Martha hurried forward. The women of the island were jostling to get into the boat. Carried in their arms or in baskets were provisions, presumably offerings to lay before the Master. Becky stood to one side, watching the proceedings apathetically. She looked even dirtier than she had in her Sparcot days, and much older, though her body remained plump. Her cheeks were sunken and her nose sharp.

Regarding her, Martha thought, She's of Algy's and my parents' generation. Amazing how some of them still survive, despite those gloomy predictions we used to hear about everyone dying young. Becky must be eighty-five if she's a day.

And, more stabbingly: What'll be left of the world if Algy and I ever reach that age?

As Martha approached her, Becky changed her position and stood with her hands on her hips. On one scrawny wrist, Martha noted, was strapped the battered old nonfunctioning watch that had once been Towin's pride. Where was he?

'Hello, Becky,' she said. 'It's a small wet world. Are you taking a summer cruise?'

Becky showed little excitement at meeting up with Martha again, or at seeing Greybeard, Charley, and Pitt as they came over to speak to her.

'I belong to the Master now,' she told them. 'That's why I'm privileged even at my age to bear one of the Second Generation children. I shall be delivered of it in the autumn.'

Pitt cackled coarsely. 'You was expecting when we left you at that fair place, however many years that was ago. Whatever happened to that kid? I reckon it was a phantom litter, wasn't it? I always thought so at the time.'

'I was married then, you coarse old brute,' Becky said, 'and the Master had not then taken on his Masterhood, so of course I had no issue. Only now I've seen the light can I conceive. If you want children, Martha, you'd better bring a gift to the Master and see what he can do for you. He works miracles, he does.'

'What's happened to old Towin then, Becky?' Charley asked. 'Isn't he on the boat with you?'

She wrinkled her face into a frown.

'Old Towin Thomas was a sinful man, Charley Samuels, and I don't think of him no more. He wouldn't believe in the Master, or take the Master's cures, and as a result he died of a malignant cancer that wasted him away until he didn't weigh above a stone and a half. Frankly, it was a blessing when he passed over. I've followed the Master ever since then. I'm now coming up for my two hundred and twenty-third birthday. I don't look a day over a hundred, I reckon, do I?'

Greybeard said, 'That line sounds familiar. Do we know this Master of yours, then, Becky? It's not Bunny Jingadangelow, is it?'

'You were always, free with your tongue, Greybeard,' Becky said. 'You mind how you address him, because he doesn't use that old name now.'

'It sounds as though he still uses the old tricks, though,' Greybeard said, turning to Martha. 'Let's go aboard and see the old rascal.'

'I've no wish to see him,' Martha said.

'Well, look, we don't want to be stuck here on this sea in this mist. We could be lost here till autumn comes, and by then we ought to be well on our way down river. Let's go and see Jingadangelow and get him to give us a tow. It's obvious that the captain of the ship must know his way about.'

They did as he said, and ferried themselves out to the steamer in Pitt's boat. They climbed aboard, although the deck was already crowded with the faithful and their offerings.

Greybeard had to wait while the women from the island entered the Master's cabin one by one to receive his blessing before he was allowed to enter. He was then shown in with some ceremony.

Bunny Jingadangelow sprawled in a deck chair, wrapped in the greasy equivalent of a Roman toga, a garment he evidently considered more fitting for his new calling than the antique collection of rabbit skins that had previously been his most notable garment. Around him – and now being carted away by an old man in shorts – were material tributes to his godly qualities: vegetables, lettuces with plushy fat hearts, ducks, fish, eggs, a fowl with its neck newly wrung.

Jingadangelow still affected his curling moustache and sideburns. The rotundity that once afflicted only his chin now covered new territory; his body was corpulent, his face assumed the pasty and lopsided podginess of a gibbous moon and was of a hitherto unprecedented blandness – though it gathered a good percentage of its area into a scowl as Greybeard entered. Becky had evidently passed on the news of his visit.

'I wanted to see you because I always thought you had a rare gift of insight,' Greybeard said.

'That is perfectly true. It led me to divinity. But I assure you, Mr Greybeard, since I gather that you still call yourself by that undistinguished sobriquet, that I have no intention of exchanging gossip about the past. I have outlived the past as I intend to outlive the future.'

'You are still in your old Eternal Life racket, I see, though the props are more elaborate.'

'You observe this hand bell? I have merely to ring it to have you removed from here. You must not insult me. I have achieved sanctity.' He rested a plump hand on the table by his side, and pouted in discontent. 'If you haven't arrived to join my Second Generationists, just what do you want?'

'Well, I thought – I came to see you about Becky Thomas and this pregnancy of hers. You've no—'

'That's what you told me last time we met centuries ago. Becky's no business of yours – she's become one of the faithful since her husband died. You fancy yourself a bit as a leader of men, don't you, without actually leading them?'

'I don't lead anyone, because I—'

'Because you're a sort of wanderer! What is your goal in life? You haven't one! Throw your lot in with me, man, and live out your days in comfort. I don't spend all my life tramping around this lake in a leaky boat. I've got a base at the south end called Hagbourne. Come there with me.'

'And become a – whatever you call your followers, and make my wife become one? Not likely! We—'

Jingadangelow raised his little bell and tinkled it.

Two old women doddered in, both dressed in a parody of a toga, one of them run to a gross corpulence and with protruding eyes that took in only the Master.

'Priestesses of the Second Generation,' Jingadangelow said, 'tell me the objects of my coming.'

With a singsong delivery, in which the thinner woman led by

223

about half a sentence, they replied, 'You came to replace the God that has deserted us; you came to replace the men who have left us; you came to replace the children that were denied us.'

'There's nothing physical in all this, you understand, Greybeard,' Jingadangelow said parenthetically.

'You bring us hope where we had only ashes; you bring us life where we had only sorrow; you bring us full wombs where we had only empty stomachs.'

'You'll agree the prose, in its pseudobiblical way, is pretty telling.'

'You make the unbelievers die from the land; you make the believers survive; and you will make the children of the believers into a Second Generation which shall refurnish the earth with people.'

'Very good, priestesses. Your Master is pleased with you, and particularly with Sister Madge, who puts the thing over as if she believes what she's saying. Now, girls, recite what you must do for all this to come to pass.'

Again the two women assumed the recitative. 'We must put away all sin in ourselves; we must put away all sin in others; we must honor and cherish the Master.'

'That is what one may term the qualifying clause,' Jingadangelow said to Greybeard. 'All right priestesses, you may go now.'

They fell to holding his hand and patting his head, begging to be allowed to stay, and mouthing pieces of jargon to him.

'Confound it, girls, I'm in audience. Leave me alone!'

They fled from his righteous wrath, and he said irritably to Greybeard as he shrugged himself about in his chair to get comfortable again, 'That's the penalty with having disciples – they get above themselves. Chanting all this repetitive stuff seems to go to female heads. Jesus knew a thing or two when He chose an all-male team, but somehow I seem to get along better with women.'

Greybeard said, 'You don't appear totally submerged in your role, Jingadangelow.'

'The role of a prophet is always a bit wearing. How many years have I kept this up? Centuries, and centuries to come yet! But I give 'em hope – that's the great thing. Funny, eh, to give people something you don't have yourself.'

A knock came at the door, and a tatterdemalion man lost in a grey jersey announced that all the Wittenham women were safely ashore and the boat was ready to move on.

'You and your party had better leave,' Jingadangelow told Greybeard.

It was then that Greybeard asked for a tow. Irritably, Jingadangelow said it should be done, if they could be all ready to sail almost at once. He would tow them as far as Hagbourne in exchange for a certain levy of work from Pitt, Charley, and Greybeard. After some consultation, they agreed to this, and put together their belongings; most of these were stowed in the dinghy or Pitt's boat while the rest came with them onto the steamer, where they were allotted an area of deck space. By the time they were under way, the mist had cleared. The day remained brooding and heavy.

Pitt and Charley became involved in a game of cards with two of the crew. Martha and Greybeard took a walk around the deck, which bore the scars of the seats on which holiday makers had once sat to view the old river. There were few people aboard: perhaps nine 'priestesses' to minister to Jingadangelow's wants, and a few crewmen. There were also a couple of idle gentlemen who lounged in the shade at the stern and did not speak. They were armed with revolvers, evidently to repel any attack that might be made on the boat; but Greybeard, disliking their looks, felt some relief that he had his rifle with him.

As they were passing the saloon, the room curtained off for Jingadangelow's use, its door opened, and the Master himself looked out. He greeted Martha ostentatiously.

'Even a god needs a bit of fresh air,' he said. 'It's like an oven in my cabin. You look as lovely as ever, madam; the centuries have left not a footmark in their passage over your face. Talking of beauty, perhaps you'd care to step in here and have a look at something.'

He motioned Martha and Greybeard into his cabin, and toward a door that stood at the other end of it.

'You're both infidels, of course, born infidels, I'd think, since it has always been a theory of mine that unbelievers are born whereas saints are made; but in the hope of converting you, perhaps you'd like to see one of my miracles?'

'Are you still going in for castration?' Martha asked, standing where she was.

'Heavens, no! Surely the transformation which I have undergone is sufficiently apparent to you, Mrs Greybeard? Crude trickery has no part in my make-up. I want to show you a genuine sample of the Second Generation.' He lifted a drape from a window in the door, and motioned them to look through into the next room.

Greybeard caught his breath. His senses rose up in him like music.

On a bunk, a young girl was sleeping. She was naked, and a sheet had fallen back from her shoulders, revealing most of her body. It was smooth and browned, molded most delicately. Her arms, folded under her, cradled her breasts; one knee was tucked up so that it almost touched her elbow, revealing the scut of pubic hair between her legs. She slept with her face into the pillow, her mouth open, her rich brown hair in disarray, scowling in her sleep. She might have been sixteen.

Martha pulled the curtain down quietly over the glass panel and turned to Jingadangelow.

'Then some women are still bearing . . . But this child belongs to none of those you have aboard?'

'No, no, how right you are! This one is just a poor old prophet's consolation, as you might say. Your husband looks moved. May I hope that after this evidence of my potentialities we may welcome him into the fold of the Second Generationists?'

'You sly devil, Jingadangelow, what are you doing with this girl? She's perfect – unlike those rather sad creatures we saw in Oxford. How did you get hold of her? Where does she come from?'

'You realize you're hardly entitled to cross-question me in this

226

way? But I may as well tell you that I suspect that there are a lot more creatures as pretty as Chammoy – that's her name – lurking up and down the country. You see I have something tangible to offer my followers! Now, why don't the two of you throw in your lot with me?'

'We are making a journey to the mouth of the river,' Martha said.

He shook his head until his cheeks wobbled. 'You are becoming the mouthpiece of your husband in your old age, Mrs Greybeard. I thought when we met so many centuries ago that you had a mind of your own.'

Greybeard grabbed the front of his toga.

'Who's that girl in there? If there are more children, then they must be saved and treated properly and helped – not used as whores for you! By God, Jingadangelow—'

The Master staggered backward, grasped his hand bell, rang it violently, and struck Greybeard over the side of the face with it.

'You're jealous, you dog, like all men!' he growled.

Two priestesses came in at once, screamed at the sight of the scuffle, and made way for the two men who had been sitting at the stern of the ship. They seized Greybeard's arms and held him.

'Tie him up and throw him overboard!' Jingadangelow ordered, tottering back into his chair. He was panting heavily. 'Let the pike have a go at him. Tie the woman up and leave her on deck. I will speak with her when we reach Hagbourne. Move!'

'Stay where you are,' Pitt said from the door. He had an arrow notched at his bow and aimed at Jingadangelow. His two remaining teeth gleamed behind the feathered flight. Charley stood by him, watching the corridor with his knife in his hand. 'If anyone moves out of turn, I'll shoot your Master without one second's hesitation.'

'Get hold of their guns, Martha,' Pitt advised. 'You okay, Greybeard? What do we do now?'

Jingadangelow's henchmen showed no disposition to fight. Greybeard took their two revolvers from Martha and put them into his pockets. He dabbed his cheek on his sleeve.

'We've no quarrel with these people,' he said, 'if they are

227

prepared to let us alone. We will go on to Hagbourne and leave them there. It's doubtful if we shall ever meet them again.'

'Oh, you can't let them go like that!' Pitt exclaimed. 'Look what a chance you're passing up. Here's our opportunity to get hold of a perfectly good boat. We can ditch this moldy crew at the nearest bit of bank. Power!'

'We can't do that, Jeff. We're getting too old to turn pirate,' Martha said.

'I felt the power coming back to me, just as when I was a young man,' Pitt said, looking at no one. 'Standing there with my bow, I suddenly knew I could kill a man again. Gor . . . It's a miracle . . .'

They looked at him without understanding.

Greybeard said, 'Let's be practical. We could not manage this ship. Nor could we get it out of the Sea of Barks.'

'Martha's right,' Charley said. 'We've no moral right to pinch their boat, scoundrels though they may be.'

Jingadangelow straightened himself and adjusted his toga. 'If you've all finished arguing, kindly leave my cabin. I must remind you that this room is private and sacred. There will be no more trouble, I can assure you of that.'

As they left, Martha saw a wild dark eye regarding them through a rent in the curtain over the far window.

When Hagbourne appeared late that afternoon, it emerged not out of the mist but from curtains of heavy rain. For the morning mist had been dispersed by a wind that brought showers with it. They died away as the steamer was secured along a stone quay, and the line of the Berkshire Downs rose behind the small town. The town Jingadangelow called his base appeared almost deserted. Only three ancient men were there to greet the steamer and help tie it up. The disembarkation that followed lent some life to the dreary scene.

Greybeard's party detached their own boats warily from the steamer's stern, although they scarcely expected more trouble from the crew. Jingadangelow did not give the appearance of a fighting man. What they did not expect was the appearance of

Becky, who came up as they were loading their belongings into the dinghy.

She set her head on one side and pointed her sharp nose up at Greybeard.

'The Master sent me to speak with you. He says you owe him some labor for the privilege of the tow he gave you.'

'We'd have done his work if he hadn't attacked Greybeard,' Charley said. 'That was attempted murder, that was. Those that worship false gods shall be damned forever, Becky, so you better watch it.'

'You keep your tongue to yourself, Charley Samuels, afore you speak like that to a priestess of the Second Generation. I didn't come to talk to you, anyhow.' She turned her back pointedly on him and said to Greybeard, 'The Master always carries true forgiveness in his heart. He bears you no malice, and would like to give you shelter for the night. There is a place he has empty that you could use. It's his offer, not mine, or I wouldn't be making it. To think you struggled with him, laying hands on his person, you did!'

'We don't want his hospitality,' Martha said firmly. Greybeard turned to her and took her hands, and said over his shoulder to Becky, 'Tell your Master we will be glad to accept the offer of shelter for the night. And see that we get someone with a civil tongue to take us to it.'

As she shuffled back up the gangplank, Greybeard said urgently to Martha, 'We can't just leave without finding out more about that young girl of Jingadangelow's, where she comes from and what's going to happen to her. The night looks stormy, in any case. We are surely in no danger, and will be glad of dry billets. Let's bide here.'

Martha arched what would, in a different lifetime, have been her eyebrows. 'I admit I don't understand the interest that untrustworthy rascal holds for you. The attractions of that girl Chammoy are altogether more obvious.'

'Don't be a silly little woman,' he said gently.

'We will do as you wish.'

A flush spread from his face over the dome of his head.

'Chammoy has no effect on me,' he said, and turned to instruct Pitt about the baggage.

The quarters that Jingadangelow offered them proved to be good. Hagbourne was an untidy ruin of drab twentieth-century houses, many of them council-built; but at one end of the town, in a section Jingadangelow had chosen for the use of himself and his disciples, were buildings and houses in an older, less anemic tradition. Over the area, vegetation grew thick. Most of the rest of the place was besieged by plants, elder, dock, willow herb, sorrel, nettle, and the ubiquitous brambles. Beyond the town, the growth was of a different nature. The sheep that once cropped short the grass of the downland had long ago disappeared. Without the flocks to eat the seedlings of shrubs and trees, the ancient cover of beech tree and oak was returning, uprooting on its way the houses where the sheep-consumers had lived.

This vigorous young forest, still dripping from the recent rain, brushed against the stone walls of the barn to which the party was directed. The front and rear walls of the barn were, in fact, broken in, with the result that the floor was muddy. But a wooden stair led up to a small balcony, onto which two rooms opened, snug under a still effective roof. They had recently been lived in, and held the offer of a comfortable night. Pitt and Charley took one room, Martha and Greybeard the other.

They made a good meal of a pair of young ducks and some peas Martha had bought off one of the women on the boat, for the priestesses had proved not averse to a haggle in their off-hours. A search for bugs revealed that they were unlikely to have company during the night; with this encouragement, they retired early to their room. Greybeard lit a lantern and he and Martha pulled off their shoes. She began to comb and brush her hair. He was pulling the barrel of his rifle through with a piece of cloth when he heard the wooden stairs creak.

He stood up quietly, slipping a cartridge into the breech and leveling the rifle at the door.

The intruder on the stairs evidently heard the click of the bolt, for a voice called, 'Don't shoot!'

Greybeard heard Pitt next door call out a challenge. 'Who's that out there, you devils?' he shouted. 'I'll shoot you dead!'

'Greybeard, it's me – Jingadangelow! I wish to speak to you.'

Martha said, 'Jingadangelow and not the Master!'

He extinguished their lantern and threw open the door. In the protracted twilight, Jingadangelow stood halfway up the stairs, a small lamp held above his head. Its light, slanting down, lit only his gleaming forehead and cheeks. Pitt and Charley came out onto the little balcony to look at him.

'Don't shoot, men. I am alone and mean you no harm. I only wish to speak to Greybeard. You may go to bed and sleep securely.'

'We'll decide that for ourselves,' Pitt said, but his tone suggested he was mollified. 'You saw earlier on that we'll stand no nonsense from you.'

'I'll handle him, Jeff,' Greybeard said. 'You'd better come up, Jingadangelow.'

The timbers creaked under Jingadangelow's tread as he pulled himself up onto the platform. Greybeard stood aside, and Jingadangelow entered their room. On seeing Martha, he made the jerk at his hips that was a portly substitute for a bow. He placed his lantern on a stone shelf set in the wall and stood there, pulling at his lip and observing them, breathing heavily as he did so.

'Is this a social call?' Martha asked.

'I've come to make a bargain with you,' he said.

'We don't make bargains; that's your trade, not ours,' Greybeard said. 'If your two toughs want their revolvers back, I'm willing to return them in the morning when we leave, provided you can guarantee their good behavior.'

'I didn't come to discuss that. You needn't use that sharp tone just because you have me at a slight disadvantage. I want to put a straightforward proposition to you.'

Martha said coolly, 'Dr Jingadangelow, we hope to be moving early in the morning. Do please come directly to what you have to say.'

'Is it something to do with that girl Chammoy?' Greybeard asked.

Muttering that someone would have to help him up again, Jingadangelow sank to the floor and sat there.

'I see I have no option but to lay some of my cards upon the metaphorical table. I want you both to listen generously, since I have indeed come to unburden myself. May I say I'm sorry you don't receive me in a more friendly way. Despite that little spot of trouble on the boat, my regard for you is unchanged.'

'We are interested in hearing about the girl in your possession,' Martha said.

'Yes, yes, you shall hear about that straightaway. As you know, I have toured the Midlands extensively during my centuries of duty. In many respects, I am a Byronic figure, forced to wander and to suffer . . . During my peregrinations I have rarely seen any children. Of course we know there are supposed to be none. Yet my reason has led me to consider that the actual position may be vastly different from the apparent one. In reaching this conclusion, I considered a number of factors, which I will now lay before you.

'If you can recall that distant epoch before the ancient technological civilizations crumbled, back in the twentieth century A.D., you will remember that many specialists gave conflicting diagnoses of what was going to happen when the full effects of the space bombs were upon us. Some thought that everything would return to normal within a few years, others that accumulating radioactivity would wipe all life of every kind from this sinful but rather desirable world. As we who have the benefit of surviving now know, both these views were mistaken. Am I right?'

'Right. Proceed.'

'Thank you, I will. Other specialists suggested that the radioactivity from the Big Accident might be absorbed into the soil in the course of years. I believe this prediction to have come to pass. And I further believe that with it, some younger women have recovered the power to bring forth young.

'Now, I have to confess that I have come across no fertile women myself, although in my new calling I have been vigilant for them. So I have been forced to ask myself, What would I do if I were a woman of approximately sixty summers who discovered

232

she could produce what we call the Second Generation? This is rather a theoretical question. How would you answer it, madam?'

Martha said slowly, 'If I were to have a baby? I should be delighted, I suppose. At least, I have spent a number of years supposing I would be delighted. But I should be reluctant to let anyone see my child. Certainly I should be reluctant to come forward to someone like you and declare my secret, for fear that I would be forced into – well, some form of compulsory breeding.'

Jingadangelow nodded magisterially. As talking soothed him, his manner acquired more of its old panache.

'Thank you, madam. You are saying you would hide yourself and your offspring. Or you would exhibit yourself and might well get killed, as happened to a foolish woman who bore a girl child near Oxford. If we suppose that a number of women have borne children, we must remember that many must have done so in the isolated settlements that now lie off any beaten track. The news of the birth would not circulate.

'Next, consider the plight of the children. You might hold that their lot would be enviable, with all the adults in the neighborhood to spoil and protect them. Deeper knowledge of humanity will persuade you otherwise. The rancorous envy of those people without children would be insupportable, and aged parents would be unable to ward off the tangible effects of that envy. Babies would be stolen by motherhood-mad harridans, by crazy sterile old men. Young children would be the constant prey of the sort of blackguards I was forced to associate with some eighty years ago, when I traveled with an itinerant fair for my own protection. By the time the children – boys or girls – reached their early teens, one can only draw back aghast at the thought of the sexual indignities to which they would be exposed—'

'Chammoy's experience must bear out all you say,' Greybeard cut in. 'Leave out the hypocrisy, Jingadangelow, and get to the point.'

'Chammoy needed my protection and my moral influence; besides which, I am a lonely man. However, my point is this: that the biggest menace any child could face would be – human society! If you wonder why there are no children, the answer is that if they exist, they hide from us in the new wilds, away from men.'

Martha and Greybeard looked at each other. They read in each other's eyes an acknowledgment of the likelihood of this theory. In its support, they could recall the persistent rumors about gnomes and small humanlike shapes in the bush that vanished when a man went near. And yet . . . It was too much to swallow at one time; in their minds and bodies they were dry of the belief in living children.

'This is all part of your madness, Jingadangelow,' Greybeard said harshly. 'Your mind is obsessed with getting hold of more of these young creatures. Please leave us. We want to hear no more – we have our own madnesses to contend with.'

'Wait! *You're* mad, Greybeard, yes, not I! Was my reasoning not clear enough? I'm saner than you are, with your crazy desire to get to the mouth of the river.' He leaned forward and clasped his hands together in a sort of agony. 'Listen to me! I have a reason for telling you all this.'

'It had better be good.'

'It is good. It's an idea. It's the best idea I ever had, and I know you – both of you – will also appreciate it. You are both reasonable people, and it has been a great delight to come across you again after all these centuries, despite that unfortunate incident this morning, for which I fancy you were even more to blame than I – but, no, let's forget that. The truth is that seeing you made me yearn for intelligent company – not the company of the fools that surround me now.' Jingadangelow leaned forward and addressed himself solely to Greybeard. 'I am offering to give up everything and come along with you, wherever you go. I shall follow your lead implicitly, of course. It's a great and noble renunciation. I make it purely for my soul's sake, and because I am bored with these imbeciles who follow me.'

In the brief silence that followed, the fat man looked anxiously at his listeners; he tried a smile on Martha, thought better of it, and switched it off.

'You collected the fools who follow you, and you must put up with them,' Greybeard said slowly. 'That's something I think I

234

learned from Martha not a million years ago: however you envisage your role in life, all you can do is perform it as best you can.'

'But this Master role, good heavens, it is not my only role. I wish to leave it behind.'

'I don't doubt you have a dozen roles you can play, Jingadangelow, but I'm equally sure that the essence of you lies in your roles. We don't want you with us – I have to be brutally frank. We are happy! For all that everyone has lost since the terrible Accident back in 1981, one thing at least we have gained – there is no longer need for the hypocrisies and shams of civilization; we can be our natural selves. But you would cause dissent among us, because you carry the old rigmarole of mask-wearing into these simple days. You're too old to drop it now – how many thousands of years old are you? – and so you would never find peace with us.'

'You and I are philosophers, Greybeard! The salt of the earth! I want to share your simple life with you.'

'No. You couldn't share it. You could only spoil it. It's no deal. I'm sorry.'

He took down the lantern from the stone shelf and put it into Jingadangelow's hand. The Master looked at him, then slowly swung his head to see Martha's face. Extending a hand, he clutched the hem of her dress.

'Mrs Greybeard, your husband's grown hard since we met at Swifford Fair. You persuade him. I tell you there are children on the downs near here – Chammoy was one of them. The three of us could hunt them out and install ourselves as teachers. They'd look after us while we taught them all our old knowledge. Convince this hardhearted man of yours, I beg you.'

She said, 'You heard what he said. He's the boss.'

Jingadangelow sighed.

Almost to himself he said, 'In the end, we're all alone. Consciousness – it's a burden.'

Slowly, he helped himself to his feet. Martha also rose. A tear forced itself from his right eye and rolled with some command down his cheek and over the expanse of his chin, where a crinkle diverted it down toward his neck.

'I offer you my humility, my humanity, and you reject it!'

'At least you have the chance of getting back to your divinity.'

He sighed and produced the effect of bowing, without, in fact, doing more than bend his knees slightly.

'I trust you will all be gone early in the morning,' he said. Turning, he moved out of the door, shut it behind him, and left them in darkness.

Martha worked her hand into her husband's.

'What a splendid speech you made him, sweet! Perhaps you are imaginative after all. Oh, to hear you say as you did, "We are happy!" You are truly a brave man, my beloved Algy. We should take the untrustworthy old fraud with us, if he could regularly provoke you to such eloquence.'

For once Greybeard wanted to silence her teasing sweetness. He strained his ears to the sounds Jingadangelow made, or had ceased to make. For after a few steps down the creaking wooden stairs, Jingadangelow had paused, there had been a muffled noise Greybeard failed to interpret, and then silence. Putting Martha aside with a muttered word, he felt for where he had leaned his rifle, took it up, and pulled open the door.

Jingadangelow's light still shone. The Master no longer carried it. He stood on the floor of the barn with his hands shakingly above his head. Around him pranced three unbelievable figures, one of them grasping his lantern and swinging it about, so that the shadows whirled around the building, over roof timbers, floor, and walls.

The figures were grotesque, but it was difficult to make them out in the dim and flickering light. They appeared to have four legs and two arms each, and to stand at a half-crouch. Their ears stood up sharp on their skulls; they had snouty muzzles and long chins. They leaped about the human staggering in their midst. An onlooker might have been forgiven for mistaking them for medieval representations of the devil.

All the hairs in Greybeard's beard crackled with a flow of

superstitious fear. Purely by reflex action, he brought up his rifle and fired.

The noise was overwhelming. A farther section of the wall at the far end of the barn fell inward into the mud. At the same time, the dancing figure with the lantern uttered a cry and fell. The light crashed amid scampering feet and went out.

'Oh God, oh Martha, bring a light!' Greybeard called, in a sudden alarm. He went lumbering down the dark stairs as Pitt and Charley ran onto the balcony. Charley carried their lantern.

With a whoop of excitement, Pitt loosed an arrow at the escaping figures, but it fell short and remained quivering, upright in the dirt. He and Charley followed Greybeard down to the ground, with Martha close behind, bringing her lantern. Jinga-dangelow leaned against the safest wall, weeping out his shock; he seemed physically unharmed.

On the floor, huddled under a pair of badger skins, lay a small boy. One of the skins was fastened low about his body, providing him with an additional pair of legs; the other was fixed so that its mask covered the boy's face. In addition, his lean body was smeared with colored paint or mud. In his belt was a small knife. The rifle shot had gone through his thigh. He was unconscious and losing blood rapidly.

Charley and Pitt dropped onto their knees beside Greybeard as he pulled aside the badger skin. The wound was a disease feeding on the smooth flesh of the boy's leg.

They hardly heard Jingadangelow blubbering over them. 'They'd have killed me but for you, Greybeard. Little savages! You saved my life! The vicious little blighters were lying in wait for me! I caught Chammoy near here, and I think they were after her. Little savages! I mustn't let my followers find me here! I must still be the Master! It is my destiny, curse it.'

Pitt went over to him, facing him squarely. 'We don't want to see anything more of you. Shut your noise up and get out of here.'

Jingadangelow pulled himself erect. 'Do you imagine I'd care to stay?'

He staggered out of the barn into the befoliaged night as Martha applied a tourniquet to the boy's leg. As she tightened it, the child's eyes opened, gazing up at the pattern of shadows on the roof. She leaned over and smiled down at him.

'Whoever you are, it's going to be all right, darling,' she said.

The dinghy was off early next morning, with Pitt's boat trailing behind it. Pitt sat in it alone, nodding to himself, sometimes grinning and rubbing his nose. When they left Hagbourne, the day was overcast, but as they moved on to the next stage of the journey that they hoped would one day take them to the mouth of the river, the sun broke through the clouds and the wind freshened.

The moldering strip of harbor, with the Second Generation steamer tied up alongside it, was deserted. To their relief, none of Jingadangelow's party had appeared to give them a send-off, hostile or otherwise. When they were some way out, a solitary figure appeared on the shore and waved to them; they were too far away to identify it.

Greybeard and Charley shipped their oars as the breeze took the sail, and the former went to sit at the tiller beside Martha. They looked at each other but did not speak.

His thoughts were heavy. The fraudulent Master was right in at least one respect: human hands were turned against children in practice, if not in theory. He himself had fired at the first child he had been close to! Perhaps there was some kind of filicidal urge in man forcing him to destruction.

It was clear at least that the drive to self-preservation was strong in the new generation – and since they were so very thin on the ground, that was well. They were wary of man. By their dress it was clear they identified themselves more with the animal kind than with the crazy Methusalehs who still inhabited the earth. Well, in a few more years, things would be easier for them.

'They can be taught not to fear us,' Greybeard said absently. 'After that vital lesson, we should be able to give them plenty of help.'

'Of course it must be as you say. But they're virtually a new race – perhaps ideally they should *not* be taught not to fear us,' Martha said. She laid a hand across his shoulder as she rose.

Greybeard chewed over the implications of that remark as he watched her walk forward. She bent over the improvised stretcher, smiling as she began gently to change young Arthur's bandage. For a minute her husband looked at her, her hands, her face, and at the child solemnly staring up into her eyes.

Then he turned his head, resting one hand on his rifle while with the other he shaded his brow and pretended to gaze ahead at the horizon where the hills were.

Brian Aldiss was born in 1925. During the Second World War he served in the Royal Signals in Burma and Sumatra. In 1948 he was demobilized and became an assistant in an Oxford bookshop. His first published SF novel was *Non-Stop*, published in 1958. By 1962 he had already won an award for his series of novellas collectively known as *Hothouse*, and during the 1960s he wrote some of his most famous novels: *Greybeard* (1964), *Report on Probability A* (1968) and *Barefoot in the Head; A European Fantasia* (1969). In addition, *The Saliva Tree* (1965) won the Nebula award for best novella. He continued his prolific output throughout the 1970s but achieved his greatest acclaim in the 1980s for the three massively researched novels *Helliconia Spring* (1982), *Helliconia Summer* (1983) and *Helliconia Winter* (1985), the first of which won the John W. Campbell Memorial Award. He subsequently turned his attention to straight fiction focusing on aspects of his own life (such as *Forgotten Life* (1988)) or autobiography (*Bury My Heart at W.H. Smith's: A Writing Life* (1990) and *The Twinkling of an Eye or My Life as an Englishman* (1998)) before returning to SF.

Throughout his writing career, Aldiss has been both an anthologist and a critic, involved in both the Penguin Science Fiction and The Year's Best SF series. Both *Billion Year Spree* (1973) and its expanded follow-up *Trillion Year Spree* (1986) are considered classic surveys of SF. The latter won a Hugo Award in 1987. He has also worked as a reviewer and essayist, writing for the *Times Literary Supplement*, the *Guardian*, and the *Washington Post*. In 2001, his short story *Super-Toys Last All Summer Long* was the basis for the Steven Spielberg film *A.I. Artificial Intelligence*. Aldiss was awarded an OBE for services to literature in 2005. He currently lives in Oxford.

SF MASTERWORKS

A Case of Conscience James Blish

A Fall of Moondust Arthur C. Clarke

A Maze of Death Philip K. Dick

Arslan M. J. Engh

A Scanner Darkly Philip K. Dick

Babel-17 Samuel R. Delaney

Behold the Man Michael Moorcock

Blood Music Greg Bear

Bring the Jubilee Ward Moore

Cat's Cradle Kurt Vonnegut

Childhood's End Arthur C. Clarke

Cities in Flight James Blish

Dancers at the End of Time
Michael Moorcock

Dark Benediction Walter M. Miller

Dhalgren Samuel R. Delany

Do Androids Dream of Electric
Sheep? Philip K. Dick

Downward to Earth Robert Silverberg

Dr Bloodmoney Philip K. Dick

Dune Frank Herbert

Dying Inside Robert Silverberg

Earth Abides George R. Stewart

Emphyrio Jack Vance

Eon Greg Bear

Flow My Tears, the Policeman Said
Philip K. Dick

Flowers for Algernon Daniel Keyes

Gateway Frederik Pohl

Grass Sheri S. Tepper

Greybeard Brian Aldiss

Helliconia Brian Aldiss

I am Legend Richard Matheson

Inverted World Christopher Priest

Jem Frederik Pohl

Last and First Men Olaf Stapledon

Life During Wartime Lucius Shepard

Lord of Light Roger Zelazny

Man Plus Frederik Pohl

Mission of Gravity Hal Clement

Mockingbird Walter Tevis

More Than Human Theodore Sturgeon

Non-Stop Brian Aldiss

Nova Samuel R. Delany

Now Wait for Last Year* Philip K. Dick

Pavane Keith Roberts

Rendezvous with Rama
Arthur C. Clarke

Ringworld Larry Niven

Roadside Picnic Boris Strugatsky,
Arkady Strugatsky

Stand on Zanzibar John Brunner

Star Maker Olaf Stapledon

Tau Zero Poul Anderson

The Body Snatchers Jack Finney

The Book of Skulls Robert Silverberg

The Centauri Device M. John Harrison

* no longer available

The Child Garden Geoff Ryman

The City and the Stars
Arthur C. Clarke

The Complete Roderick John Sladek

The Demolished Man Alfred Bester

The Difference Engine William Gibson
and Bruce Stirling

The Dispossessed Ursula Le Guin

The Drowned World* J. G. Ballard

The Female Man Joanna Russ

The Fifth Head of Cerberus
Gene Wolfe

The First Men in the Moon
H. G. Wells

The Food of the Gods H. G. Wells

The Forever War Joe Haldeman

The Fountains of Paradise
Arthur C. Clarke

The Invisible Man H. G. Wells

The Island of Doctor Moreau
H. G. Wells

The Lathe of Heaven Ursula le
Guin

The Man in the High Castle
Philip K. Dick

The Martian Time-Slip
Philip K. Dick

The Moon is a Harsh Mistress
Robert A. Heinlein

The Penultimate Truth Philip K. Dick

The Prestige Christopher Priest

The Rediscovery of Man
Cordwainer Smith

The Shrinking Man Richard Matheson

The Simulacra Philip K. Dick

The Sirens of Titan Kurt Vonnegut

The Space Merchants Frederik Pohl
and C. M. Kornbluth

The Stars My Destination
Alfred Bester

The Three Stigmata of Palmer
Eldritch Philip K. Dick

The Time Machine H. G. Wells

The Time Machine/The War of the
Worlds H. G. Wells

Time Out of Joint Philip K. Dick

Timescape Greg Benford

Ubik Philip K. Dick

Valis Philip K. Dick

Where Late the Sweet Birds Sang
Kate Wilhelm

* no longer available